BRAXTON'S CENTURY

Volume 3

J R STRAYVE JR

ADZ PRESS

ADZ PRESS
3650 Third Avenue #3
San Diego, CA 92103

Publisher's Note: This is a work of fiction. Names, characters, places, and incidents are a product of the author's imagination. Locales and public names are sometimes used for atmospheric purposes. Any resemblance to actual people, living or dead, or to businesses, companies, events, institutions, or locales is completely coincidental.

Editor: Trisha Gooch
Book Layout © 2017 BookDesignTemplates SPARK

Braxton's Century VOL 3/ JR Strayve JR. -- 1st ed.
ISBN Hardback: 978-1-7371243-9-9
ISBN Paperback: 978-1-7371243-8-2
ISBN Ebook: 979-8-9925947-0-6

"This above all: to thine own self be true, and it must follow, as the night the day, thou canst not then be false to any man."

—William Shakespeare (*Hamlet*)

TABLE OF CONTENTS

INTRODUCTION 1

CHARACTER LIST 5

1890 DOUBT, ANGER, CATASTROPHE & ABSOLUTION 7

IMPERIAL DILEMMA..23

REVELATION...33

THE COUNTESS & THE VISCOUNT 47

THE MAXIM REVEAL 61

AUNTIE VALENTINA...73

MARRIAGE 87

JOE 95

COMMONS & INTELLIGENCE 107

TWO LOVES..119

1910 – LA BELLE ÉPOQUE...137

HIS CONSTANT 151

AROUND THE WORLD 163

ANGELINA & CARMEN 173

MAXIM 181

REGENCY 187

ROYAL DISSENT 195

1916 – HUNTERS HUNTED 201

DIASPORA & DEATH 215

REDEMPTION 227

AN UNDERSTANDING 235

FREDERICK 249

UPHEAVAL 255

THE AURELIO CONFERENCE 261

COLLAPSE 271

RETURN TO CAPRI 281

REX IMPERATOR 291

THE REIGN 295

VINDICATION 313

ROYAL CARNAGE 317

WHODUNNIT? 337

WAITING AND HOPING 345

LAYING THE FOUNDATION 349

PATRICIA 355

AN ENDING 367

A BEGINNING 375

ACKNOWLEDGEMENTS 379

ABOUT THE AUTHOR 381

WORKS BY JR STRAYVE JR 383

READER'S GUIDE 385

INTRODUCTION

If you're new to Prince Braxton's story, or if you've read Volumes 1 and 2 and want a recap, the author has provided a summary for your convenience.

Set in the historical alternative world of England, the story begins in 1860 and unfolds into the 20th century. Prince Braxton is the third son of the Prince and Princess of Wales, Richard, and Mercedes.

In Volume 1, the reader watched ten-year-old Braxton's practical joke turn into a towering inferno. Then the prince, as a very young man, wins the Queen Anne Stakes at the Ascot horse races, thus creating the foundation of his wealth.

It is the height of the industrial revolution. Braxton sets off across Europe and Russia at the beginning of his one hundred-year-long adventure. He crisscrosses the globe, creating an economic empire and escaping the gilded cage that would have traditionally been his life as a member of the royal family.

While establishing his railroad and trading empire, Braxton encountered anarchists and revolutionaries. He established "Mars," based on the mythical god of war, an intelligence organization created to protect himself and his interests from conniving autocrats and zealous competitors.

His liaisons with Count Aramis and the Grand Duchess Valentina set the stage for passionate assignations and his maturation into adulthood.

We close the first book as Braxton's personification of the ancient God of War compromises nobles, aristocrats, and the rich and powerful — those threatening his burgeoning business empire.

Volume 2 finds Braxton in the 1880s in St. Petersburg, the imperial capital of Russia. His friend, The Grand Duke Prince Maxim, has survived an assassination attempt and the two men set a trap for his would-be assassins. They are aided in their efforts by Grand Duchess Valentina. The Russian noble's plot against Russia and the Grand Duke is exposed, and the guilty are held accountable, paying for their transgressions with their lives.

The saga moves rapidly through Eastern Russia and later Siberia as the trio searches for ways to replenish the looted Russian treasury.

On to the "Land of the Rising Sun! Braxton, while in Imperial Japan, finds treachery oozing through the streets of Tokyo. Nippon and Western European powers conspire to sabotage his efforts to secure favorable trade status for the British Empire. More adventure follows.

Braxton and his entourage sail south on two magnificent British Man of War battleships. He soon meets up with the "Chinese Molasses," in Hong Kong. In Shanghai, he encounters the French and a collapsing rubber trading market. The Americans and their trading ships soon enter the saga.

Hindi (India) is a challenge like none he has ever faced. He is fortunate to have made it out of the sub-continent alive. But then there is the Russian Grand Duchess, Valentina. She soon eclipses that ephemeral land, challenging our protagonist to his core.

Prince Braxton, with his dreams of love and romance shattered, returns to London before traveling to Canada and America on behalf of his father, the King of England. Along the way, he encounters the perils of mining, landslides, cave-ins, and Joe, an American millionaire turned cowboy, all of which transform Braxton's epic journey.

After losing Valentina and two years of separation, he finds himself face-to-face with her. He whispers, "Is she my dream come true or the mistake of a lifetime?"

And now—Braxton's Century Volume 3 begins.

CHARACTER LIST

Prince Braxton – A prince by birth, a titan by will, and a disruptor of empires. Over the course of a century (1860–1960), he defies tradition, amasses immense power, and navigates a world of war, revolution, and forbidden passion. His vision to reshape history fuels his ambition, but his relationships and betrayals shape his fate.

Grand Duchess Valentina – Braxton's wife, a Russian imperial Grand Duchess known for her intelligence, strength, and beauty. She is not just his partner in marriage but a formidable political force in her own right, navigating both love and duty in their complex relationship.

Cowboy Joe – A pivotal figure in Braxton's life, representing a passionate and deeply personal connection that contrasts with his marriage to Valentina. Their relationship, set against societal expectations, reveals an intimate and rebellious side of Braxton.

Prince Maxim – Valentina's cousin and the only man that parallels Braxton in power and vision.

Prince John – Braxton's brother, who plays a significant role in his life. Their relationship is layered with familial loyalty, personal struggles, and a shared history that influences Braxton's decisions.

Princess Carmen – Braxton's sister. She marries Maxim and becomes empress of Russia. But fate plays a nasty trick on her; the Russian revolution upending her life.

Angelina – A young woman of intellect and independence. Having traveled in the Far East, she carries a worldly perspective and a spirit shaped by both her lineage and her experiences.

Ramsey – A man tied to both Angelina and John's past, with a history of complicated relationships. His connection to the family, and particularly to John, adds layers of intrigue and personal conflict.

Patricia – A powerful woman charged with assuming the 'mantle' of Braxton's dream.

Dominic – Braxton's older brother and heir to the throne. His story intertwines with Braxton's world, illustrating the far-reaching effects of power, loyalty and loss.

CHAPTER ONE

1890 – DOUBT, ANGER, CATASTROPHE & ABSOLUTION

His Royal Highness, Braxton, Prince Royal of Wales, dressed in an honorary regimental commander's uniform, heard the cannon's eighteen-gun salute sounding off in the distance.

The immensely popular prince was returning home from the Americas aboard the royal yacht. Thousands of Londoners and the royal family lined the river's embankment, having turned out to welcome him home.

Braxton stood ramrod straight on the polished mahogany deck of the magnificent 250-foot steamship.

The rhythmic clanging of bells and shrieking steam whistles echoed through the air, providing a steady beat to the chaotic scene. Billowing black clouds of smoke spewed from the stacks of ships and hovered in the sky, like ominous harbingers of impending danger.

Braxton looked out over the bustling harbor, his senses embracing the sights and sounds enveloping him. Despite an unsettling feeling, the prince yielded to the allure of the harbor where the gateway to the burgeoning industrial revolution blended with the timeless beauty of the ancient River Thames, predating even the Romans. As he breathed in the less-than-pleasant river air, he mused to himself, ah, not even the Romans could have envisioned what our empire has achieved.

His eyes traced the polished mahogany handrails running along the gleaming metal gangway leading down to the dock.

There stood his parents, their majesties, the King Emperor and Queen Empress, Richard and Mercedes. Accompanying them were his brothers, Crown Prince Dominic and Prince John, as well as John's wife, Frederika. They had all come to welcome him home. Prince Braxton had not expected this. Collecting his thoughts, he wondered, why are so many of the royal family present to welcome me? Most unusual—my parents rarely greet anyone outside the palace.

Had someone died? Perhaps not: no mourning dress.

And yet, he felt an emptiness surge through his body, his heart aching. Braxton yearned to escape. Why did I return? From out of nowhere, he thought of Joe. It seemed like ages rather than a mere ten days since he had been in the Appalachian Mountains with his dear Joe.

Braxton remembered watching Joe fade into the distance as the royal yacht departed Quantico's harbor. The journey had been melancholy, each nautical mile taking him further from Joe and closer to a life he was unsure he wanted to return to.

He sighed inwardly, having vainly hoped to arrive in London unannounced, slip ashore, and make straight for the bucolic Aurelio Palace.

Prince Braxton was determined to conceal the pain of losing first his beloved Valentina, two years earlier, and now Joe. Smiling, he waved to his family and to the multitude of onlookers along the docks.

He turned to the ship's captain and returned the naval officer's salute. Braxton then turned toward the yacht's stern, saluting the Union Jack, before moving to the ramp leading down to the dock.

The boatswain's mate piped the prince ashore as his fluttering royal standard was lowered. Swallowing hard, he descended the gangplank to a cacophony of hurrahs and a military band playing a lively march.

Onlookers crowding the dock and people on smaller boats escorting the royal yacht up the River Thames waved, shouted, and sounded horns to cheer his arrival.

As Prince Braxton reached the bottom of the gangway, he noticed the king wearing a hat adorned with contentious white plumes angled in various directions—the very type of hat his father despised. Braxton couldn't quite remember which military honor or order it symbolized. Next to his father, his mother wore an extravagant hat adorned with ribbons and fruit—a departure from her usual understated headwear. Today, however, she seemed to embrace the ornate style. They're holding hands in public. What on earth? I've never seen that. Odd, but they do indeed appear quite jubilant. He chuckled to himself. I should return more often.

The prince stepped off the gangway onto the dock and saluted his father.

His Majesty returned the gesture.

Braxton's mother, her eyes sparkling above a broad smile, extended her gloved hand. Braxton leaned forward and aimed a discreet wink at his mother while performing the perfunctory kissing of hands.

She blushed, as she often had when her precocious son caught her unawares. Her favorite had grown into a virile young man.

He bowed, facing his beaming parents. Most unusual. This is the time we make small talk, wave, and depart. Why do we not get on with it?

Her Majesty looked to her side, toward her husband. The king offered her a slight nod. Their majesties then faced one another and stepped back two paces, as if beginning to dance the quadrille.

Braxton's head spun and his chest tightened.

There she stood, revealed. Her Imperial Highness, Grand Duchess Valentina, her lips curved in a smile. Disarmed and not quite believing his eyes, Braxton collected himself and returned her smile.

He thought back to the first time he'd met her in St. Petersburg, a decade ago.

That autumn dawn, he had ventured outside the Russian Winter Palace and mounted his horse for an early morning ride. St. Petersburg's sky had been clear and the air crisp. The prince remembered it perfectly. His horse shivered, snorted, and shook its head, eager to take off on a vigorous ride out of the city and into the countryside.

Braxton had heard a woman's voice from behind. "Good morning, Your Royal Highness. Welcome to St. Petersburg."

He turned in his saddle. His heart leaped; his gloved hands grew clammy. A young woman approached, riding sidesaddle, dressed in a dark, plum-colored, fur-trimmed riding habit. Her eyes sparkled; a modest smile graced her full lips. Her horse moved forward. Braxton's mount turned its head in her direction and pawed the gravel.

Now alongside him, the woman held out her hand.

"I am Valentina."

That was a different time, he reflected. The enchantment that once held us together has surely faded. Yet even now, she is stunning. Back then, she was mesmerizing. What, I wonder, are we to each other now? Is she my dream come true or the mistake of a lifetime?

Braxton removed his hat and placed it under his arm as she stepped forward. The tall, raven-haired, stately beauty stood before him. Her aquamarine eyes had lost some of their luster; her skin was less translucent. He brushed the thoughts aside, took her extended hand in his, and kissed it.

She executed a shallow curtsey.

"Valentina, what a surprise."

"Yes."

Her one-word response sent an uneasy chill through Braxton.

He stepped forward and lightly embraced her, placing his lips close to her ear. She stiffened.

Braxton whispered, "What is wrong, Valentina?"

A lively, celebratory tune emanated from the nearby military band. Raucous cheering filled the air.

She spoke so only Braxton could hear. "I am here only because my father, in his capacity as czar, has commanded me to honor the marriage contract between our two governments."

Braxton felt as if time had stopped. His heart skipped a beat. He stepped back and observed her icy, blank stare.

Who is this woman? he asked himself. She continues to punish me. Why? I cannot marry her. This once love of my life now turned shrew. I won't!

Collecting himself, he kissed her forehead and forced a smile. Inhaling deeply, he growled, his voice edged with steel, "You needn't worry, my dear. I will not force you, or anyone else, to marry me."

He stepped back, offered his arm and with a forced smile said, "Shall we?"

Valentina returned a shallow smile. "Of course."

The king had observed their embrace and inaudible whispers with concern. After a moment's hesitation, he said in a loud and cheerful voice, "This is an auspicious occasion. You both will have the honor of leading the way to the carriages!"

Braxton nodded. The couple proceeded down the red carpet concealing the wharf's ancient, uneven wood platform. The irregular surface required them to mind each step.

"Hold tight, Valentina, it is a somewhat precarious walk. We could have done without the carpet."

Valentina, acknowledging those assembled along their path, replied coolly, "You need not concern yourself; I am quite capable of walking unassisted."

Not wishing to fan the flames of her obvious discontent, he nodded. "Yes, of course."

Followed by the king and queen and the rest of the royal family, they put on their best smiles and proceeded across the dockyard.

Braxton noticed the heads of several rusty nails protruding through the thin carpet. "Valentina, please watch your skirt. It could get snared by one of those nails."

Annoyed, she replied, "Really, Braxton, I am quite capable. I've crossed the plains of Russia and the icy tundra without your assistance."

The prince's patience strained under her onslaught. Through clenched teeth, he said, "I do not understand why you are antagonizing me so. What have I done to engender such hostility?"

With a ventriloquist's precision, radiating autonomous smiles and nods while clutching Braxton's arm, she replied, "I am being forced to marry you. I will provide an heir, and then we will live separately."

It felt as though she had delivered a powerful kick. His face blanched. A phantom thought raced across his mind. How could I ever have countenanced marrying her?

The couple arrived at the end of the craggy oak dock overlooking the cobbled street below. Ten steep wooden steps, flanked by rugged handrails, led down to the street.

Four gleaming royal carriages, pulled by teams of magnificent raven-black horses, lined up to convey the royal family to Buckingham Palace.

The couple paused for a moment, looking out over the crowd. Braxton remained preoccupied, taking no note of the festive music, Union Jack bunting, and exuberant cheering.

Valentina waved again with her free hand. She removed her arm from Braxton's and used both hands to pick up her skirt. Stepping down to the second step, she wavered as the back of her skirt caught on a nail head.

The Grand Duchess stumbled forward, her body swaying as she struggled to regain her balance. Valentina tugged to free her skirt, but her foot became entangled in the folds of her petticoat, forcing her to stumble again. She grasped for the railing, in vain.

Onlookers gasped.

Valentina plummeted forward as if taking flight.

Braxton reached for her. "Val!"

His betrothed fell away, leaving Braxton clutching her silk shawl. Resolve blazing in his eyes, Braxton sprang after Valentina.

Her head slammed into the railing, a sickening crack shattering the air.

A sudden gust tore Valentina's elegant, wide-brimmed hat from her head, sending it soaring upward before it drifted down into the stunned crowd.

The bride-to-be's life force seemed to slip away as she tumbled downward, her garments flailing in a kaleidoscope of motion.

She soon lay still on the unforgiving cobblestones below.

Hearing Valentina's head hit the railing and watching her tumble down the steps, Braxton felt his chest, already tight with the weight of her words, ready to explode. His mind flew back to her earlier remarks. Surely that is not the Valentina I fell so madly in love with. She never would have said those things to me. I judged her too harshly. I am a fool! And now this!

He flew down the stairs after her, yelling, "No! No! No!"

Braxton's horrified shouts alarmed the horses and startled the bewildered crowd. Coachmen struggled to keep the spooked horses in check.

Valentina lay sprawled on the filthy, trash-strewn dockyard street, her clothing veiled in dirt. Her eyes were closed, and blood smeared the side of her face, dripping onto the grimy cobblestones beneath her.

Prince Braxton kneeled beside her, his hands trembling as he cradled her head. Desperation framed his voice. "Valentina, can you hear me? Valentina?"

She murmured, "Angeli—"

"What? What, my dearest?" His heart pounded as he strained to catch her words. "What did you say?"

But she lay silent, unconscious.

The king had clambered down the stairs behind his son. He rushed to Braxton's side and placed a hand on the kneeling prince's shoulder. Leaning down, he urged, "Son, quick, get her in the carriage. I'll have my physician meet you at the palace. Quickly!"

The prince slid one arm under her back and the other beneath her legs, lifting her as he stood. In a whisper, he vowed, "I will take care of you." Moments later, Valentina's skirts billowing around him, he rushed her into the open landau. Sitting forward on the upholstered bench seat, Braxton held her in his arms. Her bloodied face rested against his chest, her limp body and voluminous skirts draped across his lap and onto the luxuriously cushioned seat. Braxton clenched his teeth, fearing the worst.

The crowd stood silent, shocked by the turn of events.

King Richard firmly closed the carriage door and commanded the coachman, "Hurry! Take them to the palace! Immediately! Get on with it!"

Turning to the back of the carriage, the king shouted at the two footmen standing on the rumble seat, "You men, get down, get off! Your weight will slow their progress!"

Mouths agape, they jumped down onto the cobblestone street.

The Mounted Imperial Guard, dressed in brilliant red tunics and glistening helmets, formed up forward and aft of the carriage.

Unsettled horses, a confused crowd, and a barrage of frantic orders heightened the palpable tension.

The coachman grasped the reins. The horses snorted, their ears swiveling forward. With a crack of the whip, the coachman yelled, "Hyah!"

The six-horse team lurched forward. A postillion seated on the lead horse grabbed the horse's mane, struggling to remain upright and avoid falling beneath trampling hooves.

An officer shouted orders toward the Horse Guard. One mounted guardsman saluted, spurred his horse, and rode off at a gallop. He navigated narrow, winding back streets, racing toward the palace to alert them to the Grand Duchess's urgent need for medical care.

The horses, now at a gallop, sped the carriage forward, escorted by the mounted Imperial Guard.

Braxton, his recent animosity toward Valentina cast aside, stroked Valentina's cheek and prayed, My dearest, what have you done? Please, please. I can't lose you again. I love you. I always have loved you. I beg you, don't leave me.

Huge, enthusiastic crowds lined the streets, eager to welcome the betrothed royals. The city had festooned its broad avenues with celebratory bunting, banners, and flags. The throng had expected the royals to come into view at a much slower pace, at a trot, so all could feast their eyes on the young couple.

Eyeing the carriage coming into view, onlookers sensed something amiss: horses galloping, not trotting. The intensity of the guard bearing down signaled something had gone horribly wrong.

Most, though initially troubled, cheered out of habit. However, as the carriage sped by, their cheers fell silent, dumbfounded by an unprecedented sight: the imperial royal carriage racing past without the king; Prince Braxton clutching a motionless woman. Was that blood?

Braxton remained as still as he could, staring into Valentina's face.

The carriage careened through the streets; his mind frozen, oblivious to the stunned crowds flashing by.

A rough spot on the road jolted him back to the present. He removed a handkerchief from his pocket, wiping the crimson blood from her face and blotting her hair. The bleeding had stopped.

Thundering hooves on the stone pavement drowned all sounds except the coachman urging his horses forward, cracking the whip and shouting, "Go it! Go it!"

The team approached the palace as the carriage driver slowed the pace. Passing through the tall, gilded gates of the palace, the Imperial Guard broke away. The carriage continued across the outer parade deck and passed through the arched stone entrance into the interior quadrangle. The horses, now at a brisk walk, moved steadily under the porte cochère.

A footman rushed forward before the carriage had come to a stop, flinging the door open and leaping inside. He and Braxton lifted Valentina from the carriage and carefully carried her down.

Braxton held her, careful not to trip on her skirts as they wrapped around his legs.

"Your Royal Highness, may I assist?" offered the footman.

"No, I've got her!" he called over his shoulder, brushing past the footman with swift determination. "Has anyone sent for my father's doctor?"

Without waiting for an answer, Braxton bounded up the six steps and strode through the open double doors.

"Yes, Your Royal Highness!" responded the Master of the Household, chasing after the prince. "Shall we—shall we take the Grand Duchess to her rooms?"

Braxton, still running with Valentina in his arms, called back, "Yes, of course. Show me to her rooms! Send for her ladies-in-waiting immediately and have her maid come at once."

"Yes, Your Royal Highness," the Master of the Household called back, heading in the opposite direction.

The footman caught up with the prince and called out, "Follow me, sir!"

Braxton, Valentina in his arms, took two steps at a time behind the footman up the red-carpeted, double-balustrade Grand Staircase.

The prince laid the Grand Duchess on her bed. He brushed her cheek with his. She murmured, "Angelina."

He stroked her hair, gazing down at her, and wiped a tear from his own cheek.

Who is this, Angelina? He thought. I have never heard her mention this Angelina in all the years I have known her. I must find her. Surely, she is someone of importance. Perhaps someone Valentina needs. Someone she needs more than me, for it is clear Valentina does not love me—not as she once did.

"Your Royal Highness," a male voice said, "please allow me to examine her Imperial Highness."

The king's doctor, Sir Henrick, was round and short. Gray hair circled a large bald spot on the top of his head. Silver-rimmed spectacles rested on a bulbous nose. His elegant morning coat, though by necessity large, expertly cut, complemented his fine woolen trousers, and a fastidiously tied maroon cravat above a paisley silk waistcoat. His appearance attested to the fact that he was as preoccupied with fashion as he was with cuisine.

"I beg your pardon, doctor. Please." Braxton stepped aside and gestured toward Valentina.

"She fell. Apparently, her skirt caught on a nail or some sort of protrusion. Perhaps even a piece of wood." The prince paused, swallowed hard, and continued. "Her head struck a rough, possibly splintered handrail."

Examining her head, the doctor said, "Yes, I see. It is indeed a serious contusion. She is fortunate the bleeding has subsided. May I assume her head remained elevated since the fall?"

The prince nodded. "Yes, I held her the entire way from the docks."

"Good, very good."

The doctor turned to one of Valentina's ladies-in-waiting, who had just entered the boudoir. "Madame, please be so kind as to order a pitcher of warm water and clean towels?"

The middle-aged noblewoman stared blankly at the physician.

"Madame, did you not hear me?" the impatient doctor asked. "A pitcher of water and towels, immediately!"

The woman held out her upturned hands, her eyebrows knit together, and her mouth curving into a perplexed frown.

Braxton stepped forward. "Madame, auriez-vous l'amabilité de commander un pichet d'eau chaude et des serviettes propres?"

"Oui, votre altesse royal, immédiatement." She lifted her skirt, turned, and rushed out of the room.

"French, eh? Why not in Russian?" the doctor asked.

"Countess Viskanaya grew up in the French-speaking Imperial Russian court and from what I have observed does not speak her native tongue. Though I believe she speaks three languages. She cares deeply for the Grand Duchess. I spoke to her in French, hoping she would understand and comply with your request."

Loosening Valentina's collar, the doctor asked, "And her second and third languages?"

"Latin and ancient Greek."

"Well-educated for a woman. A Russian. Hmm," the doctor sighed.

Sir Henrick returned his attention to his patient and gently examined each eye. He felt for her pulse, then leaned over, placing his stethoscope's diaphragm atop her clothing, and listened to her lungs.

Henrick stood and exclaimed, "It never ceases to amaze me! Women dictate fashion, so why do they insist on these dreadfully tight corsets? I cannot hear anything. We must loosen this clothing, and I really do not know where to begin! The triage must be thorough."

Braxton turned to the boudoir door as the countess entered, two uniformed maids in tow, one carrying a large ornate Wedgwood pitcher and the other holding a stack of white towels.

In French for the countess's benefit, and then in English so the maids would understand, Braxton said,

"I will leave you now, as it is necessary to undress Her Imperial Highness so the doctor may continue his examination. Please assist Sir Henrick with anything he requires."

Braxton paused for a moment, gazing at Valentina. "I rely on each of you to render your utmost care."

The three women curtsied as Braxton strode out of the room.

CHAPTER TWO

IMPERIAL DILEMMA

Braxton's parents, the king and queen, along with his brothers, Dominic and John, and his sisters, Carmen and Dierdre, and their spouses, sat in the salon just outside Valentina's bedroom.

Queen Mercedes rose as Braxton exited the boudoir. She crossed the room and embraced her son. "How is she, Braxton?"

Princess Carmen joined them, taking one of her brother's hands in hers.

His face pale, Braxton whispered, "She's still unconscious. Sleeping, I hope." He glanced back at the closed bedroom door and grimaced. "The bleeding has stopped. We'll need to wait until the doctor finishes before we'll learn more."

Thirty minutes passed. Prince Braxton sat between his parents on a sofa. The royal family remained silent; no one felt the need to speak.

A lavish tea set and a tray of biscuits, meticulously arranged by the footmen, sat untouched. A grand mantle clock, adorned with intricate baroque designs, marked the passage of time with its slow, mournful tick-tick-tick. Each pendulum swing, every quarter-hour chime, echoed through the stillness.

Almost inaudibly, the door hinges whispered a creak.

All heads turned.

The family rose to their feet.

Her Majesty clasped hands with her husband and son.

"Sir Lawrence," the king said as the doctor entered the salon. "What is my future daughter-in-law's prognosis?"

The physician bowed. "Your Majesties, Your Royal Highnesses. Her Imperial Highness is resting. She hasn't regained consciousness. There is swelling around the contusion on her head, but I don't feel surgery is necessary to relieve any pressure on the brain. I will, of course, monitor it closely. There appear to be no broken bones, which is quite remarkable. The Grand Duchess sprained her right ankle and severely bruised her shoulder. I've ordered ice for her ankle and iced towels for her head to prevent any further inflammation. At this point, there is little else we can do."

Braxton blurted out, "When will she wake?"

His mother squeezed his hand.

"One cannot say, Your Royal Highness," the doctor said." She will need more time before we can make a conclusive diagnosis." The doctor hesitated, then added, "In all honesty, I don't know."

"Thank you, Sir Lawrence," King Richard said.

The family returned to their seats as the physician moved toward the door.

The room crackled with tension as the doctor turned and added, "One more thing."

"Yes?" the king queried.

Sir Lawrence looked directly at Prince Braxton. "It may be wise to send for someone named Angelina. Twice, during my examination, she said that name. Perhaps Angelina could attend her."

"Who is Angelina?" the queen asked the doctor, then turned her focus to Braxton.

Braxton's face went blank; he shook his head.

The doctor interjected, "I used what little French I recall asking the countess who this person might be. She does not appear to know."

Princess Carmen, Braxton's favorite sister, and betrothed to Russia's future czar, stood. "That's impossible. She's the Grand Duchess's lady-in-waiting. She knows everything!"

The following week brought no improvement in Valentina's condition.

Five days later, Braxton received correspondence from Valentina's cousin and co-regent, Princess Carmen's betrothed, Russian Grand Duke Prince Maxim.

My dear Braxton,

Thank you so very much for your Teletype communique apprising me of my cousin's condition. I have informed her father, my uncle, the czar. We are grateful to have received the information on her unfortunate accident before the headlines could make their way across Europe and Russia. We have also received accounts from my dear Carmen and others.

If only I could have joined Carmen to welcome you back from your travels, but it was impossible; as Valentina and I share the regency, neither of us can simultaneously be absent from St. Petersburg. The czar's health has deteriorated to the point we anticipate his demise at any hour. Then again, that is what his doctors have been telling us for years. As you certainly know, the czar is approaching his ninth decade.

True to form, he is more interested in the marriage contract being fulfilled than he is in Valentina's health. Some things never change.

I am not sure that you know what has transpired here. Her father demanded she fulfill the marriage contract with you and packed her off to London as soon as he heard you were returning from the Americas. On her return from India, two years ago, she kept her own counsel and surprised us all when she made it clear she no longer wished to marry you.

Braxton swallowed and shifted in his chair. He rubbed his eyes and steeled himself for what was to follow.

Valentina arrived unexpectedly in St. Petersburg. We had been under the impression she was with you and on her way to London. When queried as to her change in plans, she refused to offer an explanation. Valentina simply went about her duties as if nothing had happened.

This did not sit well with her father. The court was in an uproar for months.

One day, she disappeared. Vanished.

I received a letter a week later. She shared she was at the Svyataya Mat' Nunnery, a day's ride from the capital, stating she would take up the veil and live out her life at the convent.

This, of course, infuriated her father. He issued an order commanding her to return to the capital and prepare to journey to

London to fulfill the marriage contract. She did not obey his command. I could not then, nor can I now, understand why she took such a radical course.

I wrote to her, but when she failed to provide a reasonable response, I traveled to the convent. At first, Val refused to see me. With the abbess's help, I finally convinced her I was the only person she could trust.

My cousin agreed to see me. However, during our meeting, a screen separated us. I never laid eyes on her. I detected none of the sparkling personality she had before running off to India. It pains me to write that that lively woman, I'm afraid, is no longer with us.

Braxton placed the letter on a table and leaned forward, resting his elbows on his knees. He placed his head in his hands and thought, Poor Valentina. What could have possessed her to retreat to a convent?

Braxton's chest tightened. His mind flashed back to her abrupt departure from the train in Vienna. He remembered crying out, "Valentina! Valentina!" as she vanished into the early morning fog, swallowed up by the train's hissing, billowing gray steam.

It couldn't possibly have been my ill temper on the train that night. Certainly, I acted like a cad, but this? Why did she abandon me? It couldn't have been just me. Valentina must have been hiding something, something she couldn't or wouldn't share. It made no sense then, and it makes no sense now. We had planned on marrying when we arrived in London.

There's no logic here. She's sensible, strong, and proud. This isn't the behavior of an intelligent, courageous woman!

Braxton sat up and continued reading.

She revealed nothing except that she couldn't return to St. Petersburg. Her voice was steady, unwavering. She made me swear an oath of silence about her circumstances, binding me with a promise that left me deeply uneasy. Yet, how could I refuse her? The burden of these secrets torments me. All those years we spent rebuilding Russia together—the three of us bound in our shared purpose. I reached out to you, hoping to understand what had happened between you and Valentina. I had witnessed your love, a bond I thought unbreakable. But you never wrote back to me. Why?

As an aside, dear friend, perhaps what happened between you two is why you never replied to the letters I sent. Letters pleading with you to help me understand.

Valentina remained at the convent for eighteen months. If it hadn't been for her father's declining health and his bouts of delirium, he would have forced her to leave and return to St. Petersburg.

One day, she arrived unannounced at the palace with Countess Viskanaya. She promptly resumed her duties as if nothing had happened, as if eighteen months in hiding was a non-event!

Braxton shot out of the chair, fists clenched, and exclaimed, "That cunning Viskanaya! She knows everything!"

"Papa, Mama, I am taking Valentina to Aurelio Palace."

The king and queen exchanged glances. The queen rose, her words careful and measured. "Braxton, why? She's not well; she remains unconscious. Valentina is under the care of London's best doctors.

"Aurelio is in the countryside, hours away by train—or an entire day by carriage if no train is available." She stopped and demanded, "Explain yourself and your purpose!"

"You forget, Mama, I have my train at my disposal."

The king interjected, "Yes, son, this is highly unusual."

"I know Valentina," Braxton said. "She'll never recover here in London. The city is crowded, noisy, and the air is foul. Smoke from factories and chimneys mixed with the interminable fog isn't healthy for the sturdiest among us, much less one who is already weakened."

The three of them sat in Buckingham Palace's White Salon, silent, each lost in their own thoughts. Sounds from the street filtered faintly through the palace windows.

"And the Russian embassy?" the king asked. "Have you informed them of your plans? She's the czar's daughter. You're not her husband yet. You are in no position to remove her from London. This could create an international situation."

"Father, you know I informed the PM. You and he have met twice since her accident. St. Petersburg is fully aware." Braxton folded his hands in his lap. "Maxim is kept current and up to date on her condition. I sent a cable the day after her fall, and we've been corresponding via diplomatic pouch."

Queen Mercedes interjected, "And Carmen—your sister. We must keep her future as czarina in mind. This is not purely a family matter. It is first an affair of state with international ramifications." She turned to the king. "Our government must officially notify Maxim and the Russian government immediately."

"Yes, my dear. Both personal considerations and affairs of state must be addressed," the king said, nodding to his wife. He took the queen's hand in his and continued, "Never mind, Braxton. You attend to Valentina, and I will see that all diplomatic matters are handled."

Grateful for his parents' guidance, Braxton felt for the first time that he might be unprepared, as though he hadn't thought things through. He exhaled. "Thank you both, Mama, Papa."

The dressing gong sounded in the hall.

In a cheerful voice, grateful for the change of subject, Queen Mercedes said, "Good, we shall dress for dinner and perhaps speak of less dreary matters as we dine."

"Valentina and I will leave tomorrow morning. I've ordered my train to be ready to depart St. Pancras Station at ten."

"And who will accompany you?" his mother asked.

"The countess, Lord Ramsey, members of my staff, her two maids, and her secretary."

The king interjected, "No doctors?" He paused and said, "I will send Sir Henrick along with two nurses."

"Thank you, Papa."

The next morning, Braxton's train pulled out of St. Pancras Station at precisely 10:00 a.m. The prince had asked the engineer to forgo unnecessary whistles, to leave the station slowly, and to maintain a moderate speed to avoid jostling the train cars as much as possible.

Braxton sat beside Valentina, who lay unconscious on the bed in his private rail car. He held her hand and stroked her hair with his other. "Valentina, my darling, I'm so worried about you. It has been weeks, and little has changed. The fresh country air of Aurelio Palace and its ten thousand acres will be perfect for your recovery."

"You've never had the chance to enjoy my family's estate. My parents gifted it to me after Papa's coronation. I offered to buy it, but they insisted on making it a gift.

"The palace and the surrounding countryside are a source of my strength, my passion."

Braxton waxed on, passing the time, covering his worry with his hopes and dreams for her recovery and a future together; hoping his words might reach the silent, unconscious Valentina.

"The house was built by my ancestors, my mother's family, the Chiacontella. It's hundreds of years old—a true treasure. I have no doubt you'll come to love it as I do."

As Braxton sat beside Valentina, a familiar ache stirred inside him— a longing to bring back the love they once had, the closeness he'd thought would carry them through anything. She had been his vision of the perfect wife, the one who understood his dreams and fears, who'd shared in his ambitions. He still cared for her deeply, still felt this pull to bridge the distance she'd placed between them, hoping to find a way back to the warmth they once knew.

But he couldn't ignore the other side of him that had emerged, one that felt just as real, just as true. His connection with men like Joe, particularly Joe, had awakened something undeniable. Joe offered him a sense of comfort and belonging. With Joe, he felt seen in a way that filled spaces even Valentina couldn't touch. Somehow, he'd make his peace with loving them both, embracing each of these connections as essential in their own way.

Yet worry gnawed at him now. Sitting here next to her, did she suspect? Was that a reason, maybe one of many, for her recent distance, the sharpness in her words? If she ever truly knew, he wondered, would she see it as a betrayal? Would she understand that his love for her still burned steadily, even with this other part of him?

He took a deep breath, feeling the delicate balance he had to walk. His love for Valentina and his bond with Joe each held their place inside him, but he knew it all felt fragile, like any misstep might cause everything to shatter. He wanted to keep her safe, to protect her from any hurt his heart might bring her. And sitting there, hoping to reclaim even a piece of what they'd once had, he resolved to move carefully, to find a way to honor both sides of his heart without leaving anyone wounded.

CHAPTER THREE

REVELATION

Grand Duchess Valentina had been placed in the suite Braxton's mother once occupied in the Aurelio Palace. Decorated in the Italian Tuscan style, the suite was furnished with sculptures and paintings of vineyards and sienna-colored fields—a space that had once provided sanctuary for his mother, now serving the same purpose for Valentina.

Sunlight poured into the rooms, lifting the somber mood that had settled over what had become her sickroom. The crisp light here was a welcome contrast to the heavy décor of Buckingham Palace. Valentina's lady-in-waiting and two maids attended her, laying cool compresses on her forehead, striving to keep the semi-conscious duchess as comfortable as possible. She had not spoken since her arrival from London a week earlier.

Just the day before, Countess Viskanaya had eagerly pointed out to Sir Henrick that Valentina's color had slightly improved. The doctor prescribed a gentle diet of warm, clear chicken broth and soft vegetables, to be given five times a day or whenever she was awake.

"Doctor, I must ask—do you see any improvement of note?" Braxton inquired, sitting across from Sir Lawrence at the ornate desk in the grand-ducal study, a room built centuries ago by his Chiacontella ancestors.

Sir Lawrence paused thoughtfully. "Your Royal Highness, I cannot say for certain, but yes, I am hopeful. The countess is correct; the duchess's color has improved. However, her weight loss concerns me. If she gains strength, perhaps we can attempt a more substantial diet. Though she has not spoken, she remains awake for brief intervals. One can only hope."

"Thank you, Sir Lawrence. I appreciate both your candor and encouragement." Braxton took a deep breath. "I spend hours each day by her bedside. It pains me to see her languish, so I sit with her, recalling memories from our past, speaking of our future as I'd imagined it. I read aloud to her from the newspapers and scientific journals, hoping to spark her interest, and even revisit letters from her family. I have not lost hope." He leaned forward, concern shading his expression. "But, Doctor, am I helping her with this, or am I perhaps causing her distress?"

Sir Lawrence raised his hands from the mahogany desk and rested them atop his ample belly. "I assure you, Your Highness, there is nothing more helpful than having someone she cares for nearby speaking to her. Such familiar interaction may stimulate her mind and bolster her will to recover."

Braxton considered the words. Someone she cares for, he thought. Does she care for me at all?

He offered the physician a grateful smile. "Thank you, Doctor."

Braxton sat in contemplative silence, thoughts drifting back two years to the moment Valentina had arrived unexpectedly at the Viceregal Lodge in the northern mountains of India. He had been convalescing after eighteen grueling months, serving as his father's envoy in Russia, Japan, Hong Kong, Singapore, and India.

Noticing Braxton's preoccupation, Sir Lawrence remained silent.

Braxton's mind wandered further to his debilitating illness in India—the Idiopathic Adenitis that had rendered him nearly motionless in the oppressive, fly-infested heat of Calcutta. He could barely recall the journey from Calcutta to the mountain refuge. He continued to drift in and out of consciousness for weeks. The memory brought a sudden pallor to his face, and beads of sweat formed on his forehead.

The doctor, observing Braxton's reaction, leaned forward slightly but refrained from speaking.

Braxton, lost in thought, recalled hazy memories of voices—some familiar, some strange—piercing the silence of his feverish haze. He had endured terrifying hallucinations, his mind haunted by eerie visions he could no longer remember. Braxton would awaken only to find his limbs as heavy as stone, his throat swollen, as if he were trapped within an invisible tomb. He'd tried to cry out, but no sound came, and the ensuing panic left him weakened and hopeless. He'd slip back into fitful sleep, only to relive the same nightmares and isolation.

Sir Lawrence, concerned by Braxton's pallor and the perspiration forming on his brow, gently interrupted. "I beg your pardon, Your Royal Highness. Are you feeling unwell?"

Braxton looked up, eyes wide, and took a handkerchief from his jacket. He wiped his forehead with a trembling hand. "My apologies, Sir Lawrence. I was unexpectedly overcome by a memory of my illness in India." He composed himself and returned the handkerchief to his pocket.

A cool breeze swept through the open French doors, stirring the heavy air in the room.

The prince folded his arms, his voice softening. "You recall, of course, being informed of my illness?"

"Indeed, Your Highness. Your uncle, Cosimo, the Duke De Chiacontella, oversaw your recovery. He sent detailed letters to Their Majesties, which His Majesty shared with me as your physician."

Braxton nodded. "Yes, of course. My mother, with her unerring intuition, suspected for months that my health was failing, though I never disclosed it in my letters. To this day, it baffles me how she could sense my decline from across the world." He chuckled softly. "She was so concerned she nearly commanded her twin brother to journey from Villa Incantarre in Italy to Calcutta."

He tilted his head, considering. "The Chiacontella are wise and compassionate. I truly owe my life to my mother and my uncle."

Sir Lawrence nodded solemnly. "Their efforts may indeed be the reason you are sitting here today." Adjusting himself, he added, "And as I understand it, the Grand Duchess Valentina's timely arrival in India was crucial to your recovery as well."

Braxton's face softened, a warm smile illuminating his features. "Yes, Valentina." He looked down at his desk, his tone turning reflective. "And now here we are. She lies upstairs, convalescing, as I was, when she found me languishing in the Himalayas."

The two men sat in silence for a moment.

The prince stretched, reaching his arms above his head. "Ah."

Sir Lawrence rose from his chair.

Braxton stood as well, extending his hand. "Thank you, Sir Lawrence, for listening and for your unwavering dedication. My family and I are deeply grateful for the care you've given us."

Unaccustomed to such a gesture from royalty, Sir Lawrence slowly accepted Braxton's hand with a respectful bow. "It is an honor and privilege to serve the royal family, Your Royal Highness."

The next day, Prince Braxton rapped lightly on the towering mahogany doors of what had once been his mother's suite. This was a sacred space, her inner sanctum. She had always been his rock, a figure of endless compassion and love. Standing outside the rooms that Valentina now occupied, he felt a comforting warmth from years past, stirring emotions of love and respect for his mother.

He leaned his head against the doors, listening, but heard nothing. Braxton's heart beat faster. When will someone answer? Agitated, he rapped harder, his gentle knock becoming more insistent.

Each moment stretched, feeling endless. Unaccustomed to waiting, he grew frustrated. How am I, a prince, left waiting at the door of my own mother's suite? Even an abrupt "go away" would be better than this silence!

Conflicted, Braxton waited. He loved Valentina deeply, but she alone could summon a tempest of emotions within him. Her cold rejection at the docks had wounded him, and though his love for her remained steadfast, he questioned if she could ever reciprocate it. She had come to England not for love, but under her father's command—a journey driven by duty, steeped in irony rather than romance.

He took stock of his life, his past loves. He had always left attachments on the periphery, content with lingering connections. There had been Aramis, his first lover, years ago, and Joe, a more recent affair that had ended just weeks earlier. Now, with Valentina, he wondered: If she recovers, will she even want to marry me?

Their relationship, an arranged marriage in spirit, had been something they both had fought to orchestrate. But now, misunderstandings and time had eroded everything, perhaps even their hearts. Were they trapped, ensnared like creatures in a hunter's net?

What will happen next? What does the future hold for us?

Braxton took hold of the gilded doorknob and turned it slowly.

The door swung open, flooding the sunlit salon with warm air, the voile curtains stirring gently in the breeze.

The room was empty.

"Where the bloody hell is everyone?" Braxton muttered, irritation sharpening his tone.

Shoving his hands into his pockets, he scanned the room, his gaze sweeping over the vacant chairs and untouched surfaces. He exhaled sharply, his frustration palpable. "Absurd," he muttered, shaking his head.

His eyes drifted to the boudoir's closed door. A wry smile flickered as he tilted his head. "Behind closed doors, no doubt," he mused, irony threading through his voice. "There appears to be a pattern here."

A painting of his parents hung on the wall and nearby charcoal sketches of himself and his mother rested side by side on the mantel, momentarily pulling him from his frustration. Mama, how I treasure those times together, he thought, a smile breaking through as he chuckled softly. When Nanny would bring me to you after breakfast, while you dressed for the day.

His gaze fell on the deep green velvet settee, and he smiled. "We would sit together there."

Crossing the room, he plopped down on one end of the settee, exactly where he used to sit as a boy. Instinctively, he slid toward the middle, closer to where his mother would have sat, recalling the countless times she'd patted the cushion beside her, beckoning him closer.

What would Mama say if she were here now, listening to me reveal my deepest secrets? God forbid I'd do so today. But just imagine…how would she respond?

I dare say she wouldn't give a direct answer but prompt me to find my own. She'd plant the seeds, then patiently watch as they blossomed into insights I might not have otherwise realized.

Moments later, he rose and walked toward the double doors leading into the boudoir. He sighed and rapped on the closed door.

"Oui, entrez s'il vous plaît."

Surprised by the reply, Braxton hesitated.

He exhaled, turned the knob, and stepped into the dim bedroom.

The countess, seated beside Valentina's bed with a book in hand, rose and curtsied. "Bonjour, votre altesse royale."

He nodded curtly. "Good morning, Countess."

Braxton surveyed the room, struck by the contrast to the light-filled salon he'd just left. Gaslit sconces cast flickering light against the far wall. Heavy drapes covered the French windows, sealing out any hint of fresh air.

Switching to French, he asked, "How can you possibly read in this low light, Countess?"

She met him once again with the blank expression he had grown accustomed to. He could tell she understood him perfectly, yet his question still seemed to baffle her.

Braxton projected an unusual familiarity for a senior royal, a stark contrast to Russia, where she would have been viewed more as a high-ranking servant. And as for the dimly lit room, he imagined her attitude reflected that of many Russians he'd encountered during his years there. Light? Airy rooms? Most Russians deem it unhealthy!

He continued, "And the grand duchess, how does she fare today? Have you noticed any improvement?"

"Oui, votre altesse royale, elle semble un peu plus forte aujourd'hui."

"So, she appears stronger?" His tone turned clipped, aloof. "In what way?"

The countess swallowed audibly, and they locked eyes for a tense moment.

I should speak kindlier to her, Braxton chided himself. She's doing her best in a foreign land to care for her mistress; and kept Valentina's confidences. I ought not to judge her.

In a softer tone, he asked, "How can you even tell, in this bleak, cave-like chamber?" He glanced around the room. "Has she repeated the name…Angelina?"

The countess's mouth parted, her eyes widened, but she remained silent.

"Very well, Countess. Would you allow me a few minutes alone with the grand duchess?"

She clutched her book to her chest, bowed slightly, turned and exited the room.

The door clicked shut, Braxton strode to the nearest set of drapes and threw them open, flooding the room with sunlight. The elegant silk tapestries and fabrics adorning the walls and furniture seemed to come alive, glowing in the décor's rich Mediterranean hues.

Relishing the transformation, he strode to the other windows, flung open the remaining drapes, and unlatched the French windows, welcoming the fresh breeze that now swept through the salon, a liberating breath of life.

"Angelina."

Braxton froze.

He slowly turned toward Valentina's bed.

"Angelina," she whispered.

Stunned, he approached her bedside, gently taking Valentina's hand in his. Leaning forward, he placed his other hand on her cheek. In a moment, the warmth of her skin soothed his pounding heart, reigniting the love he'd tried to suppress. Her touch softened the years of a hardened ache that had plagued him since losing her on that foggy, chilly morning in Vienna two years ago.

Valentina opened her eyes, gazing blankly at him. "Angelina...Braxton, please bring her to me."

He caught himself pulling back slightly, then leaned in, placing his lips close to her ear. "Of course, my love. Anything. Just tell me, who is Angelina, and where can I find her?"

Valentina's eyes clouded as they closed again, her head falling to one side, several tears falling on the pillow.

"Val, please…please." His voice trembled, rising in desperation. "Dearest, where is she?"

There was no reply. Braxton felt the weight of silence settle over him, the futility of his pleas sinking deep into his soul. His heart ached with a sorrow he could scarcely contain, his strength draining with each quiet second. He leaned closer, resting his forehead gently against hers, feeling the warmth of her skin against his own. A tear slipped down his cheek, then another, until his grief flowed freely, his tears mingling with hers on the satin pillow.

"Please, Valentina," he whispered, his voice breaking. "Tell me. I'll do whatever you ask. Please, just tell me." He pressed his lips gently to her cheek, his eyes closed.

She stirred, her head lifting an inch before falling back.

His body surged with hope.

"Valentina?" He searched her face, his gaze pleading.

Her mouth opened, as if to speak.

"Darling, what is it? What do you need? How can I help you?"

Her eyes fluttered closed, then opened. In a faint whisper, "Angelina…she is—"

"Yes, my dear Val," he urged gently, "she is?"

With a voice barely audible, Valentina whispered, "Your daughter."

An electric jolt shot through Braxton.

Valentina's eyes closed again, drifting back to sleep. But before she fully succumbed, she murmured, "Bring her to me."

"Valentina!" he said, the shock siphoning the surge of energy from his body, leaving him utterly drained. He struggled to straighten himself. "What did you say?" A chill ran up his spine. "My…daughter?"

A trembling voice from the doorway interrupted, speaking in English. "Yes, Your Royal Highness. Your daughter."

Braxton sat up sharply, staring at the countess, standing by the door, her back pressed against it.

"She is lodged in a convent half a day's journey from St. Petersburg."

Breathing heavily, he locked eyes with the countess. "I don't understand. Why was I not told?"

The countess wrapped her arms around herself, her lips trembling, eyes pooling with tears.

"Countess! How old is the child? Does she know me? Who else knows I am her father?"

He shot to his feet. "I am a father! I have a daughter!"

The countess, visibly shaken, clutched the back of a chair for support, covering her mouth as tears spilled over.

"Forgive me, my prince," she cried. "But the grand duchess forbade me from revealing her secret. I'm confiding in you now because I heard her tell you to go to your daughter and bring Angelina to her. I can no longer, nor do I want to keep it from you."

Wracked with emotion, she added, "My mistress has kept this secret from everyone. From everyone, for so long."

"My daughter?" Braxton repeated softly, then added, with a touch of surprise, "And you speak English?"

"Yes, Your Royal Highness, some English."

They were silent for a moment.

"Is she healthy? How old is she?"

Crossing herself, the countess replied with a renewed composure, "Thanks be to our Sacred Holy Mother she is quite healthy, very clever, and bears a striking resemblance to you, my prince."

"To me?" A faint smile crossed his lips. "She favors me?"

"Yes, she is 15 months old."

He placed his hands on his hips. "Did the grand duchess know she was pregnant when you both left the train in Vienna?"

"She did not, Your Royal Highness."

Braxton gestured toward an inlaid table and two chairs. "Please, Countess Viskanaya, tell me everything. From that fateful morning in Vienna until my return from America. I have so many questions...I must know it all."

Crossing the room, he leaned over Valentina. "Thank you, my darling. I am a father. The father of our child. Thank you." He tenderly kissed her forehead.

Countess Viskanaya took her seat at the table. Braxton opened a concealed door within an ornate armoire, retrieving an unopened bottle of cognac and two cut-crystal glasses. Placing them on the table, he broke the bottle's wax seal and used a corkscrew to remove the cork.

"Countess, I know this may not be customary in Russia, but here in England, we'll forgo formality. We shall drink together in honor of our love for the Grand Duchess Valentina and our dear daughter, Angelina."

The countess managed a soft smile.

Braxton poured the cognac into the two glasses and handed one to the countess. Lifting his own, he said warmly, "To Valentina and Angelina."

The countess raised her glass, her voice steady but rich with emotion as she echoed in Russian, "Za Valentinu i Angelinu."

Their glasses clinked softly, the toast bridging the weight of their shared grief and the strength of their new found bond.

CHAPTER FOUR

THE COUNTESS & THE VISCOUNT

"Your Royal Highness, the grand duchess, is a very private person." The countess paused, biting her lip. "I beg your pardon if I…if I tell you things…things you may already know. I apologize, please indulge me. I am quite unsettled."

The prince nodded. "I understand, Countess. Take your time. This is important to her, to Angelina, and—"

"She shares nothing of her innermost feelings, even with me, though we have been friends since childhood." The countess's speech gained a rhythm, her voice quickening. "At times, she seems a stranger. But I love her dearly and would do anything for her. She is a good friend, a powerful soul, and a visionary. You must know how tirelessly she worked alongside her cousin, Grand Duke Prince Maxim, during your time in our country. Yet even he knows little of her private life, and certainly nothing about the child."

Braxton interrupted thoughtfully, "I would not be too certain of that. Prince Maxim is rather more astute than most give him credit. He is not, shall we say, braggadocios, but deliberate and constant. He keeps his own counsel."

"I couldn't agree more, Your Royal Highness," she demurred.

Braxton shifted in his chair. "But how did she manage it? How can one hide a pregnancy in an imperial court?"

"When we returned to St. Petersburg, she resumed her duties as co-regent. Initially, she met with the grand duke weekly and would visit her father, the czar, occasionally. His memory continues to fade, and he experiences longer spells of confusion. But then, just when everyone least expects it, he emerges from his stupor and subjects the court to weeks of lucidity. Thank God, these episodes are less frequent as he nears the end of his—"

"So, the czar depends entirely on the grand duke and grand duchess to govern?" Braxton asked, "Since leaving Russia four years ago, I haven't kept up with recent affairs."

"Yes, my lord, they rule as co-regents. But when the czar drifts in and out of his affliction, things become—unpredictable. His temperament is volatile. He often undoes their work, only to fall ill again, forcing them to restore what he has upended."

Braxton refilled his glass and smiled at the countess, noticing she'd barely touched hers. "Please, Countess, enjoy your cognac."

The countess's fingers trembled slightly, and a faint twitch crossed her face.

"Why so nervous, Countess?" Braxton teased. "I don't bite. At least not as hard as I bark."

Viskanaya let out a high-pitched laugh, took a sip of her drink, and then another, nearly emptying her glass. She extended it toward the prince.

"That's the spirit, Countess!" he said, refilling her glass.

The tension in her face softened as her eyes sparkled with conspiratorial excitement. "In one of his rages, the czar commanded the grand duchess to leave Russia and go to London to fulfill the marriage contract. She had no choice. After all, he is the czar."

Braxton remembered the fierce fire in Valentina's eyes and the disdain with which she had hissed at the czar's demand. Not long before she fell down the dockyard stairs.

He leaned over, topping off their glasses. "Countess, tell me, how did she conceal the pregnancy?"

The countess hiccupped, then giggled, covering her mouth. "Sheer genius, my lord."

"I'd expect nothing less. But how, exactly?"

"Her family, particularly her father, are known for their brooding moods and tendency to withdraw from court when it suits them. So, upon learning of her pregnancy, she laid the groundwork for her own 'retreat,' navigating the situation with careful finesse. She declined social invitations, made herself less visible at court, and allowed rumors to spread. Whispers flourished, suggesting she'd inherited some of her father's mysterious 'troubles.' These rumors served her purpose well."

Braxton raised an eyebrow. "When her condition became apparent, by what means was Valentina removed from the public's notice?"

"The convent," she said, her voice a whisper. "It was brilliant, really. She informed Prince Maxim of her decision in a letter so delicately crafted it shook the very heart of the imperial court. She declared her intent to retire within the holy walls of a convent, to live there in seclusion for an indefinite period."

"I'll be damned," Braxton murmured, astonished.

The countess shrugged slightly. "Although she was absent from the court, she remained deeply engaged in her co-regency. She refused to let her physical withdrawal hinder her duties and continued to wield considerable influence from a day's journey beyond the capital."

"And Maxim permitted this? What of the czar?"

"The czar was incapacitated at the time," she replied. "And Maxim? Well, he wasn't in a position to deny her. She is the czar's daughter. With her father still on the throne, Grand Duchess Valentina ranks higher. She outranks Maxim in the co-regency."

Braxton's lips curled into a smile. "She is indeed senior. And always a step ahead."

Following his conversation with Countess Viskanaya, Braxton summoned Viscount Ramsey from the continent. Now, the two men sat across from each other in the ducal library, near the gilded baroque desk, a small table between them.

"Ramsey, I appreciate you making the journey to Aurelio on such short notice," Braxton began.

Ramsey nodded and raised his glass of scotch.

The prince continued, lifting his drink. "When I telegraphed you, my plans were uncertain, but my purpose was clear. In the meantime, I have devised a scheme in which I require your assistance; one that may last a lifetime." He paused; his eyes steady. "And by 'a lifetime,' I do not exaggerate."

Ramsey, leaning forward to refill his glass, met Braxton's gaze.

Braxton thought back to their boyhood. Ramsey had always been like an older brother, six years his senior, and a constant family friend. The years had done little to change Ramsey's appearance. He was tall, light-skinned, with a head of dark, wavy hair and an athletic build. Always impeccably dressed, Ramsey was the embodiment of a gentleman.

Lord Ramsey and Braxton's brother, Prince John, had once shared a discreet yet intimate relationship. Though carefully concealed from public eyes, the affair had nearly been exposed but the scandal had mitigated with John's arranged marriage to the daughter of the German kaiser.

"My lord," Ramsey said, his brow furrowing, "What, by Jove, are you proposing?"

Braxton, suddenly feeling his own hesitations, blurted out, "Two days ago, I learned Valentina bore a child. I am the father."

Ramsey drained his entire drink in one swift motion, then slammed the glass onto the table, his eyes fixed on the prince in stunned disbelief.

Offering a faint smile, Braxton added, "It's true. Her name is Angelina. She is my daughter."

The prince settled back in his chair, draining his own glass.

Ramsey refilled both tumblers, then leaned back, rubbing his chin thoughtfully. "And just how do I fit into this…plan?" he asked, a sly smirk crossing his face. "Shall we say, given our shared knowledge, my interests lie elsewhere?"

Braxton's heart jolted. He fought to steady himself, forcing a calm smile to mask the unease creeping through him. "Ramsey," he said evenly, "what I'm about to ask goes far beyond the ordinary. Even beyond what a prince should ask of anyone."

Lord Ramsey picked up his own glass and tipped it slightly toward Braxton before drinking.

Braxton watched him thoughtfully. What if he refuses? And if Valentina recovers, how will she respond? What if Maxim rejects the plan? So many risks…yet Ramsey is key. If he agrees, all our lives will change forever.

Ramsey sighed, visibly affected by the drink. "All right, Braxton. What is this ominous grand plan of yours?" He dabbed his mouth with a handkerchief, settling his crossed arms on his chest, and sat back in his chair. "You know I left England after John's marriage, content to serve you. I've dedicated the past decade to building your empire across Europe, Russia, and the Far East."

They sat in silence for several moments before Ramsey asked, "So, tell me, my prince, what is it you would propose?"

Braxton hesitated before answering. "Angelina is at a convent outside St. Petersburg. I'm leaving for Russia in two days."

Ramsey listened intently as Braxton recounted all that Countess Viskanaya had shared, refilling his glass as the story unfolded.

The prince concluded, "We sail from Dover to Calais the day after tomorrow. My private train will be waiting to take us to St. Petersburg."

Ramsey tilted his head. "Us?"

Braxton shifted slightly. "That is, if you agree to my proposal."

"Of course, my lord, but what exactly do you have in mind?"

Braxton took a steady breath. "The heart of it is this: we cannot acknowledge Angelina as my child. It would shake both the Russian and British monarchies, risking scandal and possibly even political collapse."

Ramsey leaned forward, his elbows on his knees, his chin resting on steepled fingers. "The Russian monarchy would likely endure, but the British Crown? Well, that would be another matter." He refilled his glass again. "So, what has this to do with me?"

It's now or never, thought Braxton. He drew a breath and, in a swift rush, explained, "I am asking you to claim Angelina as your daughter and bring her back to England." Braxton swallowed and looked into Ramsey's eyes. "There it is. That is the plan."

Ramsey froze; his face pale as he gaped at Braxton.

The prince's jaw tightened as he noticed Ramsey's ghost-like cheeks and restless tapping of his fingers on his thighs. Leaning back, Ramsey looked uneasy.

"I know this is a lot to ask," the prince said. "You're under no obligation to accept, and I'd completely understand if you declined."

Still stunned, Ramsey stammered, "But…but you know who I am! How could I…? Are you mad? I've never even been with a woman. The thought alone is…good God, man!"

Braxton shook his head. "John married. And I'm not asking you to marry or father a child—we're straying from the matter at hand, Ramsey."

Ramsey's expression grew pained. "Must you bring up John? I once believed he was everything to me, and it still hurts to think of him. Hardly a day passes that he doesn't cross my mind."

Braxton searched for words, the right words, the words that might comfort Ramsey, but none worthy of assuaging Ramsey's agony presented themselves. "I cannot say I understand, but you know I have always respected and honored your relationship with my brother. And most importantly, I feel you and I have become lifelong friends over the years, albeit a consequence of your losing John."

Ramsey slumped into his chair and stared at the empty tumbler he held in one hand.

The prince, though looking toward Ramsey, soon centered his thoughts elsewhere, on Aramis and their month on Capris. Both were only 19 years old and full of passion. Soon his thoughts moved forward 10 years to Joe and their time in the American West. He had just lied to Ramsey. Through his own experiences, he did indeed feel Ramsey's anguish, the renting of a heart and the wounding of the soul.

It was clear to the prince Ramsey was no fool. He certainly must harbor some suspicions regarding his involvement with Aramis. They had all worked and lived side-by-side those fabulous years of horse racing and building the railroads.

Joe was another matter. Or so Braxton hoped. Braxton again searched for words that would provide Ramsey some solace. What words would have comforted him when he had to give up Aramis? What words would work now, his having just surrendered Joe? Did such words even exist?

Braxton waited for a physical sign Ramsey might be receptive to his moving forward outlining his plan.

In a hard-edged voice, the viscount blurted out, "Continue, Your Royal Highness." He sat up and poured another glass. "And how does this happen? How do I claim Angelina as my own?"

Relieved and cautiously optimistic, Braxton continued, unfolding his plot. "It really is not as difficult as one might imagine."

Ramsey placed the full glass on the side table, folded his arms across his chest, and sat back. "Hmph"

"Truly, Ramsey, with your participation, it is entirely probable my plan to bring Angelina to England will come to fruition. I have written to her cousin, the Grand Duke Maxim. If he will assist us in this scheme, all should go well."

"And Grand Duchess Valentina?" Ramsey asked.

"What about her?" Braxton asked

"One day she will recover, God willing, and realize that you have taken Angelina away from her. Think about it. You, her father, you Braxton, will have taken her away by bringing her here and giving her to me. Again, and please forgive me, but you, the child's father, will have given her away!"

Alarmed by Ramsey's exhortations, the prince pushed back in his chair, gathering his thoughts. "Consider what you are saying. Valentina is certainly aware of the consequences should arrangements not be made to protect everyone involved, including Angelina. Otherwise, why would Valentina have kept her existence secret?"

Braxton stood and placed his hands on his hips. "God Almighty! Angelina is hidden away in a convent! Something must be done. I shall not allow her to be left there, alone, motherless, fatherless."

Ramsey snapped, "Very well, damn it. Regale me with this fairy tale."

"I have sent a letter via courier to Maxim asking him to prepare the necessary documents certifying your paternal claim to Angelina."

"What? How?"

Somewhat sarcastic, Braxton responded, "I suppose you are not inquiring as to how the courier will accomplish his task, but as to the content of the letter."

The viscount glared at the prince.

Braxton ignored the look and did not wait for a response. "In the correspondence, I ask the grand duke to procure the appropriate documents attesting to your marriage to a minor Russian noblewoman. She subsequently died giving birth to a child. That part is true."

"No," Ramsey snapped. "I have never married anyone—period. So, some woman died in childbirth, and now I'm supposed to make believe this dead noblewoman was my wife? Where the hell was I when all this happened? This is a bizarre puzzle, and none of adds up or will be believed."

Braxton ignored Ramsey's comments and continued, "This part, however, is entirely fabricated."

"Braxton, this entire farce is fabricated."

"Do you mind, Ramsey?"

"I mind a great deal but do go on."

"You were not aware of the circumstances of your wife being with child, as you were in the Far East, incommunicado, tending to my affairs. In fact, the family had shared with you via correspondence, the mother's passing. But hid from you that a child had survived."

Burdened under an ever-increasing mountain of incredulity, Ramsey interrupted, "How in Hades do you expect to get away with this? You are inventing circumstances that do not exist and have not occurred. Loose ends flailing about rival the tendrils of Medusa!"

Prince Braxton returned to his seat and remained silent, allowing Ramsey time to calm down and further ponder what he was asking him to do.

"My God! The bribes, the lies, the coercion," Ramsey muttered.

In a soothing voice, Braxton replied, "Ramsey, we are talking about Russia. And yes, I advanced a large sum for Maxim to ensure 'all the I's were dotted and the T's crossed.' There is little concern that an obscure, impoverished noble family would not welcome the opportunity to enrich themselves by participating in the ruse."

Ramsey leaned forward, his elbows resting on his knees. "What would prevent them from extorting additional funds in the future?" Ramsey inhaled. "My family's wealth alone would induce anyone to ask for more."

"I addressed that in my letter. Additional funds will be held in trust and paid out annually over thirty years as long as no one, either in Russia or England, learns the truth."

Viscount Ramsey sighed and said, "You have thought of everything. No surprise there."

Braxton disagreed. "I am certain there exist matters that remain unresolved." He scoffed, "We shall address them as they rise from deep within the depths of this chicanery."

The viscount slouched back in his chair, extending his legs straight out onto the silk Persian carpet, and folded his hands atop his waistcoat.

Braxton smiled inwardly, hoping Ramsey was seriously considering the proposal. If he does not accept, I must have an alternative solution waiting in the wings. I must act now. I can keep Valentina cloistered at the Aurelio Palace for just so long. If she does not regain consciousness, the Russian Ambassador is sure to demand she be returned to St. Petersburg to the care of Russian doctors. Regardless, I will not abandon my daughter.

Braxton harrumphed. Inwardly, he struggled with the known and unknown loose ends. Russian pride. Valentina has the best medical care in the world here. Yanking her from the world's finest doctors would surely be the death of her. If the czar should rise out of his depression, have moments of clarity, and demand her return, what then? Ah, he won't demand her back. But Maxim might. One never knows. After all, she is the czar's only surviving heir.

From the far end of the column-lined library's center promenade, a knock sounded on the towering, massive double doors.

The majordomo entered. He bowed. "Your Royal Highness. A footman has arrived from Buckingham Palace bearing a letter, marked most important."

"Very well," the prince said.

The majordomo proceeded down the marbled promenade. He crossed over to the area in which the prince and viscount were sitting and extended a silver tray holding a crimson envelope bearing the monarch's ornate seal.

He bowed, took two steps back, turned and exited the library.

Braxton refrained from opening the envelope until after the servant had departed.

"I do not believe I have ever seen a red envelope and gold seal, much less the king's seal," Ramsey observed.

Breaking open the wax seal, Braxton replied, "Rarely have I. Only the most important diplomatic correspondence." He used a rose-colored jade letter opener to separate the envelope's flap from the seal and withdrew the folded letter.

Ramsey noted Braxton's eyes opening wide atop a slackened jaw while reading.

Braxton rose out of his chair and proclaimed, "Maxim is czar! The old czar is dead."

Ramsey stood. "That is indeed good news. I mean, not, not, well—not to celebrate the emperor's demise, but this does indeed increase the odds of the success of your scheme. With the passing of the czar and Maxim's ascension to the throne, Valentina is no longer co-regent." He paused. "And her cousin, Czar Maxim, has all the power he needs to assist us with our plan!"

Braxton's stomach flipped hearing Ramsey speak of 'our plan.' At the same moment, other thoughts entered his mind. Now that the czar is dead, Valentina may not have to fulfill the marriage contract. Maxim would not force her to marry. His mind churned. Angelina, our daughter, my daughter. Will I lose her before I have found her? No!

The prince's face blanched, his thoughts tumbling through seas of scenarios that might arise.

"Braxton, what is it? Are you ill? This is surely good news."

The prince breathed in, once, twice, and once again.

In an unconvincing tone, Braxton stammered, "Yes, yes, of course it is. Definitely good, very good." He hesitated and then looked directly at Ramsey. "So, I surmise you agree and will accept my proposal?"

"Well, I suppose there is little else I can do. What choice is there? This is your daughter's future." Ramsey rubbed the back of his neck and then looked hopefully at his friend, "Surely, it has always been abundantly clear I would do anything for your family, the royal family." He paused. "There are arrangements I must make before we depart. I will join you in Dover two days hence."

Ramsey hurriedly executed a bow, having assumed he had been given leave. Braxton took hold of the viscount's forearm and drew him close.

Embracing Ramsey, the prince said, "Ramsey, I shall never forget this. You are indeed a giant among men. I have always loved you as a brother and will forever be in your debt."

Ramsey swallowed and hid his face in Braxton's shoulder. He patted the prince on his back and drew away, quickly turning and hastening down the promenade toward the library doors.

Taken aback by Ramsey's rapid departure, the prince called after him. "It means everything to me, and would to Valentina, should she be awake. Please tell no one of our journey. Make up a story as to the reason for your going to the continent. I shall do likewise."

Ramsey left the library, not looking back or uttering a word.

CHAPTER FIVE

THE MAXIM REVEAL

A massive beast of iron and steel chugged furiously across France, through Germany and toward St. Petersburg. Thick plumes of dark smoke billowed into the sky, stretching in a blackened trail as far as the eye could see.

The locomotive's immense red driving wheels turned with precision; their rhythmic motion accompanied by the hiss of steam and the clank of metal. It thundered through villages, farmland, rushing rivers, and industrial centers, filling the air with powerful chuffs from its enormous cylinders and a piercing whistle.

Behind the engine a string of luxurious private cars gleamed in the sunlight. Their burgundy-painted bodies and sleek black roofs adorned with intricate gold and brass detailing; windows framed in rich velvet curtains. From afar, the train embodied a magnificent, romantic sight, gliding gracefully along the rails with its thunderous progression softened by the distance, inspiring the imaginations of all who saw it.

Inside these private cars traveled Prince Braxton, Viscount Ramsey, Braxton's longtime adjutant Major Barret, three nurses, and a small retine of servants. A dining car followed the prince's private car, another for the viscount and the major, and one designated as a nursery with quarters for the nurses. These cars trailed behind the two coal cars, a water tank, and a supply car for the crew.

During the 1,400-mile, four-day journey from Calais to St. Petersburg, Braxton found himself lost in memories. Eight years earlier, he had lived and thrived in Russia for three years, working closely with Maxim and Valentina. Together, they had expanded mining and lumbering operations and pioneered exploratory oil drilling in an effort to successfully stave off Russia's looming financial ruin. Through Braxton's ingenuity, Imperial Russia had been rescued from the brink of insolvency—and a potential revolution.

As a reward, Russia had made him a business partner, granting him 50 percent ownership in The Russian Consortium, a company created to oversee these ventures. Braxton had later spent two years in Japan as a royal envoy, followed by a year in Hong Kong and subsequently spent time in Singapore. There, he acquired an insolvent American shipping line to transport rubber from his Southeast Asia plantations and other exports. Those days seemed a lifetime ago. Now, life had taken an unforeseen turn, propelling him toward Russia once again—this time to rescue a child he had never met—his own daughter.

Under the cover of night, the train ghosted into St. Petersburg and slipped onto a secluded rail siding, where a light cavalry unit of the czar's Imperial Guard stood at silent attention. As the engine gradually powered down, a heavy hush settled over the yard, broken only by the whisper of escaping steam, the scraping of hooves, and the restless snorts of horses echoing through the darkness.

Two large, closed black carriages, each drawn by six horses, pulled up, flanked by mounted guards. An officer dismounted and made his way to the dining car where Braxton, Ramsey, Major Barret, and one nurse were waiting.

The guard saluted. "Your Royal Highness, I am to inform you that you are to ride in the forward carriage. The remainder of your party will follow in the other carriage."

Braxton frowned. "And why is that, Captain? Who has given this order?"

"His Imperial Majesty, the Czar!" replied the officer.

The prince, the viscount, and the major exchanged bewildered looks.

"Are you quite certain, Captain?" Braxton asked, puzzled as to why the czar would care about such details, especially as Maxim was not here.

"Those are my orders, Your Royal Highness."

"Very well."

The Russian officer, along with the three Englishmen and the nurse, stepped off the train and walked through the fog-laden rail yard toward the snorting horses and the clinking of harnesses.

A guard stood beside the forward carriage door. He opened it, released the folding steps, then stood back and saluted. Braxton acknowledged him with a nod and climbed halfway into the lantern-lit interior, then froze.

Sitting inside, Czar Maxim, Emperor of all Russia, wore a sly, welcoming smile sparkled with mischief, his eyes alight as he looked at Braxton.

Braxton was momentarily speechless. He himself appeared pale, gaunt, and visibly exhausted from his recent arrival in England and the flurry of events following Valentina's accident—plus the shocking revelation of his new fatherhood. The ordeal had left him emotionally and physically drained. His appearance betrayed every ounce of the strain.

Maxim's eyes widened, his lips parting in disbelief. "Braxton!" he exclaimed, drawing back slightly before regaining his composure. "My friend, it is truly good to see you." He took Braxton's hand in his. "I hope you're as pleased to see me as I am to see you."

Braxton, still only half inside the carriage, struggled to find words. He pulled himself fully into the compartment, and despite his surprise, forced a grateful smile. "Maxim…it means more than I can say to see you here. Truly, your effort to piece all of this together…well, it means the world to me." He paused, his voice softening. "You just being here…"

The two men embraced, Maxim patting Braxton's shoulder. "I couldn't bear the thought of not coming. You have my support, my friend."

They settled into their seats, and with a swift tap of Maxim's walking stick against the roof, the driver snapped the reins. The first carriage lurched forward, the loud crack of the whip echoing as the powerful horses surged ahead. Behind them, the second carriage followed, its wheels catching the rough road in tandem. Together, the two carriages plunged into the shadowed depths of the forest, the grinding of wheels and pounding hooves swallowed by the dense, looming darkness.

Braxton leaned back against the luxurious, tufted leather upholstery, feeling some of the tension of this unexpected meeting ease. The carriage jolted and swayed as the two men braced themselves for the bumpy ride.

"My letter," Braxton said, a hint of apology in his voice. "I hope my requests weren't too burdensome. I realize the notice was short."

Maxim chuckled, his voice warm and rich. "Your requests were extensive and…interesting. But I've managed to arrange everything, I hope, to your satisfaction."

"Thank you. I can't begin to repay you for such kindness."

Maxim waved off his gratitude. "Think nothing of it. Mother Russia could never repay you for all you have done."

The carriage struck a rough patch, jolting violently, and both men instinctively reached out, seizing the ornate leather handholds to steady themselves against the fierce lurch.

"And the arrangements?" Braxton asked, repositioning himself.

Maxim handed him a leather-bound portfolio. "Inside are the documents certifying Viscount Ramsey's marriage to Princess Varva and the birth certificate for their daughter, Princess Angelina."

Braxton looked at him, impressed. "You managed to produce these in a matter of days? Remarkable. They're authentic?"

"They're certified, yes," Maxim replied with a slight smile. "Factual? No. But I've used my position to make them plausible. To anyone who sees them, they are authentic."

"Autocracy does have its advantages," Braxton sighed.

"It does indeed."

For a moment, silence reigned, broken only by the rhythmic sound of hooves striking the gravel road and the grumble of carriage wheels.

"Our journey to the convent will take us into early hours of the morning. When we arrive, both you and I will remain in the carriage. The colonel of the Imperial Guard and Viscount Ramsey will retrieve the child from the monastery's reverend mother."

"And they will give Angelina directly to us?"

"Yes," Maxim nodded, "I've instructed the colonel to have the viscount, and the princess brought directly to our carriage."

Braxton gazed out the window into the vast forest shrouded in darkness, his mind far from the passing trees.

The carriage eventually emerged from the woods, rolling through open farmland. A moon, obscured by dense clouds, cast an ominous hue over the landscape. Faint carriage lanterns cast a feeble glow on the road, their light devoured by thick, looming darkness.

Braxton turned back from the window, meeting Maxim's steady gaze.

"The child is Valentina's," he said in a soft tone. "I am her father."

"I surmised as much," Maxim replied. "When she had not returned to St. Petersburg after a year of confinement, I made inquiries." The czar stroked his beard. "It appears Valentina is one of two women having given birth to baby girls within minutes of one another. The other woman died in childbirth along with her daughter."

Braxton sat up and asked. "Did you share the fact that Valentina had a child with anyone?"

"Certainly not."

"I see. Thank you for your discretion. Of course, I would have expected nothing else from you. Thank you."

"After Valentina returned to St. Petersburg of her own accord, things escalated. My uncle ordered her to London to fulfill the marriage contract with you." He paused, letting out a heavy sigh. "Tragically, Valentina never had a chance to return to the convent and see Angelina before she was forced to leave for England. The czar had placed her under guard. The armed coterie escorted Valentina and her party all the way to Calais."

"Good God! The world is better off now that the czar, that bastard, is dead," Braxton said.

The carriage jolted. Both men leaned forward, their fingers gripping the seat.

"I don't disagree," Maxim said, steadying himself before continuing. "The czar was often a difficult and unyielding man." As the carriage's jostling eased, he leaned forward, resting his elbows on his knees, and steepled his fingers under his chin. "No one—not even your sister, Carmen—knows about my suspicions Valentina may have given birth."

Braxton offered, "So would it be fair to assume Carmen is unaware of what has transpired and your business here?"

"Yes, I believe so. With the preparations for her and my coronation, she is quite otherwise occupied."

"Excellent! Now tell me, what of the mother, Princess Varvara? Her family?" Braxton caught himself, sitting back and shaking his head. "That poor woman. Her child. I count myself so very fortunate the same did not befall Angelina and Valentina."

Maxim waited a moment and answered, "She was from an impoverished noble family situated east of Moscow. Not far from where Viscount Ramsey administered your affairs while you were in India. Though it is unlikely their paths ever crossed."

The prince, his tone edged with weary sarcasm, sighed, "How very convenient."

Maxim turned sharply, fixing the prince with an exasperated glare. He took a measured breath before speaking. "Braxton, this was no simple undertaking. I trust you understand the considerable effort my staff and secret police invested in constructing this charade for you."

Braxton reached over and placed his hand on Maxim's knee. "I beg your pardon, friend. How inconsiderate of me. Forgive me, for I am exhausted, a bit overwhelmed. The last several weeks since my return from America have been nothing but a trial and discordant tribulation."

Maxim placed one of his hands atop Braxton's, smiled and said, "Forgiven."

Braxton let his head fall back against the high-backed leather upholstery and asked, "And her parents?"

"Deceased. Her father passed years ago."

"And her mother?"

"Her mother, it seems, died of despair after losing both her daughter and granddaughter. I believe her daughter's circumstances, along with her refusal to disclose the father's identity, only deepened the mother's sorrow."

"Fortunately, for our purposes, there are no siblings or immediate family. Angelina inherits the title. No money. The estates were sold to pay debts. Very sad."

"I see," Braxton said under his breath.

Maxim nodded slowly and murmured, "But again, as you said, how convenient."

Braxton shifted in his seat. "I have apologized for my insensitive remark."

"Yes, you have." The czar exhaled. "Please know that I am preoccupied with becoming czar and a bit out of sorts as well." He patted Braxton's shoulder. "But I enthusiastically support your efforts and am honored you have entrusted me with facilitating your endeavors."

"Thank you. Again, I am truly grateful."

Maxim removed a decanter and two glasses from an ornate inlaid wood box resting on the floor near his feet. "The road is much smoother between here and the monastery. I have a bottle of that American bourbon from one of the four cases you sent from Kentucky. Consider yourself lucky there's any left. I've developed quite a fondness for it."

Braxton's face lit up. "Bravo!"

Sipping the beverage, Maxim returned to his story. "I added funds to the generous fortune you forwarded to help facilitate these arrangements. I bought back Princess Angelina's family's estates. The ones sold to pay her family's debts."

The prince leaned forward. "I beg your pardon. You did what?"

"Yes, for a Russian noblewoman, albeit a minor noble, to have a respectable position in your country, she must have estates and position. And please do not forget, Viscount Ramsey's marriage would no doubt lack credulity should her circumstances not be significant. His own family's wealth and prestige demand it." Maxim tossed back his glass, refilled it and said, "Please forgive me for saying this, but Lord Ramsey's friendship with your brother Prince John has not gone unnoticed. And is not entirely forgotten. We must do everything we can to prevent Princess Angelina's reputation from falling victim to the viscount's past indiscretions."

Braxton drained his own glass and raised it toward Maxim. "Touché, Maxim. You needn't be concerned. Things are well in hand. You have played an enormous part in assuaging a predicament I had anticipated but had not yet fully resolved."

Braxton scratched his chin, adding, "Your actions will quell insidious gossip and protect the young princess."

"I thought you might approve."

In a self-congratulatory tone, Braxton said, "I say, we do make a good pair! Beginning with our joint efforts to save Russia from ruin years ago. And today, we may have saved my father's crown by avoiding the scandal associated with Angelina's birth."

The men clinked their glasses, toasting, "Za Zdarovye!" Then they settled back, each lost in quiet contemplation, sipping their whiskey in thoughtful silence.

The carriage trundled along. The road stretched out endlessly before them, leading deeper, once again, into a forest of ominous darkness.

Trees loomed menacingly on either side of the road. Their ruddy branches reached out like gnarled fingers, as if trying to snatch the carriage from its path.

Braxton asked, "Why is it always so gloomy, this Russia?"

Maxim answered, his voice tinged with a hint of sardonic amusement, "Ah, perhaps it is your state of mine, dear friend. Your inner conflicts, your tumultuous emotions, that which is your gloom.

Braxton nodded, peering out the window. "Perhaps."

The czar leaned forward, peering into the thick, gray fog. "We're nearly there." He pulled a gold watch from his waistcoat, checking the time. "Excellent. We're making good progress. It's 2:30 a.m. If you and Ramsey collect your daughter and immediately depart the monastery, you should return to your train before sunrise."

"Are you not accompanying us back to St. Petersburg?"

"I will be returning to the Alexander Palace in Tsarskoy Selo. It is best if I distance myself as much as possible from these events.

"Ah, I see. I was hoping we would have more time together on the return to St. Petersburg."

Brandishing a broad smile, Maxim rejoined, slapping Braxton's knee, "You will forget all about me and any conversation we might have as soon as you lay eyes on Angelina! Of that I am certain."

Braxton furrowed his brow and returned a shallow grin. "I suppose you are right."

"Of course, I am. But there is something more I would like to share with you."

"What is that, my friend?"

"Well," Maxim paused for a moment, then placed his hands in his lap. "It's your sister, Carmen."

Braxton turned and faced Maxim. "What, what about her? Is she not well?"

"I believe she is quite well, but very tired, bedridden, under my physician's care."

"Then Maxim, she is not well. What are you saying?"

Maxim rolled his lips and swallowed. He looked directly into Braxton's eyes. "She is healthy, but with child, we believe, well, uh, children. She may be carrying twins."

CHAPTER SIX

AUNTIE VALENTINA

Braxton and little Angelina lay side by side on their stomachs on the floor, just ten feet from where Valentina lay resting on her bed. A cool breeze drifted through the open windows, carrying the sweet scent of jasmine from the Aurelio Palace gardens.

A blue slate Jary Freres mantel clock chimed from above the unlit fireplace.

"Unca B'ax'n! Clock go ding-ding!" Angelina chirped, pointing toward the clock.

"For a toddler of only eighteen months, her English is improving quickly," Braxton thought aloud.

Angelina wore a little silk dress trimmed with blue lace and delicate white-on-white floral embroidery. Blue ribbons in her curls matched her eyes, setting off her long lashes, much like her mother's.

Skimming his fingertips along her tiny, soft jawline, Braxton murmured, "Yes, my dear, it does go ding-ding. We call those sounds chimes."

"Cheemes?" she echoed, frowning with concentration.

Braxton chuckled. "Yes, chimes."

Giggling, she picked up her crayon and with wobbly strokes, scribbled in her coloring book, spilling the color outside the lines.

"Unca B'ax'n, why you color so good? I want color like you."

He smiled. "In time, my love, with lots of practice."

She squeaked, clapping her hands. "I practice! Make picture for Auntie V'lentina!"

Braxton inhaled, a bittersweet smile on his face. Auntie, she calls her. Her mother. "Yes, let's practice every day," he said, patting her shoulder and placing a kiss on her head. "You'll make many beautiful pictures for your Auntie Valentina."

A gentle knock sounded, and the boudoir door opened. Viscount Ramsey stepped inside.

Braxton, focused on his "practice," glancing over just as Angelina's face lit up. She dropped her crayon and struggled to her feet, wobbling slightly as she toddled over to the viscount, her arms stretched out. "Papa! Papa!"

Braxton's heart tightened as it did every time he heard Ramsey addressed as "Papa." Will I ever accept this? Being relegated to an uncle—to my own dear Angelina? And how will Valentina…?

A soft voice came from the bed. "Angelina?"

Ramsey lifted Angelina into his arms, and they both turned to Valentina.

Braxton sprang to his feet.

Valentina lay back on her pillow, her eyes brilliant, fixed upon her daughter. Reaching out with a trembling hand, she whispered once more, "—gelina."

Angelina wriggled and twisted in Ramsey's arms, her little legs kicking as she reached eagerly toward Valentina. Ramsey, visibly unaccustomed to holding energetic children, struggled to keep his grip before finally setting her down on the carpet. She ran to Valentina, her chubby legs carrying her forward in unsteady little steps, her arms outstretched. "Tya! Tya!" she called out in her baby attempt to say "Tyetya," Russian for "auntie."

Both men watched as Angelina reached Valentina's bedside and gripped her mother's arm with her small hands.

Tears streamed down Valentina's face as she gathered her daughter close, her voice breaking. "My Angelina, my darling Angelina."

She nestled her face in Angelina's soft curls, murmuring, "Moya dragotsennaya lyubov. My precious love."

Angelina pulled back, bouncing on her toes, her eyes wide with excitement. She lifted her arms, clearly wanting to be held.

Valentina loosened her embrace, sinking back onto the pillow as she looked tenderly at her daughter's face.

How wise of Valentina to have taught her to say "Auntie," Braxton thought. Though it must pain her as it does me, to be called "Uncle."

The little girl pressed her cheek against her mother's arm and babbled, "Missed you, Tyetya!"

A faint smile softened Valentina's face. "I missed you too, my darling, but I kept you close in my dreams."

"Not sick no more?" Angelina asked, her voice hopeful. "Read to me? Play?"

Stroking her daughter's curls, Valentina whispered, "Soon, my little lovebug."

Each day, Braxton, Ramsey, and Angelina spent time in Valentina's rooms as her strength steadily improved. Soon, she could sit up against the pillows propped behind her. Though she rarely spoke, she often motioned for Angelina to sit beside her on the bed.

A week slipped away. The nurse had just taken Angelina for her nap when Valentina's strained, halting voice snapped the silence. "Why? Why did you bring her here? I don't understand. How could you be so cruel?"

Ramsey took a step back, his mouth slightly open in surprise.

Braxton's face tightened as he closed his eyes, holding his breath.

The men collected themselves, both gazing at Valentina, who now looked at them with fire in her eyes. "How could you do this?" she demanded. "I had Angelina's life planned out. You've ruined everything. What right had you to interfere?"

In a soft voice, Braxton said, "Now, Valentina."

She transferred her glare from Braxton to Ramsey, her tone laced with mockery. "Papa?"

Ramsey folded his arms, lowered his head, and whispered with a trembling edge, "Say something, Braxton."

Braxton sat on the edge of her bed and reached for her hand.

Valentina crossed her arms and looked away.

Gently, Braxton spoke. "You cried out for her in your sleep, Valentina. Once I knew who she was, how could I do anything else? What else could you expect from me? She is our child. Should I have left her to be raised in a monastery?"

Valentina turned toward him; her voice was low. "And how did you learn of her?"

He steepled his fingers under his chin. "You called her name in your delirium." Braxton inhaled. "You told me Angelina is my daughter."

Valentina's eyes widened, "I did?"

"You did. Countess Viskanaya, despite her initial reluctance, eventually told me the truth after hearing you plead for Angelina. After you asked me to bring her to you." He rested both hands on her folded arms. "What else could I do?"

Valentina slumped back against the pillows and turned her back to him. Her voice wavered as she spoke. "Both of you…get out."

"But I wanna see Tya Tya," Angelina whined.

"I do too, angel," Ramsey said sympathetically. "But she isn't feeling well today."

"But you say ev'day," Angelina protested, her lower lip quivering. "Now, Papa."

Kneeling to meet her eye, Ramsey said, "I know, my sweet. It feels like a long time, doesn't it? Maybe Uncle Braxton can talk to her and tell her how much you want to see her. Let's hope she feels better tomorrow."

Valentina sat alone, having just finished a light lunch of soup and sliced fruit.

Braxton knocked on the open door's frame and entered her suite.

She had bathed earlier that morning, her hair washed and styled with the assistance of Countess Viskanaya and two maids. Valentina sat in an armchair, wearing a modest floral day dress.

"Good afternoon, Valentina," Braxton said, offering a shallow bow.

"Good afternoon, Braxton."

He took a seat at the end of the divan opposite her, crossing one leg over the other, his hands resting in his lap. "I trust you're feeling better. You look lovely."

Ramsey stepped into the room, prompting a flicker of surprise across Braxton's face as he glanced up. Pausing at the threshold before crossing with deliberate steps, the viscount halted by the fireplace and leaned against the mantel. Although his arms hung loosely at his sides, a subtle tension undercut his calm façade. His gaze shifted between Braxton and Valentina, as if bracing for a sudden spark lurking in the hushed atmosphere.

Valentina had ignored Braxton's compliment and barely acknowledged Ramsey's presence. "Why does Angelina call Ramsey 'Papa'?"

Braxton looked down briefly, then glanced up at Ramsey, whose face flushed slightly.

The prince rubbed the back of his neck. "After your fall, Valentina, Angelina's name occasionally escaped your lips. We weren't sure what to make of it. But then, you told me she was my daughter." He took a steadying breath, then recounted the events that led to his and Ramsey's journey to Russia and their meeting with Maxim. Braxton ended by describing how they had taken Angelina from the monastery and brought her to the Aurelio Palace.

When he finished, Valentina sat in silence, contemplating his words.

Braxton wondered; his heart heavy.What is she thinking? Does she doubt me now? Or has she simply lost all faith in my words and intentions? How cruel it seems, her coldness and mistrust. Surely these must be temporary, just a result of her illness. But will she ever truly recover? Will she ever be the woman I loved—the only woman I've ever truly loved?

Noticing him lost in thought, Valentina softened, seeing a flicker of sadness on his face. Her own features relaxed; she remained silent.

Braxton, head bowed, inwardly concluded her heart and soul have turned to stone. Perhaps I'm wasting my time here. I can't go on like this. At least Angelina will show me some tenderness. He slowly rose. "Good day, Valentina." He rose and turned to leave.

"Please, Braxton," she called after him. "Come back and sit with me for a moment. I'd like to speak with you."

He halted mid-step, turned, and faced Valentina, carefully weighing her request. "I'll do whatever I must do to keep Angelina in England." He swallowed hard, fighting the turmoil rising within him, then returned to the divan, sitting ramrod straight, steeling himself for whatever words she might hurl at him.

Ramsey, aware of the tension, bowed and turned to leave. Before he stepped out, Valentina offered a gentle smile and a small nod—her silent gratitude for all he had done. Relief crossed his face, he then quietly slipped from the room.

In a gentler, somewhat conciliatory tone, Valentina began, "Thank you for bringing Angelina to me. I am grateful."

Braxton's mind clouded for a moment, struggling to process, her words surreal.

"And," Valentina continued, her voice softer. "I appreciate the care you've given me these past months. I realize it hasn't been easy. Rather challenging, I'm sure—especially after how I spoke to you at the dock."

Braxton's gaze sharpened, his voice a near whisper. "And since then, almost every word you've uttered…"

She adjusted her dress and folded her hands in her lap. "At the quay, I felt trapped, alone, filled with anger. I was worried for Angelina, knowing she was so far away. Please accept my apology for my behavior. You are not entirely at fault."

Braxton bristled. "At fault? I see myself as part of the solution, not the problem."

She glanced down at her hands, smoothing her skirt. "I suppose you are."

"Valentina," Braxton said, his tone firm, "do you have any concerns regarding the arrangements made for Angelina?"

"Naturally," she said, and looked down at her hands. "As any mother would. What exactly do you have in mind? How is Angelina to stay, to remain close, here, with me?"

Braxton took a steadying breath. "We have made plans with that very goal in mind, trusting that you would see their benefit. Everything has been arranged to keep her near you. Ramsey is now, thanks to Maxim, her legal father."

Valentina's face grew slack, her eyes unfocused.

"Did you hear me? Do you understand what I said, Valentina?"

She nodded.

Braxton continued, "And again, all of this depends on you. You've made it clear you object to our marriage contract. If that remains your position, especially now that your father is gone, and Maxim has ascended the throne…"

Valentina leaped to her feet, her expression breaking from indifference to astonishment. "Maxim is the czar?"

"Yes, Maxim and Carmen were crowned last week. My parents returned from Moscow just yesterday."

Valentina paced the room, a mixture of emotions flashing across her face.

"You're free now to choose your own path," Braxton said, watching her closely. "I only hope you'll consider Angelina's best interests. Maxim and I have ensured she'll be well provided for. She has her own income and the household here loves her. But ultimately, the choice is yours."

"And this plan—your and Ramsey's 'scheme'—where does it lead?"

He exhaled. "We were all dealt a difficult hand. None of us knew who Angelina truly was, or what to do with her. You were unconscious much of the time, but you kept calling out her name. There was no guarantee you would recover. And so, it was decided Angelina and Ramsey would remain here at the Aurelio Palace, at least for the foreseeable future. There's ample space, and Ramsey thought it was best she stayed close to Aunt Valentina, especially for continuity's sake. Given the state of your health, if you hadn't…if you recovered, she would be nearby. Ramsey, as you might imagine, will never marry."

Braxton eyed Valentina, her gaze lost in thought.

"I never allowed myself to tell Angelina I'm her mother." Valentina's voice trembled, barely above a whisper. "I told her she was the daughter of my friend, Varvara. She was so little then. I thought she wouldn't understand, and that her memory of me would fade quickly should I be forced to leave the monastery or be separated from her." Her gaze fell, and a tear slipped down her cheek.

"I did this knowing my child, born out of wedlock, could never be accepted by my family or society. My intention was to raise her as my ward, never to return to St. Petersburg, much less to London or to you. But eventually I realized I couldn't stay away from court forever. So, I returned to my duties in St. Petersburg, planning to make the best of it until my father passed. When that time came, I would reveal the truth to Maxim and ask his permission to leave Russia and take my child with me."

Braxton's chest tightened, a metallic taste filling his mouth. "You had no intention of telling me I was her father?"

"Of course not. Why would I? Revealing the truth would have only brought scandal to you and your family, serving no purpose whatsoever."

Braxton stood; his voice was harsh. "No purpose?" His hands clenched at his sides, his eyes flashing.

Valentina lifted her hands in a gentle, reassuring gesture. "Please, Braxton, take a seat. I chose my words poorly. I realize now how deeply you care for her—and what a good father you truly are."

Braxton tightly crossed his arms over his chest, his piercing gaze locked on hers.

She softened her tone, leaning forward. "That is all in the past, Braxton. My plans have unraveled. My father's actions destroyed them, and you seem to have done what you could to salvage them. To some degree."

His thoughts whirled with frustration. Words—just empty words. No real acknowledgment of what I, and others, have sacrificed. If only she'd answered even one of my letters over the years, I would have been by her side in an instant. Her willful silence only deepened the rift between us.

He squared his shoulders, his tone cutting and precise. "I won't pretend to fulfill some fantasy of yours or meet expectations that no longer make sense. Your father is gone, and Maxim won't hold us to the marriage contract. Your accident, any health concern—there are plenty of ways to dissolve this agreement."

Her kind expression shifted, alarm creeping into her eyes. "Braxton, is that truly what you want?"

"What I want hasn't seemed to matter since that morning you left me in Vienna."

A heavy silence settled between them.

Valentina's gaze drifted, her expression clouded as though sifting through a tangle of thoughts and memories. Her fingers tightened around the fabric of her dress. She took a slow, measured breath. After a long pause, she looked up, her eyes shining with unshed tears.

She rose from the divan, her skirt rustling softly with each step, and moved to the window. With her back to the room, she gazed outside.

In a quiet, almost tentative voice, she asked, "What do you intend to do with your life now that you are back in England?"

Braxton's jaw tightened, a trace of bitterness creeping into his voice. "My intentions were clearly laid out in the letters I wrote— though I doubt you read them," his tone sharp. "I'd planned to enter politics, to stand for Parliament, as we'd agreed. Our marriage was meant to be the foundation for it all—a family, a future, a life built together."

He paused, the words seeming heavier as he said them aloud. "But now, with everything as it is…well, at the very least, I'll still pursue politics." His gaze shifted away; the lingering frustration unmistakable.

Valentina dabbed at her eyes with a handkerchief. She turned around, her voice trembling. "Angelina is here." She took a steadying breath and continued, "Braxton, I have no reason to return to Russia. And I have every reason to remain here with Angelina. I'll marry you and give you an heir." She faltered, gripping the back of a chair for support.

Braxton instinctively stepped forward, but she raised her hand to stop him, catching herself as she straightened. "I don't have the strength—mentally or physically—to make any other commitments."

He gave a frustrated sigh. "Is it truly that difficult, Valentina? Am I so repugnant?"

She returned to her chair, her face drawn, her eyes filled with an emotion he couldn't name.

"Do you remember when we first fell in love, Braxton? How we dreamed of marrying? That magical sleigh ride across the tundra under a star-strewn sky, both of us wrapped in furs? And the long, romantic train journey through India? We were so deeply in love then. Now, how did we end up here? How could things have gone so wrong?" She buried her face in her hands. "Now, I find myself engaged to you in an arrangement we once yearned for. And now?"

"You don't have to do this, Valentina."

She lifted her head, her gaze steady. "Nor do you, Braxton," she replied quietly. "I read your letters over and over."

"What, you read them? You never responded."

"In them, I glimpsed a side of you I never saw—an empathetic man growing into someone special...that is why I'll marry you and provide you with an heir. As for what our life together will look like, only time will tell."

CHAPTER SEVEN

MARRIAGE

King Richard, Queen Mercedes, Braxton, and Valentina were having lunch when Valentina spoke up. "I'd really rather not have an extravagant wedding."

The queen reached over, patting Valentina's hand. "I understand, my dear," she said with a small smile. "I won't patronize you—it would be insincere."

Valentina straightened, glancing at each of them in turn; the queen, the king, and finally, Braxton.

Braxton shrugged, an impish grin lighting his face. "They are hungry, the public is hungry for a 'fairy-tale' wedding," he said with a hint of irony. "As usual, our government wants to keep the people entertained. Bring out the show ponies and distract them from daily hardships."

The king cast a disapproving look in his direction. "Really, Braxton."

Braxton took Valentina's hands in his, his expression softening. "And so it goes. That is our lot as royals, after all. Our lives have never been our own, you know that."

The king's face tightened. "Braxton, of all people, you have done exactly as you pleased for most of your life. Your mother and I have indulged you, as we have no other."

Valentina chuckled softly, interjecting, "True. My soon-to-be husband has indeed had his cake and eaten it too." She playfully stuck her tongue out at Braxton.

The king snorted, and the queen gave a small nod, amused.

Braxton held up his hands in mock surrender, smiling from ear to ear. It's true, he thought.

The marriage between the imperial houses of England and Russia captivated the world. Czar Maxim, Czarina Carmen, and nobility from across Europe filled London to its limits. Crowds thronged the streets, hoping for a glimpse of the procession and the pageantry of royals.

Once again, Braxton's triumphs in North America were celebrated in the press, boosting his already considerable popularity. He was heralded as the future of a changing Britain. Valentina, known for her beauty, intellect and the strength that had helped her co-rule Russia, became a figure of fascination, a blend of mystery and charm.

Westminster Abbey had seen countless royal weddings, beginning with Henry I and Matilda of Scotland in the 11th century. Now, it was once again adorned in pomp and pageantry, steeped in centuries-old tradition.

On the wedding day, London's streets overflowed with well-wishers dressed in their finest. The towering, intricately designed cathedral rose against the skyline, gilded by the morning sun. Union Jack flags waved as the crowd cheered, hoping for a glimpse of the Russian bride.

Accompanied by Czar Maxim, Grand Duchess Valentina arrived at the Abbey in a gilded horse-drawn carriage.

The carriage rolled to a stop; trumpets sounded in fanfare. Valentina stepped out, her gown an elegant cascade of white silk brocade with a minimal touch of lace and delicate blue Akoya pearls. A silver tiara, crafted in intricate filigree, glittered with diamonds, caught the light like shards of starlight. Aquamarines shimmered in soft, oceanic hues, adding a fanciful glow evoking moonlit waves cresting along a distant shore. Her veil in place spilled gracefully to the ground.

Taking her cousin's arm, Valentina looked up at Maxim, resplendent in his white uniform, adorned with gleaming medals. He leaned in, his voice soft with hope.

"Valentina, may this day rekindle what you and Braxton once shared—a truly heartfelt love."

"Thank you, Maxim. You've always been the hopeless romantic." Her smile softened, then turned wistful. "But today, simply surviving is all I hope for."

"Valentina, you don't have to…"

"Shall we?" she interjected and encouraged him forward.

Together, they moved toward the Abbey's Western Door. They entered. A triumphant second fanfare echoed, Valentina's pearl-laden train shimmering behind her, a serene river in motion.

The grandeur of Westminster Abbey rose around them: towering columns, stained glass filtering the sunlight, and lavish ornamentation creating a fanciful milieu. The fragrance of gardenias drifted in the air.

Braxton, standing at the altar in his scarlet military uniform, felt his heart race watching her approach. I've never seen a more breathtaking sight, he thought, pulse quickening.

When Valentina and the czar reached him, Maxim placed her hand on Braxton's. They locked eyes through the delicate veil, and in that stillness, Braxton felt the weight of it all. He was about to marry not just a woman of extraordinary beauty, but someone who had once held his heart completely. Yet now, a question lingered: Could they find their way back to what they once had, or had that happiness slipped away forever?

The ceremony began with the bishop's solemn prayer, followed by the Declaration of Intention.

"Do you both come willingly to marry one another?" the bishop asked.

Neither answered.

Braxton glanced at Valentina. She stared straight ahead, unblinking, her gaze fixed on a distant crucifix.

Swallowing his doubts, he answered, "I do."

The silence that followed was heavy, stretching for a moment too long. A cough echoed somewhere in the congregation, followed by whispers and the rustling of fabric.

Braxton, caught off guard by her hesitation, shuddered.

Valentina's voice cut through, soft but sure, "I do."

A subtle yet palpable wave of relief swept through the abbey as the ceremony continued. They recited their vows, exchanged rings, and, after signing the marriage register, stepped out of Westminster Abbey as husband and wife.

Stepping through the grand doors of the abbey, they met with thunderous applause reverberating across a grassy park. The park opened onto a boulevard lined with cheering well-wishers waving flags. Braxton guided Valentina to the waiting carriage, his grip gentle yet reassuring. At the carriage steps, footmen swiftly gathered up her voluminous, pearl-laden skirts, carefully maneuvering the cascading fabric into the plush interior. Trumpets resounded, church bells rang out, and the city erupted in celebration as the royal couple finally settled in, ready to travel down the jubilant boulevard.

Weeks into their honeymoon in an old family castle in Scotland, they breakfasted alone.

"Valentina," Braxton said, breaking the silence, "our time together has become so…strained. It's like neither of us is trying. Can we at least make the effort?"

Valentina drummed her fingers on the table. "I am trying, Braxton. I need time."

"But you seem angry, distant."

"I am all those things," she whispered. "But I'm still here, trying to honor our relationship."

Braxton frowned. "I want more than that. I want the Valentina I knew on the Russian steppes, the woman who stood with me in the mountains of India."

Valentina's eyes flashed, her voice sarcastic. "Is that all you want?"

He sighed. "Why are you so angry, Valentina?"

She turned away, dabbing at her eyes before standing up. "Excuse me." She strode out of the room.

The honeymoon ended. They returned to the Aurelio Palace, where Ramsey and Angelina eagerly waited.

Two months passed. Frustrated that he had not been able to bridge the distance with Valentina, Braxton approached her one morning during her walk in the garden.

"You look tired, my dear," he said. "Perhaps you should rest." He gestured to a bench. "Please, let's sit."

Valentina hesitated before nodding. "I have news," she said, pausing. "Good news, I should think."

Braxton tilted his head. "Good news? I'm fond of good news— almost as much as I am of you." He leaned in and kissed her cheek.

She tensed, pulling away slightly, but said softly, "Braxton, I am with child."

His eyes widened. Please let me love you, he thought. He gathered her in his arms, kissing her neck, her ear, her forehead.

Valentina resisted briefly, then relaxed.

"I thought you'd be pleased," she murmured.

"Oh, Valentina, I am," he whispered, pulling her close.

Braxton caught up with Valentina in the garden a couple of days later. "How are you feeling, my dear?"

"I'm worried about Ramsey," Valentina said.

"Yes," Braxton replied. "He's been through so much lately. First his father, then his mother."

"I want to do something for him," Valentina said, a hint of uncertainty in her voice.

"What would you want if you were in his place?" Braxton asked.

"Ramsey, my dear," Valentina whispered, drawing him into a gentle, lingering embrace. She could feel the tension in his shoulders as she guided him to a nearby settee, her arm still draped around him in a gesture of quiet support. Settling beside him, she let a moment pass, allowing the hush in the room to cradle their unspoken concerns.

Her voice was soft yet steady when she spoke again. "I've been terribly worried about you," compassion evident in her eyes. "I know how much you've endured—caring for Angelina, the loss of your father, and, most recently, your mother's passing." She paused, giving weight to the enormity of his burdens. "No one should have to bear so much alone."

Ramsey's voice wavered. "Thank you, Valentina. It has been, well, rather overwhelming."

"We're your family," she said. "You're like a brother to us. Braxton and I love you deeply and we could never thank you enough for all you've done for Angelina." She hugged him again.

"I love you both just as much," he replied, emotion thick in his voice.

Valentina looked at him, her eyes filled with gentle concern as she took in the weariness etched across his face. "Ramsey," she began, her voice steady but tender, "we were wondering if you might consider..."

She slid off the settee and kneeled in front of him, taking his hands in hers, her gaze earnest and full of affection. "Would you think about you and Angelina moving in with us? The four of us together, as a family. And soon there will be five of us."

Ramsey pulled her gently back onto the settee beside him, his face breaking into a warm smile. "You know, that sounds perfect. Nothing would make me happier. Nothing on earth."

CHAPTER EIGHT

JOE

The announcement of a general election sounded like a call to arms for Braxton, drawing him into the world of politics he'd long dreamed of. To officially stand for election, he would need to return to the Aurelio Palace, situated within his electoral district, and bring along his household: Valentina, Ramsey and Angelina. It had only been a few months since they'd settled into the Renaissance House in London, but now duty called them to return to the family's country seat.

Over breakfast, Valentina raised an eyebrow and with a knowing smile said, "Tell me, Braxton, what does campaigning entail? You know it's quite different in my country. The Duma may exist, but it's the czar who has the last word on appointments. I believe things here in England work differently, do they not?"

Braxton chuckled from behind his newspaper, appreciating the playful spark in her voice. She knew the system well. "Yes, my dear, you're fully aware of how the process goes. Why are you teasing me?"

She smiled, picking at her breakfast.

"In England, it means speeches, meeting the public, and the tiresome business of pamphlets and handshakes." He lowered his newspaper and grinned. "But it's quite enjoyable, in fact. Perhaps, if you are interested, you could join me on the campaign. It could bring us closer."

She looked up from her plate, her expression both amused and slightly taken aback. "Me? Campaigning?"

Braxton continued as if she hadn't spoken, shaking out his paper and lifting it again as a subtle barrier. "Think about it. You might find you enjoy it."

She let out a breath, her tone measured. "I know you'll understand, Braxton, but now that I'm with child, it wouldn't be wise for me to join you."

Braxton kept his gaze fixed on the paper.

She prodded, "Did you hear me?"

With a sigh, he lowered it just enough to peer over the top. "Yes, of course. What did you expect me to say? It's your choice to what extent you will or will not support me."

Her frustration flared, she leaned forward and said in a firm voice. "I expect you to at least listen to me! I do support you! You can be such an ass!"

Following a careless shrug, Braxton muttered, "Why bother? You do as you please, anyway. You've made your decision."

Setting his paper aside, he added, "Before Vienna, I'd hoped we'd tackle everything together, you and me. But you've made it quite clear that won't happen."

"That's unfair," Valentina said, her teacup clattering back onto its saucer. "You know I'm with child and now is hardly the time for me to be chasing around the countryside playing politics!"

"Is it? Playing politics!" Braxton set the paper aside and folded his arms. "I had hoped, maybe foolishly, you'd at least try—just make a little effort to build a marriage that doesn't feel like a death sentence. But each time I reach out, you brush me off as if I were the plague."

"The plague? I am pregnant, Braxton. How, pray tell, do you think that happened?"

He ignored the barb, pressing on. "You've avoided spending time with me, with my family. My parents worry it's something they did wrong. They adore you. They've done all they can to welcome you as one of their own. Even they're wondering if your fall has scarred you emotionally." He picked up his paper, muttering, "If only they knew."

Valentina flung her napkin onto the table, eyes blazing. "You're insufferable!" In a flash, she hurled her teacup, narrowly missing him as it shattered against the wall.

"Despite everything, I'm keeping my word!" Her voice trembled. "I will give you an heir! But that's all."

Braxton sat forward, staring into her eyes. "I'd never have imagined the Valentina I knew would turn so cold. I was a fool to believe you'd ever feel differently—that you might actually want a life with me."

They glared at one another, a silent battle of wills.

With deliberate calm, Braxton placed his napkin beside his plate. Leaning in, he lowered his voice. "I risked everything to bring Angelina back to you. And Ramsey made great sacrifices as well. But to you, it seems the love you show Angelina is the only love you'll give to anyone here. The rest of us? We're invisible, dismissed. At best, an inconvenience."

At that moment, a footman entered, bearing a silver tray. "Your Royal Highness."

Braxton took the envelope from the tray, nodding as the servant departed. A smile tugged at his lips as he opened it. "Ah, well, isn't this a pleasant surprise?"

Valentina's expression turned suspicious. "And what, may I ask, has delighted you so?"

"Joe Richards."

"Your American friend?" she asked, her tone wary.

Braxton read on, then looked up with a grin. "Yes, my dear friend. My cowboy."

Her lips tightened.

He stood abruptly, his face alight with excitement. "He's on his way here! Jolly good! Well, wife, you won't need to worry about the campaign. I'll have Joe by my side. He's offered to lend his expertise."

"Why on earth would he do that? Travel all the way from America?"

"You must have missed it, but Joe recently won a seat in the American House of Representatives. He's gained quite a bit of experience in this sort of thing, and I'll gladly have his help."

She folded her arms. "And he's crossed the ocean for...? That makes no sense."

Returning the letter to its envelope, Braxton replied, "He's part of an American delegation, touring Europe. I look forward to availing myself of whatever time he has available."

Wringing her hands, Valentina gathered her skirts and left the room.

Braxton and Joe sat side by side in the ducal study at the Aurelio Palace, a grand room adorned with portraits and lavish decor, including a Romanesque statue of the ancestral Duke Cardinal Chiacontella.

Joe took in the surroundings, nodding approvingly. "Your mother's family—they knew how to make money, like the Medici."

Braxton grinned. "Yes, and I suppose I inherited a touch of that talent. Though I try to live a bit more simply than they did."

Joe raised an eyebrow. "Who do you think is richer—your family or theirs?"

Braxton laughed. "My accountants say my wealth now rivals Carnegie's or Guinness's. Though I shouldn't boast. You're one of the few who know, so keep it between us."

"Your secret's safe with me, Prince Blowhard," Joe teased, and winked.

Braxton's gaze softened, the familiarity of Joe's presence filling him with warmth. How I've missed him. No pretense, no complications. Just us.

Joe noticed the look. "What's on your mind?"

Braxton hesitated, then mouthed a kiss. "You, us. Everything we've shared."

Joe smirked. "Any particular memories?"

"That first night in the cave," Braxton replied, his voice low. "All or nothing,' remember?"

Joe rose from his chair, and with a quiet intensity, moved closer. The air between them seemed to crackle, pulling them together.

Braxton's breath caught as Joe's lips met his, soft yet electric, a collision of longing and need. He felt himself melt, his hands finding their place on either side of Joe's face, grounding them both in that moment. He let himself sink into the kiss, savoring every sensation, every trace of warmth and familiarity.

The kiss deepened, each of them gripping the other as if the world outside had vanished, leaving only the two of them in their own universe. Braxton's fingers tangled in Joe's hair, pulling him closer, their kiss reflecting the depth of years' worth of passion and quiet understanding.

When they finally drew apart, their eyes locked and a shared grasp of one another's feelings lingered. Their love didn't need words. It was a bond etched in every stolen moment, a quiet certainty neither time nor distance could break.

Joe held Braxton's gaze, one hand gently cupping his cheek. Voice raw with emotion, he whispered, "I love you."

Braxton swallowed, his voice barely a murmur. "I love you too, cowboy."

In that quiet, stolen instant, they savored the hush and each other, both painfully aware they would soon be thrust back into a world that refused their love.

But for now, they were just two men, bound by love and memory, stealing one last moment in the safety of the study.

Joe adjusted his collar with a grin. "Well, that was nice."

Braxton, straightening his cravat, chuckled. "More to come, I hope?"

Joe grasped his lover's chin. "Find us some privacy soon, or I might just embarrass us both."

Braxton grinned, his heart light. "Consider it done."

Joe drew Braxton down on a nearby sofa and pulled him close. "Now, about you being Midas, or whatever myth you fancy yourself these days."

Several minutes passed, each man quietly lost in his own thoughts. Then, with a sudden clap of his hands, Braxton broke the silence, grinning at Joe. "Yes, perhaps I am—what was it you called me? A blowhard?" He laughed. "Well, you may be right. Care to hear more? I feel an urge to brag."

Joe raised an imaginary glass. "By all means, my prince, my lover! Brag away to your heart's content! After all, 'Who knows himself a braggart, let him fear this, for it will come to pass that every braggart shall be found an ass,'" he added, quoting the Bard with a twinkle in his eye.

Braxton slapped his thigh. "Quoting Shakespeare to me, are you? Let me guess—you've been talking with Valentina?"

Joe feigned innocence, rising from the sofa and strolling to the French doors. With a sweeping gesture, he flung them open wide, allowing a rush of cool air to billow in. "What makes you say that? You asked me, now I'll ask you: Have you been talking to Valentina? Maybe you should. And try listening more than talking. She's perceptive—usually spot-on."

He spread his arms wide, taking in the space around them. "There. The scene is set: perfect air, perfect view, perfect backdrop. Wax on!"

Braxton shook his head. "You're incorrigible, you know that?" But his grin lingered as he relaxed back onto the sofa, hands folding behind his head, fingers lacing together. "Well then, since you've set the stage, where to start? My wealth? It's hard to measure. The Russian mines, forests, oil fields—my art collections alone defy valuation. No one could ever fully afford their worth." He lowered his hands, his gaze drifting. "And then there's the shipping line, our joint ventures, and, of course, the railways and trade networks across the continent."

Joe raised an eyebrow. "How do you keep up with all of it?"

"I don't, really. Ramsey—pardon me, the Marquess of Ravenswood now—he oversees much of it with a small army of bankers and advisors. They keep the wheels turning."

"Is that what brought you back to politics?" Joe leaned in, studying his friend. "Be honest with me, Braxton. Business can be thrilling, I know, but there's more to it, isn't there?"

Braxton's gaze shifted, and he sighed. "What I miss is the thrill of Hong Kong and the rubber trade out of Singapore. That was a kind of freedom I'll never find anywhere else, certainly not in government. So yes, it was that and something else."

Joe's curiosity piqued. "Something else?"

Braxton poured scotch into two crystal tumblers and handed one to Joe.

Joe sipped his drink. "And?"

Braxton hesitated, glancing away. "Joe, you know me too well. The truth is…I suppose it's not all boredom. There's a part of me that's frustrated. With everything; with all of it."

Joe nodded. "That's what I suspected. You're a man who needs dragons to slay, uncharted seas to cross. It'll take more than just politics to satisfy you. Where are you going with this?"

Braxton's expression softened as he looked back at Joe, the flicker of restlessness now tempered by something more somber. "I've built a world, Joe. I've laid foundations, set things in motion, handed over the reins where I could. But England, England is on the edge of something enormous, a precipice, and most people don't see it. They don't understand the Empire, as it stands, can't last. If we don't shift the way we run the empire soon, we risk it crumbling from within."

Joe listened intently, his glass forgotten on the table. "You think Parliament will let you effect the kind of change necessary to thwart such an eventuality?"

Braxton sighed, swirling his drink in a slow circle before taking a measured sip. "Parliament will fight it; Whitehall will, too. Still, if I become a member of Parliament, I can do more than criticize from the outside. Once I'm inside, I'll see where the system falters and push for real change."

Joe's brow furrowed. "And your father? The king? Other than running for a seat in the House of Commons, does he know of your long-term goals?"

Braxton looked down. "I haven't spoken to him about it yet. I've written to Valentina in the past, but she has little interest in any of it."

Joe's eyes flashed. "Braxton, don't be so quick to assume. From what I've seen, she's very much aware, very much engaged."

Braxton waved a hand dismissively.

Joe reached ou and grabbed his hand. "Brax, it matters. She matters. Don't shut her out."

Braxton sat quietly for a moment, then took a long, deliberate drink. "Perhaps you're right. But England's affairs loom large and demand attention. This is about more than any one person's feelings."

He paused, a glimmer of bitterness edging his voice. "Besides, Joe, there's a part of me that has always been drawn to the impossible, to things beyond our control."

Joe let the comment hang for a moment, then cleared his throat. "So, if you're preparing for battle in Parliament, what's your plan? You want to guide the Empire out of its current state, keep it from imploding?"

Braxton leaned back, nodding slowly. "I want to initiate a transition, a graceful shift toward self-governance for certain colonies. Not the end of the Empire, but a reconfiguration. If we do nothing, if we cling to our old ways, the fall will be disastrous." He ran his fingers along the edge of his glass, his expression resolute. "And I won't let that happen while my father, or even my brother, is king."

Joe shook his head, chuckling softly. "And there you go again, Monsieur Modesty, simultaneously chock-full of humility and grandeur."

Braxton bowed. "So right you are!"

The two shared a laugh, and Joe clapped Braxton on the shoulder. "Well, my dear prince, let's get you elected, then."

Prince Braxton and Joe were returning alone from a campaign event on horseback. The early evening radiant autumn moon and star-studded heavens had vanished, the sky and the moon now obscured by ominous clouds. A gentle breeze that had embraced them now carried a bite, signaling the changing season and an advancing chill.

Braxton secured the two top buttons on his wool coat and re-arranged his wool scarf around his neck. "This is one of those 'sneak up on you' storms."

"Feels that way, doesn't it? Reminds me of those gushers we weathered out West," Joe said, patting his horse's shoulder.

"You did well today, Brax. You had them hooked the moment you stepped off the podium and climbed up on that table!"

Braxton snagged his hat with one hand just as a sharp gust threatened to carry it away. He laughed. "An old trick of mine, jumping from podium to table. I first used it in Scotland, back when I was campaigning to get Parliament to change the constitution so I could marry Valentina and run for the House of Commons. It catches most folks off guard and draws them in."

"What? You had to campaign for what? Oh, right, you told me all about it. How quick we forget. I still can't believe you needed Parliament's approval to run for office and marry who you wanted. You English are something else! Gawd!"

"I had too. I did. And I won!"

An icy rain first peppered them, then fell at an ever-increasing rate.

"We need to find some shelter, Cowboy," Braxton quipped.

"You didn't truly require my campaign efforts, did you? You've managed it successfully in the past," Joe chuckled.

"I do need you, Joe," Braxton confessed, his voice sincere.

Obscured by rain cascading down his face, Braxton couldn't see Joe's wide grin. Yet, amid the sound of the onslaught, he heard Joe's heartfelt response, "Just as I need and must have you."

The prince tugged on his reins, commanding his horse to veer left. In a loud shout, he exclaimed, "Come with me! There's an old stone house ahead, equipped with ample supplies of dry wood and water! Precisely for times like this!"

Joe turned his horse and shouted, "I thought that was only done out West. Ha! Even you English get it right sometimes!"

"Come with me, Cowboy. It's time to rodeo!"

Joe, reins in hand, gave his steed a swift smack on its hindquarters, urging it forward in hot pursuit of his lover and the privacy Braxton had promised.

CHAPTER NINE

COMMONS & INTELLIGENCE

J oe had returned to America.

Braxton stood for election as a member of the Liberal Party.

It was a turbulent period. The Great Dock Strike, one of the most significant strikes in British history, was underway.

Unbeknownst to him, the Aurelio Palace Academy upperclassmen had swamped the countryside with literature and one-on-one canvassing in support of his candidacy. Two weeks into the campaign, the opposition candidates soon fell by the wayside and Prince Braxton was elected to the House of Commons.

London, Leeds, Birmingham, and Manchester papers chronicled the election, victory, and celebrations.

HRH PRINCE BRAXTON ELECTED

MEMBER OF PARLIAMENT

ROYAL ENTHRONED IN HOUSE OF COMMONS

ROYAL FAMILY INVADES PARLIAMENT

AURELIO PALACE CELEBRATES PRINCE'S VICTORY

BUCKINGHAM PALACE SILENT ON MP PRINCE

A royal in Parliament, Braxton, was once again an international sensation. Newspapers speculated one day he would be prime minister, advising his father, the king, on how to run the country.

Braxton received a congratulatory cable from Joe in which he shared with Braxton that he would soon be running for the United States Senate.

The newly elected member of parliament answered with a congratulatory telegram and posted a letter containing a 5,000-pound sterling campaign contribution.

In the letter containing the campaign contribution, he wrote:

"My dearest Joe, my cowboy, how I wish I could be there with you; to campaign alongside you. Like you did with me."

Valentina gave birth to Prince George. He was sixth in line to the throne, behind his father, his uncle John, his two cousins, and his Uncle Dominic.

Princess Angelina seamlessly integrated into the family as Lord Ramsey returned to Russia to manage Braxton's affairs.

Braxton and Valentina immersed themselves, raising their family and attending to his political and financial responsibilities. Their relationship gradually settled into a harmonious rhythm. Several months following George's birth, Valentina found herself expecting their second child, the future Prince Arthur.

Braxton was increasingly entangled in his ever-increasing lucrative business empire. Under the astute leadership of Lord Ramsey and Viscount Everett Lawrence, the army of the Aurelio Academy graduates had grown the conglomerate to unparalleled heights, establishing it as the most powerful economic entity in the world. Not even the infamous slave-trading Belgian King Leopold could compete with the prince's riches.

Braxton, however, meticulously veiled the true extent of his wealth.

In another letter to Joe in the fall of 1898, Braxton wrote:

...and it appears with the continued onslaught of babies, number five on its way, our family has entered a very active but peaceful existence. The birth of George, followed by Arthur, Elizabeth and Elena, has brought their mother and me closer. Perhaps by necessity, but closer, nonetheless.

Upon careful consideration, I have come to believe that one thing has salvaged my marriage. When Angelina moved in with us permanently, due to Ramsey's travels, we drew closer. At first, I never could have imagined her becoming an integral part of our family. Yet it happened and has changed everything between Valentina and me, restoring our bond. Perhaps "restoring" is more of a hopeful thought than a concrete reality. Should I say, "repaired?" After all, she has left me twice before. Will she do it again? And yes, "repaired" is a more àpropos description.

Valentina's renewed, compassionate nature has brought a sense of ease to my days, whether they are consumed with politics or business. Our children's joyfulness adds a vibrant touch to our lives.

Though, I must admit, without the army of nannies and tutors our life would be quite different.

Living at the Aurelio Palace has been a delight for everyone. The Academy and stables have been a great source of inspiration for our children. Their education has flourished, thanks to the proximity to talented teachers and students. We hope this experience will better prepare them for the world that lies ahead.

It pains me to write, but my eldest brother, Dominic, and his family are going through a challenging time. While I'm not privy to all the details, there are concerns regarding his daughter's health and his son's mental and emotional development. Dominic and Mathilde are struggling. Perhaps that is an understatement.

In addition, I believe, and the family believes my father's health is declining. It weighs heavily on our hearts…

Valentina bore two more sons, Vanya and Frederick. Six children in ten years made for a full household.

"Well, my dear," Valentina remarked, entering a drawing room at Renaissance House, setting down a copy of The Adventures of Sherlock Holmes on the table. With a fluid elegance, she took a seat beside Braxton. "The children are well looked after by their nannies and governesses, and it seems we're settled in for the evening. As much as I cherish the countryside, there's something quite charming about being back in London. A bit of socializing might do us some good, don't you think?" She playfully patted his knee. "Though I do understand how absorbed you are with your work in the Commons."

Braxton leaned over and planted a gentle kiss on her cheek. "I'm so pleased you agreed to move the family to London during the parliamentary sessions. It makes everything so much easier, being together, rather than apart." Warmth filled his smile.

"Well, my dear, I must confess, it wasn't entirely out of kindness I suggested bringing the family to London," she teased. Pausing for effect, Valentina took his chin between her thumb and forefinger, locking eyes with him. "You wouldn't expect me to leave you to your own devices during the Season, surrounded by all those enchanting women and yes, handsome, charming men, now, would you?" Her coy smile hinted at the playful innuendo.

Braxton's lips curved into a half-smile. He shifted in his seat, momentarily taken aback by her double entendre. His eyes twinkled with amusement, but there was also a hint of bashfulness in his gaze. He appreciated her playful banter, but the subtle blush on his cheeks revealed mixed emotions. Nevertheless, the warmth in his expression indicated he enjoyed the light-hearted exchange, embracing the rediscovered affection they shared.

Valentina chuckled, her laughter filling the room with an infectious joy. In a graceful movement, she rose from her seat and glided over to the pull cord, giving it a spirited tug. A spring in her step, she swayed around the room, humming a Russian folk song Braxton had heard her hum in Siberia decades earlier.

Valentina stopped and turned toward the window, gazing out thoughtfully. "I've arranged for hot rum toddies to be served. I adore the delightful blend of cinnamon and sugar in them. Don't you?"

Braxton adjusted his seat, his mind swirling with a mix of curiosity and amusement. What is this all about? He wondered. What did she mean by those handsome men? His thoughts paused, leaving the rest unsaid, as he couldn't help but be intrigued by the ephemeral enigma hidden within her playful words.

A footman entered carrying a tray laden with two piping hot beverages. He placed the tray on a low table in front of Braxton, bowed and exited the room.

Valentina returned to her seat alongside Braxton. She picked up one of the thick ceramic mugs and handed it to him; then took hold of the remaining toddy, raised it toward Braxton, and said, "To us, and a marvelous Season."

My dear Joe, Braxton wrote. Thank you so much for your very kind cable to the king, Dominic's family, and my own. The tragedy of Princess Rose's passing has devastated all who loved her. The rumors of her demise from consumption are misplaced speculation. For it was scarlet fever that took her from us. As I have shared with you before, she has never possessed a robust constitution. My darling niece had recently recovered from another bout with a sore throat. Soon thereafter, while visiting my brother's family, I commented on her rubbing the pinkish skin on the side of her neck. It appeared as if she had taken too much sun. I knew that not to be the case, for she had remained indoors recuperating. The doctors were summoned. She passed three days later. I am heartsick. We all adored her so.

To make matters worse, her mother, Princess Mathilde, has gone into seclusion. Dominic is inconsolable. And there is the young prince, their son. His development remains slow. Perhaps his condition will shield him somewhat from the loss of his sister and his parents' grief.

Fortunately, my brother, Prince John and his wife have taken up temporary residence in Kensington Palace to help usher them through their melancholia.

I have interesting news to share. It appears my political life has taken a turn. I am to be elevated to Foreign Secretary. The Prime Minister finally appreciates what I can bring to the table from my world travels.

Braxton, now Secretary of State for Foreign Affairs, welcomed his visitors. "Good morning, gentlemen!" Prince Braxton strode forward, his handshake firm as he embraced each man in turn. "Lord Lawrence, Master Seiko Higoshino—it fills me with great satisfaction to see you both here. Master Higoshino, your swift journey from Hong Kong is deeply appreciated, and Everett, to have you here from Calcutta means more than I can express."

The secretary's office was stately yet inviting, its lofty expanse encased in finely carved mahogany panels. The walls, lined with shelves brimming with leather-bound volumes, stood beneath tall windows ushering in soft streams of daylight. It was a chamber that radiated dignity and power—a fitting tribute to the strength of England's heritage.

Master Higoshino, an athletic man in bespoke attire, silver at his temples, offered a deep, reverent bow. "Your Royal Highness, nearly ten years have passed since our last meeting. I have longed for this reunion and am honored to stand before you once more."

Braxton inclined his head warmly. "Thank you, Master. Please, both of you, take a seat." He gestured toward two richly upholstered, high-backed leather chairs. "Allow me to offer you refreshment. Tea? Or perhaps something with a bit more spirit?"

Lord Lawrence leaned back, a smile tugging at the corners of his mouth. "Something stronger, if you don't mind, Your Royal Highness. This is a celebration, is it not? A reunion."

"Indeed, a celebration worth marking." Master Higoshino nodded, his eyes crinkling with quiet delight. "I shall join in the toast, though I will partake in your offering of tea."

Braxton pressed a button on a nearby table. A clerk entered and placed a selection of beverages on a sideboard before slipping from the chamber.

"It is my hope," Braxton began, "we'll have a moment to catch up on family matters and other pursuits beyond the realm of duty. But for now, please indulge me as our matters are pressing. And forgive me for nearly overlooking an important detail: My wife and I would be deeply honored if you joined us for dinner tomorrow evening at Renaissance House."

Lord Lawrence inclined his head in appreciation. "You are most gracious, sir."

Master Seiko nodded in his quiet manner. "It is a privilege, my lord."

"Splendid," Braxton replied warmly. "Her Royal Highness will be delighted, as am I."

Braxton glanced around the chamber, the surroundings both familiar and strange to him. "Gentlemen, as you can see, my sphere of focus has shifted markedly since we were last together.

"These past years have been transformative," Braxton continued. "They've drawn me down a path I'd never imagined, ultimately leading here, to the Foreign Office." He paused; his voice weighted with sincerity. "I owe both of you a debt of gratitude for managing my affairs through these turbulent years. And, as you might expect, your assistance is needed now more than ever."

Master Higoshino and Lord Lawrence exchanged a knowing look.

Braxton's expression grew uncharacteristically somber. "Gentlemen, I am in crisis. I've been thrust into a role I fear I lack the courage or resolve to fully shoulder."

Lawrence and Higoshino sat transfixed, their eyes scanning Braxton's face for any sign of levity. Yet his expression held firm, grave in its honesty.

"As you may have gleaned from the briefings I've sent," Braxton said, "the British Empire finds itself perilously behind the German and Austrian military expansion. The Boer War has drained us of resources and stained our international standing. The very bedrock of the Empire is shifting."

Lawrence seemed poised to respond, but Higoshino silenced him with a slight shake of his head.

"What is to be done?" Braxton asked. Then answered himself. "We must reshape our entire imperial policy. The empire's dominion, as we know it, is slipping from our grasp."

Lord Lawrence leaned forward, his hands clasped, elbows resting on his knees. "You foresaw much of this, sir. Fifteen years ago, in the Far East, we spoke of these inevitabilities. You filed report after report warning the very government you now serve as a member of parliament and Foreign Secretary."

Braxton nodded slowly. "Indeed, I did."

Higoshino leaned back, his arms folding in measured restraint. "Forgive my intrusion, my lords, but I too recall those conversations. Were they not part of what compelled you to enter politics, my prince?"

Braxton's gaze softened as he looked at the elder man who had mentored him in his youth. Master Higoshino still teaches, he thought. I hope he isn't reproaching me, for I've done all I could. He nodded solemnly. "Yes, Master. Yet, it has taken me years to gain this footing, to establish trust within Parliament.

"We are," he continued, "caught in an unforgiving quagmire. I hold the office of Foreign Secretary only because I predicted this crisis, though my warnings had fallen on deaf ears." His gaze drifted to the ceiling, as if seeking answers. "The prime minister and his cabinet are lost, hoping I might conjure miracles to save them."

Lord Lawrence leaned back, his mouth set in a grim line. "Parliament remains the problem, my lord. I've told you this before. But you brushed me aside then. What has changed?"

Braxton winced but acknowledged the truth. "You were right. I was young, preoccupied with profits, content to leave such matters to my father's government. But I knew, deep down, the government's policies had to change."

Lord Lawrence exhaled sharply; his voice tinged with frustration. "Then you were naïve, less introspective. Years ago, you might have made a difference."

Braxton's eyes narrowed as he stood, his frame rigid. "Surely you did not make this journey to hurl accusations at me, Everett?"

Tension bore down on them like an impending storm.

Lawrence stood and faced Braxton head-on. "I did not come here to flatter, but to speak the truth. If you solicit my opinion, you shall have it in full."

Braxton muttered, barely above a whisper, "You ass."

Lawrence's face hardened. He turned and strode toward the door.

Higoshino rose slowly from his seat, his steady presence commanding the room. His calm voice cut through the thick tension. "Gentlemen, let us not dwell on the past." His eyes sparkled with patient resolve as he moved closer to Braxton, taking hold of his lapel and leaning in to whisper, "Apologize. And mean it."

"Everett!" Braxton called.

Lord Lawrence hesitated.

Braxton swallowed; his words thick. "I shouldn't have said that. My apologies."

Lawrence turned back; his expression impenetrable.

Braxton's voice softened. "Master Higoshino, you and so many others have sacrificed much. I know this. And I feel lost, Everett. I need your guidance."

Lawrence's eyes glinted with a steely reserve. "What is it you require, sir?"

Surprise and resolve mingled in Braxton's expression. "Shall we begin again?"

Higoshino filled three tumblers with scotch. "We will drain our glasses and start anew," he declared with quiet finality, raising his own.

After they drank, Lawrence set his glass aside. "How will you keep the prime minister and his sycophants from turning on you should you fail to deliver?"

Braxton sat back, crossing his arms. "Honestly, I haven't the faintest notion. But the time has come, and I am, perhaps as you said, naively committed."

"Intelligence!" Higoshino interjected, his voice firm. "What England has lacked most is intelligence and foresight."

Braxton inclined his head. "Master Higoshino, you are quite right."

The door opened, and a figure entered, his presence commanding attention. Signore Carlo Ratini strode across the room, exclaiming with a dramatic flair and in a thick Venetian accent, "Ah, did someone mention 'intelligence'? Sono Io! That's me—at least in some quarters."

Braxton stood, laughing, gesturing grandly. "Lord Lawrence, may I introduce Signore Carlo Ratini? 'Signore Intelligence,' as he fancies."

Ratini executed an exaggerated bow, his hand sweeping low. "My lord," he murmured, his gaze twinkling.

Lord Lawrence inclined his head acknowledging the introduction while Higoshino's face softened in a rare smile at the familiar figure.

Ratini said, "Ah yes, the mystical oracle himself, the man who knows all yet only speaks when plied with sake!"

Higoshino's laughter erupted, rich and unrestrained. "Ratini! You know I could split your head six ways to Tokyo without breaking a sweat!"

The two men shared a hearty embrace, their camaraderie unmistakable.

Braxton pulled a chair from the corner, buoyant, and positioned it for the Italian spymaster.

CHAPTER TEN

TWO LOVES

The 20th century had arrived. Valentina wrote to her cousin, Czar Maxim.

My dearest cousin,

I hope this letter finds you well and in high spirits. This morning, while enjoying breakfast with a view of Windsor Great Park, a smile crossed my face. Braxton, ever attentive, noticed and inquired about the source of my amusement. To our surprise, I let out a girlish giggle, filling our morning with a lightheartedness we both relished. Our relationship has become more relaxed and comfortable, and I will share more about that later in this letter.

I could not help but attribute my happy state to cherished memories of the weeks our families spent yachting on the Black Sea this past summer. Those moments hold a special place in my heart and recalling them fills me with warmth and joy.

Braxton's considerate nature was evident this morning when he was reading the papers, avoided mentioning the political unrest in St. Petersburg, allowing me to immerse myself in these sweet memories.

Together, we recounted those cherished moments throughout breakfast.

Later, strolling through the gardens, I felt compelled to pen this letter. The newspapers are filled with dreadful tales, and I worry for you, Carmen, and the twins. The catastrophic end to your war with Japan and the heartbreaking events the papers now call Bloody Sunday have left me deeply troubled.

But, my dear cousin, I will not let troubling matters overshadow the warmth and happiness of our correspondence. I believe in the resilience of our family, and you are all in my prayers. My love for our homeland remains steadfast, even in these trying times.

This letter is, in part, a celebration. Braxton and I find life taking on a whole new meaning. As our love rekindles, we realize how much we've grown and how far we've come, leaving behind past differences. The burden of discontent gently lifts, replaced by a genuine affection we embraced years ago. With each passing day, our bond deepens, making life all the more beautiful and meaningful.

Braxton faces a challenging period. It feels like only yesterday he was appointed foreign secretary, and now, as you must have heard, the prime minister has entrusted him with the role of home secretary. I shudder at the thought of the demands this role will place upon him.

Though he may have overextended himself in accepting the home secretary's role, his tenure has been remarkably successful, restoring Britain's standing as a dependable and respected player on the international stage. I could not be more proud of his achievements.

Again, I fear for his health as he tirelessly dedicates himself to his duties. We, as a family, see him rarely. However, when he is with us, all seems right in the world. The past twelve years have brought us closer than ever before.

Now, let me share an important matter. The passing of Braxton's father, King Richard, six months ago has brought our previous concerns to the forefront. You will recall we worried that Prince Dominic might not be prepared to assume the crown. Mathilde has become a recluse, rarely making public appearances. Dominic, too, seems to have withdrawn from public life, both deeply affected by the loss of Princess Rose. And as you observed when we were last together, Crown Prince Adolphus shows signs of emotional immaturity. These matters weigh on us all.

In this difficult time, Prince John has been magnificent, stepping up to assist Dominic with his kingly duties. His wife, Viktoria Louise, has been a godsend, managing the royal household on behalf of the queen. Yet the family feels as if a hammer hangs above, poised to crash down upon us. Braxton, in part, seems not in denial but evasive, avoiding the topic.

I believe his responsibilities overwhelm him. The matter of Dominic's son being unfit to succeed, and his older brother John's lack of heirs is something he has chosen to set aside for now. For reasons best left unspoken, it seems unlikely John and Mathilde will have children. Thus, it is inevitable our young Prince George will one day be king. Isn't it ironic? I renounced the Russian crown, only to find my son may bear yet another imperial burden.

The President of the United States has extended an invitation for a state visit to King Dominic. Understandably, Dominic declined, given Princess Rose's recent passing. Considering this, the prime minister and the king asked Braxton to represent them in his role as home secretary. He looks forward to visiting his "cowboy," Senator Richards, and discussing matters concerning Germany and Austria while enjoying a brief respite from his duties here. They are so very close. Very close.

I know you will keep Braxton in your prayers. The prime minister's position is precarious, rapidly losing his party's confidence. It may be inevitable that he will either resign or the government will be forced to call for elections. Braxton will unquestionably be embroiled in the events, and the consequences are beyond my imagination.

Please write to update me on your family and government. Give my love to Carmen and the boys. I am confident you will handle any hurdles with your customary grace and acumen.

Fondly,

Valentina

"We are five years into the twentieth century, but it feels like a millennium has passed. I am utterly exhausted, Joe." Braxton shook his head, brushing his hand over his face, a weary smile forming.

Senator Joseph Richards noted the changes in Braxton's 45-year-old face; lines creased his skin and his posture, though not stooped, hinted at heavy burdens.

"I think your trip to America is well-timed. We can discuss the kaiser and the Austrian emperor's machinations, and you can find some much-needed respite."

"I hope you're right, Joe," Braxton sighed. "By the way, Valentina sends her love." Joe smiled warmly. "I'm glad to hear you two are working things out and getting along better," he said, genuine happiness in his eyes for Braxton and Valentina.

"Yes, she has been a great help, especially in these past five years, offering solid counsel when I was foreign secretary and now as home secretary."

"Well, you always said she was a stellar regent when she and her cousin ruled Russia in her father's stead."

"Speaking of which, Maxim has, following the October Manifesto, surrendered some power to the Russian parliament, the Duma."

Joe scoffed, a wry smile tugging at the corner of his mouth. "Parliament? Duma? That assembly of sycophants? They're nothing but a facade, a thin veil of legitimacy cloaking his reign. He remains a czar, the ultimate authority. This so-called surrender of power is nothing more than clever theatrics, a strategic display for the public. It's window dressing, not an actual transfer of power. He holds the reins tight, letting the people think they have a voice while he whispers commands from behind the curtain."

Braxton crossed his legs, his gaze steady. "Be that as it may, Maxim appears weak. Even the illusion of lost power—the mere suggestion that the czar is loosening his grip—could be enough to embolden Germany and Austria. They've been watching, waiting for any sign of vulnerability. This display could give them the pretext they need to stoke the fires of war, under the guise of 'restoring stability' or 'defending order.' The perception of weakness, even if it's all for show, can be as dangerous as weakness itself."

"Is that the primary reason you're here and meeting with the president?"

Braxton leaned forward, his eyes meeting Joe's with a mix of determination and affection. "Yes, we absolutely need a contingency plan if war should break out. The kaiser is reckless, and the Austrian emperor…well, he is, for the most part, his general's marionette." Braxton paused, allowing a gentle smile to surface, glad to be there, sharing this moment with Joe. After all their years together, the trust and connection between them was still a rare solace amidst mounting international tensions.

Joe's gaze softened, a glint of appreciation in his eyes. "Braxton, the president has asked that I accompany you to the White House." He lingered on the words just a bit longer than necessary, letting his tone carry the unspoken truth—he was glad to have Braxton here, by his side, the political demands notwithstanding.

Their eyes met, holding each other's gaze for a brief, unspoken moment that transcended words. The prince smiled. "I'm not surprised. Does this have to do with him choosing you as vice president for his re-election?"

Joe pursed his lips, then replied, "I can neither confirm nor deny."

"Well, congratulations!" Braxton said.

Joe folded his arms. "The president believes you will be the next prime minister."

Braxton's face, impassive, said, "God forbid."

A profound silence fell over them as they each considered the unspoken burdens looming over them.

"By the way," Joe added, his tone lightening, "I've arranged for my private rail car to take us to the Virginia mountains for a hunting trip."

Braxton inhaled deeply, resting his head back. "You know," he said wistfully, "it's been over 15 years since our days in the American west. Some of the happiest days of my life."

Joe rose, crossing over to Braxton, and leaned in, pressing his lips against Braxton's. Hope surged through Braxton. Joe's touch banished the fatigue that had weighed on him, filling him with strength.

"I am always here for you," Joe said, kissing him again.

Braxton, savoring the kiss, closed his eyes. "Yes, Joe, I know. I am counting on you." He reached up, clasping Joe's shoulders, pulling him close. "I love you, Joe."

"I know," Joe whispered. "That is why I am here. I will always be here for you. I will forever love you."

The mountain cabin was as primitive as it was perfect. Tucked deep in the woods, it provided all the seclusion they could want, a world stripped down to just the two of them. With no comforts beyond what they made for themselves, they spent their days hunting in the thick woods, fishing in the river, and then gutting and dressing their catch side by side, the quiet work a language of its own.

Nights were theirs alone, with no one around for miles. They'd sit close, talking softly or saying nothing at all, the wild sounds of the forest wrapping around them. Here, they didn't need anything but each other. It was simple, raw—just the two of them.

Lying together on the bearskin rug, they watched the fire flicker and crackle within the stone hearth, its warmth casting a soft glow across the room. Animal skins draped over their bare bodies, still warm and damp from their lovemaking. Braxton rested on his side, propped on one elbow, watching his finger as it traced gentle, meandering lines along Joe's chest and abdomen.

Joe lay on his back, his gaze fixed on the split-log ceiling beams above, hands clasped behind his head. His dark hair, longer than usual, framed his face with a certain boyish charm, softened by the quiet intimacy of the moment.

"There's something I've been meaning to say, Joe," Braxton began, his fingers tracing slow, lazy circles down Joe's torso, almost as if the act itself gave him the courage to continue.

Joe tilted his head toward Braxton, watching his lover's gaze fixed intent on the movement of his hand gliding down his skin. "Share away, but please—don't stop what you're doing."

Braxton chuckled softly and kept his hand moving, savoring the quiet intimacy between them. "It's about…you and me. And, well, our families. Our wives."

Joe's gaze drifted back to the ceiling, his face settling into a thoughtful stillness. "Oh, that."

"I know it's not fair to them, what we're doing," Braxton said. "I mean, I can't exactly justify it. But—is it wrong?" His voice softened, almost as though he were asking himself as much as Joe.

Joe stayed quiet for a moment, letting the words hang in the fire-lit silence, both comforting and exposing. "Braxton, I've thought about this more than I'd like to admit." He took a slow breath. "Sometimes, I feel guilty. I look at my wife, and I know I love her. I know I'm committed to her. But this—." He glanced over at Braxton, his eyes softening. "This thing between us…it's different. It's not something I could walk away from, even if I wanted to."

Braxton nodded, the lines of his brow deepening. "I feel the same. I love Valentina, and I know you love—but with you…" He paused, searching for the right words. "With you, it's like a part of me that can't exist anywhere else. It's not just desire. It's…well, it's us. You're the only one with whom I can be completely me."

Joe reached out, his hand brushing Braxton's cheek. "I think that's what makes it worth it. We both know what we have at home, what our lives look like on the outside. But in here…" His voice grew softer. "In here, we get to just be us. Even if no one else can ever know."

Braxton looked down, a flicker of uncertainty crossing his face. "Are we all right with that? Hiding this? Living between two worlds?"

Joe's hand settled on Braxton's, grounding him. "As long as we're honest with each other, I think we can be. I know we're both going to keep loving our wives. But you and I, we're something else. Something I don't want to lose."

Braxton exhaled, as if some heavy weight had lifted, and leaned into Joe's touch, his own hand finally coming to rest over Joe's. "Then let's keep it. For as long as we can."

Joe gave a small smile, lifting Braxton's hand to his lips, pressing a gentle kiss there. "Then let's keep it. Whatever this is, it's ours. And that's enough."

Braxton leaned closer, his mouth brushing Joe's, soft at first, as if savoring the taste of him. Joe's hand traced up his back, fingers pressing into the tense muscles of Braxton's shoulders.

They felt the essence of spoken and unspoken words, in the way they moved against each other, close enough to feel the heat of their passion, the warmth of their bodies.

The firelight flickered over them, casting shadows on the walls as Braxton's hands slid up Joe's arms, tracing the shape of him, the familiar lines of his body that still brought something new each time. Joe pulled Braxton closer until their bodies pressed together, skin against skin, the warmth between them spreading as naturally as a heartbeat.

They moved in quiet rhythm, their bodies instinctively finding each other, every touch deepening their connection. Braxton's hand ran down Joe's back, his fingers savoring the strength beneath them, feeling Joe arch into him. They breathed in sync, each quiet gasp, each shiver becoming a shared language spoken in silence.

The world outside had disappeared as they surrendered to each other, letting the fire's warmth carry them into the night, the intimacy between them filling the quiet spaces as they lost themselves in the connection, the quiet passion, and the shared certainty of their love.

After six days' sailing aboard the opulent White Star luxury liner RMS Celtic, Braxton's homeward journey to England was nearing its end.

Though he couldn't be certain, he sensed a subtle shift in the ship's motion. The hum of the engines took on a more urgent pitch, and the floor beneath his feet tilted at a slightly different angle. The Celtic had adjusted course and gained speed, Braxton had no proof, but he knew something had changed, something was amiss.

The ship's captain entered the large, first-class stateroom's grand parlor.

"Excuse me, Your Royal Highness," the captain bowed respectfully.

"Good evening, Captain," Braxton replied, rising from the desk.

"Sir, I have a telegram."

"Really?" the prince asked, his eyes widening in surprise. "Captain, you, you are delivering this to me personally?"

"Yes, Sir. Under the circumstances, I thought it best," the captain said, his voice low but urgent. "The message is encrypted, and it's from His Majesty. There is also an immediate directive from the Admiralty's First Sea Lord to make full steam for Southampton."

He handed Braxton the telegram, bowed, then turned and left the cabin, closing the mahogany door behind him.

Braxton gazed at the compact sealed envelope in his hand. He picked up a dagger-shaped letter opener resting atop a stack of papers and sliced open the seal. He placed its contents on the desk and turned toward the bulkhead and removed a small painting attached to the cabin wall, revealing a wall safe secured inside the bulkhead.

Moments later, a cypher key in hand, Braxton sat and decoded the telegram:

From:

HRH King Dominic I, Buckingham Palace, London

December 15, 1905

To:

Foreign Secretary, HRH Prince Braxton, RMS Celtic, At Sea

Message:

PM RESIGNED STOP FORM NEW GOVT ON YOUR RETURN STOP

PROCEED TO LONDON UPON ARRIVAL STOP DOMINIC STOP   **Words: 16**

Braxton sank into a nearby sofa, his eyes fixed on the vast darkness of night beyond the oversized porthole. Up until that point, he had been unaware of the ship's movement, absorbed in the telegram.

He lost his balance for a moment as the deck heaved beneath him. Catching himself, he glanced toward the porthole, where he caught sight of towering waves. The liner shuddering, surging forward, plowing into 14-foot swells.

The weight of government affairs had kept him from noticing the roiling seas. Braxton said to the empty stateroom, "These seas, should they be sentient, would ease their tempest, knowing misbode foretelling greater storms brewed in London."

Prince Braxton was aware his party faced a crisis. The prime minister and chancellor of the exchequer had been found to have been incredibly careless and indirectly implicated in a financial scandal destined to destroy their reputations. While their only sin might indeed be stupidity, they had been professionally and personally compromised. Their political careers were surely over. England had recently assisted the United States in negotiating the Treaty of Portsmouth, ending the Russo-Japanese war. The British government was sorting out labor unrest and inevitable unionization inside the Taff Railway and other industries plagued with labor strife. The Suffragette movement and the implementation of the Aliens Act had consumed the governments and Braxton's every moment. Every moment, except, of course, those he had spent with Joe in the Blue Ridge Mountains of Virginia.

The so-called "hunting trip" had been a precious escape, a time spent solely with each other, away from the complexities of the world. There had been no aides-de-camp, no footmen, stewards, or secretaries. No one. This had been their time together alone, intensely physical and romantic. When would they have that chance again? To be caught in the dystopic world where it was just the two of them? Joe would soon be Vice President of the United States. Certainly, one day, he would become president. Braxton's thoughts continued. And me? Prime minister? Of course. I've buggered myself with raw ambition and foolishly not given a thought to reality. I'm done. Even more troubling, George, my dear son, will one day ascend to the throne. All my goals and aspirations, my endeavors to enrich my family and keep them as far away as possible from the throne, have been a waste of time and effort.

Braxton's face contorted with fury, and a ragged cry tore from his throat. "All I have fought for is for nought!" he thundered, each word reverberating through the cabin. In one swift, violent motion, he seized a small table and hurled it across the space. The crash of splintering wood echoed against the paneled walls—a sharp, final punctuation to his anguish. His breath came in harsh gasps as the weight of shattered dreams pressed relentlessly upon him.

Amidst the biting London winter cold, Braxton and Valentina stepped into the White Drawing Room of Buckingham Palace. Inside, they found John and their mother, Mercedes, gathered close to a roaring fire. Outside, a relentless winter wind and sleet battered the palace, causing the windows to shudder with each gust.

Dominic entered, somber. "I apologize, but Mathilde is, as you might expect, not feeling well." He turned to his brother, Prince John. "Vicky, is she joining us this evening?"

"I'm afraid not, brother," Prince John responded, shaking his head slowly. "She's attending to your Adolphus. It's been a challenging day for the crown prince."

Overwhelmed by the weight of his responsibilities, Dominic buried his head in his hands, seeking solace on a stool by the hearth. He turned to Braxton, his voice laden with concern, "Braxton, I must ask you, what am I to do? I mean, as king, not just for Adolphus, but for the entire kingdom, the empire?"

Mercedes, the queen mother, rose from her chair and moved over to Dominic, kneeled beside him, and gently wrapped her arm around her son's shoulder. "Dominic, we are here for you. Please do not concern yourself. The family stands ready to support you in whatever you need, whatever you may require."

Valentina stood. "I know this is a very trying time for everyone, but may I suggest we discuss our options?"

She turned toward her husband. "Braxton, do you mind if I be the one to share our thoughts with the family?"

"Certainly not, my dear. Under the circumstances, I prefer you to do it. Knowing what you are about to put forth, it would be rather disingenuous on my part."

The family exchanged uneasy glances and remained silent.

"Braxton is the natural choice of the party to lead the government. He is the most qualified and a favorite of the people," Valentina stated. "Dominic, you know, as you have done so in the past, it is the king's duty to appoint someone to form a new government.

Ultimately, it is up to parliament and the people to decide who remains prime minister."

Dominic looked up and over at Valentina, then turned his gaze to Braxton, and nodded in reluctant agreement.

Meanwhile, Braxton observed the conversation as though he were detached from the ongoings, looking down on the family from above. The weight of the situation bore down heavily on him. How did this happen? This is not what I wanted, he thought. Dominic was supposed to provide an heir. If he could not, then John, the spare, was meant to provide a successor. And now this! Prime Minister! I do not want to be the first minister. I only wanted to help from within parliament as a backbencher, to facilitate preparations for the new century!

Conversation in the White Drawing Room came to an end. Family members acknowledged Braxton's undeniable leadership abilities. Yet, they couldn't help but be taken aback by the fact that the little boy who once caused the Cupula Inferno, and now one of the richest men in the world, would ascend to the position of prime minister, becoming the de facto leader of the most powerful nation on earth.

The next day, the newspaper headlines around the world read:

KING ASKS BROTHER TO FORM NEW GOVERNMENT!

CONSTITUTIONAL CRISIS!

ROYALS TO FORM NEW GOVERNMENT!

PRINCE BRAXTON TO BE PRIME MINISTER

BRITISH PEOPLE SURRENDER TO CROWN!

His Royal Highness Prince Braxton established a government, subsequently ratified by Parliament.

On the other side of the Atlantic Ocean, the sitting Vice President of the United States resigned, citing unspecified reasons.

Senator Joseph Richards emerged as the nominated candidate for the vice presidency. The United States Senate soon ratified the nomination.

Six months passed and the President of the United States was assassinated, resulting in Joseph Richards assuming the office of the presidency.

Braxton addressed the men seated around the cabinet table at Number 10 Downing Street. "My government has governed for only a year. What did they expect? The papers are blowing things out of proportion. Yes, the situation is messy, but it's under control. There's no constitutional crisis! That issue was settled!"

"Perhaps," one of the ministers countered. "An Act of Parliament can alter England's constitution. However, it flies in the face of tradition. And tradition cannot be legislated."

"Indeed," the prince responded. "We will take charge of the discourse. I expect each of you, gentlemen, to contribute articles to the newspaper, opinion pieces, spreading our message. And, naturally, we shall utilize the government press office. I want each of you to organize press briefings and interviews to ensure our views are properly conveyed."

"Prime Minister, may I propose an idea?" suggested the President of the Local Government Board. "Let us organize rallies and meetings across the country to introduce, rather, re-introduce our policies, principles, and program."

"Excellent suggestion," Braxton replied. He cleared his throat and said in a slow and deliberate tone, "Make every effort to present the government favoring the populace, the people. Ensure no member of the royal family or the House of Lords are present at these events. I am to be referred to as the prime minister, not His Royal Highness or Prince Braxton. Present our programs as the government's initiative, with no reference to the crown. Eventually, I hope, sooner rather than later, we can return to referring to His Majesty's government's policies. But until that happens, we will do everything possible to project our government as a government of the people!"

CHAPTER ELEVEN

1910 – LA BELLE ÉPOQUE

Valentina and Braxton lay side by side on a canopied wrought-iron garden lounge, its cushions adorned with faded floral patterns. A gentle breeze stirred the air in the Renaissance House gardens, carrying the scent of late summer blooms.

Braxton turned to Valentina; his smile soft as he met her gaze. A rare tranquility wrapped around them, soft and fragile, until a shattering, anguished cry tore through the air, slicing the peaceful silence. The bellow reverberated from the stables, rolling across the gardens like a thunderclap, filling every corner of the estate with a raw, primal sound.

Valentina jolted upright, eyes wide as the harrowing sound rippled through the gardens.

Braxton, calm but attentive, slid his hand over hers, grounding her with a gentle squeeze.

"My dear," he murmured softly, his voice a steadying balm against the alarm in her gaze. "It must be Vainglorious III, likely struggling in foal."

Her breathing slowed under his touch, and she leaned into the warmth of his hand. "Of course," she whispered, her shoulders easing, "I knew that. But still, it was so sudden."

Braxton brushed a thumb over her knuckles, reassuring. "She's strong, Valentina. All will be well."

Valentina relaxed, a faint smile tugging at her lips. "Ah, yes, of course. I'd nearly forgotten. My mind was…elsewhere."

She adjusted her skirt as they leaned back once more, the moment of alarm passing. Braxton turned toward her again, a warmth in his gaze. "So, where were you just now? You seemed content. Do you think you could return there?"

A blush crept into Valentina's cheeks. "Well, actually, I received a letter from Angelina in Shanghai."

Braxton's eyes lit up. "Marvelous! And how is she?"

"Her letter sounds vibrant. She's thriving. These two years in the Far East with Ramsey have done wonders for her."

Braxton squeezed her hand. "I know how hard it was for you to let her go. But would you agree it's been for the best? She's grown into the strong, independent woman we hoped she'd be."

Valentina nodded, a sigh escaping her. "Yes, it's exactly what I wanted. But she's made a request. And I find myself torn."

Braxton's smile softened. "Let me guess. She wishes to keep working with Ramsey and appears to thrive in his company."

Valentina bit her lip, her gaze dropping. "Yes, you're right," she said, her voice barely a whisper as she looked away. "I miss her terribly. It's not fear for her safety but the longing to see her grow, to be present as she becomes this complex, beautiful woman; a mother's dream." She placed a hand over her face, fighting back tears.

Braxton gently brushed her hand away, tilting her face toward him, and wiped a tear. "On a lighter note," he murmured, "it seems she's quite the sought-after young lady in society. Lady Anson wrote recently hinting Angelina might have a romantic interest."

Valentina smiled, collecting herself, her eyes brightened. "Yes, I've heard rumors. What else could we expect? She is our daughter, after all."

Before he could respond, a low, distant hum caught their attention. Both shielded their eyes as they looked toward the sound, watching a swarm of biplanes appear overhead.

The hum intensified; a rhythmic droning reverberated through the air. Twelve planes spun, dove, and climbed, moving as dancers in a synchronized ballet.

Valentina shot to her feet. "Braxton! Those planes—they're fighting! Are we at war?"

Braxton rose, slipping his arms around her waist. "Not yet, my dear. They're practicing. Preparing, perhaps, for what may come."

That evening over a quiet dinner, Valentina, before looking up, stirred her tea. "Did you see The Times article about the 'Belle Époque?' Utter nonsense. All this sugar-coating of the era's art and industry. It only masks the storm that's brewing. How can anyone pen such naïveté?"

"My dear," Braxton began.

"It's foolish, Braxton! It's dangerous. Why can't they see what's looming over Europe? This isn't some misnomered idyllic belle époque—it's laide époque, ugly times creeping in."

Braxton placed his napkin on his lap and leaned forward. "There's something I want to discuss with you."

Valentina, her brows raised. "Are you changing the subject?"

"Not entirely. Your observations provide the perfect follow-on." He took a breath. "I'm considering stepping down from the premiership and resigning my seat in parliament."

She slowly lowered her glass, her face a mixture of shock and curiosity.

Braxton met her gaze, nodding, as if reassuring her. "Perhaps I could have been more delicate in my approach. But, yes, I am serious."

She blinked, collecting herself. "Is it in any way related to this faux belle époque?"

"It is."

Her expression softened. She leaned forward. "Tell me more, Braxton. I'd like to understand."

"As you know, my intelligence network—the Mars organization—has been gathering insights from across the globe for years; from my early days in Vienna onward. They're far more effective than British Intelligence."

"Yes, I know," Valentina replied, her eyes narrowing thoughtfully. "Mars' reach is vast. What is troubling you?"

"Germany's military strength is growing while Austria stumbles with its own preparations. Maxim's army, while large, lacks training. And France maintains a carefully crafted façade of ignorance, feigning obliviousness to the impending storm.

"For the past five years, I've been preparing Britain for war. But our allies are not ready and we cannot do this alone. I'm at a loss."

Valentina paused and then inhaled.

Braxton detected her angst and looked into her eyes.

Holding his gaze, she asked, "And Joe? Will he support us, Braxton? You share a bond with him unlike any other."

Braxton's face tightened. "As president, Joe shares my concerns, but there's a strong isolationist faction in America. It complicates things."

"Well, your relationship is complicated," Valentina said.

Braxton stiffened at her remark.

Her gaze shifted as she further considered his words, then focused on him once more. "So, if you step down, what will you do?"

Braxton leaned back, his voice calm. "I'll begin consolidating our assets, slowly divesting our European interests. Quietly."

"That would take years, Braxton."

"It would have. But I've taken steps to expedite things. The absurd idealism of this so-called belle époque has actually worked to our advantage. I've come a long way these past months acquiring favorable terms, contracts, agreements."

Valentina leaned in; her hands clasped beneath her chin. "And Russia? Surely you don't plan to hold on to the Russian Consortium."

"Maxim and I have reached an agreement. Russia's economy is faltering, and Master Higoshino suggested a barter: Russian art, icons, jewels, all in exchange for my equity in the consortium."

"Such an exchange would require entire shiploads of those treasures," Valentina pointed out.

Braxton nodded, smiling. "Indeed, it does. Master Higoshino and Angelina are currently managing the logistics."

A laugh escaped Valentina's lips, her face lighting up with admiration. "Of course, you've been planning this for years. Angelina's involvement has been the keystone, has it not?"

Braxton searched her face, a trace of concern in his gaze. "Does that trouble you?"

"Trouble me? It's exactly what I would have hoped. She's navigating a life as adventurously as the one we once shared in Siberia. I couldn't be prouder." She took his hand, her eyes bright with excitement. "Braxton, in spite of you, after 30 years I still love you."

With sudden energy, she rose, pulling him up with her, her hand firmly clasped around his. She led him toward the closed door of the dining room, her smile brimming with anticipation. "Come, my love. Let me show you just how much."

Braxton let Valentina lead him down the quiet halls, her fingers laced tightly with his, her touch gentle yet firm, as if afraid to let him slip away. When they reached their bedroom, she closed the door with care, then turned to him, her gaze warm and open, filled with a softness that seemed to dissolve all distance between them. Her hand moved to his cheek; her touch delicate yet unwavering.

She whispered, her voice barely above a murmur, "Tonight, let it be only us. You and I alone."

He cupped her face in his hands and looked into her eyes, a quiet smile playing on his lips. "Then that's all it will be, Valentina," he replied, his words a tender promise. He leaned down, pressing his forehead to hers, savoring the shared warmth between them. His lips found her brow, then her cheeks, lingering there as if memorizing each soft curve. When their mouths met, it was gentle, unhurried, a kiss that spoke of years of devotion and trust, a silent understanding of all they had been through together.

He removed his jacket and untied his white tie.

Valentina's fingers found the buttons of his shirt, slipping it from his shoulders, letting it fall to the floor. He mirrored her movements, helping her slide out of her gown and undergarments, her skin gleaming softly in the evening light. She looked up at him, her eyes bright yet vulnerable and he felt a swell of tenderness. He reached out, his fingers tracing the delicate line of her collarbone, skimming over her shoulders, down her arms, his touch as light as a whisper.

They eased onto the bed, bodies entwined, as he held her close, their faces inches apart, their breaths mingling in the quiet. His hands moved along her back, fingertips mapping every familiar curve, his touch infused with a gentle reverence. She melted into his embrace, her own hands tracing over his chest, her touch featherlight, each movement intentional and tender, as if savoring the quiet moment as much as he did.

Their bodies drifted in sync, guided by a silent harmony that spoke volumes of longing and understanding, each kiss imbued with tenderness and care. He brushed his lips over her shoulder, down her arm, the softness of his breath a caress, while her hand found its way to his face, fingers threading gently through his hair. They lingered this way, their closeness a balm, their touch a shared vow, each moment deepening the connection between them. With every gentle kiss, every caress, they rediscovered the love that had weathered so much and still held strong.

As they lay together, breath slowing, Braxton stroked her hair, brushing a stray lock from her face, his finger tracing her brow.

"I love you, Valentina," he whispered, his voice a soft vow.

She looked up at him, her eyes glistening with emotion. "And I love you, Braxton," her voice barely above a whisper, her gaze never leaving his. She rested her head against his chest, and he wrapped his arms around her, drawing her close, their heartbeats gradually finding a shared rhythm.

In the quiet, their world faded, leaving only the warmth between them, the strength of their love anchoring them to each other, a love deeper and truer than words could ever capture. And as they drifted into sleep, still wrapped in each other's arms, they knew that whatever lay beyond the door, whatever challenges or heartaches, they would face it together.

Months later, Braxton wrote the following letter:

My Dearest Angelina,

Your aunt and I are immensely proud of the remarkable progress you have made in understanding the intricacies of our family enterprises and assisting your father, Ramsey.

Though it saddens us, we could not be present at your wedding to young Everett Lawrence, our hearts brim with joy for you both. Everett's impeccable reputation and distinguished lineage promise a strong foundation for your future together. We are utterly delighted with your choice.

Ramsey has informed me you and Everett, per my request, have agreed to remain in the East for the foreseeable future. Later in this letter, I'll explain the reasoning behind my request.

In the wake of the Titanic tragedy, we are left to mourn the loss of many dear friends and associates. Families like the Astors and Strauses, and our own dear friends, the Spencer Silverthornes, have been deeply affected. Mercifully, none of our family or employees were listed among the manifest. Still, so many of us are grappling to reconcile the sinking of the "unsinkable."

Your aunt and I eagerly await your safe return to England when you, your father, and Everett have achieved the objectives we agreed upon.

When you both finally arrive in England, I'll need your help to manage the proceeds from the sale of our European holdings. I will share my thoughts regarding making significant investments in British armaments and heavy manufacturing; our family's way of supporting the nation's war preparations

There is another matter weighing heavily on my mind. Our king's health is frail, undoubtedly worsened by parliament's recent vote declaring Crown Prince Adolphus ineptus servire—unfit to inherit the throne. This news strikes painfully, especially for my brother John, though he guards his sentiments too closely to share them on paper.

And then there is my son, George. It seems he is destined for the throne one day. Yes, I am aware I follow John in the line of succession. Therefore, my close proximity to the throne, combined with my role as prime minister, creates an unsustainable tension. Undoubtedly, a constitutional crisis looms. Therefore, I intend to tender my resignation by year's end.

This letter is full of all manner of news, yes?

These developments will undoubtedly affect both the family, of which you and Ramsey are a part of, and our business. As such, you and Everett, along with your father, may find yourselves shouldering considerable responsibilities during this transition.

Once my duties as prime minister conclude, I plan to have George accompany me on an international trip. This journey is vital for him, as it will prepare him as a future king by broadening his knowledge of the world.

I have directed the proceeds from our European sales to be invested in machinery manufacturing across England, Canada, America, and South America. I welcome any input you might have on these matters.

In a separate letter, I instructed your father to travel to Russia to reduce capital expenditures while increasing logging, mining, and oil drilling operations. We must extract as much capital as possible, for I believe Russia stands on the precipice of revolution. The socialists are no friends of capitalism. Discretion is essential, and we must forestall any talk of panic selling as we divest our Russian holdings.

While your father is in Russia, he will find that we have redirected our top engineers from the Russian oil fields and mines to South America to explore potential mining prospects.

My dearest Angelina, I understand this is a tremendous amount to absorb. I would have confided in you and your father sooner but the risk of our plans becoming known to competitors was too great.

George and I will soon depart from England with our journey eventually bringing us to you through the Americas. The thought of seeing you fills my heart with joy.

Yours affectionately,

Uncle Braxton

Prince John and Braxton sat in the study at Number 10 Downing Street, each holding a glass of scotch as they gazed at the fireplace's flickering flames.

"Brother," John said, his voice unsteady. "I cannot be king."

Braxton said nothing, his eyes locked on the dancing flames, allowing the crackle of the fire to fill the silence.

"Well, what are we to do, then?" John's voice wavered, barely above a whisper.

"Our duty," Braxton replied, his voice firm. "Yours and mine alike. Who could have imagined it would come to this?"

The fire snapped as sparks leaped into the air, jumping about with the shifting of a smoldering log. Braxton leaned forward, using the poker to push it back into the flames.

"As prime minister, I'm pushing you into the fire, John. "You must begin preparing for the responsibilities that await you once you ascend to the throne."

"Into the fire, am I?" John laughed bitterly. "What are you talking about? Utter nonsense!"

Braxton set down the poker and met John's gaze. "You know exactly what I mean. You need to be prepared, sooner rather than later. I won't be there to protect you this time."

"Bugger off, Brax!" John muttered, taking a long swallow of scotch.

"Funny. It's your buggering, as you put it, that's played no small part in bringing you to this point."

John's eyes flashed, and he leaned forward. "You're an ass, Braxton."

"And you're not the first to say so," Braxton replied, a faint smile tugging at his lips. "But I'm the ass who's bailed you out time and time again."

"Enough with the lectures!" John said, tossing back his drink and refilling his glass. "I'm here to tell you I cannot be king. If Dominic dies and they proclaim me king, I'll abdicate. You'll end up with the crown."

Braxton turned, his gaze piercing. "You will do no such thing. You will not abdicate. You will not disgrace yourself, our family, or the legacy of England's monarchs. You have a duty, John."

John swallowed, unable to meet his brother's eyes.

"Look at me, John!"

"I can't. I'm terrified they'll find out. Discover the truth about me."

Braxton's tone softened. "We're all afraid. But there's a chance they won't. If the worst comes to pass, we'll face it. But you must be ready. The empire teeters on the edge of war. I'm stepping down to manage our family's assets and invest in our country's future. Now is not the time to falter."

John hurled his empty glass into the fireplace, shattering it against the bricks, sending shards and embers flying. The crash echoed through the room.

Braxton remained unmoved. A moment later he said, "I'll take that as a 'yes.'"

"Yes, damn it!" John snapped, sinking back into his chair.

Braxton rose and with a deliberate calm, strolled over to the sideboard, plucked a fresh glass and filled it to the brim. He handed it to his brother, saying nothing before resettling into his chair.

"Dominic is declining. The doctors say his grief over Rose's passing has taken its toll. I'm stepping down as prime minister to focus on our affairs—and, more importantly, to be here for you and Dominic. We have no other choice."

John shook his head. "You're repeating yourself, Brax."

"I am."

John's voice trembled. "I'm completely unprepared, Braxton. I lack the will…the skill…"

Braxton reached over, clasping his brother's hand. "John, I've known about you for years. Since that morning I saw you with Ramsey at the Aurelio Palace. I must have been only ten."

John's eyes widened, a smile breaking through his angst. "You knew? Of course you know. I know that. But back then, you knew?"

Braxton nodded, a softness in his eyes. "My dear brother, you've always underestimated yourself. But be that as it may, you have always been there for me. How could I forget those days sneaking into garden parties, racing horses? You've lived fully, following your heart—a rare gift. And now, England needs you. You're far more capable than you think."

They sat in silence; the fire casting warm shadows around them. Braxton handed John his glass of scotch before adding another log to the flames.

Braxton retrieved his glass and returned to his seat. "I love you, brother," he paused, his voice quiet but steady. "And because I do, I have a plan, a way to help you prepare for the throne, ready or not."

As prime minister, Braxton arranged for Prince John to tour Europe to observe the continent's political and military developments.

Though John had never shown much interest in such matters, he accepted the task, knowing his brother needed him to embrace a sense of duty.

Fully aware of John's limitations, Braxton crafted detailed briefings, guiding him on how to gather insights and make impactful assessments. Every encounter, every conversation John undertook, was carefully orchestrated, providing him purpose.

Intelligence from the British government revealed Germany's covert military exercises in Bavaria and Austria. Braxton arranged John's itinerary so he would "coincidentally" arrive in these regions just as the exercises began, sending ripples of uncertainty through German and Austrian ranks. With his diplomatic entourage embedded with British intelligence officers, John's observations evolved into a vital source of information.

When John returned from the continent, he looked Braxton in the eye, his gratitude unmistakable. "Thank you," he said, his voice resolute. "For the first time, I feel transformed—like I've truly served the empire and, perhaps, taken my first tangible step toward the future awaiting me."

CHAPTER TWELVE

HIS CONSTANT

Braxton rose, facing the assembly with grave resolve. "Honorable lords, ladies, and gentlemen of this house. For nearly two decades, I have served as a member of parliament, giving my all to this great nation. It has been both a privilege and a duty, and I have worked tirelessly to keep our empire secure and prosperous. I believe, in large part, I have succeeded. I have also labored to prepare our nation for the looming conflict that now shadows our future. With the unwavering support of this chamber, the government has secured mechanisms to uphold our nation's strength and readiness. As prime minister, I believe I have done all I can."

Whispers swept through the high-vaulted chamber, the solemn gothic revival walls seeming to bear witness. Members of parliament filled the benches along each side of the rectangular hall, their murmurs blending with the faint creak of wood, attendees taking their places, creating a charged atmosphere under the lofty ceiling.

From the spectators' gallery above, a soft shuffling indicated onlookers adjusting to witness the momentous occasion. The charged air hinted at the quiet weight of anticipation.

"Order!" the Speaker of the House thundered, his gavel's sharp crack slicing through the hum of voices.

Braxton stood motionless, allowing the room's restlessness to die down before he continued, his voice measured, each word carrying a gravity deepened the stillness. "Once again, the seasons have turned, and I must face the inevitable. I have come to terms with what must be." He paused, his gaze sweeping over the chamber. "I offer my deepest gratitude to you—the people of the greatest empire the world has ever known—for granting me the honor of serving as your Member of Parliament, Foreign Secretary, Home Secretary, and Prime Minister."

Braxton paused, lowered his voice and delivered the final blow with unwavering resolve. "Today, I will tender my resignation to His Majesty."

Gone were the customary throat-clearings and quiet side remarks. The silence was so profound it felt as if the room held its breath. One member, as later reported in the London Times, leaned over and whispered, "One could have heard a moist fart."

Then, as if on cue, a wave of murmurs swelled into a roar, spreading like wildfire. Journalists scrambled from the press gallery, the banging of doors and hurried footsteps echoing through the halls as they raced to break the news.

The House of Commons erupted with frenetic energy as members and spectators alike grappled with the sheer magnitude of Braxton's resignation as prime minister. The speaker, rising once more, pounded his gavel repeatedly. "Order! Order!" he commanded, his voice growing hoarse with frustration. The sea of voices crashing in waves of disbelief and confusion was deafening. "Order in the House!" His face hardened as he glared at the unruliest members, one by one, until their voices faltered.

Gradually, the tempest of voices ebbed, replaced by a tense, uneasy quiet.

Braxton continued, "England and the empire stand secure, strong in both military and economic matters. The government is prepared to defend our nation against whatever may come. Our people are united in advancing the empire. That is my gift to you, my dear fellow citizens. God save the King!"

Everyone sat, digesting the reality of what lay before them. For nearly two decades, Braxton had served in parliament for the last ten years as their unwavering leader and anchor.

A member of parliament rose, clapping slowly and steadily. More joined in, until members from both sides were on their feet, applause swelling in intensity. Eventually, cheers and hurrahs filled the air, the sounds carrying into the streets beyond.

Braxton steepled his hands against his chest, bowing as he departed through the sea of supporters who wished they could shake his hand or embrace him. Yet, as a royal, they could only bow as he passed, many suspecting that one day, this man would be king.

The applause trailed him down the corridor, growing faint as he exited and disappeared into a waiting car, which bore him to Buckingham Palace to formally tender his resignation to King Dominic.

Prince Braxton, Prince George, and a retinue of business managers and clerks embarked for the United States at the end of December, a month following Braxton's resignation.

"The president has kindly offered to meet us when we arrive in New York," Braxton told his son, George, as they sat on the stern of the royal yacht, bundled in heavy overcoats against the sharp winter wind gusting over the churning Atlantic.

George glanced at his father, curiosity in his gaze. "Quite remarkable, isn't it?" he mused. "Why go to such lengths? We're scheduled to be in Washington D.C. a week later. Odd, don't you think?"

Braxton, knowing well the reasons behind Joe's arrangement, replied, "He's offered us the use of his brownstone during our stay in the city. It's a rare courtesy."

George seemed unconvinced. "But his family remains at the White House. Surely, this level of hospitality is hardly necessary, even for royals. I could see it if the king himself were arriving, but—"

"You know well enough, George. Joe regards our family as his own," Braxton said with finality.

George shrugged. "Yes, he has been like an uncle. We've always called him Uncle Joe. Yet Mama seems less fond of him. Hmph, though she adores Mrs. Richards and their children."

Braxton inwardly acknowledged his son's keen insight, though he chose not to share Joe's motives for the special arrangements. "Regardless, this will give you the chance to experience the city in all its magnificence, with none of the usual constraints."

George adjusted his scarf. "I suppose I understand." After a pause, he asked, "But why place me at the forefront, Papa? I am not next in line for the throne. Uncle John is, and after him, you. I see no need to elevate my role."

Braxton smiled, a glimmer of understanding in his gaze. "Tell me, George, how many years have I?"

George replied, "Fifty-two."

"And you, my son?"

"Twenty-two," George said, shaking his head slightly.

Braxton looked at him with a hint of gravity. "Then understand this. The likelihood of my ever ascending to the throne is slim, and even if I do, my reign may not be long. But you, George, are 30 years younger than me. You must be ready, no matter what the future holds."

Later that evening, as George slipped into his overcoat, he noticed movement through a partially open door. Stepping inside, he found Braxton and Joe in quiet conversation.

"Good evening, Papa. Good evening, Mr. President—Uncle Joe," offering a polite bow.

Braxton grinned. "Enjoy your evening, son. The city is yours tonight."

"Make the most of it, George," Joe added. "There is much to see and do."

Once George left, Joe turned to Braxton, the warmth in his gaze shifting to something deeper. "I've sent the servants off for the evening. We're alone."

Braxton's breath caught. "You've truly gone above and beyond, Joe," he murmured. "After all this time."

They left the drawing room, hand in hand, and crossed the foyer, mounting the stairs.

Reaching the landing, Joe led Braxton into a dimly lit bedroom, a faint glow from the corridor trailing in behind them. The air felt charged, a quiet anticipation layering over them as they stood close, breaths mingling in the low light.

They shed their coats with familiar ease, hands moving to untie each other's ties, loosening the elegant knots with a sense of reverence yet growing urgency. Joe's fingers worked swiftly, tugging at Braxton's waistcoat; Braxton responded in kind, their laughter and quiet murmurs blending into the space. Joe's shirt slipped off, leaving his skin exposed to the warm glow of the low lamplight. He looked up, his eyes meeting Braxton's with a depth of feeling that spoke louder than words.

"Braxton," Joe murmured.

Braxton's mouth curved into a smile as he pushed Joe gently back onto the bed. He kneeled to remove Joe's shoes, his hands slow, almost reverent, before moving to undo the fastenings of Joe's trousers, sliding them away with the practiced grace of familiarity and care.

The dim light danced over Joe's form as he lay on the bed, his muscled frame a testament to years of hard work, his chest rising and falling with each breath, calm yet charged with anticipation. Braxton took a moment, savoring the sight, the intimacy of their closeness as he quickly removed what remained of his clothing.

Braxton leaned over, lowering himself slowly, savoring the closeness as he and Joe came together. Their arms wrapped around each other with fierce tenderness, pulling one another into a tight embrace. They felt the warmth and strength in each other's touch, each heartbeat syncing with the other's, rising from somewhere deep between them. Every subtle movement, every touch, every whisper, affirmed the trust and intensity binding them.

Braxton and George's party had hired three private train cars for their journey from Washington, D.C. to Chicago, then on to Denver and San Francisco. Father and son, seated across from one another at a mahogany table in the parlor car, found themselves alone as snow-covered fields swept past the windows.

George gazed absently at the white, endless landscape. Braxton broke the silence. "Well, my boy, I trust the newspapers have reported accurately on your time in New York and Washington." He rustled the paper he'd been reading. "It appears you acquitted yourself quite well. An enjoyable adventure, I gather." Braxton offered his son a warm smile, then returned to his reading.

George's voice, touched with introspection, broke through the quiet. "Father, the reports were fair. I did enjoy myself."

Braxton looked up, smiling with satisfaction. "Excellent, George. That was the intent." He resumed his reading.

George's tone grew serious. "I must say, though, the trip became something of an unexpected and rather unsettling education."

The remark caught Braxton's attention. He glanced over the top of his newspaper, brow slightly furrowed. "Unsettling, you say. In what way?" He sensed the same subtle tension he'd noticed in George since New York, though he had assumed it was just the thrill and distraction of new surroundings.

George watched the passing scenery, his thoughts caught between loyalty and turmoil. "How long have you and Uncle Joe been together?"

Braxton's heart skipped. Lowering the newspaper, he took a moment to compose himself before speaking. "More than two decades, George. Before you were born; even before your mother and I married."

George turned from the window and faced his father. "People assume Uncle John is, well, inclined toward men. Perhaps that's why he's never had children. But you. You have six children. Are you…?"

Braxton shifted in his seat, a hundred thoughts racing through his mind. The train plunged into a tunnel; the car suddenly consumed by the dark. A few moments later, they emerged into bright morning light.

Braxton spoke carefully. "I've never felt bound by a single term. My affections have never been confined to one gender. My relationships are with individuals who hold a place in my heart."

George crossed his arms, his expression one of conflicted surprise. "This is…unfamiliar." He hesitated. "You were the last person I'd have suspected of being a sodomite."

Braxton's expression iced over. He jumped up, angry eyes flashing. "Watch your tone and your words," he said, his voice low and steely.

George's jaw dropped. "I beg your pardon, Papa. I didn't mean any disrespect."

"Thoughtless," Braxton snapped. "You, my son, are careless and arrogant."

"I apologize, Papa. It's simply a lot to understand." George's face softened, his words nearly a whisper. "It's all new to me. I'm just struggling to understand it all."

Braxton paced the length of the parlor car, hands clenched tightly behind his back, his steps sharp and controlled. His jaw set, and his brow furrowed, every movement charged with an edge of restrained fury. He muttered under his breath, barely audible, each step a way to release his simmering tension.

He reached one end of the car, paused, then turned sharply to walk back, his shoulders slowly relaxing as he moved. His strides grew less rigid, his breathing steadied, and his fingers began to unclench. With each pass, the fire in his eyes softened, and the tension around his mouth eased. Finally, he halted mid-pace, exhaled slowly, and let his shoulders drop, the anger dissipating into a composed calm.

Braxton took a deep breath, letting the tension ease. "A drink, then." He poured two whiskeys, handing one to George.

"You didn't know me as a young man," Braxton said with a wry smile. "I was rebellious in my youth, you know. Surely, you've heard the stories of my escapades."

George chuckled, "The Cupula Inferno."

"Indeed," Braxton replied, a hint of nostalgia in his voice. "I've never let conventions dictate my life." He cleared his throat, choosing his next words with care. "George, my relationships with men and women alike have each held meaning. I don't expect you to agree or even understand, but I have always chosen to live on my own terms."

George looked into his father's face; his admiration tempered with concern. "I worry that your legacy—your extraordinary achievement—might be tarnished if such things were to become public knowledge."

Braxton nodded, acknowledging the reality. "That's fair. I've been cautious; up until now, at least." He hesitated, then said quietly, "I'm only sorry it had to be you who discovered Joe and me."

George's expression softened. "When I saw you and Uncle Joe together, everything suddenly made sense. All the little things fell into place." He took a breath, his voice gentle yet strained. "I didn't know what to feel—shock, confusion, maybe even betrayal—but one thing was clear. I had to protect you." He glanced away for a moment before meeting his father's eyes again. "So I closed the door and turned off the light."

Braxton turned to the window, his gaze distant, eyes glistening. George's voice broke the silence, soft and steady behind him. "What I saw wasn't shameful. It was beautiful."

Braxton slowly faced him, and for the first time, he saw understanding in his son's eyes.

"It reminded me of an Alma-Tadema painting," George continued, his voice barely above a whisper. "It felt timeless, like the love between two souls."

George rose and crossed the room, placing a firm yet comforting hand on his father's shoulder. "Papa, do you love him?"

Braxton nodded; his voice thick with emotion. "Yes. Deeply."

George embraced him warmly. "I may not understand it completely, but I love you."

Braxton pressed his son's head against his.

After a moment, they returned to their seats. Braxton raised his glass. "Thank you, son."

"Of course, Papa." George took a sip, then ventured, "Does Mama know?"

Braxton inhaled deeply, exhaled slowly, and took a long drink before nodding. "I believe so. She's never asked, but she's hinted over the years. She's shown me grace in ways I'll never fully comprehend."

"Truly? How?"

"Your mother and I have a passionate but complex love. She's left me twice, and I've caused her pain as well. But through it all, she has been generous and forgiving. I believe, in an odd way, she understands Joe has been my sanctuary, my constant. And in a way, she accepts it."

George fell silent, taking in the depth of his father's words. "She must love you deeply."

Braxton nodded. "She does. And so does Joe. I'm a fortunate man, George. I have loved deeply, and in turn, I have been loved in ways few could comprehend."

CHAPTER THIRTEEN

AROUND THE WORLD

George pressed a small ivory button, lowering the window with a quiet hum. In the dense, fog-laden mist, a lone figure emerged at the guardhouse door.

Prince George extended a folded document through the open window. The figure examined it under the beam of a flashlight before snapping to attention and saluting.

"Sir!" He turned to his right and signaled. A heavy, resonant clang echoed through the air, announcing the iron gates as they slowly swung inward.

Their vehicle proceeded through, coming to a halt in the yard. The chauffeur stepped out, moving briskly to open the rear door of the maroon Rolls Royce Silver Ghost Thrupp & Maberly limousine.

The car's polished aluminum body, black fenders, silver beltline, and gleaming brass headlights radiated an air of power and immense wealth.

"Welcome, gentlemen," greeted another uniformed guard, addressing Braxton and George as they emerged from the car.

Braxton and George took in the surrounding scene—row upon row of warehouses, each partially obscured by the thick fog that softened the edges of the morning light, casting a muted, almost ethereal glow.

From across the bay, a foghorn groaned a mournful, resonant note.

"The last time I stood here was 30 years ago, and this damn fog!" Braxton broke off, addressing the guard. "Is Mr. Carlton here?"

"Your Royal Highness, over here!" called a tall, portly man, impeccably dressed save for a well-worn porkpie hat. "A true pleasure to see you again, Sir!" he nodded, acknowledging George with a slight bow.

"Ah, Mr. Carlton, a pleasure to see you," Braxton greeted warmly. Gesturing to his son, he added, "Allow me to introduce my eldest, George."

George extended his hand. "Mr. Carlton, the pleasure is mine. I've heard much about you and your invaluable partnership with my father."

Mr. Carlton beamed. "Well, young prince, your father and I have shared a fine business alliance for decades. May there be decades more."

Braxton chuckled. "Yes, 30 fine years indeed."

Carlton glanced toward the bay. "This fog should lift soon, and we'll be able to inspect the warehouses. Other than maintenance, they've remained untouched all this time."

"Exactly as I instructed. Excellent work, Mr. Carlton," Braxton said approvingly.

A thin layer of mist settled on their coats, adding a sheen to the fabric, while the dim lights from nearby buildings flickered faintly through the haze, lending a ghostly air to the scene.

The morning chill sharpened as they stood in the open. Drawing their coats closer, they listened as Carlton briefed them in hushed tones, his words seeming to dissolve into the fog, preserving the secrecy of their task.

An hour later, as the fog retreated, 50 warehouses, in five neat rows of ten emerged. Each warehouse an imposing 25-foot-tall brick structure spanning over 20,000 square feet. Inside, crates were stacked high, labeled with the innocuous title, "Agricultural Machinery."

Within the crates lay a wealth of treasures from Russia, Japan, China, India, and Singapore, each item a testament to Braxton's meticulous foresight and decades in global trade. More than artifacts, they were assets of immense value, gathered through resource exchanges and strategic purchases, now primed to finance Braxton's vast, multi-generational plan.

Braxton and George inspected each of the 50 warehouses. By sunset, as they climbed back into the Rolls Royce, George extended an invitation to Carlton.

"Mr. Carlton," George said, "we'd be honored if you would join us for dinner."

"Thank you, Your Royal Highness. I'd be delighted."

"Excellent. We dine at the Palace Hotel at eight," George replied. "I've reserved a private dining room."

Stepping through double mahogany doors adorned with gold filigree handles, Mr. Carlton arrived in the hotel's private dining chamber. Inside, rich emerald-green flocked wallpaper covered the walls and was accented by marble wainscoting with gilded molding.

A meticulously set table for three graced the room, laden with fine porcelain, sterling silverware, and cut crystal. At its center, a striking floral arrangement of miniature blue roses and Swarovski nautical figurines brought a touch of maritime elegance to the opulent setting.

Princes Braxton and George stood by the fireplace, cigars and glasses of scotch in hand. Both wore evening dress—white tie, tailcoats, intricately detailed waistcoats and black velvet slippers adorned with discreet embroidery.

"Mr. Carlton," Braxton greeted him, "we're glad you could join us."

Carlton wore appropriate evening attire; minus the pork-pie hat.

Dinner proceeded, conversation light and free from business until dessert had been served. Afterward, they retired to the fireside, where cigars and brandy awaited.

"Shall we sit by the fire?" George suggested, gesturing to the armchairs.

Once settled, brandy glasses in hand, Braxton broke the silence. "Mr. Carlton, I require that you double our warehouse capacity."

Carlton's eyebrows shot up. "Double it, Sir?"

Braxton nodded. "Yes. Double."

Carlton leaned forward; curiosity piqued. "When would you like it completed? And is there anything specific we need to prepare for? Customized facilities, perhaps?"

Braxton's gaze shifted briefly to George, then back to Carlton. "Within three months. It will house a similar inventory, so no additional requirements. Just additional capacity."

"More agricultural machinery?" Carlton asked, his tone a shade doubtful.

Braxton's smile held a glint of amusement. "Of course."

George, seated with hands clasped, interjected, "Mr. Carlton, we'll need Pacific Transport Shipping—our joint venture—to arrange shipments from Vladivostok, Odessa, St. Petersburg, and Sevastopol to the expanded warehouses."

"How many ships?"

George paused. "Difficult to say, though my cousin, Princess Angelina—"

Carlton interrupted, "Yes, I had the pleasure of meeting her in Singapore and Calcutta. A formidable businesswoman."

"Yes, thank you," George replied. "Princess Angelina will coordinate the logistics. My father and I have laid the groundwork to initiate shipments—"

Braxton's attention drifted at the mention of Angelina, carrying his thoughts miles away across the Pacific. Angelina, he thought, a faint smile appearing. I can't wait to see her again. It's been almost three years.

He leaned back, his mind painting a vivid picture of his daughter's recent life. How she must have changed, he thought. Twenty-one years old now, a grown woman.

In his mind's eye, he saw her confidence, stronger now, no doubt, than when she had set sail for Calcutta. Married to Lord Lawrence, he recalled, envisioning her radiant in her wedding photograph. A businesswoman now, well-traveled and educated; her intellectual curiosity and discipline two of her many qualities. Ah, how I miss her. Braxton's heart swelled with both pride and a keen yearning.

"Papa?" George's voice pulled him from his reverie. Braxton turned to his son, then to Mr. Carlton.

"I apologize. My mind wandered."

"Quite all right, Papa. Mr. Carlton was asking if you'd like to meet with our various division managers while we're here in San Francisco—the mining, forestry, drilling, and shipping heads."

"Of course," Braxton said, gathering his thoughts. "I mentioned that in my letters. Please set up meetings over the next week and ensure their latest accounting portfolios are ready a day prior to each meeting."

"Very good, Sir," Carlton acknowledged.

George rose, "We sail for Singapore one week from tomorrow."

The lush, jungle-like garden glistened in the morning sunlight. A symphony of birds filled the air: Javan Mynas, Black-naped Orioles, Asian Glossy Starlings, and Coppersmith Barbets flitted through the vibrant foliage. Above them, the layered canopy concealed the source of an eerie, witch-like cackle…the elusive, yellow-billed Oriental Pied Hornbill.

Babbling softly, a stream wound its way alongside crushed gravel paths, flowing beneath ornate bridges and into tranquil pools where koi fish displayed dazzling colors, their scales shimmering in the dappled light.

Princess Angelina and her father found a peaceful reprieve on an intricately carved wooden bench beneath a pagoda covered in entwined vines. The ornamental pagoda sat on a small island, connected to the shore by a gracefully arched bridge. The pond was adorned with blooming water lotus in every hue imaginable, the soft, elegant honey citrus fragrance embraced them.

"I am so happy to see you, Uncle," Angelina said, her face alight with youthful radiance. Her white lace-gloved hands rested gently in her father's grasp.

Braxton couldn't suppress a smile, a rare warmth spreading across his features. "It has been an eternity, my dear Angelina. You appear well. Your aunt and I have missed you terribly. Nearly three years, and look how you've flourished, blossomed and matured."

Angelina blushed, a soft rosy hue coloring her cheeks. "Thank you, Uncle. I've longed to see you and Aunt Valentina." She paused, tilting her head thoughtfully. "How is she?"

Braxton responded to her question and shared updates on family and friends. In turn, he asked after her life, inquiring with particular interest about her marriage. Time slipped by, morning easing into midday as they caught up, genuinely interested in one another's lives.

Angelina reached into the folds of her dress and brought out a fan crafted from sandalwood and silk, painted with delicate phoenixes. She raised it above her head, signaling to a servant who waited nearby on the pond's shore. Moments later, he brought a tray of iced gin and tonics to their table. Angelina handed her father a glass before taking her own and raising it with a smile. "To the soul's joy—gin—and the body's cure—quinine."

Braxton laughed knowingly and lifted his glass, enjoying the cold drinks' refreshing taste.

Conversation shifted to matters of business, their words blending into the serene, almost mystical ambiance of the garden.

"My dear," Braxton began, "we've kept each other informed through our letters."

Angelina nodded, placing her glass down and folding her hands in her lap, her attention focused entirely on him.

"My letters may have hinted at the difficulties facing the crown with Dominic's ill health and the specter of war looming ever closer."

She rested a reassuring hand on his forearm. "I suspected as much," she replied thoughtfully. "I could read between the lines, both in your letters and in those from Everett's family. It's all so very sad."

"Indeed," Braxton said. "As I mentioned, Dominic is emotionally and physically drained. For the most part, John has taken on the responsibilities of kingship. I fully expect him to be declared regent before I return to England."

"But, Uncle," Angelina said, frowning, "establishing a regency is no small matter. Surely, you should be there to guide such a transition?"

Braxton gave a nod of approval. "Astute as ever, my dear. Yes, you're absolutely right. And I've taken certain steps to ensure that transition."

"Steps?" Angelina leaned back, crossing her arms. "You anticipated all of this while still serving as prime minister?"

"Yes," Braxton admitted. "The Declaration of Incapacity was drafted during my final month in office. John, a few senior council members, and I had been discussing it for months leading up to my resignation. We all agreed: John will submit the declaration to the full Privy Council soon. Once the council approves, Parliament will be required to act."

"My word," Angelina murmured, her eyes widening. "You laid all the groundwork and then left the country, distancing yourself so it wouldn't appear you orchestrated the change in line of succession."

"Precisely." Braxton finished his beverage and placed his glass on the table. He gazed across the lake at the verdant landscape. "That, in fact, was my primary reason for resigning. I am too closely tied to the throne to govern as prime minister. Importantly, the constitution will not allow it."

Angelina stifled a soft laugh behind her hand, quickly regaining her composure.

Braxton raised an eyebrow, amused. "What amuses you, my dear?"

"My apologies." She let her hand fall from her mouth, revealing a mischievous grin. "This is all so…convoluted. I couldn't help but feel there's more to this story than meets the eye."

Braxton tried to suppress a smile; aware she had seen through him. With a slight cough, he conceded, "Well, I suppose there's often more than meets the eye."

"Of course there is." Angelina picked up the pitcher, refilling their glasses before looking back at her father. "Please, Uncle. Continue."

The soft murmur of the garden filled the pause as they each settled deeper into the tranquil afternoon. Somewhere nearby, the faint hum of bees mingled with the occasional rustle of leaves in the breeze, creating a cocoon of stillness around them.

ANGELINA & CARMEN

Braxton leaned back in the corner of the garden bench, folding his hands in his lap and crossing one leg over the other.

"Are we preparing for a summer's tale?" Angelina asked, a teasing glint in her eyes.

"Indeed, we are," he responded with a smile. "A true story, mind you, more an expedition than a mere tale."

Angelina exclaimed, feigning a childlike interest. "Uncle, an expedition? I adore expeditions!"

Braxton laughed aloud. "You provide great amusement, Angelina."

"Well, when you are pleased, I am pleased," she responded. "Now, an expedition? Really!"

Utterly amused, yet intent on moving forward with his story, Braxton said, "Exactly so. An expedition where you shall assume a leading role."

She leaned forward and placed her elbows on her knees and cradled her face within her lace-gloved hands, smiled and locked her gaze on him.

"As you know from my previous letters, I am intent on divesting myself of most of my interests in this part of the world. The globe is in an uncertain place. Battle lines are being drawn in Europe. German, Austrian, and Turkish ambitions for colonial empires loom large. Russia is in turmoil and is on the brink of revolution. The Japanese, too, have imperial ambitions. China is a den of banditry and fractional warfare."

Angelina sat up and drew a deep breath.

He stared down at his hands for a moment and returned his gaze to Angelina. "I require your assistance as well as the support of your father. I have spoken to him at length on this topic and we are in accord."

"In accord?"

"Yes. However, it also necessitates you and Everett's wholehearted commitment."

"This sounds rather ominous, Uncle,"

"It will require several years of dedicated efforts, far from home, amidst rapid escalating tensions and danger. I would undertake all this myself, but circumstances at home require my presence. That being said, I have no recourse."

Angelina wrung her hands, her brow furrowed with tension. "Uncle, this intricate and seemingly multi-faceted intrigue is undeniably fascinating, but it also leaves me deeply unsettled."

Braxton leaned forward, his gaze steady and reassuring despite the weight of his words. "Angelina, I understand your concern, but don't let it overwhelm you. Instead, I ask you to focus. Listen carefully to what I'm about to share—it's crucial."

He paused, allowing her a moment to still her restless hands and meet his eyes. "You possess the clarity and strength to understand this, even if it feels daunting now. The path ahead is fraught with uncertainty, yes, but it's also one of immense purpose. It is not a task I assign lightly, but I trust your resolve, as my father trusted mine in my youth."

Braxton's voice softened, though its conviction remained unshaken. "What I'm about to unfold may challenge you, but it will also shape you in ways you cannot yet imagine. There is a delicate balance in this, Angelina, and you are far more capable than you give yourself credit."

He reached out, gently taking her hands in his. "Now, listen closely. Everything depends on this."

Braxton outlined what he required of Ramsey, Angelina, and Everett in overseeing the sale of his assets in Japan, Hong Kong, China, and Singapore.

"It will take several years to locate buyers willing to pay the true value of these assets," he explained.

"Yes, no doubt." She took a moment to reflect, then continued, "I can speak for my husband. We will remain in the East and fulfill your wishes." Her fingertips lightly and briskly tapped her lap. "And what about Russia?"

He chuckled. "Ah, Russia. Indeed, Russia. That poses the most formidable challenge within my scheme."

Angelina said, "As uncertain as the world stage may be, I find it hard to believe there are buyers eager to pay full price.

"Indeed, none with the necessary capital," he confirmed.

"Perhaps through trade or barter," Angelina suggested.

"Exactly," he nodded, "and this is precisely where the three of you enter the equation. The czar has consented to exchange antiquities, icons, and similar treasures in return for my stake in the Russian consortium."

"Ah, yes," Angelina acknowledged.

"However," he continued, "he has indicated Russia may not have enough of what we require for fair compensation."

Angelina let out a sudden, involuntary snort, her hand flying to her mouth, her eyes sparkling with amusement. Stifling a laugh, she composed herself and said, "Forgive me, Uncle."

Braxton smiled.

"Uncle, just consider this. Russia is brimming with mountains of icons and treasures. Opulent gilded ornaments are scattered the length of the empire. The imperial jewels, historical relics, and museum-grade treasures could undoubtedly serve as the means to secure your equity.

"I've personally seen paintings by European masters adorning palace walls, and oh, the Fabergé eggs alone! Russian is a cornucopia of wealth."

She paused, rising from her seat with the fluid grace of someone who commanded attention. Pacing thoughtfully around the pagoda, her gaze drifted over the tranquil pond as she weighed the next point. "However, these aren't simple assets," she said, her voice growing sharper. "Transporting and storing them will require meticulous planning. Where do we safely house such valuables while searching for buyers? And flooding the market haphazardly could send international values into chaos."

"Master Higoshino," Braxton said.

Angelina whipped around, placed her hands on her hips, facing her uncle, "Genius!"

"Thank you, I thought so," quipped Braxton.

"And as for storage? Where would he accommodate the—?"

"San Francisco. I have made the necessary arrangements," Braxton replied.

"And transportation, shipping?" Angelina pressed.

"Once more, accommodations have been made. And back to my point. You, Ramsey, and Everett, along with Master Higoshino, will oversee the cataloging of the bartered items and their shipping."

"Hmm," Angelina mused, once more pacing the pagoda. "We are burdened with a significant cargo, not to mention the size and number of shipments required," she added, shaking her head, then rubbing her white gloved hands together, "I can hardly wait! When do we start?"

"Her Imperial Majesty, the Czarina," the majordomo announced. Braxton's older sister, Carmen, entered the Mauve Room in the Alexander palace.

She rushed over and threw her arms around her taller brother. "Oh Brax, I have been so desperate to see you. Thank you ever so much for coming." She pulled back and straightened her pastel silk day dress and motioned to the sofa. "Please join me," she said, pulling him down beside her.

"Carmen, my dear. It is so good to see you. George sends his best."

"George, where is he? I was under the impression he would be joining us for tea."

"Ah, I did as well. But the twin archdukes got hold of their cousin and took him fishing with Maxim on the lake. I guess the twins are what, early twenties now? Well, Maxim insisted you and I have time alone. Actually, he said you had…"

"Oh, absolutely!" she exclaimed, her voice carrying a note of forced enthusiasm. "Very true. I did suggest I have time with you." Her hands fluttered briefly before she reached for the tea service, hesitating for a moment as if gathering her thoughts. "Besides, I rarely have the opportunity to speak English, save with the British ambassador. Everything at court revolves around French—speaking French, dressing in French fashion, indulging in French music, literature, and even the works of French philosophers. Would you believe there are Russian nobles who cannot even speak Russian?"

Braxton pulled on his ear and remarked calmly, "Yes, I do."

Her hands trembled as she handed him the teacup and saucer, the porcelain rattling softly in the quiet room.

He continued, his voice steady and measured, "I too marveled at that absurdity when I was first here some 30 years ago."

She nodded quickly, her lips pressing into a faint, nervous smile, though her fingers lingered on the edge of the tea service, betraying a flicker of unease.

Carmen, overly enthusiastic, asked, "Your family, well, our family. How do they fare? Please, catch me up on their lives. Living in St. Petersburg feels worlds apart from places I cherish—Aurelio, London, home,"

Braxton internalized the angst in his sister's voice and mannerisms. "My dear sister, perhaps you know more than I. It has been six months since departing England. Let me tell you what little I do know."

Carmen sat rapt, unwavering in her determination to hear every detail about his resignation from the premiership and the journey that led him to the Alexander Palace.

"Now, Carmen, it's your moment to confide in me, to share what you couldn't express in your letters."

"Well, as you are aware," she leaned in and lowered her voice, "I am compelled to limit my correspondence to familial matters. The Secret Police scrutinize all letters, purportedly to shield us from revolutionary threats. Maxim has been working to eradicate the remnants of the mad czar's reign, but I am afraid his success remains uncertain. To this day, I am not convinced he is an absolute monarch. That is another matter entirely.

"Maxim has been diligently striving to reform the government, yet he faces unwavering opposition. The anti-monarchists are growing increasingly militant and gaining popularity by the day. I'm genuinely concerned for our safety," she confessed, reaching for an embroidered handkerchief from her skirt to dab her eyes.

Overwhelmed by her emotions, she leaned into Braxton, her tears flowing freely.

CHAPTER FIFTEEN

MAXIM

Braxton's time in St. Petersburg was drawing to a close. He and Maxim had arranged a clandestine meeting in the czar's private study. To Braxton's surprise, the room was smaller and gloomier than he had anticipated, furnished in a stark, masculine style.

Settling into a chair that he'd hoped would offer some comfort, he found it devoid of any luxury. Puzzled, he wondered why his dear friend, once a connoisseur of refinement and sophistication, now seemed to embrace a nearly Franciscan austerity. For heaven's sake, he thought, this man rules one-sixth of the world and is reputedly as wealthy, if not more so, than I.

Gesturing to the dimly lit room, the prince inquired, "Maxim, when did you take up the life of a monk?"

Maxim, startled, replied, "What? What on earth are you talking about?"

"This chamber—it's as spartan as a monk's cell," Braxton continued, though he smiled as he observed, "though I'll admit, the L-shaped desk is quite…efficient."

With a defensive edge, Maxim responded, "While my people suffer, I find it difficult to enjoy the more lavish rooms of the palace. It feels…inappropriate."

Braxton shook his head. "Did Siberia not offer you enough sacrifice and discomfort, Maxim? We spent months hunting for oil and ore to bail out your bankrupt empire."

Maxim sighed. "Perhaps it did. But since those days, nothing has been easy. I find myself beyond despondent, dreading each day."

The czar shared how the country had rapidly succumbed to anarchist infiltration. War with Germany and Austria—or no war, he feared—the monarchy itself would not survive. The nobility, he believed, had grown ineffective, incapable of protecting or sustaining the autocracy.

With the formation of the Duma, a body meant to represent the people, landowners, and businessmen, a semblance of a parliament had been created. Yet, as Maxim explained, the Duma was ineffective and lacked the capacity to support a strong monarchy or operate as a democratic entity. Without intervention, he feared, the power vacuum would be filled by anarchists and extremist factions.

"I must plan for the inevitable," Maxim admitted. "It's essential I transfer as much of my personal wealth out of Russia as possible— and it must be done in utmost secrecy. If word of my actions spread, the anarchists will declare treason and the little authority I hold will vanish."

Braxton's mind traveled back three decades to his arrival in St. Petersburg from Venice, just days after the God Mars scheme and Carnivale Bacchanal. Maxim, then a young noble, not yet czar—had met him under cover of night, accompanied by the Imperial Guard.

During that time, Maxim had just survived an assassination attempt. The dangers seemed grave then, but Braxton realized that today, the stakes were far higher.

Gazing at the czar, Braxton's thoughts shifted inward. How had I failed to consider the full implications of this situation for my sister and the imperial family? Their lives now dangled precariously over the abyss. Could they survive the coming upheaval? Would they escape with their lives?

Noticing the prince's pallor and the beads of sweat forming on his forehead, Maxim allowed Braxton a moment to regain his composure before continuing.

"I have a substantial quantity of gold, silver, Swiss notes, English bonds, and jewels I'd like to send to London," Maxim said. "It's only a fraction of the family's wealth, the most we could set aside discreetly without attracting suspicion. I estimate it's worth at least £72 million."

Braxton felt a chill run up his spine. "If that's just a fraction of your wealth, where is the rest?"

The czar shrugged. "Much of it is tied up in land, investments, monopolies, art, sacred icons, precious jewels, and outstanding loans," he explained, then added, "And let's not forget the Russian Consortium. When you divest, that will effectively cripple or end the consortium."

Braxton let out a sigh. An involuntary groan escaped his lips.

Sensing his friend's distress, Maxim offered reassurance. "And that's as it should be. Without you, none of this would exist. Everything I have is a direct result of your efforts in saving the empire from financial ruin all those years ago."

Braxton rose from his seat and walked the room, examining the floor-to-ceiling shelves filled with books, photographs, and paintings. Holding a model triplane in his hand, he asked, "You would like me to arrange for the transport of those assets?"

The czar, his attention fixed on a photograph of his twin sons, murmured, "Yes, that would be my preference."

Prince Braxton took a thoughtful moment, carefully returning the model plane to its shelf. "I'll be leaving for Italy within the fortnight. And plan to stay with the Chiacontella family at the Villa Incantarre before heading to London. My diplomatic immunity should allow me to cross Europe without declaring anything, but I worry Austria might present an obstacle. I'll need Austrian documentation to ensure safe passage. I doubt they'll honor my British passport, let alone my diplomatic status. Can your government procure the necessary papers?"

The czar gave a curt nod. "Yes."

"With luck, those papers will secure my passage through Italy as well. I've arranged for the British navy to transport me from Naples to London."

Maxim remained silent, the prince detailing his improvised plan.

Braxton paced slowly, each step deliberate, his voice low and precise. "Here's what I propose. Over the coming weeks, we'll discreetly move the trunks—gold, silver, jewels—all of it, onto my train, piece by piece." He paused, glancing at Maxim with a knowing look. "If questioned, we'll say they're personal belongings I've acquired over the years. Or perhaps that they belong to Valentina."

He stopped directly in front of Maxim, the weight of the moment hanging between them.

"But we must tread carefully," Braxton continued, his voice barely above a whisper. "Any exposure could trigger a crisis of international proportions. With the state of things, it would be a disaster we can ill afford."

He met Maxim's gaze, his words sharp and laden with warning.

"This operation," he said, "must remain unseen, unheard, and absolutely untraceable. One misstep, one loose word, and the whole thing unravels."

CHAPTER SIXTEEN

REGENCY

"I cannot fathom what keeps him so long. He summoned us, and now an hour has passed," Braxton remarked, stubbing out his cigar in the crystal ashtray.

Prince John tossed back his third glass of scotch. "King or no king, it's inconsiderate and, frankly, habitual at this point."

The double doors opened.

"His Majesty the King," announced the footman.

Dominic entered Buckingham Palace's White Drawing Room.

"What on earth, brother?" John demanded, his frustration evident. "We've been waiting for over an hour. Why summon us, then leave us waiting?"

Without responding, Dominic strode to the side table, took hold of the decanter, and poured himself a whiskey.

Braxton and John stood, bowing in unison. "Your Majesty."

King Dominic gave no indication he'd even heard them.

"How are Mathilde and Adolphus?" Braxton asked.

The king shrugged as he lit his cigar, his gaze fixed distantly as he drew in a deep puff. "Same as ever. Nothing has changed," he replied, the words drifting out with his exhale.

With a casual wave, Dominic motioned for his brothers to sit. "The prime minister will be joining us."

He took his seat opposite them, his expression weary, his gaze forlorn. "The prime minister was detained, and I thought it better to wait until he'd left Downing Street before my joining you."

John's voice was measured but edged with irritation. "And you didn't think to inform us of this delay? Very thoughtful."

Dominic pressed his lips together but said nothing.

Moments later, the king's secretary appeared in the doorway. "Your Majesty, the prime minister has arrived."

"Very well, send him in."

The prime minister stepped into the room, offering a series of bows, each calibrated to the rank of the royals before him. He exchanged brief pleasantries with the king and the princes, his tone courteous yet efficient. As the secretary exited and closed the doors behind him, the four men were left alone in the hushed, charged atmosphere. Braxton noted the prime minister's tense expression and pallor.

His voice taut, the prime minister said, "Your Majesty, Your Royal Highnesses. Please accept my apologies for the delay. State matters required my attention."

The king grunted. "And have you confirmed the government's suspicions?"

The prime minister exhaled slowly. "Yes, Your Majesty," he replied, pausing. "The Austrian Emperor's heir, the Archduke and his

Archduchess, were indeed assassinated. Shot—murdered—in Sarajevo."

Braxton and John exchanged wide-eyed looks; brows raised. Their attention returned to the prime minister and then to Dominic.

The king faced John. "Now, do you see why I insisted on waiting for the prime minister?"

Chastened, John replied, "I beg your pardon, sir."

The prime minister overlooked what was clearly a private exchange.

His tone solemn, Braxton asked, "Would it be accurate to say, Prime Minister, that war is upon us?"

"Not immediately, sir. But the Austrians and Germans are hungry for conflict. They may seize this as a chance to lay blame on all of Europe for one assassin's actions."

"A false flag, then," Braxton mused aloud.

"Let us hope not," Dominic interjected. He turned to John. "Given your time in Germany two years ago, what do you think? Might they use such a pretext for war?"

"I wouldn't rule it out," John replied, arms crossed. "I wouldn't be surprised if they hired the assassin."

"Really!" Dominic, running his fingers through his hair, turned to the prime minister. "What say you, Prime Minister?"

"I can't say with certainty, but I don't disagree with His Royal Highness."

Turning to Braxton, the prime minister continued, "Sir, let me say, when you resigned as prime minister nearly three years ago, you left us well-prepared for any conflict. For that, the nation is deeply grateful. The government also values the intelligence you continue to provide from your private sources."

Braxton gave a brief nod, intrigued by what he presumed to be the minister's line of thought.

The prime minister seemed to gather himself before he spoke again. "With that in mind, I believe it's essential to discuss the safety of their Imperial Majesties, Empress Diedre and Empress Carmen."

A heavy silence settled over the room. The three brothers sat stunned; their shoulders weighed down with concern.

"Our sisters," the king murmured. "Their lives, at the mercy of men intent on war."

Straightening, Braxton shook off the despondency. "I presume you're here to request some form of service. Perhaps a diplomatic mission?"

The king's voice was tentative, almost musing aloud. "A mission? For what purpose?"

The prime minister's attention remained fixed on Braxton. "You're correct, sir. The era of diplomacy in matters such as these has largely passed."

Dominic leaned back; his eyes closed. "Gentlemen, I find myself quite fatigued. I suggest you continue without me."

John rose and moved to his brother's side, gripping Dominic's arm gently. "Dom, let me help you to your chambers."

"Thank you, Johnny," Dominic murmured.

Braxton spoke up, concern evident in his tone. "Is there anything I can do?"

Resolute, John replied, "You and the prime minister should discuss the necessary steps. If you would be so kind, keep us apprised."

With John's support, Dominic stood. Bent slightly, he looked to the prime minister. "It appears the time has come for the Privy Council and government to appoint my brothers as co-regents."

Though they'd anticipated this, the reality of Dominic's words struck heavily. The prime minister, who had also risen, bowed. "Yes, Your Majesty."

John led Dominic from the drawing room.

After a moment, Braxton resumed his seat, folding his hands in his lap. "Well, Prime Minister, it appears our work is cut out. Shall we begin?"

"Where to start?" the prime minister asked.

"As the king's directive concerning the regency is now in your hands, let us address the welfare of my sisters, the empresses."

The prime minister nodded and settled back into his chair. "Indeed, Your Royal Highness. Following your return from your world travels, including Russia, I began discreet inquiries."

"Inquiries, Minister?"

"Yes, I instructed our embassy in St. Petersburg to gauge the czar's concerns for his family's safety," he explained, his tone grave. "The report was…alarming. Both the Winter Palace in St. Petersburg and the Alexander Palace in Tsarskoy Selo are minimally fortified and poorly guarded. A well-sized mob could breach either with little resistance."

Braxton frowned. "But why such neglect, Minister? Surely the czar's security apparatus recognizes the danger. When I met with the czar, he was overwrought, but aware of the situation."

The prime minister nodded. "The ambassador reports the Imperial Guard is stretched thin protecting the family and various state sites across the empire. Some units were recently deployed to the western border in case of war."

Braxton shook his head slowly. "I know the terrain well around St. Petersburg and Tsarskoy Selo. May I draft a plan to ensure their safety? Dieu nous en préserve, un sauvetage est necessaire. God preserve us, a rescue is necessary."

"Yes, God forbid," the prime minister agreed. "Sir, with your past experience in Berlin and Vienna, your guidance would be invaluable. Your, shall we say, 'exploits' have suited you well for this task."

Braxton's mind drifted to the kaiser's ill-fated arms smuggling to Vienna in 1881; a plan he had unwittingly disrupted during an encounter with anarchists.

"We might consider Crimea, the Livadia Palace," Braxton suggested. "If, by chance, they could be brought to Crimea, matters would simplify. Could you contact the ambassador and prepare three contingency plans?"

The prime minister inclined his head. "Agreed."

"As for my sister, Empress Diedre, and her position with the kaiser, it is different. She has been estranged from the emperor for years."

"Precisely," The prime minister replied. "Our ambassador in Berlin notes that she rarely stays at the Stadtschloss. She favors the

Marmorpalais in Potsdam. Or, more frequently, takes to the Rominten Lodge in East Prussia."

Braxton steepled his fingers, a look of understanding passing over his face. "That aligns with her letters. So, we have three possible locations if extraction becomes necessary."

"If it comes to that, Your Royal Highness. Prudence calls for preparation. For now, German agitators show no signs of targeting the German royal family, but such matters can turn swiftly.

"Indeed. Especially in wartime," Braxton agreed. "I'll have a plan drafted and sent to you promptly."

CHAPTER SEVENTEEN

ROYAL DISSENT

"It gives me great discomfort, Your Royal Highness," began the prime minister, "to address the matter of the royal family's participation in the war effort."

"Minister, you and I have discussed this matter before, and now that war has been declared, it is indeed time to act," Prince Braxton replied, seated with his sons in the ducal library at the Aurelio Palace.

Traditionally, members of the royal family were compelled to adopt high-profile roles in times of war. Prince George, as third in line to the throne, had anticipated a mostly ceremonial position. His duties would be largely symbolic, "window dressing" for the crown, securing a place on the General Staff, and inspecting combat units.

"Papa, it is unjust," Prince George asserted. "Keeping me from the front lines gives the impression I'm shirking my duty. As a future king, should I not be remembered for serving, not as a noncombatant?"

The prime minister interjected. "The government understands and respects your stance, Your Royal Highness. But in these times, no heir or monarch is ever placed in the line of fire. It simply isn't done. The nation cannot risk the life of its future king."

"Why not, minister? There are spares to the spare! Egads! I have five siblings!"

Braxton's tone firmed. "George, we've spoken about this before. "As I said, your role is determined by the crown and the government." Both your Uncle John and I have weighed this matter carefully with the prime minister."

George sprang to his feet. "But Papa!"

Braxton's patience thinned. "We have invested years in preparing you for the throne, with intensive study and training and at considerable expense. The empire's stability is vital.

"We cannot burden our people with uncertainty simply because you choose to defy the obligations imposed by the crown and the king's government."

Braxton rose, his gaze steady and unyielding. "As a future king, George, you must think beyond yourself. Think of how your actions affect the empire and its people."

His son looked away, jaw clenched before storming down the long colonnade and out of the study.

Prince Arthur and Prince Vanya exchanged glances, rose in unison, and bowed to their father. "Good day, Papa."

"Gentlemen, please remain seated," Braxton insisted. The two brothers complied, focusing their attention on him.

"Minister, could you outline the roles the government envisions for them in the war effort?"

The prime minister leaned forward. "Your Royal Highnesses, each of you will play a crucial part. As Prince George's involvement will be restricted, it is essential that both of you serve honorably."

The two princes remained still, faces unreadable.

"Prince Arthur, you are to report to Sandhurst for officer training. We'll expedite your commission to the army."

Prince Arthur nodded with a serious expression.

Prince Vanya chimed in, "I assume I'm headed for the navy."

"Indeed, Your Royal Highness. You'll report to the Royal Naval College at Dartmouth."

Vanya sighed, glancing at Arthur. "Come, brother, it seems we have much to prepare for."

"Thank you, Minister. Thank you, Papa," Arthur said, bowing.

Vanya nodded to his father and exited alongside his brother.

The prime minister then turned to Braxton. "And His Royal Highness Prince John? Has he agreed to continue as co-regent and represent the crown in His Majesty's stead?"

Braxton stroked his chin thoughtfully. "That, minister, is another matter."

The prime minister waited, puzzled. "Sir?"

Braxton's face held no expression. "My brother will not agree to anything other than serving on the front."

The prime minister's face blanched. "Impossible! He's the heir."

"Yes, he is."

"I don't understand, Your Royal Highness. We've just told Prince George—"

"Exactly, minister. However, Prince John's decision is firm. He is currently with the Secretary of State for War arranging his assignment to the front."

The prime minister rose abruptly. "This cannot happen, Your Royal Highness."

Braxton met his gaze, unwavering. "I know. John has served honorably and, with his wife, has given much in support of their Majesties. But he dreads the day he might sit on the throne. He is…different, as you know."

The prime minister returned to his seat, his expression grim.

Braxton continued. "As heir and co-regent, if the government denies him permission to serve on the front, he will relinquish his claim to the throne. And when he does, the press will have no reason to restrain themselves from uncovering his past. The government and the crown will face a storm that could very well destabilize the monarchy."

The minister clasped his hands, his gaze distant.

Braxton thought, my dear John, are you seeking fame or escape— or something darker? The cruelties of life have relentlessly pursued you. Is it my duty to shield you from yourself, or to let you walk your own path?

Just then, Princesses Elizabeth and Elena entered the study, their skirts rustling as they crossed the room, four lively corgis bounding behind them.

"Hello, Papa," Elizabeth greeted, curtsying and kissing her father on both cheeks. Elena followed suit.

The pups pawed at Braxton's legs, hoping for treats hidden in his pockets. He kneeled on the carpet, giving them their due attention, as the princesses offered their hands to the prime minister.

"It is so lovely to see you, Minister," Elena said. "We've missed your company. Where have you been hiding?"

The prime minister blushed, as he always did when the princesses greeted him. Their warmth and graciousness had that effect.

Elizabeth took the chair beside him. "I do hope you have plans for us in this dreadful war, Minister. Elena and I are eager to serve—provided you let us join the front lines!"

The prime minister, accustomed to their playful charm, replied, "Of course, Your Royal Highness. The front it is."

Elena grinned. "I told you, sister! The prime minister wouldn't keep us idle. So, what are our roles? Artillery? Pilots?"

Braxton chuckled. "Girls, mind yourselves."

The prime minister smiled. "Your father and I, along with His Royal Highness Prince John and His Majesty, have agreed you both could contribute greatly. First, by assisting with the Queen's Imperial Military Nursing Service, and later with staff duties on the continent."

Elena clapped her hands. "Wonderful."

The princesses rose. "Thank you, Minister," Elizabeth said. "We're honored to serve."

The prime minister stood. "Royal princesses in service will inspire all classes to volunteer."

Turning to their father, Elena said, "Thank you, Papa."

"Yes, thank you, Father," Elizabeth echoed.

Braxton embraced them. "I'm so proud of you both."

They curtsied, exiting, their enthusiastic pups tumbling along behind. Elena leaned close to Elizabeth. "George will be mad with envy!"

Elizabeth giggled as they disappeared through the doorway.

The prime minister turned back to Braxton. "Forgive me, Your Royal Highness, but I can think of no finer representatives of the crown than the princesses."

Braxton's face softened. "Nor could I."

He sat back, contemplative. "Frederick…now, there's a matter. Sharp as he is, he lacks maturity. His judgment has been questionable, to say the least."

The prime minister inclined his head.

"I've decided to send him to America," Braxton said, his tone firm. "Perhaps in Texas learning the oil business he'll stay out of the newspapers."

"A wise choice, Your Royal Highness."

CHAPTER EIGHTEEN

1916 – HUNTERS HUNTED

The mid-morning sun rose over the distant hills, casting a gentle golden light across the Aurelio Palace gardens. The Grand Duchess Valentina sat alone in her bedchamber, a space reflecting her Russian heritage intertwined with the English countryside. She was surrounded by snow-white pillows adorned with embroidered landscapes reminiscent of her beloved mother Russia.

A breakfast tray lay across her lap, holding an array of toast, preserves, ripe fruit, and a petite teapot with a matching cup and saucer. Awaiting her perusal, a folded copy of The London Times rested nearby on the silken bedcovers.

Valentina reached for the teacup and, while raising it to her mouth, pulled the newspaper close. Her eyes caught sight of the headlines, and her breath stilled. She bolted upright, upsetting the tray, scattering toast, jam, and porcelain across the silk coverlet.

"No! No! Maxim—no!" she cried, her voice trembling with disbelief.

On leave from the front lines, the czar's 27-year-old twin sons had invited their father on a hunting and fishing expedition to their cherished lodge at Langinkoski, a modest retreat along the Kymer River in the Grand Duchy of Finland. Known for its salmon-rich waters and secluded forest, the dacha offered the imperial family an escape from court life—no servants, no ceremony, only the solace of nature.

Buoyed by the success of the previous day's fishing, the czar and his sons, joined by a small military escort, set out into the woods, eager to take on the challenge of hunting.

Overnight rain had soaked the forest, leaving the ground soft and the air thick and cold, the kind of chill that clings to the skin.

They remained undeterred, their focus on the hunt ahead. As they ventured deeper, a strange quiet settled over the trees, a silence interrupted only by the faintest of sounds—unfamiliar and easily dismissed. Twigs cracked in the shadows, and every so often, a sudden rustle of underbrush rose and then died away.

Yet, with their sights on the prospect of game, the men took little notice, unaware of the watchful eyes tracing their every step. They moved on, their laughter and voices punctuating the stillness, never realizing that the forest itself seemed to be holding its breath.

A light drizzle fell, chilling them to the bone. Unprepared for the persistent rain, their spirits dampened and even the guards' vigilance waned. Thus, missing subtle signs they were not alone.

Headlines cried across Europe and beyond:

CZAR AND PRINCES SLAUGHTERED IN THE WOODS OF LANGINKOSKI!

"I just spoke with my sister, Carmen," Braxton said, having returned to Aurelio the day after the assassination.

Valentina sat in the garden, her gaze lost in the gray, cloud-laden sky. She nodded faintly. "I can only imagine what she must be enduring."

She looked up at Braxton. His face was drawn, his expression hollow. Valentina patted the bench beside her. "Please, sit with me."

He took the seat beside her and wrapped his arm around her shoulders. They rested their heads together, searching for comfort in the silence.

A chill breeze stirred, prompting Braxton to unfold a blanket he had brought with him. He draped it around Valentina before settling in beside her once more.

"How did she sound? Were you able to hear her well?"

"Enough, though it was garbled at times." He took Valentina's hands in his. "The events have drained the life from her."

"Understandably so," Valentina murmured.

Braxton nodded. "She sounded as if she had nothing left to give. Alone now, in a foreign palace surrounded by enemies, in a country at war."

Gently, Valentina asked, "What did she say?"

Braxton exhaled, gathering himself. "She gave me the barest account, but from what she shared and what I learned from Lord Hemperly, the imperial family's physician, here is what I make of it.

"It seems the czar was struck fatally in the chest, his body tumbling into a ravine. Gunfire horribly disfigured the young princes, enough that their coffins were sealed." He paused, the horror of it hanging between them. "Three coffins were taken to Kazan Cathedral.

Carmen arrived before the public viewing began. When she learned her son's coffins were sealed, she ordered them opened."

"Oh my God," Valentina shuddered. "Whatever for?"

Braxton's voice grew softer, as if recounting a dreadful dream. "Hemerly told me, Carmen approached Maxim's coffin first, she was barely able to stand. She whispered, 'My dearest Maxim, how has it come to this?' and touched his face with her bare hand, murmuring, 'I will love you forever.' Then, she requested that they seal the coffin.

"She turned toward her sons' coffins, found a nearby chair, and slumped down. Hemperly advised against opening them, telling her, 'Your Imperial Majesty, forgive me, but both grand dukes are…well, all but unrecognizable.' But she demanded that he open them."

Valentina's hand tightened on Braxton's as he continued.

"At her command, the physicians reluctantly complied. One by one, the coffins were unlocked, revealing bodies disfigured beyond recognition. Still, she insisted on looking upon her sons one final time."

Valentina shivered. "How could she bear it?"

Braxton's voice faltered, heavy with emotion. Hemerly said that Carmen stood motionless, silent, as tears streamed unchecked down her face. Finally, she moved, her steps slow and unsteady, each one burdened with unbearable agony. Carmen was able to gaze down on her first son, but when approaching the second coffin, she faltered, overcome, unable to bear the sight. She turned away, her sorrow too great to face.

"They had to steady her as she left the cathedral, her body weakened by the crushing weight of her grief. By the time she arrived at the Winter Palace, she was unable to walk."

Valentina turned to Braxton, her voice trembling. "What can be done for her?"

Braxton looked away; his expression hardened with a grim resolve. "I don't know," he murmured, barely audible. "But whatever it is, I'll see to it."

Following the murder of her family, the Empress Carmen rarely ventured beyond the palace walls. Haunted by threats against her life, she ordered additional guards not only around the palace grounds, but throughout St. Petersburg and Moscow. Though she held the title of consort to the late czar, she had no aspirations to follow in his place. Unlike the notorious Catherine the Great, who had dethroned and dispatched her husband, Czar Peter III, Empress Carmen had no desire to rule. But she knew that others, driven by political ambition, would see her as a threat. She sensed, with chilling clarity, that as long as she remained in Russia, those seeking power would not rest until they had removed her.

Resolving to end speculation and ensure her own safety, she determined to publicly renounce any claim to the throne.

Dressed in stark black, she arrived alone at the Tauride Palace. As she stepped from the Daimler, the chill seemed to press in, bitter and unyielding. Her long mourning dress, plain and severe, swept to the ground, her veil softly framing a face set in quiet determination.

She glanced up at the towering double doors, her gloved hand momentarily steadying herself on the car. Then, without hesitation, she moved forward, each step purposeful, her dark figure a striking silhouette against the stone. Her gaze remained fixed on doors ahead, shoulders squared, as if each step brought her closer, not just to the building but to a fate she neither welcomed nor feared.

As she approached, two uniformed guards in black armbands drew the doors open.

Empress Carmen ascended the steps, each step steady and purposeful. She entered through the grand doors, her gaze fixed ahead, undistracted by the murmurs in the hall. Crossing the threshold into the chamber, she paused, poised and resolute, prepared to face the assembly.

Three thunderous strikes echoed as the chamberlain's staff hit the floor.

"Her Imperial Majesty and Most Serene Highness, Carmen, Empress of All the Russias!"

A hushed silence fell over the hall. The 442 delegates turned as one, all eyes on her. Carmen moved confidently toward the platform, her gaze steady, meeting no one's eyes. Ascending the steps to the podium, she ignored the throne-like chair on the dais prepared for her presence and remained standing.

Drawing herself upright, she addressed the hall with extemporaneous resolve. "My lords and gentlemen, I am here today to speak on the question of succession."

Murmurs stirred through the assembly.

"It has been my honor to serve as your empress," she continued, her voice clear and unwavering. "I have come to love and cherish my adopted country. And it is with this love for 'Mother Russia' that I hereby renounce any claim, real or imagined, that I might have on the Russian Imperial Throne."

The words struck the hall into profound silence, each delegate grappling with the implications. They stared, stunned, absorbing the gravity of her statement.

"As your Empress," she went on, "I decree that this assembly shall appoint the successor to the late Czar Maximilian. The people shall decide the matter of succession through you, their representatives. I charge you to choose from among the extended Imperial Family, and while there is no clear heir, consider both lineage and individual merit. Let primogeniture alone not decide this."

Her gaze swept over the hall, commanding its attention. "May God grant you wisdom and strength as you bear the weight of this grave responsibility."

She turned to descend from the dais, then paused, her gaze once more sweeping the room. "In the interim, if it is your wish, I shall stand ready to collaborate with the government to ensure a seamless transition. Once the heir is ratified by this assembly and the upper house, I shall bid farewell to Russia."

With that, she descended the stairs and moved steadily through the hall. The only sound was the gentle rustling of her gown as it brushed across the floor. When she reached the back, applause erupted, filling the chamber with a thunderous cheer. She turned, offered a single nod, and departed.

Inside her car, she leaned back, her head resting against the seat, her eyes closed. She had done all she could for Russia. Yet she felt little faith in the duma's ability to carry out her wishes. Russian history was steeped in autocracy. She feared the people were unprepared for a government of compromise and cooperation

Weeks passed. Carmen felt her position within the palace deteriorate. Cold indifference replaced deference she had always been shown. As the Duma remained mired in deadlock, St. Petersburg erupted in riots, the Winter Palace a symbol of the people's frustration. Palace staff vanished one by one.

Five weeks after her public renunciation, a furious mob descended upon the palace. Blood stained the gardens, and hundreds lay dead before the violence finally subsided. It was then Carmen understood her fate had been sealed. The palace walls held little protection, and she had no one to protect her. She was trapped; her survival dependent on escape.

Britain's ambassador sought a private audience. He suggested they walk in the gardens, alone.

"Your Majesty," he whispered as they walked, "I bring a proposal."

"A proposal?"

"Yes, Your Majesty, a scheme to ensure your escape."

Her breath caught. "Thank God."

"Indeed," he replied. "Here is what I suggest: In two nights' time take a solitary stroll in these gardens."

"Unattended?" she asked, her voice barely audible. "That is impossible. I am but a prisoner here. I am always attended."

The ambassador nodded. "It must be so, or the plan will fail. If we are discovered, the consequences would be catastrophic. There would be little our government could do."

Carmen wrapped her arms around herself, trembling. "I will do what I must. Continue."

They reached the far edge of the garden. He motioned her to a secluded bench. "When you reach this point, look for an unmarked car," he said, indicating a side street. "The rear door will have a small white ribbon tied to the handle. Open it, get in, and you will be safely taken from here."

Two nights later, still shrouded in her mourning attire, Carmen dined quietly with her one remaining lady-in-waiting. She adjusted her bodice, shifting uncomfortably.

"You seem unwell, Your Majesty," the countess remarked.

"Oh, it's nothing."

Toward the meal's end, the Empress suggested a stroll in the garden. She requested a light cloak, despite the chill.

"But it's bitterly cold," her lady protested.

"I need the cool night air," she insisted. "I'm feeling overheated."

The countess hesitated, but relented, and soon the two stepped onto the terrace. A footman offered to accompany them.

"No, thank you; we shan't be long," Carmen replied, refusing the lantern as well. "The moon is lovely tonight and will provide sufficient light."

Adjusting her bodice once more, she descended the steps, lifting her skirts. Several minutes into their nocturnal stroll, she turned to the countess. "It seems you were right. I am chilled. Would you fetch a warmer shawl?"

The lady-in-waiting nodded and hurried off. As soon as she was out of sight, Carmen moved swiftly toward the meeting point, keeping to the shadows to avoid the watchful eyes of the palace guards. She noted the guards had grown lax, distracted by cigarettes and drink.

The empress slipped through the garden unnoticed, a renewed sense of purpose driving her forward.

Carmen reached the designated spot and made for the waiting car. She crossed the street and took hold of the handle and removed the white ribbon. About to step inside, a figure exited the car, dressed in a similar gown. The figure extended her hand. Carmen surrendered the light shawl and her hat, gloves, and shoes. The stranger disappeared into the garden—a decoy, cleverly planted to mislead her pursuers should they come.

Heart pounding, Carmen climbed into the car. The door closed behind her, and the vehicle rolled away, leaving the palace, and her former life, behind.

In the dim interior of the car, Carmen found a neatly folded winter coat, gloves, a pair of sturdy shoes, and a traditional kokoshnik hat. She pulled on the heavy shoes and slipped on the gloves, feeling the comfort of the fine leather. Wrapping the coat tightly around herself, she placed the kokoshnik atop her head.

The car glided onto the boulevard, tires whispering over the damp pavement. Soon, they turned onto a side road heading inland, putting distance between them and the bustling port. An hour passed in silence as they drove through winding, darkened lanes flanked by towering warehouses.

When the car stopped, a man dressed as a longshoreman opened the passenger door. Carmen stepped out, her gaze lifting to meet eyes partially obscured beneath a dark hat. Without a word, he gestured for her to follow. As she did, she caught faint scents of the sea and kerosene lingering in the chilled night air. When the car pulled away, she felt the weight of the unknown settle heavily on her shoulders.

A distant clock chimed, each toll of the bell breaking through the cold silence, a slow heartbeat in the night. She stood waiting beside her silent guide, the stillness between them thick with unspoken tension. Then, from the depths of the fog, a low rumbling sound emerged. She turned, her breath hitching as a weathered truck crept into view, its dim headlights barely piercing the dense mist, casting eerie, shifting shadows across the cobblestone. The truck rolled to a stop, and the engine shuddered into silence, leaving only the ghostly haze and her rising sense of fate.

Three men descended and opened the rear doors, revealing rows of barrels labeled "vodka." With brisk efficiency, they cleared a path among the casks, guiding her to a hidden compartment at the truck's rear. Carmen took a seat in a sturdy chair within the confines of stacked barrels, each side forming a wall of shadow and wood. Once the doors were closed, she was encased in a silent mobile fortress.

The truck groaned forward. Carmen, feeling the confinement of her situation, took a deep breath, holding her hands tightly in her lap. "What a choice I've made," she murmured. "Here I am, a fugitive in the company of barrels." She lifted her head and whispered, "For Maxim, for my sons, I will survive this."

The truck bumped along. She reached for her cigarette case nestled in her dress pocket. Savoring the sense of defiance in that small gesture. She muttered to herself, "One must keep some comforts, after all."

Time passed slowly as the truck continued its journey, eventually reaching a dimly lit pier. The driver exchanged brief words and cash with a guard, then proceeded to the far end of the dock. Fog thickened, veiling them in an eerie silence broken only by the faint sound of faraway foghorns. A large freighter loomed at the edge of the pier, its outline barely visible in the murk.

Once again, after the barrels had been unloaded, and the empress released from her rolling fortress, the men assisted her off the truck ushering her toward the ship's gangway. Without hesitation she crossed and stepped aboard, her black-clad figure vanishing into the vessel's shadowed recesses. A steady rumble from the engines reverberated through the hull, punctuated by distant shouts and clanking chains as the ship prepared to depart.

On the quarterdeck, a man waited in near darkness, his face hidden as he gestured for her to follow. Carmen felt an inexplicable comfort as they ascended ladders and wound through narrow passages, each step heightening her sense of safety and resolve.

At last, they stopped before a stateroom. Her mysterious guide unlocked the door and gestured for her to step inside. A dim light glowed from a corner of the room, casting long shadows across the space. She entered, feeling his presence linger behind her as he shut the door. A flicker of fear crossed her mind.

Slowly, she turned.

He switched on a bright light. Carmen's breath caught as the room filled with warm light, and she saw his face.

"Braxton!" she gasped, tears welling in her eyes.

"Of course, sister," Braxton murmured, his own eyes glistening.

She rushed forward, throwing her arms around him. His embrace tightened, but as he pulled back slightly, his hand brushed the hard bodice beneath her gown. Braxton's brows furrowed with sudden curiosity, his eyes narrowing.

"Carmen," he began with a small, incredulous smile, "what are you wearing?"

She laughed, wiping a tear from her cheek. "Jewels, of course," she said, almost breathlessly. "Did you think I'd leave Russia empty-handed? They're sewn into my corset, my skirts, everywhere!"

Braxton chuckled, relief and admiration mingling in his eyes. "I should have known," he murmured, holding her close once more.

Braxton sighed, a hint of relief breaking through his serious expression. "Maxim provided for you, remember?"

"One can never be too careful, dear brother."

CHAPTER NINETEEN

DIASPORA & DEATH

Prince Braxton watched the prime minister depart, then leaned back in a leather wingback chair by the marble fireplace. The fire's faint glow danced across the walls, casting flickering shadows as he stared up at the intricately carved ceiling. His recent conversations weighed heavily on his mind. *Sending them to war,* he thought. *I am their father, yet I am the one who must send them off. They embrace their duties as members of the royal family, but do they truly grasp what lies ahead? What will this war make of them? How will they return to us—if they return at all? My God. What will be left of them?*

A gentle touch roused him from his thoughts. He looked up to find Valentina's sparkling green eyes, her presence and soft smile filling him with a measure of comfort.

"Darling," she whispered, "are you unwell? Perhaps you're simply weary."

A subtle smile tugged at the corners of Braxton's lips, a fleeting expression that hinted at unspoken thoughts. "Maybe so, my love. I was thinking of the war…and how it might shape our family."

Valentina took his hand and eased herself onto the arm of his chair. "I understand," she murmured, her voice gentle and low. "All parents across the empire bear this same weight."

He nodded. "If that's true, then perhaps…perhaps the crown has an opportunity here." He sat up, his voice gaining strength. "An opportunity to show compassion, to reach out to the people."

"What are you suggesting?" Valentina asked, intrigued.

"What if the king expressed his gratitude to the families of the empire for their sacrifices—for sending their sons to war?"

Valentina's face softened. "That's a splendid idea. Perhaps you should draft a statement for the prime minister to review and then present it to Dominic."

He rose and kissed her forehead. "You would have made a fine empress in Russia. Perhaps, one day, England will have that same blessing."

She blushed and gently tugged his hand. "Speaking of our empire, I received a letter from Angelina."

"She's in Hong Kong, isn't she?" Braxton asked, tilting his head slightly.

"Not anymore," Valentina replied, a knowing glint in her eyes. "She's returned to the rubber plantations in Singapore."

Braxton raised his brows. "I hadn't heard. She didn't share those plans with me. Tell me, Valentina—are you part of all this?"

Valentina's lips curved into a faint smile. "There's competition for our rubber supply—Australia and Japan, she writes. I thought it prudent to stay informed."

Braxton exhaled, feeling a small weight lift from his shoulders. "Well done, Valentina. Your insights are invaluable, as always. With

John often occupied at the front, having your keen mind focused on these matters is a blessing. You always seem to have a handle on things, even when my attention is pulled in other directions. I don't take that for granted. Thank you."

Her expression softened, her eyes meeting his. "You've had enough to carry, Braxton. It's only right that I shoulder some of it."

She smiled. Her voice warm yet confident, she said, "Our years managing the Russian Consortium have served us well. Sharing my knowledge with Angelina has been a personal joy—and it keeps us close."

Braxton squeezed her hand. "You've done brilliantly, both of you. And Everett too, of course."

Valentina kissed him on the cheek. "Of course, my dear. Whatever else could you expect from us?"

Three months later Brigadier General Prince John wrote Braxton from the Belgian front.

My dearest brother,

I have now spent a full week on the front lines and the reality is worlds apart from my expectations. Soldiering, it seems, is a far cry from Sandhurst's drills and the splendid London parades.

British forces are exemplary in their discipline and training, yet we are significantly outnumbered. The weight of potential loss gnaws at me, knowing lives hang in the balance. We are entrenched, and any hopes of advancing seem bleak.

Braxton's brow furrowed as he read, the ink on the page growing fainter.

I am fortunate to have Lieutenant Robert Cranshaw as my adjutant, a fellow cadet from Sandhurst, robust in spirit and intellect. His company is a comfort in this grim place.

Braxton felt his heart sink. Oh, John, he muttered, alone in the study, please be careful. He continued reading.

This dual role of co-regent and army officer is a challenge, and it troubles me here at the front. My position puts the senior officers in a bind. To ease their burden, I intend to resign as co-regent.

Braxton sighed, setting the letter aside.

In the months that followed, Prince John's courage in battle became the subject of countless dispatches. His unwavering dedication to his brigade, a force of over 3,000 men, resonated throughout England. Reports from the front, published in local papers, celebrated his efforts to lift morale and his bravery in venturing beyond the trenches to recover wounded soldiers. Yet some official reports voiced concerns that his disregard for personal safety threatened compromising the brigade's command structure. And perhaps other units as well.

Prince Braxton, headquarters generals and the prime minister convened around a large table at the War Office in Whitehall.

"I understand, Prime Minister," Prince Braxton said, "that as a commander, I would take issue with Prince John exposing himself to such danger."

"While we agree, Sir," General Whitcomb responded, "his actions have boosted morale to unprecedented levels."

The prime minister shook his head. "How high will morale be if he is injured—or worse, killed?"

"Or taken prisoner?" Whitcomb added.

A heavy silence fell over the room.

That night, Prince John emerged from the fortified bunker near the front line. Wrapping a woolen scarf around his neck, he fastened the top button of his field jacket, holstered his revolver, and made his way to the forward trench line.

Intermittent flares lit the narrow no-man's-land. Icy mud crunched under his boots as he moved, quietly encouraging those on duty. A mortar shell exploded nearby, scattering dirt and debris. John threw himself into a small shelter, finding himself enveloped in darkness.

"Got through that one," muttered a soldier beside him.

"Here's hoping we make it through the next," another murmured.

John sat up against the damp wall; his uniform covered in mud.

"Got a tab?" asked a man.

"Wish I did," replied another.

John pulled out his cigarette case. "Gentlemen, care for a fag?"

"Who's that?" someone whispered.

"Careful," muttered another. "Sounds posh."

"Do you want one or not?" John asked, amused.

"Yes, sir, please!" someone said.

A match flared, briefly illuminating the prince's dirt-covered face as he extended the gold case.

"Blimey!" one soldier whispered, helping himself.

"Here, take a few more. Be sure to share them," John chuckled, and lit his own cigarette.

Three mortars exploded nearby. The men dusted themselves off, grateful for the reprieve of tobacco and another near miss. "Thanks, sir," one murmured, his voice filled with genuine gratitude.

"Well, gentlemen, carry on. Keep your heads down." John stubbed out his cigarette and crawled out, pausing just outside the shelter, his back to the entrance, out of sight, but within earshot.

"That was the prince," a soldier whispered.

John grinned,

"He's a brave one, that," another said.

But another voice muttered, "I heard he's a puff, him and his adjutant."

John froze, his heart plummeting. Icy night air cut through his heavy coat, creeping into his very core. The chill he felt was more than winter's bite—it was a hollow, numbing dread.

"Robert, you understand, don't you? If our relationship were ever exposed, everything would be lost. You'd be stripped of your rank, likely imprisoned. I'd have to renounce my claim, banished from my family, from society—perhaps even from England."

Robert pressed his face onto John's shoulder, his voice trembling. "Are you leaving me?"

Prince John turned, wrapping his arms around his lover, his own voice barely steady. "No, Robert. I'm not leaving you. Nor will I abandon you. I'm saving your career…perhaps your life."

Details of Prince John's final mission were sketchy, for journalists were rarely permitted near the front. At the war's outset, Britain's

Secretary of State for War kept journalists far from the action, allowing only limited, supervised visits as the conflict continued.

Prince John had developed a friendship with a journalist for The Times, a man of little fortune but keen insight. They shared many personal thoughts and ambitions, yet each had kept certain secrets—private matters though presumed—neither dared to reveal.

Just days before the assault, John summoned his friend. They dined together in the officer's mess, sharing cigars and cognac late into the night. John spoke freely, encouraging his friend to take notes—a candid, almost memoir-like account. The journalist, surprised by this openness from a royal, documented John's reflections on duty, honor and the complexities of war.

The next morning, as battle loomed, Prince John convened his command for final preparations. He went over every detail with the battalion commanders, ensuring all understood their orders.

"Gentlemen, may fortune favor you," he said and dismissed his officiers.

Two men stayed behind—the Brigade Major and Lieutenant Robert Cranshaw.

John addressed the Brigade Major with calm authority, "are we prepared?"

The Brigade Major snapped to attention. "Yes, General. As ready as we'll ever be, sir."

"Good," John replied with a measured nod. "I'm entrusting you with the execution of the plan. I'll take my usual walk through the trenches to bolster morale and assess the situation firsthand."

The colonel hesitated, concern flickering in his eyes. "Sir, the attack is nearly upon us."

John's expression softened, but his tone remained resolute. "I'm aware, Colonel. I'll be cautious."

"Your uniform will make you a target!" the colonel protested.

John motioned toward a plain overcoat draped over a chair. "I'll wear that. It should suffice."

Though still visibly uneasy, the colonel saluted. "Yes, Sir."

Executing a crisp about face, the colonel exited the command tent.

Robert removed the coat from the chair and held it open. "John, this is madness. You're needed here—not out there in the line of fire."

John gently placed a hand on Robert's cheek. "I must be where my men are. They deserve that."

Robert's face grew pale. "Then let me go with you."

"No," John said firmly. "You'll remain here. If anything happens to me, you will carry on. You have your life ahead of you."

Robert swallowed; his voice a faint protest. "You know I'd rather face it beside you. I can't bear—"

"Robert," John whispered, leaning in until their foreheads nearly touched, "you must do this for me. If anything happens, I need to know you're safe, here…where I can keep my promise, even if from afar."

Robert's jaw tightened as he fought back tears, his voice trembling with emotion. "At least let me watch for you, wait for you. I'll be here, waiting, until you come back."

John took his hand, guiding it to his chest, pressing it firmly over his heart. "Then keep faith for me, Robert. I'll return to you if I can."

With trembling fingers, Robert steadied the coat as John slipped it on, smoothing the collar with a touch that lingered, unwilling to let go.

John turned to him, his gaze locking onto the fragile smile Robert wore, thin and forced.

"Then I'll do as you ask," Robert breathed. "But know this—I'll wait for you; forever if I must."

John's smile was bittersweet as he gently kissed Robert's forehead. "I know you would. I will return if it's within my power. But if I cannot? Remember, you are stronger than you know."

With one last look, Robert reluctantly stepped back, watching as John turned and strode out of the command tent and toward the waiting trenches. Only when he disappeared from sight did Robert turn away, his hand pressed tightly against his heart.

The mist hung thick over the scarred land as dawn broke, casting a muted glow. Prince John moved through the trenches, stopping to offer words of encouragement. The distant, rhythmic artillery's thunder reverberated, a brutal prelude to the attack.

British artillery opened with ferocity, raining shells upon the German defenses. Explosions shook the earth, churning mud and smoke into the air as the Germans retaliated with relentless mortar fire. Undeterred, John continued his rounds, guiding medics to the wounded, offering a hand where he could.

At the trench's edge, he picked up a Lee-Enfield rifle from a fallen soldier and, strapping ammunition pouches across his shoulders, took aim into no-man's land. He fired steadily, his shots precise, the practiced marksmanship of a seasoned big game hunter. Amidst the chaos, he pressed forward with his men, crawling, running, fighting.

The prince's courage blazed, a beacon rallying the men around him as they watched in awe. He plunged into the muddy chaos, hauling the wounded to safety. Dirt caked his hands as he dragged men across the battlefield, heedless of the shells whistling through the air and bursting mere yards from him. He flinched as fragments sliced past, tearing at his uniform and embedding in his coat sleeves.

The Germans took note of his heroics and relentless drive and adjusted their aim to rain fire on him. Explosions cracked around him, throwing soldiers off their feet, flinging limbs askew, and blasting deep craters into the earth. Prince John dropped low, the force of the detonations pounding through his chest. He scrambled forward, elbows and knees sinking into the mud as he reached another fallen soldier, heaving him up, ignoring the screams of agony as he hauled the man toward cover.

Returning to the lines, he rounded a makeshift barricade. A German soldier charged from the smoke, bayonet fixed, his boots sliding through the slick mud. John used his own bayonet to deflect the thrust aimed at his chest. They grappled, feet slipping, hands clawing for a grip in the sludge. The German's knife sliced John's thigh, a hot sting of pain cutting through the cold mud soaking his trousers. Gritting his teeth, John tightened his grip on his rifle, angled it like a spear, and drove the bayonet into the enemy's side. The German gasped, eyes wide, blood spreading across his uniform as he crumpled forward against John before collapsing, lifeless, into the churned mud.

Another explosion erupted, flinging dirt and debris against John's neck and jaw, coating him in a gritty layer of earth and smoke. Gasping for air, he pressed forward, sidestepping severed limbs and scattered equipment. He charged back into the thick of battle, his lungs burning as he braved the relentless chaos.

Enemy shells pounded the field, sending up geysers of mud. The prince pushed on, his grip tightening on his rifle, firing steady shots as he advanced. Each step sank him deeper into the mire, his body aching under the strain. He paused only to aid the wounded, to lift a comrade from the mud, slinging an arm over his shoulder, steadying him, blood from his own wounds mingling with the grime that caked their skin.

The Germans honed in on his position. A barrage of artillery fire tore apart the ground around him. He dove to the side, his arm scraping against splintered wood, blood soon streaking down his sleeve. Still he rallied, urging his men onward with a fierce cry that cut through the cacophony. Those who witnessed him fought with renewed ferocity, galvanized by his fearlessness.

John fought through the swirling smoke, his vision blurred by the haze and the sting of sweat mingling with blood. As he pressed forward, he dragged yet another fallen man to safety.

As dawn bled into morning, the enemy's marksmen zeroed in on John's position. It was just past ten o'clock when the final barrage found its mark.

German rifles trained directly on him. He locked eyes with his men, unwavering, until a barrage of bullets tore through him, throwing him to the ground. His body lay still, his final act one of courage and defiance, his legacy etched in the hearts of those he led.

The battlefield, drenched in mud and blood, lay silent for a moment as men on both sides bore witness to his sacrifice, a royal prince transformed into a soldier in the heart of war's grim reality.

That night, under cover of darkness, Robert Cranshaw ventured into no-man's land and brought back the fallen prince.

The world awoke to the headlines:

HEIR TO BRITISH THRONE
SUFFERS HEROIC DEATH AT FRONT

HRH BRIGADIER GENERAL, PRINCE JOHN, KILLED

The man once destined to lead the British Empire had fallen in battle, his bravery forever sealed in the annals of war and sacrifice.

CHAPTER TWENTY

REDEMPTION

Upon Braxton's return to the Aurelio Palace, a diplomatic pouch awaited him. He and Valentina, just back from Prince John's funeral at Windsor Castle, removed their coats, the weariness of the past days evident in their movements.

"I'll leave you to your work, my dear," Valentina said softly. "But don't be too long. It's late, and these past days have been trying. You need your rest." She patted his forearm.

He took her hand, kissed her forehead, and replied, "I agree. These last days have been arduous. I'll join you once I've tended to these matters."

They shared a parting smile before she retired to her suite and he turned toward the ducal study.

Braxton stirred the fire to life and drew a key from his waistcoat. The lock on the leather satchel clicked open, and as he lifted the flap, he drew out a thick, cream-colored envelope. His breath caught—it bore John's seal.

Stunned, Braxton dropped into his leather desk chair, broke the seal, and pulled out the pages. Adjusting his glasses, he read:

My Dearest Braxton,

You're likely to read this soon after my passing. I'm deeply sorry for the burden I leave with you, the weight that will now alter the course of your life: regent now, and quite possibly the next king. In time, I hope you might find it in your heart to forgive me. I must share a painful truth. My relationship with Robert is no longer a secret—it has spread among the men. The notion of a future king with such— inclinations would shake our family, the government, and the monarchy itself to the core. In a time of war, it would be a ruinous scandal. So, I see no recourse.

You are owed an explanation, Braxton. I trust you to ensure my life has not been in vain. Destroy this letter when you've finished reading it.

Braxton's grip tightened as he read on, absorbing John's words with growing grief and anger.

Dominic's anguish and subsequent incapacity, following his acknowledgment of Adolphus's situation and the loss of Rose, have left both him and the monarchy vulnerable. Our role as regents has only underscored Dominic's frailty. I could not, in good conscience, allow myself to inherit the throne under these circumstances, knowing my secret would inevitably come to light.

You, dear brother, must be the one to bear the crown and uphold our family's honor. You always stood apart from Dominic and me, possessing a strength and dependability we could never match. Your ability to live freely, to love both women and men, protected you from suspicion. My own marriage has suffered for this. I've trudged forward each day, haunted by the knowledge that my nature, if exposed, would see me condemned as unfit, sinful, monstrous.

I know your own secrets, dear brother—Aramis, Joe, others. You've been wiser, more cautious than I. You found love without sacrificing your freedom. I, though, have walked a different path, one shadowed by fear.

My life has been a constant balancing act, living for duty but yearning for love. The shadows of judgment and rejection have haunted me for so long. But you've shown me a better way, Braxton. Your compassion and loyalty were a beacon for me, a rare source of strength. And I have one last request, my dear brother—make this empire a better place. Improve the lives of those like us who live in fear of condemnation. Use your influence to create a world where no one must suffer as I have.

I trust you to honor this request, for I know that, above all, you embody kindness.

Your Loving Brother,
John.

The night passed in sleepless anguish as Braxton read and reread John's letter. By dawn, he had wandered outside to the ornamental lake, where he collapsed onto the grass, his head cradled in his hands, muffling his sobs. The cold mist clung to the lawns, the trees stood in solemn witness, and the early light spread thin and pale across the silent grounds.

How could this be? he thought, his mind a torrent of pain and disbelief. Johnny was meant to be king. He was kindness, gentleness, love itself. And now he lies dead, taken by war, surrounded by blood, mud, and death. What kind of God allows this?

Braxton's anguish swelled, and he raised his voice to the sky, trembling. "Why, God? Why did you not protect him? Were his sins so grave that you forsook him? He would have been a great king!"

He collapsed backward, gazing up at the heavens as dawn's first light broke through the drifting clouds. "Do not try to comfort me with a glimpse of the sky's beauty," he whispered in anger.

"Always the poet, my love," came a familiar voice. Valentina stood nearby, spreading a blanket on the grass beside him. He watched as she lay down and patted the space beside her. "Come, you'll catch your death lying on the cold ground."

Braxton shifted onto the blanket, resting his head in her lap. They looked at each other in silence, her fingers brushing through his graying hair, calming his turbulent thoughts.

An hour passed, and as the morning brightened, Braxton stirred. Gazing into her kind, warm eyes, he whispered, "Hello, my dearest."

"Hello, my love," she replied softly.

He adjusted his position to take in her face fully. "I don't believe I've been this close to you since India."

She chuckled, "You may be right."

"I needed you so desperately then," he murmured, "just as I do now."

She nodded, leaning down to kiss him. "And just as I was then, I am here for you now."

Pulling back, he sighed, "I don't deserve you."

She quipped, "Perhaps not. But neither do I deserve you. We are, as they say, undeservedly blessed."

Braxton smiled, then lay back, his head cushioned on her lap. "Johnny's death—his actions—it wasn't accidental. It was deliberate."

"Of course it was," she replied, unruffled.

He frowned. "What do you mean?"

"His letter, Braxton. It's clear he knew he couldn't keep his secret in the trenches. Secrets don't last on the battlefield."

"You read the letter?" His eyes widened.

"Yes, I found it on your desk. Better me than a maid tending the fires."

"My God! Where is it now?"

"On my person, safely tucked away," she assured him, stroking his hair. "Now, calm yourself."

"You read all of it?" His head careening with what had been revealed."

"Yes."

"So, you know."

"Yes, Braxton. I have known since reading your letters when I was in the monastery."

"But you stayed with me." His eyes growing moist.

She swallowed.

"Why?" He asked.

"Braxton, must we always indulge your thoughts and questions, your emotions? Let it be. Let me have—" She looked up at the sky. "Let it be."

The sun rose and the gentle chorus of morning unfolded: birds trilled from the trees, their songs blending with the soft hum of activity from the estate's outbuildings. The scent of newly kindled fires drifted through the air, filling the palace parkland with warmth and promise, each sound and fragrance a quiet celebration of dawn.

His voice lowered. "Johnny's choice, to sin so gravely—"

"Which sin?" Valentina interrupted, her tone unyielding.

He closed his eyes. "Both, taking his own life and forbidden love."

"And he ensured that legacy was hidden," she replied. "Your brother staged his death to secure the family's reputation. John's courage saved his honor, in a way."

"You don't mince words, do you?"

"Would you have it otherwise?" she asked, smiling.

"No, not entirely."

He sighed. "I rather enjoy resting on your lap."

"And I, sir, enjoy keeping you precisely where I want you."

After a brief silence, her tone grew serious. "With John gone, our lives are no longer ours."

"They never were," he countered.

"But now they are even less our own. More than ever, you are bound to the throne." She hesitated. "The family's enterprises, Braxton. What are your plans? Dominic's failing health makes it clear he won't live out the decade. With you now the heir, should we consider divesting?"

Braxton lifted his head, gazing at her. "Divest? No. Not until the war ends. To sell now would be impossible; no one could pay what it's worth. We'll wait, and even then, I won't divest. I have other plans."

Valentina looked thoughtful. "Plans?"

"I intend to form a series of trusts, each masking our ownership while retaining control."

"Braxton, you're aware that a monarch's involvement in commerce is forbidden," she cautioned, resting a hand on his. "Once you're king, you'll are not permitted to engage in commerce.

"I'll manage," he replied. "The trusts will shield our involvement. The crown's stability need not hinge on our holdings."

He intertwined his fingers with hers.

"It's not just about the assets, Braxton. It's about ensuring your neutrality."

He sat up, wrapping an arm around her shoulders. "You're right, but these plans will outlast us both. I must move forward."

"When will you share them with me?" she asked, smiling. "I recall that much of this dates back to our days in Siberia."

Grinning, he cupped her face, his excitement shining through. "I can't wait to share it all with you, my love," he said, drawing her close for a lingering kiss.

When they finally parted, Valentina smoothed her skirts and suggested with a playful smile, "Perhaps we should continue this conversation in my room."

CHAPTER TWENTY-ONE

AN UNDERSTANDING

Valentina opened a letter from Princess Elizabeth. She read aloud.

"This morning marked the first time I truly observed the enchanting sunlight in Paris."

She glanced up from the elegant stationary.

Braxton, behind his newspaper, smiled. "Ah, sunlight in Paris. After the war, we really should plan a visit. It's been ages since we were at our home there—it was well before the war began."

Valentina lowered the letter. With a raised brow, she said, "Yes, dear, I remember quite well. I joined you there after you and George completed your gallivanting global journey." She took a sip of tea, savoring her sarcasm. "Shall I go on?"

Without waiting, she resumed reading.

Over breakfast, I mentioned to Elena how the sunlight seems warmer, as if it wraps around you. Although the sun sits lower in the sky, it feels different. Maybe it's the city itself that's changed—a touch more hopeful, less burdened. I feel at ease, more able to appreciate my surroundings.

Braxton sighed. "September in Paris…how wonderful for her. Since the Americans joined the war—"

Valentina raised her hand. "Do you mind, dear? I'd rather hear what she has to say."

"My apologies," he said, gesturing for her to continue.

Valentina shook her head, amused, then continued reading.

1918, and who would have thought, four years ago, that we'd still be fighting this ghastly war? It has been dreadful, losing Uncle John and so many others. But I digress; there's news to share.

Valentina looked up, a twinkle in her eye. "Shall I continue?"

Braxton's eyes widened and nodded.

Valentina read on.

As you know, Elena and I spent most of the past four years nursing on various fronts. Now, finally, we've managed to carve out some well-deserved time for ourselves. Our position within the family has added certain distractions; and in Paris, we're quite the attraction. Since Papa was created Prince of Wales, it appears Elena and I have acquired a certain cachet.

"Oh my," Braxton chuckled. "Our girls, making the most of it."

"Yes, it would appear so," Valentina agreed and continued.

During the war, we concentrated on doing our duty, deeming it unseemly to draw attention. But now…well, both Elena and I have met someone special. Not the same person, mind you—two separate individuals. I feel nervous even writing this.

Valentina looked up, blushing. Braxton winked, encouraging her to continue.

Elena has met a French diplomat, recently back from years in the Near East. I'll leave it to her to tell you more. And as for me, I met an American officer. We actually met years ago, though I found him rather dull at the time. It seems the years have transformed him. His family once stayed with us at Aurelio, when his father was president—Paul Richards. Do you remember Paul?

Valentina lowered the letter, stunned. Braxton's blue eyes sparkled, his mouth dropping slightly.

Wordlessly, he rose, fetched a decanter of scotch and two glasses, and returned. Pouring each of them a generous drink, he handed Valentina hers before downing his own in one gulp.

She followed suit, then held her glass out for a refill.

He obliged, raking his fingers through his hair as he fought back old memories.

Valentina cleared her throat and resumed reading.

He's kind, ambitious, and speaks warmly of our family. It seems his father filled his head with stories of Papa's travels across America before any of us were born. I look forward to hearing more, Papa, especially about your friendship with Paul's father.

Valentina grinned. "This should be interesting. I'd suggest you leave out certain details when regaling her with your friendship."

Braxton snorted, took a deep breath and said, "Would you mind reading on?"

Valentina chuckled. "Ah, wartime romances. It will be fascinating to see what comes of it." She paused, studying him, but he was lost in thought, his gaze drifting out the window.

She returned to the letter.

Vanya and Arthur recently visited, having taken leave from their military units. They've grown so much, both physically and in demeanor. I hardly recognize the mischievous boys they once were. Mothers with eligible daughters are eager for introductions, and finally, my having brothers has its benefits.

Braxton huffed. "Too bad there's been no news from Frederick."

Valentina looked up. "But you were pleased with his handling of affairs in the Americas, weren't you?"

"I was, but his conduct in society has been another matter entirely," Braxton coughed, "I had hoped that focusing on business might keep him grounded, but it seems he inherited my, shall we say, talents for pursuits beyond just business." He softened slightly. "It appears he might have a bit too much of me in him."

Valentina arched a knowing eyebrow. "Does that really surprise you?" She glanced at the letter, a hint of a smile tugging at her lips.

"Frederick might be holding up a mirror you're not entirely ready to face, dear."

"Valentina?"

"Yes, love?"

"You seem to take satisfaction in dredging up chapters of my past I'd rather forget."

She smiled sweetly as she reached for the tea service. "More tea?"

Braxton gazed at her in silence as she poured. "Yes, I suppose I do." He sighed, crossing his arms. "I thought we'd put all that behind us."

"I don't recall any such agreement," she replied, cocking her head and placing the tip of one index finger aside her chin.

Braxton pressed his lips together. "I thought we'd moved on. I thought we were, well—"

"Perhaps it's seeing you reflected in Frederick," she replied. "Remember, he is your son. The apple does not fall far from the tree, and I urge you to look for the good in him, as you would wish others to do with you."

Braxton rubbed the back of his neck, pondering her words. "You've never been so direct."

"I should have been, years ago. It would have been kinder if I'd been more forthright, instead of leaving you in Vienna."

Braxton's face flushed, pain flickering in his eyes as he looked down, absorbing the weight of her words. Valentina searched for his gaze, her hands resting calmly in her lap.

He looked up after a moment, his tone softened. "Is there anything more?"

"Yes." Her voice was gentle but resolute. "It would serve you well to take to heart what I've shared. I want the best for you, Braxton, and others may not be so understanding."

She paused, then continued, "If you are to ascend the throne, those past escapades, that sowing of wild oats, must end. Otherwise, you may not appreciate the harvest they bring."

"This morning marked the first time I truly observed the enchanting sunlight in Paris." She glanced up from the elegant stationery.

Braxton, behind his newspaper, smiled. "Ah, sunlight in Paris. After the war, we really should plan a visit. It's been ages since we were at our home there—well before the war began."

Valentina lowered the letter with a raised brow. "Yes, dear, I remember quite well. I joined you there after you and George completed your gallivanting global journey." She took a sip of tea, savoring her sarcasm. "Shall I go on?"

Without waiting, she resumed reading. "Over breakfast, I mentioned to Elena how the sunlight seems warmer, as if it wraps around you. Although the sun sits lower in the sky, it feels different. Maybe it's the city itself that's changed—a touch more hopeful, less burdened. I feel at ease, more able to appreciate my surroundings."

Braxton sighed. "September in Paris...how wonderful for her. Since the Americans joined the war—"

Valentina raised her hand. "Do you mind, dear? I'd rather hear what she has to say."

"My apologies," he said, gesturing for her to continue.

Valentina shook her head, amused, then continued reading. "1918, and who would have thought, four years ago, that we'd still be fighting this ghastly war? It has been dreadful, losing Uncle John and so many others. But I digress; there's news to share." Valentina looked up, a twinkle in her eye. "Shall I continue?"

Braxton's eyes widened and nodded.

Valentina read on. "As you know, Elena and I spent most of the past four years nursing on various fronts. Now, finally, we've managed to carve out some well-deserved time for ourselves. Our position within the family has added certain distractions; and in Paris, we're quite the attraction. Since Papa was created Prince of Wales, it appears Elena and I have acquired a certain cachet."

"Oh my," Braxton chuckled. "Our girls, making the most of it."

"Yes, it would appear so," Valentina agreed. "During the war, we concentrated on doing our duty, deeming it unseemly to draw attention. But now…well, both Elena and I have met someone special. Not the same person, mind you—two separate individuals. I feel nervous even writing this."

Valentina looked up, blushing. Braxton winked, encouraging her to continue.

"Elena has met a French diplomat, recently back from years in the Near East. I'll leave it to her to tell you more. And as for me, I met an American officer. We actually met years ago, though I found him rather dull at the time. It seems the years have transformed him. His family once stayed with us at Aurelio, when his father was president—Paul Richards. Do you remember Paul?"

Valentina lowered the letter, stunned. Braxton's blue eyes sparkled, his mouth dropping slightly.

Wordlessly, he rose, fetched a decanter of scotch and two glasses, and returned. Pouring each of them a generous drink, he handed Valentina hers before downing his own in one gulp. She followed suit, then held her glass out for a refill. He obliged, raking his fingers through his hair as he fought back old memories.

Valentina cleared her throat and resumed reading. "He's kind, ambitious, and speaks warmly of our family. It seems his father filled his head with stories of Papa's travels across America before any of us were born. I look forward to hearing more, Papa, especially about your friendship with Paul's father."

Valentina smirked. "This should be interesting. I'd suggest you leave out certain details when regaling her with your friendship."

Braxton snorted, took a deep breath and said, "Would you mind reading on?"

Valentina chuckled. "Ah, wartime romances. It will be fascinating to see what comes of it." She paused, studying him, but he was lost in thought, his gaze drifting out the window.

She returned to the letter. "Vanya and Arthur recently visited, having taken leave from their military units. They've grown so much, both physically and in demeanor. I hardly recognize the mischievous boys they once were. Mothers with eligible daughters are eager for introductions, and finally, my having brothers has its benefits."

Braxton huffed. "Too bad there's been no news from Frederick."

Valentina looked up. "But you were pleased with his handling of affairs in the Americas, weren't you?"

"I was, but his conduct in society has been another matter entirely," Braxton coughed, "I had hoped that focusing on business might keep him grounded, but it seems he inherited my, shall we say, talents for pursuits beyond just business." He softened slightly. "It appears he might have a bit too much of me in him."

Valentina arched a knowing eyebrow. "Does that really surprise you?" She glanced at the letter, a hint of a smile tugging at her lips. "Frederick might be holding up a mirror you're not entirely ready to face, dear."

"Valentina?"

"Yes, love?"

"You seem to take satisfaction in dredging up chapters of my past I'd rather forget."

She smiled sweetly as she reached for the tea service. "More tea?"

Braxton gazed at her in silence as she poured. "Yes, I suppose I do." He sighed, crossing his arms. "I thought we'd put all that behind us."

"I don't recall any such agreement," she replied, cocking her head and placing the tip of one index finger aside her chin.

Braxton pressed his lips together. "I thought we'd moved on. I thought we were, well—"

"Perhaps it's seeing you reflected in Frederick," she replied. "Remember, he is your son. The apple does not fall far from the tree, and I urge you to look for the good in him, as you would wish others to do with you."

Braxton rubbed the back of his neck, pondering her words. "You've never been so direct."

"I should have been, years ago. It would have been kinder if I'd been more forthright, instead of leaving you in Vienna."

Braxton's face flushed, pain flickering in his eyes as he looked down, absorbing the weight of her words. Valentina searched for his gaze, her hands resting calmly in her lap.

He looked up after a moment, his tone softened. "Is there anything more?"

"Yes." Her voice was gentle but resolute. "It would serve you well to take to heart what I've shared. I want the best for you, Braxton, and others may not be so understanding."

Christmas 1918, following the end of the war, marked the first time in four years Valentina and Braxton had gathered their entire family together.

Valentina, overwhelmed with joy at their reunion, refused to let anything dampen her spirits. For their children, young adults eager to leave the war behind, life had changed irrevocably, and the world they'd left behind no longer existed in the same way.

Braxton and the princes, George, Arthur, Vanya, and Frederick, were dressed in white-tie attire. Valentina, and the princesses, Elizabeth and Elena, wore Paul Poriet gowns and adorned themselves with jewels. Valentina's tiara, a gift from her brother, the czar, years ago, reflected Russian imperial elegance, with exquisite diamonds, rubies, and emeralds evoking a sense of festive wonder and tradition.

Earlier that evening, Valentina had dismissed her dresser and now stood alone in front of her mirror, a knot forming in her stomach. She wondered if her gown, her jewels, and even her way of life had become relics, echoes of a past at odds with the world as it now was. But the thought melted away as her daughters, Elena and Elizabeth, entered the room.

Valentina's gaze softened, taking in the sight of the young women, radiant in their gowns, now returned from war and unmarred by its specter. A profound warmth filled her, a sense that, despite everything, all was as it should be. Her daughters were safe, poised, and with bright futures ahead of them.

"Shall we go down, my dears?" she said, the pride clear in her voice. "I believe your father and brothers are waiting for us."

"Mama," Princess Elena began as they gathered in the Aurelio Palace's festively decorated salon. She absentmindedly tugged at the gown's beaded embellishments. "Have you thought about Elizabeth's and my request to invite—"

"Invite who, Sis?" Frederick interrupted with a grin. "Does Ellie have a new beau?"

Vanya leaned in with mock surprise.

"Do not call me Sis!" Elena shot back. "Or I shall call you Fredo!"

Frederick, sporting a mischievous grin, strolled to the decanter, and poured himself a generous refill. He raised his glass high with a dramatic flourish, his voice full of jovial pride. "To the Americas and to all the wealth I've brought back to this family while you were, well, otherwise engaged. Our coffers are far fuller than they were before the war, and I'll humbly accept that I, for the most part, am to thank!"

Braxton, listening while watching his son, responded dryly, "Yes, Frederick. We do indeed have you to thank. Thank you."

Frederick, caught mid-sip, nearly choked on his drink, sputtering in surprise before recovering with a delighted laugh. "You're welcome, Papa!"

Laughter erupted around the room.

"Be kind to your sister," George interjected, "or Papa may just send you back to the Americas."

Valentina's eyes sparkled with quiet amusement.

The family stilled, each face reflecting intrigue as they watched Elena press forward, an excited glint in her eye. "What about our question, Mama?"

Valentina took her time, pausing to sip her port. The surrounding anticipation palpable, her children hanging on her every word. "Oh, that. Yes, your father and I have discussed it," she said, in an off-hand manner.

The siblings exchanged surprised, delighted glances, a murmur of anticipation sweeping through the room as they sensed their mother's approval. Elizabeth's hand flew to her mouth in barely contained excitement, while George's brow lifted in surprise, the corners of his lips curving upward. Vanya leaned back grinning and crossing his arms as he waited for the verdict.

"We think it best you invite both acquaintances at the same time—avoid unnecessary tension. But wait until spring, perhaps late April," Valentina concluded, her tone both indulgent, amused.

Elena and Elizabeth exchanged gleeful looks, both women soon bouncing with excitement.

Vanya and George shared a knowing, teasing grin, clearly entertained. Frederick, ever the showman, raised his glass in a silent playful toast to his sisters.

Each of the five siblings looked toward Vanya, who, predictably, did not disappoint.

"This woman," Vanya declared, pointing at Valentina with a grin, "cannot possibly be our mother. Make sure she doesn't leave the palace with that tiara! Mama would be heartbroken to learn an imposter had run off with one of her sparkly things!"

Rising to pull the servant's bell, Vanya announced, "I'm ordering the 1913 Veuve Clicquot before Mama and Papa return! Champagne for everyone!"

A brief silence filled the room as all eyes shifted to Braxton, who broke the tension with a smile. "An excellent idea."

The following year saw Elizabeth marry Paul Richards and move to America, while Elena wed her French diplomat, Comte Henri Montmorency, and settled with him in the Near East, where he served in foreign affairs, and she became active in her father's business interests.

CHAPTER TWENTY-TWO

FREDERICK

"Frederick," Braxton began one day on the Aurelio Palace shooting range, "now that your sisters are moving forward with their lives, what do you plan for your own life?" He raised a Boss & Co. break-action shotgun. "Pull!" Two shots cracked through the air as he obliterated the skeet.

Frederick, not one to be shown up, raised his own shotgun. "Pull!" He shattered two targets in mid-air, handed the gun to the reloader, grabbed another, and shouted, "Pull!" Two more skeet disintegrated.

Braxton nodded approvingly. "Is that your answer, son?"

Frederick, accepting another gun, shrugged. "Not exactly, Papa. But I sense you have something in mind. Otherwise, you wouldn't have called me back from Monte Carlo."

"Are you content idling away in the casinos and drifting about the Mediterranean on your yacht?"

Frederick gave a wry smile. "It's frightfully expensive financing all that 'doing nothing' sort of thing."

"My point exactly," Braxton replied. "Since your return from the Americas, you've spent two years—"

"Wasting my life away?" Frederick interjected.

Braxton handed his gun to the loader. "The crown needs someone they can trust, someone to be hands on, rule in India."

"Sounds more suited to George, Arthur, or perhaps pithy Vanya," Frederick quipped. "Pull." He fired off two shots, missed, and muttered, "Well, thank you, Papa, for spoiling the shoot."

"Son, India needs a reliable presence. Someone who embodies both the wisdom of Solomon and the discipline of Henry VII."

He lowered his gun. "I'm no Solomon, Papa."

"Why are you afraid of your own ambitions?"

Frederick paused, his hand gripping his shotgun as he looked over at his father, a glint of surprise in his eyes. "Afraid of my own ambitions?" He tilted his head and grunted as he exchanged guns with his loader.

"Papa, I spent two years putting those ambitions to good use across the Atlantic. You can't deny the coffers are fatter thanks to me."

Braxton didn't respond immediately. He simply watched, his expression steady, his patience evident.

The silence, usually a comfort between them, now pressed down on Frederick. Feeling the weight, he glanced at his father and muttered, "Monte Carlo's been a pleasant diversion…perhaps a bit too pleasant."

Braxton's gaze softened further. "I think it's become a hiding place."

Frederick stiffened, then took a deep breath, lowering his gun. "Perhaps you're right," he admitted, almost reluctantly, a hint of sincerity creeping into his voice. He glanced back toward the field, watching as a skeet soared into the sky before disintegrating into shards from his father's perfectly aimed shot.

Braxton handed the shotgun off to his loader and turned back to Frederick. "India needs a leader who can navigate both the empire's interests and the complexities of a changing world. Someone with ambition—and the steel to face what lies ahead."

Frederick looked down at his shotgun, turning it over thoughtfully. "You'd trust me with India? I'm…well, not exactly known for restraint, nor for matters of state."

Braxton, a glint of pride in his eyes said, "Nor was I, once. You'd be surprised what responsibility can reveal in a man."

Frederick scoffed, but there was a glimmer of something in his eyes—a hint of pride, a dawning excitement. "Sort of like vice-king of India," he mused, playing with the words. He straightened, adjusting his collar with a newfound purpose. "Quite the undertaking, Papa. I can't say I expected it."

Resting a steady hand on Frederick's shoulder, he said, "Sometimes, a challenge is the best way to find one's place."

With a grin and a flourish, Frederick shouldered the gun and saluted. "To ambition, then," he said, letting his voice carry the weight of both jest and something deeper.

Braxton harrumphed and with mild exasperation shook his head. "Come along," he said, guiding Frederick across the park toward the palace gardens after they had handed their guns to the loaders.

They walked in silence until they reached a spot under a sprawling oak. Finally, Braxton turned, his gaze steady. "Would you accept the post, Viceroy of India?"

Frederick stopped short, raising an eyebrow with exaggerated surprise. "Viceroy of India? So…King of India?"

"Not king, Frederick. Viceroy. Dominic's the emperor; you'd be representing him."

Frederick gave a mock sigh, tilting his head thoughtfully. "Feels a lot like 'king' to me."

"Why aren't you taking this seriously?" Braxton asked, trying to keep his voice steady but giving his son a shrewd look.

Frederick rubbed his arms, shivering theatrically. "Maybe it's because I just returned from sunny Monte Carlo to this damp, miserable place, only to have India dropped in my lap on a silver platter? Honestly, I'm stunned. It's so unlike you to hand over the keys to anything that actually matters."

"You mean my handing the America's over to you during the war?"

"Other than that."

Braxton exhaled, half-laughing. "And what's so surprising about me offering you this?"

Frederick grinned, relaxing his posture. "Because, Papa, I never thought you'd trust me with something quite so…imperial. I know I'm not exactly your golden child."

"Maybe not golden," Braxton admitted, "but you're more capable than you let on. And India's no Monte Carlo. It's a challenge—one to which you can rise."

Frederick's grin faded, a hint of sincerity breaking through. "I suppose, if you insist," he said with a theatrical sigh, his eyes brightening with a gleam of curiosity, "India could use a touch of Monte Carlo's flair."

Braxton gave him a long look, barely concealing his smile. "If by flair you mean wisdom, then yes. It could."

Braxton's expression softened as he looked at his son. Favorite? he thought, sensing that Frederick's quip was more than idle talk. There was something beneath the surface.

"Frederick," he said gently, "besides all this, what's really on your mind?"

Frederick's confident façade faltered slightly. "Well," he admitted with reluctance, "I was turned down by someone I'd hoped to marry."

"The German baroness?"

Frederick nodded, looking away. "Yes. I had high hopes for that, and, well, it didn't go as planned."

Braxton placed a reassuring hand on his son's shoulder. "I'm truly sorry, son. She would have made a fine match—and a remarkable addition to the family. But disappointments have a way of teaching us. Don't let this defeat your confidence or cloud your ambitions."

Frederick cleared his throat, clearly wanting to move on. "About India—if I accept, would I still be free to pursue my own business interests?"

"Of course," Braxton assured him. "As long as you're discreet. But remember, this role demands commitment to the crown. India isn't just another post—it's a responsibility that will challenge you on every level."

Frederick managed a grin, clapping his father on the back. "Thank you, Papa. I'll take the appointment. This challenge—it's exactly what I need right now."

Braxton gave him a measured look, his tone kind but resolute. "Then go, Frederick, and prove yourself; not to me, but to yourself.

Seize this chance to continue to grow into the man you're meant to be."

The British government had largely neglected India, despite the subcontinent's significant contribution of over a million soldiers to the war effort. This neglect fueled deep resentment among the populace, leading to widespread civil unrest and severely impacting commerce.

Braxton saw Frederick's skills as an opportunity to revitalize the economy and divert focus from the grievances simmering among the Indian people.

Before he departed, Frederick married Lady Catherine, a British noblewoman of intelligence and beauty who approached their union pragmatically, understanding Braxton's role in arranging the marriage.

A month later, as the newly titled Duke and Duchess of Kent, they boarded a ship for India, where unrest awaited, and where they would shape a new chapter in the history of the British Empire.

CHAPTER TWENTY-THREE

UPHEAVAL

King Dominic appeared from a hidden door concealed by the bookcase in Buckingham Palace's Audience Room, his usually discreet entry echoing in the empty chamber. Unaccompanied, his figure cast a solitary shadow on the ornate carpet. Prematurely gray hair framed a face etched with weariness, and his back, once straight with confidence, bore the weight of his years: stooped and fragile. Each step came slowly, his cane a steadying but insufficient support.

Halfway to his chair, his foot caught on a sofa's leg. The moment hung suspended as he lurched forward, his cane slipping from his grasp. His head struck the table's edge with a sickening thud before he crumpled to the floor, unmoving, the room swallowed in an eerie silence.

Outside the room, the prime minister and the king's equerry awaited the signal indicating the king was ready for his weekly appointment with the prime minister. Braxton joined them, apologizing for his late arrival.

"Strikers delayed my car," Braxton explained, glancing at the doors. "Prime Minister, has the king not arrived for your audience?"

The prime minister shifted uneasily. "It appears he's delayed, Your Royal Highness."

Braxton checked his watch, raising an eyebrow. "Twenty minutes? I doubt it." Moving swiftly, he darted past the minister and equerry, thrusting open the Audience Room doors. Inside, he took one look and called out, "Send for the king's doctor!"

The equerry rushed to the wall phone, rotating the hand-crank, while the prime minister followed Braxton into the room.

Braxton kneeled beside Dominic, his voice tense as he checked for a pulse. "Dominic, can you hear me?" He thought he felt a faint pulse but wasn't certain.

Two footmen hurried in. At Braxton's command, they gently lifted the king and carried him to his bedchamber. The doctor arrived shortly and attended to the king,

Braxton turned to the prime minister. "It may be best for you to return to Downing Street and inform the cabinet," he suggested.

"Yes, Your Royal Highness."

"Until we know more, let us keep the king's condition confidential." Braxton's voice held a calm authority. "Agreed?"

The prime minister hesitated, then nodded. "However, I advise the palace prepare two statements, should the need arise."

Braxton's brow furrowed. "Two statements?"

"One for recovery, and another…should it be necessary."

The words hung in the air as Braxton, expressionless, gave a single nod. The prime minister bowed and left.

Queen Mathilde entered the bedchamber, clad always in the black of perpetual mourning since her daughter Rose's death two decades ago. Her ashen complexion and waist-length white hair lent an ethereal, almost spectral quality to her presence. She swept past Braxton and the medical team, all of whom respectfully bowed.

Ignoring the king's doctor, Mathilde leaned over Dominic, kissed his forehead, and in her thick German accent said, "Mein liebster Dominic, you vill soon join our beloved Rose. I vill meet you both der."

Braxton noted her strange, languid demeanor and thought, *Laudanum, or perhaps something stronger.*

"Mathilde," he said gently as she moved away from the bed, "would you like to stay, or shall I accompany you to your rooms?"

She barely acknowledged him. "Nein, no need to trouble yourself. I vill prepare for my journey to join dem."

Braxton watched her depart, the rustling of her skirts echoing a mournful dirge in the silent hall. He rubbed his forehead, trying to make sense of her words. *What does she mean by "prepare?"*

Dominic lingered in a vegetative state, sustained on broth and soft foods. Mathilde remained in seclusion, visiting only once, on the eighth day, when she placed a bouquet of chrysanthemums and a letter on his bed. She kissed his forehead and left without a word.

The family gathered in mourning attire in Buckingham Palace's White Drawing Room. Braxton held the unopened letter Mathilde had left on Dominic's bed.

"Is that the queen's letter to Uncle Dominic?" Prince George asked.

Braxton nodded, a somber expression crossing his face.

Princess Elizabeth whispered, "She passed not long after leaving the letter with Uncle Dominic."

Valentina interjected, "This is why we wanted you all here when we read it. Initially, we considered reading it to Dominic, hoping he might rally if made aware of her passing."

Vanya furrowed his brow. "Do you think he would understand? He remains unconscious, doesn't he?"

"It is impossible to know," Braxton replied.

A murmur of agreement spread through the room.

"Do you think it explains why she took her own life?" Prince Arthur asked, a little too bluntly.

Valentina shot him a sharp look. "We don't know for certain that she did."

Arthur shrugged. "Come now, Mama. She simply threw back an entire bottle of laudanum, and that's that."

George admonished him, "Arthur, have some respect."

Braxton took the letter opener, sliced through the seal, and removed the single sheet of paper within. The family tensed, anticipation filling the room. Clearing his throat, he read:

My Dearest Husband,

It pains me deeply to see you confined to this bed, unable to join our precious Rose as heaven surely intends. How unfair it is you were nearly reunited with her, only to be denied at the last.

It wounded me to learn of your attempt to go without me. I, who have borne the heaviest sorrow in losing Rose, should be the one to join her first. We both knew this. I would have followed had you shown the slightest wish to be with her now. It was selfish of you to attempt to leave me behind.

"Nutter," Vanya whispered. Arthur stifled a snicker, but Braxton silenced them with a raised brow before continuing:

With that said, I have made my own arrangements to join her. I shall be with you both in time, but please, do not delay overlong.

Regarding our son, I have considered taking him along. He, too, feels Rose's absence keenly. But he is away at school—or a hospital, as they say. I trust he will find his own path.

So, I forgive you, dearest, for trying to leave me behind. But I will have much to say about it when we meet again. Do not tarry,
Your devoted wife,
Mathilde

CHAPTER TWENTY-FOUR

THE AURELIO CONFERENCE

The king remains in a vegetative state, and we wait," Braxton said, seated in the ducal study with the prime minister. "I remain regent, the empire marches on, and yet I feel as if one hand is tied behind my back. As regent, my options are limited, are they not?"

"Not entirely, sir. You are regent and, for all intents and purposes, acting king."

"We have a nation reeling from the cost and consequences of war," Braxton said. "And we're burdened with a constitutional monarchy that's unable to respond effectively."

The prime minister looked puzzled. "I apologize, sir, but I don't entirely grasp your concerns."

"As regent, I must work to keep the nation's morale high, to act on behalf of the king, and to see us through the tough times as we rebuild. Prince George will one day be king, and it's essential we leave him an intact and flourishing empire."

The prime minister's shoulders slumped as Braxton observed him, the man's weariness evident. The war had drained him. Braxton observed the prime minister with a growing sense of disquiet. The man appeared visibly unfit, wearied by the strain of recent years. A capable figure was sorely needed to steer the country through the uncertain aftermath of war.

"Prime Minister," Braxton ventured, carefully, "what are your thoughts on how we proceed from here?"

The question seemed to startle the prime minister, who sat up, blinked, and glanced through the French doors, his gaze unfocused on the gardens beyond. He cleared his throat. "Well, yes, I agree entirely, Your Royal Highness. But where, indeed, do we begin?"

Braxton felt a pang of disappointment. The prime minister's answer lacked the conviction he'd hoped for. Here sat the man meant to lead the government's recovery efforts, yet he seemed to flounder, lacking both clarity and energy. And with the monarchy itself limited by Dominic's incapacitation, it was becoming painfully clear someone needed to step up with a plan, not just for leadership—but for action.

The prince leaned forward, speaking slowly. "Perhaps it might be time to consider a collaborative approach," he said, choosing his words carefully. "I am, after all, here to act as regent. If I could be of any assistance, even behind the scenes…"

The prime minister looked at him, relief flashing across his face. He nodded slowly, though he seemed almost reluctant to admit it. "Your Royal Highness, with all that's been on my shoulders, I must say—your guidance would be invaluable."

Taking in the minister's fatigued expression, Braxton recognized the unspoken approval he'd been seeking. He would need to take the reins, subtly but decisively, if he were to see the empire through its recovery.

"Allow me to propose a course of action," Braxton said. "I suggest summoning a select group of parliamentarians to the Aurelio Palace—those who represent innovation, thoughtfulness, and the vigor of youth. Men who may lead one day."

The prime minister looked taken aback. "Aurelio? Here? And younger men? Why?"

"By bringing them out of London, Oxford, Manchester, or wherever they are—away from their individual agendas, we can focus their energy on the needs of the nation."

Understanding dawned on the minister, fidgeting with his watch chain as he mulled it over. "I see…yes," he muttered.

"I have a few individuals in mind," Braxton went on.

"Not from the cabinet, I presume?"

"Certainly not. We need fresh perspectives, energy, and ambition."

"And who will oversee this assembly?" the prime minister pressed.

"They will," Braxton replied firmly.

"They, Your Royal Highness?"

"Yes, Minister."

Over the years, alumni from the Aurelio Academy had risen in both the Labour and Conservative parties, through the ranks of parliament, quietly forming a coalition bound by shared values and unwavering loyalty. Today, 12 of those alumni had been summoned to the palace, a rare honor that left them intrigued—and a bit uneasy.

As they entered the ornate Romanesque library, a ripple of astonishment ran through the group. None had ever set foot in the magnificent ducal library, which Prince Braxton used as his private study during his time at the Aurelio Palace.

"Good God, is this real?" one young member of parliament said, his gaze sweeping over the soaring arches and shelves brimming with ancient volumes. "I feel like I've walked into a Roman Temple full of books."

"Or a museum," another quipped, craning his neck to admire the gilded Romanesque ceiling. "I half expect a docent to appear and shush us."

"Not likely," a third member of parliament countered, gesturing to a footman offering a tray of drinks. "You don't get champagne in a museum."

They mingled, accepting the champagne and delicate sandwiches; the banter, laced with curiosity, continued.

"So," one asked, lowering his voice, "any guesses why we've been summoned? This feels…significant."

"Maybe it's about party unity?" another ventured. "You know how he's always been a master of bridging divides."

A skeptical chuckle rose from the group. "Unity? At this moment? We're more likely to find consensus on the color of unicorns."

"Well," a quieter member interjected, "we're all Aurelio men. That has to count for something. He knows he can trust us."

"That, or he's going to give us a dressing-down for some monumental failure we've yet to discover," another joked, prompting a round of nervous laughter.

The youngest of the group, still clutching his first glass of champagne, glanced around with wide eyes. "You realize we're standing in his study from the Academy days, right? The ducal library. This was the place."

A hush fell over them as they took in the weight of that revelation.

"Hard to believe we're here now," one of the older members said. "Back then, we could barely get through a debate without quoting Cicero—or cracking a joke about his toga."

"Some things never change," another quipped, raising his glass.

As footmen circulated with a second round of drinks, the room grew more animated, their initial awe giving way to easy camaraderie. Speculation ran wild about the purpose of the gathering, from strategies for the Empire to whispered rumors of reform.

The room fell silent, however, when the footman announced, "His Royal Highness, Prince Braxton."

Every conversation halted. Glasses were lowered. The young men turned as one to face their host, bowing deeply as the prince entered the library, his presence commanding the room without a word.

"Gentlemen, please," Braxton said with a smile. "Thank you for accepting my invitation." He knew each by name and had developed friendships with several over the years. "Bring your drinks and join me at the table."

They followed him to the conference table where Braxton began with tales of his mother's family, the Chiacontellas, and their acquisition of the land to build this palace eight centuries earlier. He recounted his own childhood mischief, including the infamous Rotunda fire.

Braxton then shared why he had founded the Academy, and the responsibilities expected of its graduates. He congratulated each man individually for their achievements and serving in parliament.

"Gentlemen, I have never desired to be king. As the third son, I believed I was safe from such a fate." He chuckled. "Yet it appears my brothers have left me with little choice. It is now my duty to serve as regent, and, if necessary, to assume the throne should my brother Dominic pass."

He paused before continuing, "In the aftermath of the Great War, our nation and Europe are desperate for stability. You now hold the power, the means—and the responsibility—to help bring that about."

The twelve members exchanged glances around the table, their expressions shifting as Braxton's words settled over them. A few adjusted their posture, sitting straighter, while others looked momentarily taken aback, brows furrowed in contemplation. One or two reached for their glasses, quietly sipping, as if buying time to absorb the profundity of his statement. The room grew still, a shared understanding passing among them, internalizing the gravity of Braxton's words.

The prince let his words settle and continued, outlining his proposal, interweaving it with anecdotes from his time as royal envoy, member of parliament and prime minister, emphasizing his deep familiarity with their world.

"Unity within our government is essential if we are to lead the Empire into the 20th century as the world's preeminent power. The global landscape is changing, and so must we."

He then disclosed that he had personally invested over a billion pounds in England and across Europe to stimulate growth, prompting surprised glances from those around him.

"Gentlemen, it is up to you to forge a unified government capable of leading the Empire. That is your purpose here. Find a way to serve and unite the people."

As he spoke, the Aurelio graduates left their drinks untouched, hanging on his words.

"Will you, gentlemen, commit to this vision for our country?"

The young members exchanged glances before standing one by one. A murmur of agreement grew louder until one of them raised his glass. "I pledge to do so, Sir!"

The others followed with a resounding, "God Save the King!"

Braxton raised his glass. "Thank you, gentlemen. God Save the King!" He looked each man in the eye before adding, "I suggest you don't leave the Aurelio Palace until you've formed a government with both parties represented." He chuckled, then continued, "And, naturally, Labour will lead the government—initially. This will bring broader support from across the populace, ensuring our unity is visible, not merely declared. A unified government is essential if we are to survive in a world spinning out of control."

"Hear, hear!" they chorused, exchanging looks signaling a camaraderie forged in shared purpose.

"Now, gentlemen, I'll leave you to your work. Stay as my guests until you've created a government to present to the crown. I look forward to tea later, and dinner."

He bowed and exited the library.

The young men remained at the Aurelio Palace for three days, meeting between sessions of shooting, fishing, fox hunting, and lawn tennis. Braxton treated them as lords and gentlemen of fortune, ensuring they felt empowered.

On the morning of the fourth day, he invited them to breakfast in the library. As the meal concluded, Braxton asked, "So, gentlemen, what have you devised?"

One of them, evidently chosen as their spokesperson, replied, "Your Royal Highness, we outlined our plan the afternoon we began."

"Congratulations on building a framework so quickly," Braxton said.

"With that framework, we spent the remaining days refining the government and shaping a legislative agenda for the coming year."

Braxton looked at them, astonished. They had surpassed his expectations.

"Excellent. Who do you propose for prime minister?"

They eagerly shared their choice, presenting their agenda in detail over the next two hours. Though Braxton didn't agree with all their ideas, he saw the potential and knew he could guide them. There was hope.

"Well done, gentlemen. I am honored to have had you as my guests and look forward to supporting your government—or, rather, the king's government. God Save the King!"

The room echoed with a unified response: "God Save the King!"

News of the "Aurelio Conference" swept through the papers, stirring both alarm and anticipation. The formation of a Unity Government left the establishment and much of the empire confounded, as the unprecedented coalition signaled a departure from tradition. Yet, for a nation weary and battered by war, this unexpected alliance ignited a spark of hope—a chance, at last, for recovery and renewal. All eyes turned toward the Aurelio Palace, eager to see if this new government could indeed steer the nation toward stability and success.

The newly structured parliament functioned with remarkable efficiency. While opposition remained, debates transformed into meaningful discussions, and disagreements led to compromise. For over two years, it was as if the legendary Camelot had been revived.

The economy grew, wages rose, employment reached record highs and poverty diminished. England appeared to be moving forward as a united nation.

Leadership from the British Isles emboldened the Commonwealth, and the British Empire presented itself poised to recover from the ravages of war.

As regent, Braxton kept a close eye on the government and his sprawling global ventures. But after over 60 years—building an empire, running the country as prime minister, and now standing in as regent—he felt weariness settling in.

Each day chipped away at his strength, leaving even his steadfast resolve feeling stretched to its limits.

CHAPTER TWENTY-FIVE

COLLAPSE

"It's wonderful to have this time together, away from London and its pressures," Valentina said, her arm linked with Braxton's as they descended the steep incline. "Look! The cobblestones seem to stretch on forever."

The path along the Royal Mile from Edinburgh Castle perched on Castlehill, wound down into the heart of the city, ending at the Palace of Holyroodhouse.

Valentina's step was light, her spirits high. "Perhaps we could slip inside one of those charming shops in the old town. I hear the restaurants are lovely. Do you think we'd go unnoticed?" She smiled, giving Braxton's arm a playful nudge. "Come, dear—relax, look around. Try to enjoy our little escape."

He stopped abruptly and turned to face her, a clouded look in his eyes. "I need your help, Valentina," he began, his voice strained. "I—I just can't carry on like this." His voice faltered as he swallowed.

Valentina paused, meeting his troubled gaze, and gently squeezed his arm. "What's weighing on you, my love? You know I'm here, always. Whatever it is, we'll face it together." Drawing closer, she whispered, "I've sensed something was troubling you, especially as Dominic's health has declined these past years."

Braxton looked past her, almost as if he hadn't heard her words, and murmured, "Please, allow me to admit my shortcomings."

Valentina studied his worn face as he continued, "I feel incapable—trying to manage our family's affairs, governmental matters and act as regent for Dominic. It's crushing me, Valentina. I hold myself to a certain standard, and this…well, I'm falling short. I see no clear way forward."

She tightened her grip on his arm, her voice steady and reassuring. "Dearest, it's not as dire as it seems. I'm certain you have everything under control."

Braxton only shook his head.

Valentina patted his arm, her expression warm. "I'll gladly help however I can. I have more than enough time in my schedule."

He looked at her earnestly. "It's more than help, Valentina. It's a partnership—like when we were side by side in Russia. You understand, don't you?"

Her eyes softened. "Some of the happiest days of my life were spent working beside you. I'd love nothing more than to do it again." She leaned in and pressed a gentle kiss to his cheek.

Braxton offered a faint smile. "Perhaps so. My duties as regent—"

"Yes?" Valentina prompted.

"Your co-regency with Maxim was remarkable. You served Russia admirably. I need you to stand with me like that here."

She remained silent, fully grasping the weight of his request. Though her role as co-regent had been officially recognized in Russia, a similar arrangement would be impossible in England's constitutional monarchy, especially for someone foreign-born.

Not having an official title, Valentina took on a quiet, supportive role. She and Braxton worked side by side, reviewing the government reports in the leather-bound red boxes brought each day by the Page of the Presence. These boxes contained parliament updates, national concerns, news from the colonies, and international developments, along with matters needing royal assent. Together, they reviewed and addressed everything the boxes held, Valentina's participation a steadying force.

In the next three years, a vibrant new world emerged. Jazz, cocktails, cinema, and industry flourished, and a carefree spirit swept society. Paris was the heart of this cultural awakening, drawing people from around the globe, keen to join the brilliance of the "Lost Generation." Known as Les Années Folles, or the Roaring Twenties, this era came alive with the voices of F. Scott Fitzgerald, Ernest Hemingway, Josephine Baker, Salvador Dalí, and Pablo Picasso, all icons of art and innovation.

Braxton and Valentina often visited Paris, spending time at their 18th-century château, which Braxton had restored some 40 years earlier. The château's cellars held a treasure trove of antiques from Braxton's long career in the art world. His art business thrived, funding efforts to address post-war poverty in Paris. He also continued to build children's hospitals in honor of his parents, King Richard and Queen Mercedes.

In this thriving world, Valentina came to life. Braxton encouraged her to embrace the role of a grand duchess, fulfilling her every wish. For the first time, they could live as the partners they'd long wanted to be, their days filled with love and laughter.

Braxton returned frequently to London for his duties as regent, leaving Valentina to enjoy the company of their grandchildren, who filled their Parisian residence and the Aurelio Palace with youth's vitality and music.

The French economy boomed, driven by the automobile and aviation industries—both sectors in which Braxton had invested heavily. Though initially reluctant, Braxton eventually saw the value in working with German firms. The devastation in Germany and the harsh reparations of the Treaty of Versailles compelled him to encourage his colleagues to support the recovery of German industry.

The Parisian dusk had softened into a velvet night, the lamps along the Champs-Élysées casting a warm, golden glow on the busy street. Crowds bustled by, glancing at the elegant women seated at one of the finer cafés, their identities obscured yet undeniable. The scent of fine perfume and cigarette smoke hung in the air, mingling with the heady energy of 1920s Paris. Zelda Fitzgerald, lively as ever, leaned back with a grin, casually gesturing with her cigarette holder. Opposite her sat Valentina.

"Call me Val, please, as friends do."

"Val," Zelda tried the name with a playful lilt, laughing as she exhaled smoke into the night air. "It's so fitting for you, really. But I must say, Val, even for an American, it's strange not calling you your royal highness!"

Valentina gave a light laugh. "Oh, Zelda, if anyone in Paris recognized me, they'd be gaping in our direction, pointing and gossiping instead of going about their merry business. It's freeing and refreshing to be myself, your friend and not a royal."

"Well, Val," Zelda opened her diamond encrusted cigarette case and held it out toward Valentina, "I can't imagine anyone not gaping at us, but it's probably for the best if we go unnoticed. Imagine Scott, or Braxton, seeing us here!" She rolled her eyes with a laugh, taking a sip of her champagne. "Scott would write it up in some essay. 'My wife and the grand duchess, plotting on the Champs-Élysées!'"

Valentina's laughter was rich, genuine, and threaded with that subtle poise that came from years of royal life as she accepted the cigarette, and said, "Oh, don't tempt me—I'd almost like to see his version of our espionage. And I assure you, you are the only one allowed to call me Val. If the press catches wind, they'll think I've gone thoroughly mad."

Zelda leaned forward, her tone growing more thoughtful. "Tell me, Val, doesn't it…doesn't it get lonely? You, a royal, with all the mystery, all the spectacle of it? Braxton's so…well, he's like Scott in a way. Off on his adventures. There must be so much you shoulder alone."

Valentina's smile softened, and she nodded. "You know, Zelda, there's a comfort in the traditions and expectations—they're like armor. But yes, there are times I feel like a ghost in my own life." She paused, her gaze distant. "Braxton, for all his public life, has his private world; the parts of himself he shares only with those who understand him. And yet, no matter where he wanders, he always returns to me. In his way."

Zelda's eyes twinkled, both empathetic and mischievous. "Scott and Braxton—they're like magnets for people, aren't they? Scott has a world of his own, too—a world I sometimes wonder if I'll ever fully belong to. But his drinking may prove ruinous. And yet, like you said, he always comes back. Though Lord knows I don't think I'd mind if he brought Hemingway back a little less often."

Valentina chuckled, lifting her glass in solidarity. "Oh, I could say the same about certain diplomats and generals…" She took a sip, the corners of her mouth quirking upward. "But as infuriating as it can be, there's something irresistible about the mystery of them, isn't there? It's what keeps the intrigue alive, what makes me…well, love him."

"Love, indeed," Zelda sighed, raising her glass as well, her voice a little softer, wistful. "For all the wildness, I wouldn't trade it. But Val, I do wonder…when you're with him, is he ever entirely…yours?" She glanced around, a quick, darting look, as if the question were something almost forbidden.

Valentina's eyes lit up with understanding; with something both knowing and unknowable. "In moments, yes. There are moments that feel more precious because they're fleeting. Perhaps that's why I treasure them." She paused, her gaze turning serious. "But I think that's what sets us apart, Zelda. We don't need to hold them tightly. We're not of them; we're with them."

Zelda's laugh was bright and devil-may-care, matching the rhythm of the bustling street as she tossed her head back, her golden hair catching the light. "Yes, with them but not of them! Cheers to that, Val. A toast, to the women who keep their own secrets, who can stand beside men who think they run the show, yet only we know what they don't see."

They shared a quiet moment, gazing out at those passing by. Valentina turned to Zelda, her voice tinged with hope. "But sometimes, I truly feel he is mine. There are moments when he's with me, really with me, that feel like we're the only two people in the world. It's fleeting, but it's real. And I think—I hope—it's enough."

Zelda let out a soft sigh, nodding slowly. "Yes, those moments. Sometimes I think they're all I need to believe he's mine, or almost mine. Maybe that's what love is—a bit of reality and a bit of illusion. Enough of both to keep us holding on."

A wistful silence settled over them as Valentina placed her hand gently on Zelda's. "Perhaps it's our own magic, then, that keeps them coming back. I don't need him to be only mine. I just need to feel that, in those quiet moments, he chooses me."

Zelda's smile returned brighter this time. "Then here's to that magic, Val. To believing it…maybe, hopefully." Their glasses met with a soft, hopeful clink, each woman holding her own sense of possibility close, just out of sight, like the stars above the bright lights of Paris.

Valentina raised her glass, "To us, then. For the real queens, darling, are always in the background. And no one even notices we're the ones pulling the strings."

In the summer of 1927, Braxton experienced fatigue, aching joints and fevers. He kept his condition to himself and eventually visited a highly regarded London physician.

"Well, doctor, am I imagining things, or is there something wrong?" he asked with a weary smile.

The doctor's tone was grave. "I'm afraid there is, Your Royal Highness. You seem to have contracted a form of asymptomatic malaria, likely from years ago."

Braxton was stunned. "Malaria? Are you certain? That's impossible!"

"It may have been lying dormant since your time in India or Singapore. It's not unheard of. Did you experience symptoms then?"

"Yes, I had a prolonged illness in India," he admitted. "We took quinine as a preventative."

"That may have been what kept you safe all these years. But the symptoms have returned."

"Good heavens. What can be done?"

"You require quinine, and absolute rest. There's no other cure."

Valentina noticed the shift in Braxton's energy and mentioned it to Vanya at breakfast, her tone tinged with concern. "Your father seems…more worn out lately. And he hasn't come down for breakfast this morning."

Vanya looked up; his eyes filled with worry. "He canceled a Privy Council meeting yesterday afternoon. That's not like him." Vanya took a deep swallow of his Bloody Mary, then turned to the footman. "Has the Prince of Wales left the palace this morning?"

The footman bowed. "I don't believe so, sir."

Vanya turned to his mother, a frown deepening on his face. "He's probably in his rooms, buried in work, but still…" He hesitated, then nodded toward the footman. "Ask the majordomo to look in on His Royal Highness."

The footman hurried off. An uneasy silence filled the room.

Moments later, Prince Braxton's secretary rushed in, his face flushed with alarm. "Your Royal Highness, the prince—he's taken ill. Very ill."

Vanya shot to his feet, knocking over his juice glass in his hurry. "I'll go, Mother," he said, hurrying out, Valentina following close behind.

They found Braxton in his sitting room, half-reclined on a divan. The secretary explained, "The majordomo and I helped him onto the divan after finding him partially on the floor. The doctor's on his way."

Valentina spoke calmly, though her face was drawn. "This must remain confidential. No one is to speak of it."

Vanya kneeled beside Braxton, checking his pulse. "He's breathing, and it seems he has lost consciousness."

Braxton's letter to Lord Arlington, Lord President of the Council, lay on the carpet along with another letter addressed to Valentina. The secretary handed them to her. She glanced at the names and, in a firm tone, "Help Prince Vanya move His Royal Highness to his bed, then inform the majordomo to restrict entry to this wing."

CHAPTER TWENTY-SIX

RETURN TO CAPRI

Prince Braxton lay unconscious in bed under the doctor's attentive care. Nearby, Valentina and Vanya sat together on a settee, waiting quietly.

"Exhaustion," Valentina murmured, recalling her memories from India. "I've seen it before. Your father spent years building his business empire, and I witnessed much of it, as you know. His work ethic was legendary, but despite his convictions, he is not invincible."

"How long did it take him to recover last time in India, Mama?" Vanya asked.

"Months," she answered.

Vanya's gaze drifted to the painted rococo ceiling as he mused aloud, "A regent can hardly afford the luxury of illness, let alone a prolonged one. With Uncle Dominic incapacitated and now Papa in this state, what can we do?"

Valentina placed the letter for the council on a nearby side table and opened the one addressed to her. Meanwhile, Vanya stood and walked over to the doctor and looked down at his father.

"What's the prognosis, doctor?" he asked, with both urgency and dread.

The doctor sighed, as if this diagnosis was all too familiar. "I fear it's the same as it was over 30 years ago, Your Royal Highness."

"You were with him, then?" Vanya asked in surprise.

"Yes," the doctor replied. "That's why I'm here now," he added with a gruff sigh. "Her Royal Highness is correct—it's exhaustion, compounded by age." Then, after a pause, he added, "And malaria."

Vanya looked startled. "He's only in his sixties." He paused. "I suppose that is not young. But I have never thought of him as old."

"Longevity is relative, Your Highness. Most men don't see much beyond 60. His Highness has enjoyed remarkable health, but he's also worked relentlessly his entire life. To recover, he'll need to reassess how he lives and conducts his affairs."

"But the malaria?" Vanya pressed. "He hasn't been anywhere near malarial regions recently."

"I suspected malaria back in Calcutta. At that time we moved him to Shimla's Viceregal Lodge to isolate him. He showed few classic symptoms, but I prescribed a substantial amount of quinine. In time, his strength returned. He must have been asymptomatic since then."

Vanya nodded slowly and returned to the settee beside his mother. "Did you hear all of that, Mama?"

She patted his knee with a reassuring smile. "Darling, don't forget, your mother has quite the knack for handling complex situations. I served as co-regent in Russia during the most trying of times—when my father's condition deteriorated. Those were challenging, even dangerous days, but I survived them."

Her smile turned playful as she added, "And, of course, thanks to your childhood escapades, I've honed the art of listening to multiple conversations at once. I suspect that skill alone is what helped me navigate the chaos of court life in St. Petersburg."

Vanya scoffed; a bit surprised. "That's rather grim, Mama."

"Yes, it was," she replied softly. "My mother didn't survive those times."

She paused, then continued, "Your father's letter shows he's well aware of his illness. He's asked the Privy Council to appoint me co-regent."

Vanya stared at her. "You? But wouldn't George be the obvious choice?"

"Yes, however, George is currently in South Africa. He can hardly act as co-regent from there."

"Or Arthur, or even one of the girls—"

"Perhaps you can discuss that with your father once he recovers. Not before."

"True," Vanya agreed, though still surprised. "The council respects you, but you're not a counselor of state. And you're Russian."

"We shall see, Vanya. With all your father has done, the Privy Council holds him in the highest regard. That respect should assuage concerns they may have."

Vanya crossed his arms, frowning in thought. "I still don't quite see why he asked you to take on that role."

Valentina met his gaze steadily. "Our partnership goes back a long time. Sometimes, men simply overlook what's plainly before them. Let us hope for his swift recovery."

Vanya's frown deepened. "Did Papa say why he thought co-regency was necessary?"

"Yes," Valentina replied. "I'm curious—why do you ask?"

"Regency is typically handled by one person to avoid confusion and discord. It seems…unusual."

"Your father says in his letter he's justified the request, partly because he'll be out of the country."

"Out of the country? I didn't know he had plans to leave."

"You're to accompany him to the Chiacontella villa in Capri."

"Good Lord, Mother! What is this all about?"

She offered a wistful smile. "The villa is special to him. He spent a month there with Aramis after he earned his first fortune."

"Ah, Cousin Aramis. He and his father worked closely with you and Papa." Vanya rubbed his chin thoughtfully. "We went to their home, Villa Incantare, once as children. The Italians truly know how to live life. I had planned to see more of Europe on my Grand Tour, but the war put an end to that."

"So, you don't mind accompanying your father to Capri?"

"Not at all. But it seems a bit strange. Why not recover at the Aurelio Palace? Or in Paris? Why Capri? It's so remote."

"Perhaps isolation is precisely what he needs. And I expect you to keep me updated on everything."

"Yes, Mama."

"Oh, and Vanya," she added as she stood, "no mention of malaria." She glanced around. "Hmmm, I'm sure we'll find some quinine around here somewhere."

The warmth of the Mediterranean sun mingled with the scent of salt and blooming flowers, casting a golden glow over Capri's rocky shores.

Reclining on a cushioned rattan chair on the fourth-story terrace overlooking the Mediterranean, Braxton soaked in the sun. Hs bare torso and legs warm under its rays.

The villa had never been wired for electricity and had no phone. Here, the world seemed to slow down, only to reawaken on another plane, infused with a new sense of peace and beauty.

The unexpected visit, from Braxton, and the long gap since their last meeting left Aramis curious but unprepared for his cousin's exhausted state.

A victrola sat just inside the loggia spinning a jazz record by the famed Louis Armstrong. The lively strains of Heebie Jeebies filled the air.

"You may want to give some thought to moving before you roast," Aramis teased, bringing two gin and tonics, each garnished with a lime slice. He handed one to Braxton, his former lover.

Braxton took a sip, savoring it. "Hmmmm. Where were these delicious things when we were here 40 years ago?"

"It was all wine back then, remember?"

"Indeed," Braxton nodded.

"We were younger, thinner, ready to conquer the world—and could down several bottles. Look at us now!"

"You did conquer the world, Brax."

Ignoring the comment, Braxton continued, "Now, one more of these and we'll be utterly finished."

Aramis sighed, reminiscing. "Those five weeks we spent here in our youth might just have been the happiest of my life. Do you remember swimming au naturel and sharing moments of intimacy in that turquoise grotto?"

Braxton laughed. "I'll never forget your father showing up in the grotto with wine, cheese and bread. He too, naked as a Jay bird; as if it were the most natural thing in the world."

"When he swam into the grotto, I wanted to vanish. He talked as if catching us 'en flagrant délit' was of no importance, as long as no one else did! I still marvel at it," Aramis laughed, drinking deeply.

"I loved you then, Ari. I wanted to spend my life with you here. I had my fortune. We could have made it work."

Aramis looked into his drink thoughtfully, then at Braxton. "Why have you come back here after all these years? And why ask for me? What if my family didn't have the villa anymore? You could go anywhere. You're probably the richest man in the world."

Braxton smiled. "God, Ari, so many questions."

Aramis refilled their glasses and watched Braxton chug his down.

"Let's have another, and I'll answer every one."

"Of course." Aramis took Braxton's glass and strolled across the sunlit terrace, passing through the villa's ancient loggia into their bedroom—a spacious room brimming with cherished memories.

Several months had passed since Braxton's arrival in Capri. The first few weeks were a blur, but by the third month, he had regained his strength.

"Here you are, Your Majesty-to-be," Aramis teased, carrying a tray ladened with chilled gin and tonics. A pitcher sat in a bucket of ice.

Braxton laughed and said, "Brilliant idea, cousin!"

"Thank you," Aramis replied, setting up an umbrella over Braxton. "No more sun for you today. Now, take your medicine," he added, handing him his drink.

Braxton shaded his eyes, looking northwest. "Do you hear an engine? Odd. I never noticed aircraft here before."

"Likely not. The Wright brothers only flew in 1903. You haven't been here since well before that."

"Well, I mean recently."

The plane roared closer, passing over the hills and out of sight.

"Ah, that seaplane looks just like the one that brought you in," Aramis observed, nodding towards the horizon. "Though, to be fair, you were half-dead at the time, so you might not remember."

Braxton grimaced and took a long drink. "Thank you for the reminder, Aramis. I hope neither the family nor the government are here to cart me off. I'm finally beginning to enjoy myself."

"We shall stand our ground and fight them to the end!" Aramis teased.

"You know, plenty of other seaplanes exist—not just in the Royal Air Force," Braxton said.

"True enough. Could be French, even. Definitely not Italian, though," Aramis scoffed. "We're still trying to get the trains to run on time, much less land and take-off on water!"

Braxton nodded. "Right then, your questions. I'll take them in order, though if I skip one, consider it ignored rather than forgotten."

Aramis laughed, a bit unsteady and slurred, "You're still the same—a charming bully. A leopard doesn't change its spots." He belched.

Braxton, grinning from ear-to-ear, raised his glass. "Bravo, old friend. I feel a solid buzz coming on."

"Right you are!" Aramis barked, toasting.

Leaning back, Braxton said, "To answer your questions: I came here because this might be the most beautiful place on earth. Capri holds happy memories…and you, my dear Aramis, were my first love."

Aramis swallowed, a touch of color rising to his cheeks. "If I weren't so drunk, I might blush. Men do blush, don't they?"

Braxton tilted his head. "I suppose when one man tells another he was his first love, blushing would be appropriate. Perhaps we should consult The American Blue Book of Social Usage."

Aramis laughed. "I've heard it all now! An Englishman referencing American etiquette. You could be sent to the Tower for less!"

"To the Americans and to Joe!" Braxton toasted.

"To the Americans for great jazz!" Aramis added, then paused. "But…who is Joe?"

Braxton ignored the question, shifting gears. "Now, about why I came back. I intended to return before my brother passed. Once he is gone, there will be no more freedom for me. There's always a retinue, an entourage—no escape from it. I didn't plan on this illness either, but…perhaps I did. I sensed something coming. Then, just like in India, it hit and I made my arrangements. But here I am, knocked down once again."

"And Joe?" Aramis asked, undeterred.

Braxton's eyes lit up.

At that moment, Vanya stepped onto the loggia, came to attention and bowed. "Your Majesty—God save the King!"

Braxton sobered, instantly, and asked, "The king?"

Vanya nodded. "Uncle Dominic died this morning."

Braxton's chest tightened. The moment he'd prayed would never come had arrived. He, the third son, never expected this fate. Yet here he was—King of England, Emperor of India.

A jolt of realization coursed through him, stark and unrelenting. Has my life—all its struggles, ambitions, and sacrifices—been for nothing? The question hung, raw and echoing, as he stared into the depths of his own reflection. Or had it, in some strange design, shaped him into something rare? Am I not, perhaps, more prepared for this crown than any king before me?

CHAPTER TWENTY-SEVEN

REX IMPERATOR

"It's been over three years since your recovery and ascension to the throne. How would you say are you holding up, Papa?" Prince George asked.

"Better than I expected," Braxton replied. "Your mother has been an immense help. We've truly been partners since Edinburgh and the coronation."

In his early forties, Prince George, now the Prince of Wales, was gradually stepping back from family business matters to focus on studying the constitution and his future duties as king.

Braxton placed a hand on George's shoulder. "Son, it's a comfort knowing you're handling things so well. Frederick thrives as viceroy, and Vanya and his duchess embrace their roles. Elena's in America, Elizabeth in Damascus. Arthur has his naval career, so that leaves you and me."

George raised an eyebrow. "And where is this going, Father?"

"He's about to give you more work, George," Valentina called as she entered from the garden.

Braxton smiled, relieved his wife had so easily bridged his intentions. "Thank you, dear."

George grinned. "Very well. What needs doing?"

"Not to worry—I'm well," Braxton assured him. "It's more a matter of shifting focus. I need to wrap up some family business on the continent and in the East."

George's face grew serious. "This wouldn't have anything to do with the social unrest in Germany, would it?"

Braxton nodded thoughtfully. "Watching the Germans, I've noticed certain darker tendencies beginning to resurface, driven by radicals. I plan to divest the family of our interests in that region."

Valentina, busying herself with a vase of flowers, added, "And what of our holdings in Singapore?"

Braxton replied, "Rubber is precious now, almost like gold. With Japan's making economic and military incursions in Manchuria, it's time to sell off our interests before further escalation."

George leaned back. "Sounds like quite a bit is changing."

"Indeed," Braxton confirmed. "Angelina will handle the final steps in Singapore and China. Then she, her daughter Alicia, and granddaughter Patricia will return to England."

Valentina beamed. "I can hardly wait to see them again!"

George chuckled. "Didn't you just see them in Paris last year?"

Valentina smiled. "Yes, but it feels like an eternity."

When the Great Depression hit, hunger and anger drove people into the streets. The masses turned their frustration on the government, anti-monarchists directed their ire at the crown, and political unity disintegrated. Parliament, once unified, descended back into discord.

Braxton, still well-connected with both parties, knew conflict was inevitable. As tension simmered, people took to the streets.

"Papa, it's time the crown stepped into the national crisis," George urged one evening during dinner with Braxton, Valentina, and the prime minister.

Braxton placed his hands on the table. He said, "George, have you forgotten your constitutional lessons?"

"Braxton," Valentina interrupted, "you don't have to speak to him like that."

Braxton sighed and resumed eating.

The prime minister, ever diplomatic, addressed George. "The constitution is clear on the crown's limited role in government affairs. How do you envision the crown helping in this crisis?"

George placed his hands on his lap. "I believe the government can involve the crown—indirectly, of course—by focusing public attention on it. People still respect the monarchy. Let's use that to redirect their frustration."

The prime minister leaned forward. "May I ask how you suggest we do that, sir?"

"Create a campaign centered around the king's life," George proposed. "Weekly articles, exhibitions, concerts, parades—anything to remind people of our shared heritage and stability."

Braxton glanced at George with renewed respect. A wise strategy, indeed.

CHAPTER TWENTY-EIGHT

THE REIGN

Following Braxton's return from Capri, he and Valentina established a routine of sharing morning coffee in the comfort of their spacious bed.

"Isn't it peculiar," Braxton mused, "now that we're king and queen, we're back to sharing a bed?"

Valentina, hidden behind her newspaper, quipped, "Ah, modernity, my dear."

Braxton chuckled. "Speaking of modernity, it seems our daily 'guests' are on their way."

"Splendid! My favorite part of the day," Valentina replied with a smile.

"Mine too, Val. Brace yourself!"

As if on cue, a footman entered and approached the bed, collecting their breakfast trays. Seconds later, six grandchildren, still in their nightclothes and ranging in age from three to seven, burst into the room, followed by four lively corgis.

"Good morning, Grandmama! Grandpapa!" the children chorused.

"Good morning, darlings," Valentina greeted them, reaching out to the little ones.

Braxton scooped one of the younger children onto his lap, and before long, the rest had clambered onto the bed, nestling between their grandparents. A footman arrived with small woolen throws, which Valentina gently tucked around the little ones, ensuring they were warm and snug. Moments later, another servant entered, balancing a tray of biscuits.

"I love Grandmama's biscuits," one said, while two others chimed in with their agreement.

One grandchild asked innocently, "Did you snuggle with your grandmama?"

"Not that I can remember," Valentina replied. "Things were quite different when I was a child."

"That's so sad, Grandmama," a youngster said.

Valentina smiled.

"Grandpapa, did you snuggle with your grandparents?" another asked.

"Not quite like this," Braxton said, thoughtful. "In fact, I don't recall ever seeing my grandparents' bedroom. "He squeezed one of the children. "Though I think I would have liked to do this with them."

After a few moments of chatter, the grandchildren busied themselves with biscuits and the dogs, leaving Valentina and Braxton to read their papers. But just as they relaxed, both their expressions changed, scanning the headlines.

They both leaped up out of bed, startling the children and sending pastries and coffee scattering.

Following Braxton's coronation, anarchists and anti-monarchists attempted to infiltrate his family's affairs, nearly breaching his financial empire. A team of 35 "investigative journalists" meticulously unraveled parts of his vast empire, disclosing the intricate web of holdings: lands, factories, ships, railroads, mines, and oil fields, estimated in billions.

Global headlines exploded:

KING'S FINANCIAL EMPIRE SHOCKS WORLD

**CRASSUS & SOLOMON DWARFED
BY ROYAL FORTUNE**

ROYAL WEALTH RIVALS MANSA MUSA'S GOLD

The revelations sent shockwaves worldwide, echoing across radio broadcasts and painting a picture of a monarch's financial empire, vast and fantastic beyond all imagination.

"Get the prime minister here immediately!" Braxton barked, heading for his dressing room and shouting for his valet.

Valentina calmly but urgently instructed, "Children, fetch your parents and have them meet us in the Pavilion Breakfast Room!"

The children scrambled from the room in a flurry of excited whispers, leaving Valentina to steady Braxton.

"Calm down," she said in a low, steady voice. "We've prepared for this possibility since Russia, nearly 50 years ago. It's time to manage the situation." She raised an eyebrow as she added, "I rather like the first headline—King's Financial Empire. The other headlines are vulgar and grossly inaccurate."

Braxton's huff indicated his agreement.

An hour later, the family gathered around a grand table in the Pavilion Breakfast Room, a beautiful space decorated with Asian artifacts from the Royal Pavilion in Brighton. The opulent chandelier and porcelain vases evoked a miniature, exotic world, softened by the morning sun.

Braxton and Valentina entered, nodding to the assembled family. "Good morning," Braxton said, gesturing for them to continue eating. "The prime minister will be here shortly."

"You've all seen the papers, I assume?" he asked, and most nodded solemnly.

Moments later, the footman announced, "The Prime Minister, Your Majesty."

The minister entered, visibly tense.

Braxton gestured for him to sit. "Please join us, Prime Minister. I imagine you haven't had the chance to breakfast yet, given the early hour."

"Thank you, Your Majesty," the minister replied.

The prime minister settled into his chair; heavy silence fell over the table. Braxton finally broke it, addressing the news they'd all read that morning.

"As you may have seen, one of our greatest fears has been realized," Braxton said, his hand briefly tightening around his glass. "I'm disappointed the government was not alerted to these articles ahead of publication, Prime Minister."

The minister looked down, his face grave. "I am as astonished as you are, Your Majesty."

Braxton continued, his voice measured but firm, "The information gathered on our family's financial holdings is remarkably thorough. The substantial breach of our private financial matters is shocking. I have never shared our personal holdings with the government, nor any of its officials. Personal holdings are separate."

King Braxton paused, then reached over and took Valentina's hand. "I was the third son, free to pursue my interests without a thought of the crown. Becoming king was never part of the plan." His voice steadied. "And yet here we are, our family's private matters now exposed for all to see. Her Majesty and I considered the possibility over the years, but we never thought it would truly come to this."

The room's familial warmth chilled. Braxton continued, his voice unwavering. "We will face this directly, with full disclosure. The people deserve the truth—indeed, perhaps more than they think they want. If the facts do not mollify them, then I will abdicate. The throne was never my ambition, but now it is my burden."

Younger members of the family shrank back, their eyes wide with surprise observing their grandfather's uncharacteristic intensity. The adults sat in tense silence, each one absorbing the potential ramifications.

At last, the prime minister, who had barely touched his meal, cleared his throat. "Your Majesty, as you've called me here—what exactly do you intend to do?"

Braxton's response was brief, resolute, and left no room for doubt. "That is why you're here, Prime Minister. Listen closely."

"George, please join your mother, the prime minister, and me in my study." He rose and placed his serviette on the table. He Looked at his family, smiling. "I do so apologize for your morning and breakfast being interrupted. I look forward to all of us having luncheon together."

The king leaned back and folded his arms, tapping his fingers thoughtfully. "It is time we face this head-on. The wealth—my wealth—it's out in the open now."

Valentina nodded with a small smile. "Agreed. But if we're open about how we're using it, turning it back to the people, that could change everything."

"So, you're saying we go public with your plan, Papa? Show them exactly where the money's going? George asked.

"Yes. Social housing, hospitals, scholarships—all of it. But there's more: I want to give the newspapers a full account detailing our decades of philanthropy, every blasted farthing!"

Raising an eyebrow, the prime minister asked, "An open record, Your Majesty? That's…bold. It has never been done, but it could work."

"Bold is what we need right now, isn't it? We've got critics claiming I'm hoarding wealth, exploiting our colonies like some despot. If they can see the funds flowing back into the public good, they'll have little to shout about."

"And if you make it clear in your messaging, Braxton—frame this wealth as a tool for everyone's benefit—the people will understand that your intentions are honorable," Valentina said.

"Maybe even share some stories about the work you've done for Britain over the years, Papa," George suggested. "The public should know you didn't just inherit riches. You worked tirelessly, building connections and looking out for British interests worldwide."

"That's exactly the idea. I've done my share of racing, yes, and what-not, but I've also worked. Hard. And they should see that. Let's release photos and articles—pieces from my time abroad in Europe, Russia, Asia, all the diplomatic groundwork."

The prime minister nodded his approval. "If the public sees that Your Majesty has been serving them all along, expanding British prestige, they may think twice before they label you a profiteer. It could even be a rallying point for national pride."

King Braxton said, with a touch of determination, "That's the aim. If they still want me gone after this, I'll step down. But I won't walk away without a fight—and without showing them what the monarchy stands for."

"I think this will do more than just keep you on the throne, Papa. This could be what restores faith in the crown for good."

Valentina reached over, placing a hand on Braxton's arm. "Then let's start right away. They need to see the real Braxton—the king who works for his people."

At the king's weekly audience, the prime minister asked, "Sir, did you happen to read The Times' recent article detailing Your Majesty's thorough preparations for war during your time as prime minister and later as regent?"

Braxton shifted in his seat. "Yes, I've read it."

"It appears," the prime minister continued cautiously, "that further revelations may be forthcoming."

"Oh?" Braxton leaned forward. "What, precisely?"

The prime minister folded his hands in his lap. "Two tenacious journalists have uncovered information alleging Your Majesty's family enterprises profited from the war."

"Profited?" Incredulous, Braxton raised his voice. "We lost money—never even came close to breaking even."

"Of course, Your Majesty. I am simply relaying what I have been told."

"Thank you, Prime Minister. Please keep me informed."

The prime minister stood, preparing to leave, when Braxton asked, "Do you know who these journalists are? Their political affiliations?"

"Socialists, communists, anti-monarchists, primarily, sir."

"I see. Perhaps we should be prepared to counter this narrative. It always strikes me as odd how socialism and similar ideologies gain traction among the masses. Yet it's never the aspects of idealism these philosophies represent that thrive and endure—only the darker elements metastasize."

"As in cancer, Your Majesty?"

"Yes. It's always the idealists who first rise to power, yet inevitably, it's the power-hungry, not the true ideologues, who prevail. Take Karl Marx: there is a degree of idealism there, even a few noble ideas. Lenin, too, initially championed lofty principles. But once in power, ideals give way to ambition. In Russia, Stalin has inflicted horrors rivaling those of Ivan the Terrible or Genghis Khan."

The prime minister considered this for a moment, pensive. He cleared his throat. "Precisely, sir, how do you suggest we manage the looming strikes, sir?"

Braxton placed his hands on his lap, his gaze fixed on the patterned carpet. For a moment, he was silent, the internal conflict swirling in his mind. The prime minister was supposed to govern—his duty was to lead parliament. Yet here he was, asking for the king's guidance on governance. Yes, the king was to advise and consent, but this? He sighed quietly before responding, "I suggest Parliament establish a commission. Delay too long, and all the goodwill we've worked to build could evaporate."

The prime minister nodded. "A delay would provide fuel for every socialist paper to stoke doubt about the crown, damaging both its and the government's reputation."

"Indeed," Braxton replied. "You'll arrange for the commission, Prime Minister?"

"Yes, Your Majesty."

Braxton continued, his tone reflective. "I've spent much of my life building schools, hospitals, and countless other causes for those less fortunate. Looking back, I wonder if I was naïve. Certainly, I was young—how could I have known then what I do now? But enough of that," he said, waving a hand as if to brush the thought aside.

"Is there anything else, Your Majesty?"

"No, Prime Minister," Braxton replied, standing. "Rest assured, I'll make available all necessary military contracts and financial records to prove our family's losses on wartime supplies and weaponry."

With that, Braxton pressed a button on the nearby table. "Good day, Prime Minister."

The prime minister bowed. "Your Majesty." He stepped back, turned, and left the Audience Room.

Braxton returned to his chair, his thoughts simmering. How could this happen? I sacrificed health, time with my family and countless millions to save this nation.

Determined to tear down the monarchy, anti-monarchist journalists unleashed a barrage of salacious headlines and incendiary editorials. One radical newspaper thundered, "War lines the royal pockets while our soldiers bleed on foreign soil!" Another ran a front-page exposé claiming, "The king's advisors foresaw the conflict, yet refused to intervene—preferring the clink of coins to the cries of the dying." Sensational pamphlets, circulated in factory districts and working-class neighborhoods, railed that the crown and its government were "trading English lives for aristocratic fortunes," accusing them of orchestrating the entire war purely for profit.

These self-styled reformers spared no tactic, forging anonymous "testimonies" and doctoring official documents to stoke public outrage. Day after day, they printed new allegations with little to no supporting evidence, insisting they had "proof of collusion" between royal advisors and arms dealers. Their strident editorials challenged readers to "rise against imperial greed" and to cast off "the blood-soaked shackles of a parasitic crown." Despite denials from the palace and Parliament, the anti-monarchist press pressed on, whipping up anger and suspicion throughout the nation.

In response, the graduates of the Aurelio Palace Academy rallied. Parliament established a commission to investigate the king's actions during his years as a member of parliament and prime minister in preparation for the Great War. For three months, the commission scrutinized every accusation. Meanwhile, socialist agitators stirred anti-monarchist sentiment, bolstering unions and inciting riots in major cities.

The revelation of the royal family's private wealth brought the prestige of the crown crashing down, unleashing a wave of public outrage. Bands of agitators roamed London's streets, shattering windows, torching vehicles, and igniting chaos. The King's Guard and additional regiments were called to secure Buckingham Palace and government buildings, while the royal family, children, grandchildren, and their spouses sought refuge at Windsor Castle.

Braxton turned to Valentina. "Valentina, perhaps you should join the family at Windsor until things settle down."

She clasped his hand, her gaze firm. "I'll stay by your side for now. The guards are holding the crowds back, though the sight of smoke billowing over the city is unnerving."

Braxton exhaled. "I'm worried about your safety, my dear."

"And I yours," Valentina replied.

Braxton looked out at the bedlam below. "I can hardly believe the shouts echoing through the streets. Nothing like this since Charles I lost his head. Some of them want me dead!"

Valentina wrapped an arm around his waist, her voice a whisper. "Yes, it's terrifying. My dresser told me what she's heard from the streets. It's worse than we thought."

Braxton's jaw tightened. "Molotov cocktails were thrown through the windows at St. James Palace. We were lucky the fire was put out. Several policemen were injured—two killed near Westminster. Anger is consuming the populace."

She rested her head against him. "We'll talk in the morning," she murmured, hiding her own fear.

The next morning, Braxton and Valentina looked out from Buckingham Palace, watching a crowd swell along the half-mile Mall.

"What's that noise?" Valentina gasped. "The shouts are so loud I can't even think!"

Braxton squinted, tension lining his face. "Two guards down. Someone threw a stone!"

Shouts, jeers, projectiles hurled at guards and the sporadic crack of rifle shots filled the air, putting everyone inside Buckingham Palace on edge.

That night, at precisely eleven o'clock, a Molotov cocktail shattered the Music Room's window. Flames leaped from the broken glass, crawling up the draperies and scorching the ornate walls. Smoke billowed, blackening the marble columns as centuries of treasured compositions went up in a torrent of fire.

A maid had just stepped out of the room when the exploding glass struck her, sending her staggering into the hallway. She let out a panicked cry, "Fire! Fire! Fire!" and at once, the clang of brass bells rang through the palace corridors.

No one had retired for the night—the riot outside, fueled by pounding drums, firecrackers, and even the occasional dynamite blast, still raged. The city was in turmoil, injuries mounting and havoc spreading through its streets.

Outside, guards held their posts around the palace perimeter, watching the fires blaze.

The palace fire chief ordered the gas main shut and rallied the fire brigade and palace staff. A call was sent out to the London Fire Brigade, but the rioting crowds slowed the fire trucks, allowing the fire to spread quickly.

Flames fed on draperies, rugs, and antique furnishings; oil paintings blackened, curled, and ignited. With the fire brigade unable to penetrate the crowd, the palace staff hastily formed bucket lines.

Braxton, his heart pounding, raced up two flights of stairs to alert the servants. "Fire! Everyone out!" he called.

Members of the royal family, servants, and guards formed a makeshift bucket line, passing heavy pails of water hand to hand. Palms reddened and blistered from the relentless motion as soot and ash clung to weary faces. Then, almost as if by divine intervention, sirens wailed in the distance. Fire trucks rumbled through the gates, and rioters and onlookers scattered, clearing a path. A hush fell as hoses unleashed a powerful spray onto the raging flames.

Lightning split the sky with a deafening crack, and the heavens opened, unleashing sheets of rain that pounded the earth. A roar of relief erupted from the crowd—now hundreds strong—united in that moment of salvation.

Despite the chaos, a sense of camaraderie bound the crowd, and they drew together to renew their efforts to save Buckingham Palace. Thick smoke burned eyes and lungs, and many coughed or wiped sooty streaks across their cheeks.

Braxton felt his arms grow heavier with each pass of the bucket. Yet he refused to stop. Driven by the loyalty of the citizens, and his determination that for the future of the Empire, this palace—the home of England's rulers—must endure—he struggled on.

Valentina glanced around her, catching glimpses of weary faces illuminated by sporadic flashes of lightning. She couldn't help but see the same desperation and resolve mirrored in her own heart. Footmen and servants who'd once bowed to her now brushed against her in a chorus of frantic purpose, their usual deference replaced by urgency and sweat.

Now and then, someone would pause, trembling from exhaustion or stifling a sob at the sight of the palace's gilded halls consumed by flames. Another helper would nudge them gently to keep going. A guard, tears welling in his eyes, thought of the countless nights he'd patrolled these corridors, never imagining he'd one day fight for them in such an unrelenting way. Still, bucket after bucket made its way down the line, each individual gritting their teeth against the sting of heat and the soaking rain, each one clinging to the belief their efforts mattered.

Buckets passed from hand to hand, while lightning cut across the sky. By 3:00 a.m. the flames had been doused, leaving only embers. Parts of the palace lay in ruin—blackened walls and once-grand rooms reduced to charred remains.

The storm quieted. A palace guard captain suggested the king and queen withdraw. Braxton shook his head. "Absolutely not! Get these people in out of the rain, first."

Weary men, women, and children filtered through the charred hallways; their sodden shoes muffled on blackened floors. The crowd filed into the palace's ballroom, untouched by fire or rain. Palace staff offered blankets and steaming refreshments. Grand hearths crackled back to life, bringing welcome relief from the cold. Braxton and Valentina moved among them, pausing to thank each exhausted face for their tireless effort, their voices filled with gratitude despite the weight of the devastation around them. Each gesture of thanks seemed small compared to the monumental task ahead, but still, they offered it, knowing that even in the ruins, every ounce of aid had tremendous value.

After everyone had settled, Braxton stepped onto the dais, his voice carrying over the crowd. "Who wants to sit on these grand chairs?" he asked with a laugh, gesturing to the royal thrones.

A cheer erupted from the crowd, and a small boy raised his hand, shouting, "Me! I do!" Braxton laughed, motioned him forward, and, with a theatrical flourish, hoisted him onto his throne. Laughter bubbled up around the room as more children—along with a few daring adults—lined up for their turn, the atmosphere lightening in an infectious wave of joy and raucous laughter. The room was alive with a sense of shared mirth, every giggle and playful shove adding to the growing sense of community and camaraderie.

An hour passed, and finally, Braxton sat down, gesturing for quiet.

"Tonight, has been the most eventful I've experienced in years. I owe all of you a great debt. Thank you for helping save our home."

The crowd quieted.

"But I know why you're here," he continued. "This fire brought you to the palace, but something else led you into the streets. It saddens me that you're upset with the crown. I am the crown, and I take that personally. As your king, I owe you an explanation. I never thought I would wear the crown. I was a third son, and I pursued business, thinking I'd always remain a private citizen. But fate had other plans."

Braxton took Valentina's hand. "Through my life, I've worked for my success. I took what advantages I had and built something with them. But I never stopped working. And yes, we've become wealthy. But we haven't done anything wrong. We've worked hard, and we've sacrificed."

He paused, his voice heavy with the weight of his words. "You may not know this, but my family has paid an unbearable price. My sister, Carmen, narrowly escaped assassination in Russia. My brother, Dominic, your late king—he and his wife, along with their daughter, died in unfathomable sorrow. And my brother, John, gave his life in the Great War, sacrificing himself to save his men. And now, here I am, standing before you—doing my very best to serve you as your king."

A murmur rippled through the crowd as he continued.

"Tomorrow, I'll show you records. You'll see that my companies never profited from war or took advantage of government contracts. I've given millions to hospitals and schools. I've never taken a penny from the government—not as envoy, not as a member of parliament, not as prime minister, and not as your king. My family maintains the palaces at our own expense. We don't ask the people to provide financial support."

Quiet murmurs grew as his words sank in.

"I know you see us as wealthy—and we are. But that wealth has come through hard work, wise investment and giving back. That's why we're sharing this with you now. Tomorrow, we'll rebuild this palace together. And soon, we'll face challenges across the channel. I hope we can face them united."

The room stood silent until one voice called out, "God Save the King!" and others joined in, repeating it until the ballroom echoed with the sound.

A journalist, present in the ballroom, meticulously transcribed the entire impromptu speech. The early afternoon edition of the London Times reported the events of the previous evening, including the speech, word for word.

CHAPTER TWENTY-NINE

VINDICATION

The day came for the prime minister to address parliament. Standing at the dispatch box, he began, "Mr. Speaker, esteemed colleagues, the commission charged with investigating the actions of the crown and government in the lead-up to the Great War has now delivered its conclusions."

A hush fell over the chamber. "Allow me to outline the findings…" The prime minister detailed each accusation, finally concluding, "In summary, His Majesty personally incurred a loss of £75 million in preparing for the war." He paused, then raised his voice: "Long Live the King!"

Newspapers responded with triumphant headlines:

KING'S ACCUSERS DEFEATED UNDER SCRUTINY

HONOR RESTORED: CROWN VINDICATED

EMPIRE RELIEVED: SOCIALISTS REBUKED

ANTI-MONARCHISTS FORCED UNDERGROUND

In the wake of the announcement, public sentiment swung against the king's critics. Anti-monarchists faced fierce condemnation, with several socialist shops attacked and isolated cases of individuals tarred and feathered in vigilante acts. Those who had raised accusations quickly retreated from public view.

Meanwhile, Valentina continued to assist Braxton with his daily "boxes," while overseeing the family business tasks taken on by Prince George's siblings. As the younger generation assumed more roles within the family enterprise, rumors about the royal family's extensive financial interests continued to swirl.

Setting down her newspaper, Valentina remarked, "The Fascists are wreaking havoc in Germany and Italy."

Braxton nodded, his expression weighted with concern. "It's worse than I thought." For years, he had tracked incoming intelligence through the Chiacontella banking network, as well as his clandestine "Mars" organization—quietly funded since Carnivale in Italy in 1880.

The government, increasingly reliant on Braxton's intelligence, began to show signs of unease over the crown's influence. Frustrated by constant inquiries into his sources, Braxton responded firmly to the prime minister.

"Minister, your demand for my private intelligence is not only offensive, it's short-sighted," Braxton said. "I've long gathered intelligence for myself, for my businesses, and often for the good of this government. You may recall it was my sources that provided critical information during the Great War, saving thousands of lives.

Now, as we approach yet another conflict, you would risk dismantling those sources?"

The prime minister stammered, "But, Your Majesty, surely the government has both the need and the right to this information."

"No, Prime Minister, you are mistaken," Braxton replied. "This information is mine. Complying with your request would potentially compromise valuable sources, not only for me but for the nation. Threaten that, and I will dissolve parliament and appeal directly to the people."

The minister faltered. "That would be…constitutionally precarious."

"We shall see," Braxton answered evenly. "Let me be clear: any action that jeopardizes these resources will prompt me to dissolve parliament."

The matter was never raised again.

Global tensions rose; figures such as Hitler and Mussolini brought Europe to the brink. The atmosphere echoed the unrest of 1912, now reignited nearly 20 years later.

CHAPTER THIRTY

ROYAL CARNAGE

The opening of parliament in 1939 was heralded as a grand exhibition of the enduring might, authority, and historical legacy of the British Empire spanning centuries.

Traditionally, the monarch, accompanied by their consort, proceeded from Buckingham Palace to the Palace of Westminster in the Coach of State. The coach is a fairy tale-inspired, extravagantly gilded carriage drawn by six horses, attended by footmen and two coachmen.

The Royal Guard and Imperial Regiment escort the coach on horseback. It is a momentous pageant displaying all the pennants and standards associated with the monarch.

On this occasion, Braxton wore the Imperial State Crown and Valentina wore the Queen's State Crown. They were clothed in coronation robes, each one resplendent with the full array of honors.

Police and security lined the route, containing the immense, enthusiastic crowds. A thunderous roar greeted Their Majesties, as the people pinned their hopes and dreams on the king and queen, convinced they alone could shield them from the looming specter of war.

Both Braxton and Valentina discreetly held one another's hands and marveled at the love and enthusiasm emanating from the crowd. As they rounded the last turn approaching Westminster Palace, Valentina squeezed Braxton's hand. He glanced toward her and found love, assurance, bravery, and peace reflected in her gaze.

A blinding light erupted followed by an ear-splitting explosion, turning the majestic carriage into a whirlwind of splintered wood, twisted gold, and shreds of flesh. Shards of glass and metal sprayed outward, a storm of razors tearing through the air in a lethal frenzy. The explosion ripped the horses to pieces, their bodies sent sprawling, fragments of bone and muscle scattering across the street.

The blast ripped through the carriage, the once-elegant vehicle obliterated as coachmen were hurled backward, limbs and bodies torn as they crashed through the shattered partition. Queen Valentina, crushed beneath the collapsing carriage and the weight of debris, lay pinned, her life extinguished under the merciless rubble.

The king was flung from the wreckage, his body landing on the unforgiving pavement with a sickening thud. Footmen riding on the back of the coach, caught in the explosion's blast, morphed into ghastly missiles, flung into the crowd, striking spectators with grotesque force. The street transformed into carnage; bodies strewn like broken dolls, mingled with the anguished cries of the wounded.

The twisted carriage remains crashed backward, slamming into the mounted guards. The scene an apocalyptic tableau of shattered bodies, splattered blood, and billowing smoke—a grotesque monument to the devastation of the moment.

The motionless king lay sprawled on the blood-smeared pavement covered in debris. Slowly, acrid smoke dispersed, revealing a scene of unspeakable horror. Amidst the cacophony of screams, agony, and panic, blood from the mangled bodies of both animals and men formed a gruesome tapestry, drenching the ground, splattering horrified onlookers and weaving rivulets of crimson blood in every direction.

Amid the smoldering wreckage, staggering through the devastation, police officers found King Braxton. Clad in tattered coronation robes, his figure seemed to loom larger than life, as if conjured from some grim, epic legend—an image of ruined majesty cast across a landscape of death and despair.

Around him, the air pulsed with the agony of the injured: cries from battered bystanders, wounded soldiers, and bloodied cavalrymen mixed with the tortured screams of dying horses, creating a chilling symphony of suffering.

Sirens sliced through the chaos, growing louder as emergency vehicles fought their way through the choking smoke and wreckage, while police and soldiers scrambled to direct medics to the fallen.

An ambulance, encircled by a platoon of soldiers, cautiously navigated through the scene of devastation, eventually halting beside the fallen king. The soldiers erected a protective barrier around the king and the medical personnel attending him. The king was transferred to a stretcher. Four medics clad in stark white uniforms bore the weight of the injured king, bearing him solemnly across the brief expanse to Westminster Palace.

Rumors spread of Braxton's survival in critical condition, making him the focus of deep, widespread concern.

Despite a lack of visible broken bones or apparent damage to his head and extremities, Braxton remained unconscious, his breathing shallow and his complexion resembled that of a lifeless figure. He lay motionless, offering no signs of life other than the faint rise and fall of his breath.

In the gravity of the situation, the Archbishop of Canterbury was summoned to administer last rites, an ominous presence adding to the tense atmosphere.

Prince George was absent from London when news of the assassination attempts on his parents reached him in Scotland. Swiftly mobilizing, the military provided a plane for his transport to the capital. By evening, radio broadcasts and newspaper headlines blared the shocking news:

QUEEN VALENTINA KILLED! KING BRAXTON ON DEATHBED!

ROYALS SLAUGHTERED!

KING AT DEATH'S DOOR!

HRH QUEEN VALENTINA ASSASSINATED!

The prime minister declared a State of Emergency and imposed martial law, placing the entirety of London under a strict 24-hour curfew. Police conducted thorough searches, combing the streets, buildings, sewers, and subways within a mile radius of the incident.

Prince George asked the prime minister to order the shutdown of trains and aircraft, forbidding ships from leaving their docks. London was shuttered—no buses, taxis, or subway cars moved. Businesses and schools closed, sheltering employees and students in place.

Addressing the nation via radio from Scotland before his departure for London, Prince George delivered somber news of his mother's assassination and provided an update on the king's condition:

"In the wake of the recent tragic events, I stand before you to implore your assistance in our collective pursuit of justice and resolution. It is imperative for each and every one of us lend our utmost cooperation to the authorities.

"I urge you try and recall anything that could remotely have bearing on today's events, both before and after the explosion. And to promptly report any suspicions or pertinent information to Scotland Yard. Our combined vigilance and diligence are indispensable in uncovering the truth behind this heinous act.

"Courage, patience, and unity are the virtues upon which we must now rely. Together, we bear a solemn responsibility to aid in the apprehension of those responsible for this treasonous and murderous deed. Let us not falter in our resolve to seek justice for the innocent lives lost.

"Rest assured, my fellow citizens, that I shall soon join you in London. I pledge to provide continuous updates and support throughout this trying time. With unwavering determination, let us unite under the timeless refrain, God Save the King! Thank you, and may we find solace and strength in our collective resolve."

The resounding chorus of "God Save the King" was played on the radio and soon singing voices of those listening to the broadcast joined in echoing across London, the British Isles, the Commonwealth, and beyond.

Six hours later, the prince arrived at Harmondsworth Aerodrome in London, greeted by the remnants of the Royal Guard and several Scotland Yard officials. Escorted through deserted streets, he reached Westminster Palace. Confronted with his father's frail form in the infirmary, the prince staggered, momentarily losing his strength until his adjutant braced him. Steadying himself, he approached his father, whose aged appearance bore grim witness to the toll of the tragedy. "Doctor, how serious are his injuries?" Prince George asked, his voice tense.

The lead physician, replied, "Your Royal Highness, we're still assessing. Remarkably, there are no visible fractures. Externally, he presents with abrasions, contusions, and likely multiple soft tissue injuries. His Majesty is in a state of profound shock, complicating prognosticating internal trauma. We're particularly concerned about possible internal hemorrhaging and cranial trauma."

"What measures are you taking?"

"We've initiated triage procedures to stabilize him. His head is being cooled to reduce any risk of cerebral swelling, though we can't yet confirm if there's intracranial bleeding. Intravenous fluids are being administered to counter shock, and we're monitoring his blood pressure and respiratory patterns. We're prepared for any surgical intervention should abdominal or thoracic injuries be present."

"And signs of paralysis?"

"As of now, we detect no motor impairment. His reflexes are responsive, which is promising, but only time will reveal the full extent of any neurological effects."

"Thank you, doctor. Keep me updated on any changes."

The doctor nodded, a respectful determination in his gaze. "Of course, Your Royal Highness. We'll do everything possible for His Majesty."

"Again, thank you. My family and I appreciate all you are doing. "When do you anticipate he might be stable enough to move to the palace?"

The physician shook his head. "Moving him at this stage would be ill-advised, Your Royal Highness. Without a full assessment of his internal injuries, any transfer poses significant risk. We need to monitor him closely here until we are certain of his stability."

Prince George nodded, digesting the weight of the words. "I understand."

He paused, then quietly asked, "Where…where have they taken my mother?"

The prime minister, standing nearby, stepped forward. "Her Majesty's body has been moved to Buckingham Palace, Sir."

A shadow passed over the prince's face. "Understood," he replied, his tone subdued. He turned back to the prime minister. "Prime Minister, I intend to address the Empire on the current situation. Arrange a radio broadcast for me at the soonest possible moment."

The prime minister inclined his head. "At once, Your Royal Highness."

Within half an hour, Prince George addressed the nation.

"My dear friends, loyal subjects of the Empire, and members of our world community.

"I have just returned from my father's side at the infirmary in Westminster Palace. I have seen His Majesty, your king. He lives, though he is gravely injured.

"I earnestly ask you to join me in prayer for his recovery. By some miracle, he bears no visible wounds, yet his internal condition remains uncertain. I vow to keep you informed regularly and with utmost honesty about his progress. I urge you to hold him in your hearts, alongside our Empire and the soul of your beloved queen.

"Today, many have suffered great losses. My heart, and the hearts of my family, are heavy with sorrow for those who have given their lives or suffered in service to the crown. We stand with you in this pain, our tears falling with yours, and our love and gratitude toward you unwavering.

"God bless you all. God Save the King!"

Over the next 12 hours, the desolate streets of London remained eerily still, shrouded in a dense atmosphere of whispered conspiracies that turned the once bustling metropolis into a haunting enclave of the sinister.

Scotland Yard found itself inundated with a deluge of clues and conjectures of potential leads, paralyzing any effort that might focus on solving the crime. Amid the chaos, the Yard meticulously sifted through the myriad calls, homing in on the intricate web of activities surrounding the site of the horrifying explosion.

The first glimmer of hope emerged from Dover, where the activities of a private transport surfaced with a tale of a suspicious cargo that had clandestinely arrived earlier in the week from an undisclosed port. The ship's captain had dutifully reported the dubious cargo to the local military office. In an era overshadowed by an impending war and heightened security measures, incoming transports underwent rigorous inspections. Crews were instructed to report any semblance of suspicious cargo. The captain, in his detailed statement, described the crate.

A detective asked, "So, tell me, captain, what caused you to report the shipment?"

"Aye, been out at sea for about a month, I reckon. My missus has been bawling for my return. Her birthday came and went four days back, so I was in a right hurry to make the homeward stretch. But the blooming harbor master starts yapping about dodgy cargo. So I spill the beans, spill them good, and then I high-tail it home, sharpish-like."

"Captain, would you please recount what you told the harbor master?"

"Well, that crate—it wasn't English craft. Not French either. It was proper rough, mate. Not put together well, like something out of Romania or near Russia or Poland, you know? And the letters on it— pure bonkers. I hadn't a clue what they meant. Definitely not English, that's for certain."

By the time the Scotland Yard Inspector arrived, the crate had vanished into the shadows, whisked away in a discreet private conveyance. A dead end.

A second vital clue surfaced at a motor vehicle repair garage. The owner reported that two of his mechanics had recently repaired a medium-sized lorry that had broken an axle on a road between Dover and London. Its cargo had to be unloaded for repair. The garage owner described a large crate similar to the one reported by the captain in Dover. This crate also bore foreign markings.

"Mr. Scoggins," the Scotland Yard detective inquired, "when did you repair the vehicle?"

"That would be about three days past, detective, Sir."

The pieces of the puzzle converged, weaving a tale of covert movements and concealed plots, leaving Scotland Yard to untangle the intricate threads of the unfolding mystery.

Scores of members, peers, staff, and visiting families, eager to witness the opening of parliament and glimpse the king and queen, found themselves marooned in Westminster Palace. The younger children, cooped up in the muggy government edifice, sought merriment by embarking on grand adventures, delving into every conceivable corner and crevice of the expansive complex. The linked buildings offered a plethora of opportunities for exploration.

Thirty-six hours passed. A multitude of public edifices, shops, schools, hospitals, and places where people had been engaged in their daily affairs prior to the lockdown found themselves in a state of limbo. Supplies dwindled, and a sense of scarcity loomed. People, understandably restless from confinement, sought diversion; they explored and invented ways to amuse themselves.

"This is the BBC, bringing you news and stories from across the nation. Good evening, listeners. We begin tonight's broadcast with an update on the condition of His Majesty, the King. While he remains in a delicate state, doctors report his resilience is showing. His Majesty has, against all odds, stabilized since the tragic events of the last few days. Though he has not yet regained consciousness, his vital signs remain steady, and we are told his doctors remain hopeful. The royal family and medical team ask for the continued prayers of the nation as the King rests and recovers.

"Tonight, we are adapting our program to bring the people of London—and all those still confined wherever they were when Their Majesties were attacked—closer together. We hope that sharing stories of how our fellow citizens are managing and what is happening in our streets and beyond will bring you comfort and a sense of strength.

"Now, dear listeners, let us share with you some of what we know.

"The curfew over London and surrounding areas holds firm, bringing a strange rhythm to the city's days and nights. Police and military patrols are a common sight, marching past shuttered shops and empty streets to ensure the curfew remains unbroken.

"For the most part, the public has shown remarkable patience, staying indoors as requested while life is put on pause. In households across the city, neighbors and families are learning how to live in close quarters, many spending time by the wireless, sharing stories, games, and even revisiting old tales of Britain's resilience. Curiosity, and perhaps a touch of cabin fever, have led to colorful speculations about who might be responsible for the tragic events that have struck the very heart of our royal family.

"But of course, there are those more daring—or some might say restless—souls who have ventured outdoors despite the restrictions. While the odd defiant wanderer may have thought twice about breaking curfew after finding themselves directed to a local police station, others have been less fortunate, and these stations have filled beyond capacity. For such cases, Whittington Barracks, Victoria Barracks, and even the Royal Artillery Barracks have stepped in to house those brave but misguided enough to breach the curfew.

"Our servicemen and women have not left the public wanting for supplies. The military has been swift and effective in distributing rations, ensuring that our city's residents are fed, even if confined. And among this makeshift routine, a peculiar spirit has begun to emerge—one of support and resolve. Families gather around the radio, sharing wild theories about the king's condition and the loss of our beloved queen.

"Some of the stories circulating on the airwaves have stretched the bounds of credulity. Radio stations, it seems, are now in something of a contest to capture the most attention with ever-more speculative narratives about how such an attack could have unfolded. But if there's one thing this trial has revealed, it is that the people of Britain will stand together, resilient and resolute, even in moments of tragedy and inconvenience. As one listener called in to us earlier today, 'We are undaunted; we are together; we are patient.'

"This is the BBC, keeping you company through these quiet days and asking you to stay safe, stay indoors, and remember: we are all in this together. God Save the King."

King Braxton lingered in the Westminster Palace infirmary, attended by doctors and specialists flown in from Switzerland and America. His presence was marked by stillness, with barely audible breaths serving as the only sign of life.

No new credible information had reached Scotland Yard since the report regarding the repair of the truck. The prime minister and Prince

George, along with Scotland Yard, were desperate for leads. They could not continue to hold the people "hostage" much longer.

"Good evening, listeners. This is the BBC.

"Tonight, we bring you a special broadcast from His Royal Highness, Prince George, the Prince of Wales. The prince will address us directly, sharing an important message with the people of Britain. In these challenging times, our collective efforts and steadfast support are more crucial than ever. His Royal Highness now calls upon each of us to aid in the search for justice.

And now, listeners, His Royal Highness, The Prince of Wales."

"My dear people of Britain, I want to begin by offering my deepest gratitude to all of you for your prayers, your support, and your unwavering concern for my father, the king, and for our family during this difficult time. The strength and kindness of the British people has been a great comfort to us, and I cannot overstate how much it means.

"But tonight, I must turn to you once more, in earnest, for your help. As we work to identify those responsible for this terrible attack, we need your assistance in gathering vital information. To that end, the government has decided to share some important details with you so that we might uncover the truth together.

"Here is what we have learned: in Dover, a suspicious crate bearing foreign markings was loaded onto a dark, ruddy green lorry, featuring a boxy cab, tall wooden sideboards, and a heavy-duty, open cargo bed. The vehicle broke down and was subsequently repaired. The crate itself was large and unfamiliar, accompanied by three individuals who may hold the answers to the questions we now face.

"Consider what you have just learned. Reflect deeply. Search your memories and inspect the locations where you find yourselves now. It could be that someone has seen something, or that even the smallest detail might shed light on this heinous attack. Any information you have—no matter how small—should be reported directly to Scotland Yard.

"In times like these, our strength lies in our unity, in the dedication we show to protect one another and our empire. I ask that we stand together now, with courage, vigilance, and unwavering resolve. 'God Save the King.'"

In the hours following the radio broadcast, the Yard persisted in meticulously scrutinizing the wreckage at the explosion site. Investigators assembled the puzzle pieces. Remains lay strewn about—both animal and human—succumbing to decomposition. Fragments of fabric, wood, metal and leather, ranging from large pieces to those smaller than a coin, littered the pavement. The air harbored putrid decay.

Resolute, the tireless investigative teams sifted through the debris, working around the clock. Frustrated and hard-pressed, they considered closing down the site. Then, by chance, they discovered fragments resembling a projectile casing.

This unexpected discovery left Yard detectives and military inspectors baffled, forcing them to question their initial assumptions about the explosion. They began to suspect it wasn't merely a simple bomb, prompting a complete reevaluation of the catastrophic event.

Intrepid aristocratic youngsters, confined to Westminster Palace, organized a game they dubbed, "Find the Clues."

Their exploration led them to a musty, vacant room where they discovered a large map of England hanging on a wall. Curiosity drove one enterprising soul to look behind the map and uncover a large chalkboard. The older boys and girls swiftly compiled a roster of potential clues that might unravel the mystery: guns, rifles, bombs, clothing, maps, daggers and more.

The brainstorming continued haphazardly.

A five-year-old girl chimed in, "What about the lorry? Isn't that a clue? The prince said there was a lorry. I heard him!"

A hush fell over the room.

An older boy retorted, "Do you see any lorries around here?"

Undeterred, the youngster stuck out her chin. "No, but we haven't looked for one!"

Murmurs and snickers rippled through the group.

A 12-year-old girl having stood patiently listening and assessing the situation, shouted, "Alright, everyone, listen up!" a grin spreading across her face. "We've got a list of clues and a whole palace to explore! So, here's the plan: Spread out, keep your eyes sharp, and don't come back until you've uncovered something fantastic! This is our adventure—let's make it count!"

She raised her fist in the air, rallying the younger children. "Together, we're going to solve this mystery! Now, off you go—go find those clues!"

And so, the game was afoot. Laughter and shouts filled the air as the children, energized, dashed out of the room, venturing to the far corners of the Westminster Palace complex.

Oblivious to any potential danger, their parents—engrossed in social and political circles—were pleased to see their little ones happily engaged in their search for clues.

A group of four boys gazed over at the towering structure before them, its shadow stretching long and ominous in the fading light. Big Ben loomed overhead, magnificent and mysterious, its ancient stonework seeming to whisper secrets hidden for centuries. The boys had always been drawn to this grand clock, its presence both comforting and intimidating. Standing on the rooftop of an adjoining building, with the promise of discovery ahead, their excitement mingled with a hint of awe.

Descending from the vantage point where they had first spotted Big Ben, they wound through the palace's dim corridors toward the base of the tower. As twilight settled, eerie shadows played upon the ancient stones, sapping their initial enthusiasm and replacing it with a cautious trepidation. Each footstep echoed ominously, as if unseen perils hovered. Yet they pressed on, driven by a quiet resolve to discover whatever secrets awaited them in the gathering dark.

Upon reaching the entrance, their excitement turned to dismay. The door was tightly locked-up, seemingly impenetrable. A hefty steel bar spanned the double-wide, twelve-foot-high wooden door, secured by massive padlocks fastened to the stone wall.

Their hopes dashed; their imaginations flourished. One of the boys shuddered, "I reckon there's a monster in there."

A younger, wide-eyed boy inquired, "Why do you think that?"

The older boy pointed out, "Look there," he whispered, wide-eyed. "It's like something's tried to push its way out. See how the wood's starting to splinter, bulge?"

Another boy exclaimed, "Look, one of the hinges is damaged—like it's going to break off!"

With that revelation, the four boys screamed in terror and bolted as fast as their legs would carry them back towards the safety of their parents.

At the same time the boys had laid siege to Big Ben, a spirited group of six pre-teen girls made their way towards the utility garages next to the palace. Their enthusiastic leader, weaving tales of the adventure inspired by Prince George's words, convinced them that discovering this elusive vehicle would surely secure them an invitation to the next royal ball. The prospect thrilled the girls. Thoughts of Cinderella and Prince Charming danced through their heads as they skipped, laughed, and shared their ideas of an ideal prince with one another.

The grandeur of the palace gave way to dingy utility spaces—a sobering transition as they entered the realm of those responsible for maintaining the palace. The surroundings were bare and utilitarian. With evening descending, most of the staff had left for the day, seeking a place of rest for the night.

The girls explored the expansive facility, passing through kitchens, storage areas, and boiler rooms, encountering the massive, indescribable machinery that serviced the palace.

On the brink of giving up, one of the girls spotted what looked like garage doors through a window. "Come over here and see what I see!"

They huddled together, excitement mounting in the way only a group of giggling friends can experience. With infectious glee, they let out a collective shriek of delight, their laughter echoing through the air. The girls surged forward, bursting through an adjacent door, and dashed across the stone courtyard toward the garage.

By now, these young ladies, adorned in their elegant attire, had accumulated the grime and dirt resident in maintenance shops. Engrossed in their adventure, they were oblivious to their disheveled appearance, and even if they had noticed, they cast it aside, fully absorbed in their mission.

The group of young girls huddled together in front of the massive garage door, their eyes bright with excitement. Their leader placed her hands on the rough wood and turned to her friends. "Alright, everyone, shoulder to the door! On three…ready?"

The girls lined up beside her, pressing their small shoulders against the weathered wood, giggling nervously. On the count of three they pushed together. The door didn't move.

A couple of them winced, one rubbing her shoulder. "This door's solid as a rock," muttered one girl, grimacing. "My shoulder's already sore!"

"Mine too!" another chimed in, shaking out her arm.

"Come on! We can't let a door get the best of us!" the leader urged, undeterred. She raised her hand. "One…two…three!"

They all braced their aching shoulders once more, pressing harder than before, their faces scrunched in concentration. The door didn't budge.

"Again!" the leader commanded, breathless but smiling.

"I think I'll lose my shoulder for real this time," a younger girl groaned.

A smaller girl beside her, fists clenched, added, "We're not giving up now!"

"Push harder, girls! Imagine we're storming a castle!" their leader encouraged, her voice rising with excitement. With a shout, they hurled themselves against the door one last time. The wood groaned, finally relenting, a deep, satisfying creak that sent a thrill through them all. And then, with a sudden jolt, it gave way, swinging open in a dramatic crash.

The girls careened forward in a chaotic whirl of limbs, falling into a gaping maw of darkness, their bodies landing on the unforgiving concrete floor.

As if possessed by a malevolent spirit, the door they had triumphantly breached moments before seemed to taunt them, its ancient hinges emitting sinister creaks and groans as it slammed shut with a resounding thud.

Sprawled across the cold, grimy floor, the stunned damsels found themselves enveloped in a void of utter blackness.

CHAPTER THIRTY-ONE

WHODUNNIT?

One of the girls yelped, "Ow, that hurt. I think I might have—"

"My mama is going to be very upset with what I have done to this dress," another harrumphed.

"I'm scared," one whimpered.

"There has to be a light switch somewhere," another whined.

The older girl barked, "Everyone stay still. It is too dark to move around. Is everyone alright, anyone hurt?"

"I can't find my shoe."

"I think it landed on me," a voice in the darkness said, with a half-hearted giggle.

One of the more resourceful young ladies stood and shuffled in the direction of where she hoped they had entered, her hands outstretched in search of an exit.

Her fingers brushed against the cool surface of the wall, feeling for the familiar contours of a doorknob. But found something quite different. She had discovered a sizable lever. With a surge of daring, she pulled down with all her might.

In an instant, overhead lights sputtered on and illuminated a garage. The vast space extended as far as her eyes could see, filled with boxes, vehicles, and equipment.

The luminescence also revealed the raucous sight of the girls flung across the floor, their dresses billowing around them like colorful sails caught in a tempest. Limbs tangled and skirts askew, they lay sprawled across the unforgiving concrete, a tapestry of disarray amidst the dreary garage's background.

The girls blinked in the sudden light, glancing around with wide eyes. They could now see a towering stack of crates in one corner and dusty tools strewn across a workbench.

"This is not fun anymore. I want to go back to my mama," a dazed girl lamented.

The older one retorted, vigorously attempting to brush the accumulated dust and grit from her dress, "Stop it! Collect yourself. We did not come here to act like a bunch of silly ninnies!"

The girls glanced around, a few chuckles escaping as they took stock of the chaotic scene they now found themselves in. Most were wrestling to regain composure, hastily straightening their clothes and attempting to tame their hair with fingers stained by the grime of the garage floor.

Soon, all now standing and bedraggled, they drew close to one another, peering into the vast, densely packed garage.

"There must be thousands of crates and things in here!" exclaimed one girl.

"Not likely, but indeed, many," the older girl agreed.

One girl asked, "Ladies, remember what His Royal Highness said on the wireless about the lorry?"

Anticipation buzzed among the young girls, their eyes wide with excitement and curiosity. Some whispered excitedly to each other. Fingers tapped nervously against thighs, and smiles tugged at the corners of their lips as they imagined the sought-after lorry hidden just beyond their grasp. Each breath hummed with the thrill of possibility, filling the air with an electric energy that sparked with every thought racing closer to the prize they hoped to uncover.

"It's here! I know it! Let's find it!" An excited girl squealed.

"Let us go two-by-two and see what we can find," the older girl said.

The girls counted off by twos, paired off, and set out scouring the garage, their chatter echoing throughout the huge facility.

Excitement soon waned as the search yielded nothing resembling the vehicle the prince had described.

Disheartened, their vigor diminished, they began to regroup, heads hung low.

They glanced around, frustrated that the elusive lorry was nowhere to be found. The younger girls, their shoulders sagging, exchanged worried looks. One of them tugged on her companion's sleeve, voice quavering. "Can we go back now? I just want to see my parents." A collective sigh followed—exhaustion and disappointment settling over the group like a heavy cloak.

"Come here! We found something!" a voice called from the far reaches of the garage.

The harried girls hurried toward the beckoning voice, tripping over each other, one or two of them skinning their knees along the way.

Unconcerned about their torn dresses and ruined shoes, they reached two of their friends standing in front of a vehicle covered in tarps.

The shrouded vehicle loomed ominously, its bulk obscuring any hint of its true form. It faced a double garage door like a silent guardian of secrets. Underneath the tarp, its contours hinted at unfathomable size and mystery, stirring the imagination of the girls gathered around it. Could it possibly be the lorry they sought?

Its wheels were partially revealed from under the draping canvas.

Counting the wheels, the girls confirmed six, just as the prince had described. Four of the girls pulled on the canvas, revealing the vehicle's ruddy green color they had been seeking.

The youngest among them curiously asked her sister why one of the tires seemed "nicer" than the others.

One of the young ladies, realizing that this was very likely the sought-after truck, could not contain her excitement and peed her pants.

The girls erupted into a frenzy of jumping up and down, screaming, "We found it! We found it!"

Then, as suddenly as they had erupted, they fell silent, stared at one another in disbelief and in unison turned and ran pal mal, squealing and laughing, exiting the garage.

Their sprint through the maintenance areas, kitchens, and long passageways leading to the public rooms resembled a chaotic ballet, with occasional collisions and shrieks.

Meanwhile, the boys entered at full tilt from the opposite end as the girls careened into the hall.

The children, both boys and girls. raced toward the grand palace's central lobby, arms flailing and voices rising in unison. Their parents, pulled abruptly from their own activities, looked on in astonishment. The girls, disheveled and looking like angels having tumbled into a grease pit, stood before them, their messy appearance deeply unsettling.

The boys, with their vigorous tugging and uproarious shouting, dominated the room, creating such a clamor that it took several minutes for parents to restore order to the chaotic gathering.

Outside on Parliament Street, investigators pressed on, determined to piece together the puzzle amid a grim scene of scattered debris, mangled human bodies and horses, and the shattered remnants of the carriage.

The prime minister stood next to where the king had lain, listening to the Scotland Yard Commissioner. "Based on the evidence we have gathered, we've dismissed the possibility of a bomb causing the blast. Instead, the Yard's detectives lean towards the theory of a projectile-like device being the culprit. Our attention has pivoted towards uncovering the source of the projectile. We are currently modeling possible trajectories."

Shaking his head, the prime minister asked, "How long do you think it will take? The circumstances are extraordinary and baffling. How could such an event have transpired?"

"It is hard to say, sir. What makes it so perplexing is police were stationed on rooftops, closely monitoring the buildings along the procession route, making it improbable for a projectile to be launched unnoticed. Furthermore, all the buildings had been thoroughly inspected and secured earlier in the morning," the commissioner said.

A man rushed towards the prime minister and the commissioner. "Come quickly; the lorry has been found! We believe the assassins are trapped in the Clock Tower!"

In short order, the police had Big Ben surrounded: its tower's lone entrance, standing open, its padlocks having been removed. Inside, a squad stood guard, ready to secure the premises.

The policemen launched their ascent up the tower's 334 steps with grim determination, the echo of their boots pounding like war drums against the stone walls. The stairwell echoed with the fierce rhythm of their march, every step sending up a challenge to whatever—or whoever—lay ahead.

Suddenly, a single gunshot ripped through the air. Instinctively, the men pressed themselves against the walls, seeking cover behind any scrap of stone they could find. The silence that followed felt thick, suffocating, as though the tower itself were daring them to continue.

Without a sound, the police regrouped and crept forward, weapons at the ready, senses straining to detect the next ambush. Their once-steady climb had transformed into a desperate siege, every step a nerve-wracking gamble as they advanced up the stairwell in tense, measured bursts. Each landing a potential battleground, every shadow an ominous threat.

They pushed onward, each man's pulse pounding as fiercely as his footsteps, their movements taut with the readiness to fight, the stairwell above them no longer just a route, but a gauntlet.

They moved on, inching their way up the winding stairwell. The silence broken again by another crack—a second gunshot ricocheting down the stone walls. They flattened themselves against the cold rock, searching desperately for cover in the narrow confines. Heartbeats thundered as they scanned for the source, guns poised, breaths held.

The men continued for what seemed an eternity, creeping upward with the same fierce resolve. They hadn't climbed ten more stairs before another shot rang out, closer this time The sharp echo seemed to slice through the air. They dropped to a crouch, pressing themselves into crevices and alcoves in the stone, weapons raised, eyes darting.

Every step was a fresh ordeal as they moved in staggered bursts, one policeman covering another. Shadows pulsed with danger; every corner held the possibility of an ambush. They continued their advance, bodies coiled tight, the sounds of gunfire spurring them onward, committed to reaching the summit, whatever the cost.

When they reached the clock level, they were met with a grim scene. Two men lay sprawled on the ground, their bodies gruesomely mangled, possibly from a weapon malfunction. This malfunction might explain why the projectile may have fallen short of its target. Nearby, a third man sat slumped in a corner, weapon still in hand, the back of his head blown apart, suggesting a desperate, final act.

Scotland Yard investigators, summoned to the scene, examined the damaged weapon with a mix of fascination and concern. The weapon bore a resemblance to an American Bazooka, yet it was larger and appeared even more powerful. Army weapons experts identified it as a possible German prototype, potentially designed to destroy tanks.

Detectives pieced together the evidence. They found a maintenance panel on the clock face left ajar. They deduced that the panel had been opened during the royal procession, allowing the assailants to fire the weapon. It seemed likely that the lone survivor had not fully secured the clock face's utility window after the weapon had fired.

Further investigation led detectives to believe the three men had entered the tower the previous night, hiding until the attack. Among the evidence scattered around were cigarette butts and a matchbox labeled in German, along with a scrap of paper bearing faint foreign writing. The men carried no official identification but had German, English, and Belgian currency. Locked inside when security forces sealed the tower earlier that day for the opening of parliament, the lone survivor must have realized escape was impossible. Hearing the soldiers closing in, he chose to end his life rather than be captured.

A detective was overheard saying, "Thankfully, the security measures for the tower were taken seriously. It's been 350 years since Guy Fawkes attempted to blow up parliament—seems we've learned our lesson."

CHAPTER THIRTY-TWO

WAITING AND HOPING

King Braxton had been brought to Buckingham Palace under a somber cloud, the physicians attending to him around the clock. For weeks, he remained in a murky haze, drifting in and out of consciousness, unresponsive to all but the bare necessities of treatment. The palace moved at half-speed, an uneasy stillness gripping the halls as his family and closest advisors waited, hoping for a sign.

Nearly a month after the explosion, he awoke with a start, his eyes snapping open, alert and intense. The fog of his lengthy recovery still lingered, but his determination was unmistakable. He pulled himself up, refusing to lie back any longer. "Brief me," he commanded.

Around him, the medical staff exchanged uncertain glances. Some tried to deter him, offering him rest.

He dismissed them with a wave. His gaze never faltered, focused solely on the task ahead. It was clear, despite his weakened body and hoarse voice, nothing would stop him from picking up exactly where he left off.

"Your Majesty," a senior physician spoke cautiously, "there is still much recovery ahead. You must take things slowly."

"And the queen?" He asked, knowing all too well the answer.

No one made a sound or stepped forward to answer.

Braxton's eyes pooled. He turned away and waved his hand dismissively. "I have been resting long enough, Doctor. My country will not wait for an old man's comfort." He shifted in his bed and looked out the window, his gaze distant yet focused. He remembered locking eyes with Valentina just before the blast. It was that brief, searing memory that haunted him now. And the vision of her clear eyes, full of love and strength, that final wordless exchange between them. Promise me we will always be together, he had mouthed, just before everything went dark.

She was gone. Her absence settled around him, a cloak he couldn't shed.

The funeral was a subdued event. The nation mourned quietly, each citizen feeling the loss without the usual public spectacle, out of respect for the king's fragile health. And Braxton, though he had not been conscious when the funeral was held, felt Valentina's departure in the marrow of his bones.

One afternoon, Braxton summoned George to his rooms.

"Thank you, George," he said, his voice still bearing the weariness of his recovery, "for seeing to the royal boxes."

George nodded, a touch of pride in his response. "It was an honor, Papa. I've been fortunate to have had your guidance—and Mama's. She was wise, pushing you to familiarize me with the responsibilities and duties of kinging."

The king, amused, looked away for a moment, something distant in his expression. "Yes. Your mother's idea. She was always right about the most important things."

As George left, Braxton closed his eyes, letting the quiet of the room surround him, then chuckled. Kinging, he thought.

Ten years passed and Braxton was now in his 80s, each year weighing heavily upon him. His injuries a decade earlier only aging him further. And yet, though physically weakened, his mind clung to its duties. He resolved to conserve his energy for what mattered most: his service to the realm.

A new daily regimen had taken shape, one that gave nearly all of his business responsibilities to his children and grandchildren. Focus on the kingdom, he reminded himself, focus on the people.

One evening, George joined him by the fire where Braxton stared into the flames before speaking with a mix of sorrow and determination.

"We are all that stands between Britain and despair," he said quietly, "but it is in our nature to rebuild, George. We shall rise again, brick by brick."

"Yes, Papa," George replied, his voice steady with conviction. "The people believe in the future. And so do I."

Braxton nodded, sensing his son's resolve. "It is not the king who gives a country its strength, but its people. And in this, we are blessed beyond measure."

Although he seldom spoke of her, those closest to him knew he carried Valentina's memory with him, drawing strength from the life they had shared. She had been his light, his compass. And now, as he led Britain, he honored her legacy by fighting for the country they both loved so deeply.

One evening, as he watched the sun set over London, Braxton felt a sense of quiet peace. Britain was rebuilding, and so was he. His purpose was clear, his spirit unwavering. I may not have deserved her, he thought, but I can honor her by serving this land until my final breath.

Braxton soon suffered another loss. His dear cowboy, Joe, passed away after a brief illness.

He clung to their memories, each one a fragile thread tethering him to the love and wisdom Valentina and Joe had left behind. Their presence settled in his heart. With every step, every breath, he willed himself to honor their imprint on his life.

CHAPTER THIRTY-THREE

LAYING THE FOUNDATION

Crown Prince George, now in his 70s, held the potential to ascend the throne if he outlived his father. Meanwhile, Braxton recognized great promise in George's son, Prince Michael, nearing 30. The king believed it was vital for Michael to connect with the public and project both vigor and strength. To that end, Michael's siblings were brought on board to assist. George, fully supportive, collaborated with the prime minister to craft a plan ensuring the younger royals played an active and visible role in public life.

Braxton spent considerable time at the Aurelio Palace, regaining his health and laying out what he called his "Foundation for the Future."

In the early 1950s, Braxton turned his attention to a rugged corner of the Scottish Highlands where a long-neglected fortress had captured his heart decades before. The crumbling and weather-worn, structure had served as a favorite hideaway for him and Valentina—a place untouched by modernity—yet brimming with historical charm. Rather than build a private estate elsewhere, Braxton poured his resources into refurbishing what he now christened "Braxton Castle," determined that this grand restoration would serve a higher purpose.

Drawing on his experience building hospitals and schools, Braxton incorporated essential mid-century upgrades to make the castle both practical and comfortable. Gone were the drafty corridors and temperamental wood stoves—central heating now coursed through newly insulated walls and the once-dim hallways sparkled under electric chandeliers. Telephones were installed throughout, and a modern kitchen replaced the ancient hearth and iron range. Every detail was chosen to preserve the castle's storied heritage while renovating the castle.

Braxton Castle was more than a personal retreat. The castle would serve as the heart of a worldwide academy, blending the castle's history with the evolving demands of the modern era. It would become the centerpiece of his greatest ambition, the Aurelio Academy, and the establishment of the Braxton Initiative—a dream within a dream. The academy would offer a world-class education rooted in timeless principles while open to contemporary innovation. His vision stretched well beyond its ivy-covered stone and thick battlements. Braxton ensured the castle would not only endure, but stand as a beacon of learning, progress, and hope for generations to come.

It was time to tie it all together.

For more than seventy years, Braxton had diligently safeguarded the vast treasure trove hidden away in San Francisco warehouses, and another secret cache in Paris. The Nazis, in World War II, despite their occupation of Paris, had failed to uncover his vaults there. Only

Braxton and the late Master Seiko knew the full extent of these hidden stores, packed with artifacts and priceless artwork veiled as ordinary crates marked "books and documents."

The caretakers of the San Francisco warehouses remained oblivious to its true value, and for 50 years the treasures lay untouched. In many cases they had been hidden away since the 1880s.

Now, however, Braxton faced a dilemma: How to monetize these assets and use the proceeds to fuel his dream? Selling the collections publicly would be unthinkable: it could reignite the scandal of his family's wealth that had nearly led to an uprising before World War II. He had no wish to revisit those flames.

The world was changing fast. Vast fortunes had emerged, particularly in the Middle East where oil wealth had created nouveau riche magnates with a taste for grandeur. America, too, was wealthier than ever, its affluent class seeking outlets for extravagant displays.

One afternoon, Braxton quietly slipped away from Buckingham Palace without fanfare, arriving unannounced at Lord Ramsey's London residence. Although now ninety-five and long retired, Ramsey remained one of Braxton's closest confidants. Braxton found him lying in bed. The two old friends spent little time on pleasantries and soon found themselves bantering back and forth.

"You know, Ramsey," Braxton began with a chuckle, "I never told you, but as a young man, I'd spy on you and my brother John during your little…rendezvous. I learned a few things that came in handy later on."

Ramsey raised an eyebrow, a smile playing at his lips. "Don't flatter yourself, you old rogue. John and I knew you were there, enjoying the show. Why do you think we kept dragging you to all those society events? We were keeping an eye on you."

Braxton laughed, half in disbelief. "You mean…you knew all along?"

Ramsey leaned back, smug. "Of course, Braxton. I even guessed what you and Aramis were up to before his father did."

"What else did you know?" Braxton asked, raising an eyebrow.

Ramsey smirked, jabbing a playful finger at him. "Mars!"

A flush crept across the king's cheeks.

"Yes," Ramsey went on, "you never really fooled your closest friends. We've all been collaborating behind the scenes for seventy plus years, keeping you out of harm's way."

Braxton's jaw dropped.

Ramsey snorted, clearly enjoying himself. "We all knew. Ratini, your Italian spy, had a nickname for you. Remember Monsieur Abberline, the renowned detective from Scotland Yard?"

"For God's sake, you old coot, of course, I remember Inspector F. Abberline."

"Cosimo, Maxim and your beloved Valentina were in on it too. She often ran interference for you. We just figured it was best if you didn't know how often we cleaned up behind you."

Braxton stared; speechless.

Ramsey grinned and continued, "Now, tell me, why are you really here?"

Braxton exhaled, finally conceding. "I need your help."

Ramsey, adjusting his pillows, said, "Isn't that always the way? Well, at least this time you came to me."

They fell into reminiscing, trading old stories until Ramsey nodded off, with Braxton not far behind, falling asleep in a wing-backed chair.

They woke up to a servant bringing tea, but Braxton had other ideas, retrieving a flask from his jacket.

"Fancy a drop?" he asked.

"Do I ever need to be asked?" Ramsey chuckled. They spiked their tea, and Braxton explained his predicament regarding monetizing the treasures.

Ramsey's eyes gleamed as he listened, the thrill of scheming rekindling his spirit. "I think we can work with this," he said finally. "Though it'll take time. Possibly more than either of us has left. But I know it can be done. But why as me? Surely there are others?"

"For God's sake, Ramsey, why on earth would I bother asking anyone else?"

Ramsey grunted. "I quite agree. How—why would you?" He refreshed his tea with more than a dollop from the king's flask. "Ah, the king needs his old friend yet again. Now, what do you plan to do with all this treasure you've hoarded?"

Braxton leaned back. "Give it away."

"Give it away?" Ramsey scoffed. "To whom?"

"It's more about to what," Braxton said quietly, his eyes distant.

They shared another drink, discussing logistics. "I have someone in mind," Ramsey said. "My nephew, Alexander Jeffries."

"Do I know him?"

"No, you don't," Ramsey replied with a half-smile. "He's young, intelligent, and knows his way around art and antiquities. Back in the day, I thought his education was a bit frivolous, art history, ancient studies and the like, but I funded it. He's grown into it."

Braxton nodded. "Sounds promising."

Ramsey held out his glass. "A bit more, if you please." Braxton poured. Ramsey continued. "Jeffries has been involved in retrieving stolen art for the government and Jewish communities. He's good— resourceful and connected, in need of a new challenge. This could be it."

Braxton considered Ramsey's proposal. Prince George, having been waiting in Ramsey's library for his father for over two hours, walked into the room. "What's going on here?" he asked, a smile tugging at his lips.

"Out!" Ramsey barked, waving his glass. "This is no place for you, boy! We're plotting the takeover of the world."

George laughed, retreating. "Carry on then, gentlemen. Carry on."

When the door closed, the two friends exchanged a glance and, raising their glasses, laughed heartily.

CHAPTER THIRTY-FOUR

PATRICIA

Braxton and Ramsey met a week later in London at Renaissance House.

"I never thought you would get out of that bed. And here you are, spinning around like a whirling dervish!"

"Your command of the obvious has often been lacking Mr. King, so what's new?"

"Don't be crabby!"

Ramsey caught his breath and leaned back in his wheelchair, still grinning. "Very well, to business." He grew serious, leaning forward in his chair. "Alexander and I have discussed establishing an auction house in Cyprus. The local regulations there are…minimal, which works to our advantage. We'll partner with British expatriates, an old family you might recall, the Osbournes. You hired them for shipping and trade years ago and Alexander's already connected with their sons. They served together during the war."

Braxton listened intently. Ramsey's mind was as sharp as ever, and with Alexander's help, they were designing a plan that was as thorough as it was ingenious.

"We'll compensate the Osbournes generously," Ramsey continued. "They've got connections that'll be valuable when dealing with the Turks, Greeks, and various officials. If we keep everyone satisfied, it'll be smooth sailing—but costly."

Braxton marveled inwardly at Ramsey's vision and foresight. Even at his advanced age, his old friend had lost none of his creativity.

Ramsey motioned for something to drink. "Water?" Braxton offered.

"Oh, come now, you dolt. Gin and tonic," Ramsey said with exaggerated disdain.

Braxton chuckled. "How foolish of me. I forgot you prefer gin transfusions." He pressed a button on a table next to his chair, A footman entered through a service door. "A pitcher of gin and tonics, if you would," Braxton said.

Ramsey resumed, "We've also located a secluded property formerly owned by an exiled, fortunately for us, an impoverished noble. Name escapes me, but it doesn't matter. The compound is walled in. There are cliffs on three sides and an inlet for moderate-sized ships on the other. Secluded yet near enough to the commercial district for easy access."

"How will we transport everything to Cyprus? And the Osbournes will manage what, exactly?"

"We're still working out the logistics." Ramsey's voice held a hint of exasperation. "It's only been a week since you proposed this scheme."

Braxton nodded, leaning back. "Understood."

"We estimate 10 to 15 years to convert everything to cash," Ramsey added. "Alexander's young he'll see it through. You and I, on the other hand, will be long gone. But tell me, Braxton, what's this all about? What's the grand purpose behind this wealth?"

Braxton's gaze softened. "Ramsey, it's been right before your eyes for seventy years."

"Enough riddles, Braxton. Just tell me."

"It's not a riddle. It's a dream—one I've had since we returned from Europe after setting up the trading companies in Spain, France and the Low Countries. I've been building toward it for seventy years."

"Just tell me what it is," Ramsey pressed.

"In due time," Braxton said, holding his friend's gaze steadily. "For now, let's remain focused on Cyprus."

Ramsey sighed and adjusted his seat. "Fine. But we might need a backup plan should the Cypriots get too greedy. For now, I think it's our best option. What say you?"

Braxton looked out the window, his face contemplative. "Agreed. We must move quickly. I'd prefer not to leave my family with this burden." Braxton closed his eyes for a moment and then said, "France is as unpredictable as ever. If they swing toward communism, our assets could be seized."

Ramsey nodded. "We'll need the Chiacontella Bank in Zurich to handle the financial transactions."

"Absolutely," Braxton said.

Over the following weeks, Braxton and Ramsey met regularly, disguising their encounters as visits between old friends reminiscing about shared memories. By design, Braxton never formally met Alexander Jeffries, maintaining an added layer of discretion.

Lady Patricia, granddaughter of Princess Angelina, was a poised and capable businesswoman. Though not conventionally beautiful, she possessed Braxton's shrewdness, impeccable memory and a powerful intuition. Braxton saw her as a worthy confidante and partner.

He invited Patricia to meet him at Renaissance House. Seated in the family drawing room, he watched the fire flickering on the hearth. Except for his recent meetings with Ramsey, it had been years since he had visited this London residence. With no guests present, it was the perfect setting for a confidential conversation.

Lady Patricia entered, moving with the assured grace that Braxton admired. Though he had often been tempted to tell her of their true relationship, he hadn't yet done so. Perhaps she knew already, perhaps she didn't.

"Your Majesty, dear uncle, it's truly a pleasure to see you." She curtsied, then leaned in and kissed him on each cheek.

Braxton beamed.

"Patricia, thank you for coming."

Dressed in a tailored Hardy Amies light gray two-piece suit, Patricia exuded elegance. Her jacket, cinched at the waist and paired with a pleated skirt, accentuated her figure with sophistication. Patricia's richly textured dark hair, was styled fashionably yet conservatively. She carried a black portfolio purse slung over her shoulder.

He gestured to the chair beside him. "Please, sit by me."

She settled into the chair and took his hand. "What is on your mind, Uncle?"

For a moment, Braxton felt as he had on that last carriage ride with Valentina, a sense of closeness and companionship. Patricia's calm presence and strength reminded him of his wife. He felt certain that she was capable of bearing the responsibility he was about to place upon her.

For half an hour, Braxton recounted the story of the treasures he had acquired in Russia, his investments in oil, lumber, and precious artifacts, and the troves stored in Paris and San Francisco. He shared his vision for transferring the collection to Cyprus, with Lord Ramsey and Alexander Jeffries leading the way.

Patricia sat, her gaze steady and composed. Inwardly, she was working hard to comprehend and catalog what he was sharing. This man was far more than she had imagined. She had respected him all her life, but his revelations cast him in a new light, far beyond her expectations.

"Have I overwhelmed you?" Braxton asked.

"Yes," she admitted, "but I'm intrigued and eager to help in any way I can."

"Wonderful," he replied, smiling. "I've arranged supper for us here."

Braxton shared details of the plan to move the treasures from Paris and San Francisco to Cyprus, mentioning the Osbournes' role and Alexander Jeffries' involvement.

Patricia's eyes lit up. "Alex Jeffries—I know him! We were at the Aurelio Academy together, though not in the same year."

Braxton raised an eyebrow. "Does that present any difficulty?"

She looked thoughtful for a moment, then shook her head. "No, uncle, none at all."

Patricia's mind drifted over her past interactions with the king, her Uncle Braxton. Their exchanges had always seemed distant, bound by family decorum and the regal protocols of gatherings. However, there had been rare occasions when the king, breaking from formalities, would sit her down for a genuine talk, asking her questions with a depth of curiosity that puzzled and touched her in equal measure. She'd seen him as a figure of grandeur, dignity, and accomplishment—yet mostly always distant. And here he was, sharing secrets that went beyond the world of propriety, laying before her a side of himself she had never glimpsed and certainly never imagined.

Tonight, everything felt laden with a strange familiarity, something almost mythological. The king's eyes, his gaze piercing yet kind, as if weighed with secrets buried deep within. Patricia realized she might never truly know this man, now revealing parts of a legacy concealed in shadows, dangling before her vast fortunes and responsibilities that felt both alluring and dangerous. The thrill sent a shiver down her spine, igniting a desire for something beyond her predictable life in finance.

Here was the challenge she had silently yearned for; a venture into uncharted realms, promising liberation from the confines of a world dominated by men. She had always been likened to her Uncle Braxton.

Though no one had ever directly revealed it, Patricia had quietly pieced together the connections and come to believe that King Braxton and Queen Valentina were her great-grandparents. Strangely, it did not trouble her that no one had explicitly told her so. Instead, the knowledge filled her with a quiet confidence. The unspoken truth felt natural, as though some things, like heritage, didn't need words to be understood. She felt reassured, as if her place in his life—and her role in this grand scheme—had always been a certainty.

With his hand steady, Braxton refilled their glasses and raised his in camaraderie. Leaning toward her, he continued, "Patricia, your role will be to manage and oversee the finances and logistics of this operation. You'll handle the sale proceeds with the utmost discretion to safeguard the privacy of all involved."

Patricia held his gaze. "And where am I to deposit these funds?"

"I've arranged accounts with the Chiacontella Banks in Zurich and New York."

She raised an eyebrow. "And you won't let the proceeds sit idle, of that I am certain."

Braxton gave a small smile, his eyes full of approval. "Certainly not. That's where your expertise comes in. I trust you'll invest with care—long-term properties, manufacturing, utilities, emerging technologies." He paused, as if ensuring the gravity of the moment settled between them. "Patricia, no one must ever know about this. The details are yours alone. You will control what will amount to billions."

Her gaze fell to the fire as she absorbed the weight of the task.

After a moment's silence, he asked, "What are you thinking?"

She took a breath before speaking, her voice calm. "It's quite deal to absorb. I see your intent, but I need to know. What is your ultimate goal? Surely this secrecy goes beyond simple discretion or profit. What becomes of these assets once you're gone?"

Braxton leaned back, then answered with a mischievous grin. "And?"

Though her composure remained steady, a note of caution crept into her voice. "You'll draft a Royal Pardon for both Jeffries and me—purely as a safeguard, since we both know this skirts the edge of legality. I'll secure the documents in the most confidential place possible."

Braxton reached into a worn satchel by his side, retrieving two leather-bound portfolios. Handing them to her, he said, "I doubt you'll need them. But here they are."

Patricia held the portfolios for a moment, a touch of awe softening her expression. "You are a mystery," she murmured.

"You have no idea, my dear."

Braxton poured a little more into their glasses, and Patricia placed the documents carefully with her bag. Then, measuring her next words carefully, she looked up at him. "What exactly do you want to achieve with this wealth?"

Braxton's expression turned solemn; his voice weighted with purpose. "I want these funds to power innovation and uplift people who have vision but lack resources. I set up a family trust years ago to ensure our descendants would be cared for. This wealth—from hidden treasures—is meant to go further: to fund education, advances in science, technology, and commerce, to stabilize nations, and perhaps, just maybe, to foster world peace."

Patricia nodded, struggling to comprehend the magnitude of his vision. "One person can't accomplish this alone. You must have a plan for how it should be managed."

Braxton's expression softened with satisfaction. "I do. What would you consider fair compensation?"

Patricia held his gaze. "I hadn't thought on it just yet."

"Both you and Jeffries will receive a commission from the proceeds. Out of that, you'll cover all necessary expenses—underwriting, administration, marketing, and delivery."

Patricia took a deep breath. "This will be an undertaking of immense cost. The scale alone…"

Braxton cut in, "You'll share forty percent of the sales. I'll provide you a loan for initial expenses."

She raised an eyebrow, smiling faintly. "For such a project? I'd say forty-five percent is more reasonable."

Braxton chuckled. "Perhaps it is." He rose to his feet, taking her hand in both of his. "Thank you, my dear."

They spent hours outlining details, refining the plan until it sparkled with clarity.

Over the next six months, they met weekly, devising a structure that would endure, creating a board to guide the wealth's distribution.

Braxton signed a charter appointing Patricia as trustee of his trust.

In Paris, Alexander Jeffries moved in calculated stealth, navigating a world of shadows to recover the treasure Braxton had hidden decades before. The château held its secrets close, but with each night, the contents of the vaults dwindled, disappearing piece by piece into crates bound for Cyprus.

The operation was a study in secrecy. Jeffries orchestrated the shipments under layers of pretense, using shell companies and falsified shipping documents to mask the troves as innocuous goods.

The pieces slipped out of Paris with ease, each shipment a clandestine victory.

Patricia and Alexander communicated only through the trusted Mars Couriers, forsaking telephone, telegraph and radio to avoid interception. The couriers, fast and discreet, flitted between cities, bringing updates and instructions as if they were passing ghostly messages.

As the last of the Paris pieces made their way to Cyprus, Patricia enlisted an international art dealer to act as her liaison to the world's wealthiest collectors. This dealer, well-connected and discreet, approached his clients with caution.

The first buyer—a wealthy Russian industrialist—showed interest in a collection of Russian icons, a purchase wrapped in secrecy and discretion. From Master Seiko's cataloged photographs, preserved over decades, each piece was presented with a quiet elegance.

Patricia knew the reputation of these artifacts would precede them; interest spread in hushed whispers through the art world's upper echelons. Patricia had no intention of flooding the market; each sale, a carefully orchestrated affair, offered only to those who could appreciate the significance of their acquisition.

As each sale concluded, funds were transferred to Chiacontella accounts in Zurich and New York. The proceeds, carefully allocated, and seamlessly distributed.

Meanwhile, in San Francisco, Alexander oversaw the emptying of the warehouses. The crates were swapped out for modern shipping containers and marked for transport under the guise of aid for post WWII reconstruction.

The first shipment left San Francisco on a fog-covered night, the ship gliding beneath the famous San Francisco Bridge with a silent purpose. Ten days later, it arrived in Cyprus, its arrival a signal that the last leg of Braxton's legacy was in motion. The treasures would be safeguarded within the compound, overseen by Alexander with the assistance of a local network of allies who kept prying eyes at bay.

With each transfer, Braxton's ambition crept closer to realization. Over the next three years, Patricia and Alexander solidified their network, embedding their work within the art world's deepest corridors. However, the burgeoning conflict in Cyprus—driven by nationalist fervor and demands for self-determination—brought the entire operation to an abrupt halt. Rising guerrilla activity, along with violent clashes that spilled onto city streets, forced Alexander to shutter the compound under urgent conditions. In a final rush, he locked the remaining treasures away in the fortified vaults of the Chiacontella Banks, knowing that returning to Cyprus would be impossible.

In the dim light of Braxton's private study, he sat across from Patricia, thoughtfully swirling a glass of brandy. Patricia leaned forward, her face glowed in the light of the fire, anticipation evident in her eyes. She'd just returned from Cyprus and was eager to share update Braxton.

"It's done, Uncle," Patricia said with a small, triumphant smile. "Alexander has closed the compound. The last of the collection is secure within Chiacontella vaults."

Braxton nodded, a look of relief mingling with pride. "I had my doubts about how long we could continue under those circumstances.

You've done remarkably well, Patricia. Jeffries, too. Truly remarkable."

Patricia shrugged, though a hint of pride gleamed in her eyes. "We had to adapt quickly. The guerrilla activity was becoming too close for comfort. But Alex handled the security flawlessly."

Braxton leaned back; his gaze steady. "You two have solidified this project more swiftly than I could have imagined." He paused, leaned forward, his expression darkening with a trace of worry. "Patricia, tell me, what's next? Are you truly confident the remaining treasure is safe, leaving everything there—the art, the icons. It worries me. I can't shake my concern. This collection is precious, and so much is at risk if we're wrong."

Patricia gave a resolute nod. "The banks' vaults are as secure as any fortress. The Chiacontella Bank has a reputation to uphold. They'll guard our interests well."

Braxton considered her, a faint smile touching his lips. "I knew you were capable, Patricia, but I never realized how you would carry out such a vision so seamlessly." He paused, choosing his words. "This dream was mine alone for so long. But now… Now, it's yours too."

Patricia reached out, placing a hand on his. "It's an honor, truly. A perhaps a dream passed on lives forever and grows more powerful."

Braxton squeezed her hand, his eyes softening. "Let's hope so, my dear. You've done more than I could have hoped." He raised his glass in a silent toast. "To seeing this vision through, whatever may come."

CHAPTER THIRTY-FIVE

AN ENDING

Braxton was ninety-five-years-old. His heir, Prince George, was in his early seventies and not in good health. The next in line, George's son, Prince Michael, was entering his late thirties.

"Prime Minister," Braxton said, addressing the eighth person to hold the premiership since he became king. "No doubt, the cabinet has concerns regarding Prince George's health."

"Yes, Your Majesty. I have been reticent to share the government's concerns regarding this with Your Majesty."

"Ah, yes, Minister. My son and I have discussed the matter at length. The situation is what it is and we've come to terms with it." Braxton leaned forward slightly, his hands resting heavily on his knees. "George is resolute in his commitment to carry out his duties as king, as long as he is physically able. But let's be clear: both he and I agree that the people are tired of seeing an old man propped up on the throne, barely able to fulfill their responsibilities."

"His son," the premier asked, "Prince Michael, do you feel he is up to the task of regent—should the crown prince be unable to perform his duties?"

"Of that, I have no doubt," the king replied, adjusting his jacket's cuff. "He is well acquainted with the constitution and as you are aware, he often confers honors and deputizes when his father and I have been unavailable. Michael is young but possesses intelligence and judgement." The king folded his hands in his lap.

The two men sat for a moment, the prime minister waiting for the king to end the audience.

"I am beyond old and my son and heir is not far behind. The sooner a young man sits on the throne, the better."

One evening, Prince George welcomed the royal family to Clarence House for a night of dinner and entertainment. Candlelight bathed the dining room in a warm, inviting glow. The gentle clink of fine China mingled with the low hum of conversation, filling the air with a sense of quiet elegance and familial ease.

At the head of the table sat Prince George.

His father, the king, sat at the other end of the 20-foot table.

A radiant smile spread across George's face as he pushed back his chair and rose to his feet, his eyes sparkling with excitement. Taking up his crystal champagne coupe he tapped it with a knife, drawing the attention of his dinner guests. When the room quieted, George spoke, his words brimming with anticipation.

"I have splendid news," he began. "My doctors have finally cleared me to fly again, and soon my passion for the skies will be fulfilled once more!"

Braxton felt his breath catch, his fists clenching under the table as his face paled. Still, he steadied himself, determined to join in the celebration around him.

All eyes were on Prince George as the prince raised his glass, and with cheers filling the room, guests raised theirs in turn. "Hip-hip-hurrah! Hip-hip-hurrah! Hip-hip-hurrah!"

Braxton, assisted by a footman, rose, lifting his glass to honor his son.

Dinner resumed; the room alive with familial warmth. George embraced each moment, reveling in the joy and companionship of his children and their families. Despite the shadows of his recent battle with cancer, his spirit was vibrant, his energy seemingly boundless, devoting himself to those around him.

Later, Braxton, preparing to depart, placed a hand on George's shoulder and leaned close. In a quiet, tender voice, he said, "You know I love you with all my heart. You're the perfect son. I am blessed beyond words to be your father. I only ask that you reconsider piloting—perhaps with a co-pilot?"

George's eyes misted. He quickly wiped the tears away and nodded. "Certainly, Papa. And thank you. Your words mean everything to me."

Later that night, as Prince George lay in bed, he felt a faint, unsettling discomfort—an old, unwelcome sensation.

The next morning, Prince George had his driver take him to Stapleford Aerodrome.

Just after the war, ten years earlier, his love for aviation had led him to purchase and oversee the restoration of a WWII military fighter aircraft, a Supermarine Spitfire.

Known for its speed and maneuverability, this single seater had been a prominent workhorse during the war, captivating George's imagination. He relished flying the magnificent machine for hours, often crisscrossing England and the English Channel, with a preferred route back from the French coast towards the sunlit chalk cliffs of Dover.

Prior to taking that morning's flight, the prince conducted his customary inspection, commending the meticulous check carried out by mechanics who had been briefed about HRH's planned flight earlier that morning.

Southern England's airspace was duly notified of the crown prince's flight, leading to clearances and rerouting of military and commercial traffic.

As was the custom, several military aircraft were deployed for security reasons and discreet observation. This request had been made by the palace two years earlier, respectful of Prince George's flying skills, but concerned with his advancing age.

The prince strapped himself into the fighter, completed his checklist, and taxied to the main runway. Invigorated by the power of the Griffon engines, the aircraft stole down the runway, effortlessly rising into the translucent morning skies, inviting the prince to envelop himself in its beauty.

The following two hours found him flying high above southwestern England. He soon piloted his craft toward the Aurelio Palace and circled high above, reminiscing about his time as a child and student at the Aurelio Academy. The aircraft banked southwest towards Windsor Castle. Peering down at the 1,000-year-old fortress, he spied St. George's Chapel and considered his grandfather and grandmother entombed below. He knew it would not be long before he, too, would join them there for eternity. Circling back towards London, he caught a bird's-eye view of the Houses of Parliament and Buckingham Palace. His home, Clarence House, shimmered in the light. The aviator prince set a course to the east and the English Channel.

"Stapleton Tower to Golf Romeo One, Golf Romeo One, this is Stapleton Tower. Be advised, our calculations indicate your fuel levels are critically low. Your aircraft does not have sufficient reserve capacity for a safe journey across the channel and back. It is imperative, Your Royal Highness, that you return to Stapleton immediately. Acknowledge. Over."

George did not respond to the urgent radio transmissions. Ignoring all warnings, he pressed on towards the Channel, ascending relentlessly from 10,000 to 20,000, and then to 30,000 feet. The pilots trailing his aircraft grew increasingly alarmed at his daring ascent and deviation from the expected flight path.

The Royal Air Force pilots closed the distance between their aircraft and the prince's plane. They attempted to make radio contact and received no response. Two aircraft pulled alongside the Spitfire. It was obvious Prince George was conscious and in full control of the aircraft. They drew closer. One pilot extended an arm horizontally out to the side and made a circular motion with his hand, signaling to turn around. The prince returned a thumbs up and a wave.

He maintained his course, crossing the Channel at 400 knots, dangerously low on fuel.

The air controller at Stapleton radioed Calais-Dunkerque Air Base, informing them of the prince's flight path, critically low fuel levels and concerning behavior.

The prince's fighter aircraft entered French air space and was soon hugging the French coast.

King Braxton received a phone call from the Chief of the Air Staff. "Your Majesty. We have a situation. The crown prince took off from Stapleton this morning—"

"I beg your pardon. Did you say Prince George flew earlier today?"

"Sir, he is airborne as we speak and is flying up and down the French coast, with little or not enough fuel to make it back across the Channel, sir!"

Braxton's head swam, uncertain of what he had heard. "He's an exceptional pilot! But…are you absolutely certain? We can't afford any mistakes. Order him to land in Calais immediately, anywhere he can touch down! Now! Anywhere! Now!"

"Your Majesty, he is not responding to the radio, nor has he complied with acknowledged hand signals to return to Stapleton."

"I see. Can you patch me in?"

"Give us a moment, sir."

Braxton listened as the operator patched him through to the control room, where George's radio transmissions were being monitored. A few faint clicks and the operator's voice came through.

"Your Majesty, we have a line open to the prince's craft. I'll connect you now."

"Thank you, Field Marshal," Braxton replied, his voice calm but edged with tension.

"Stapleton Tower to Golf Romeo One, Golf Romeo One," the operator transmitted, using the prince's designated call sign. "His Majesty is on the line. Do you read? Over."

A burst of static hissed in reply, then faded into unsettling silence.

The operator adjusted his headset and tried again, his tone firm, urgent. "Golf Romeo One, Golf Romeo One, this is Stapleton Tower. His Majesty is requesting you acknowledge. Please respond. Over."

Another pause followed. Braxton's jaw tightened as he heard the operator key the mic again.

"Golf Romeo One, this is Stapleton Tower," the operator repeated, his voice steady but insistent. "You are instructed to return to base immediately. Please acknowledge receipt of this transmission. Over."

The silence lingered, heavy and oppressive, broken only by faint bursts of static.

The line remained silent, and the operator tried again. "Sir, did you hear my last transmission? His Majesty requests your immediate return."

Again, no answer. Braxton pressed the phone's receiver firmly against his ear and chin, his voice carrying a quiet strength. "George, it's your father. If you can hear me, please land the plane while you can."

Static.

The king exhaled slowly, overcome as the knowledge of his son's intentions became clear.

Static.

In a halting voice, he said, "I think I understand, my son, and I love you."

Static.

"Goodbye George. God Bless."

Eventually, Prince George turned his plane back over the Channel toward England. Warning lights and alarms had long since signaled the pilot he was dangerously low on fuel.

He climbed to 40,000 feet. The white cliffs of Dover loomed ahead. Ten miles out, the engine sputtered.

Evening headlines read:

CHANNEL PLANE CRASH KILLS PRINCE GEORGE!

CHAPTER THIRTY-SIX

A BEGINNING

"**M**ichael, I truly appreciate all you are doing, but why all the fuss, the expense? It is just one more birthday, preceded by many, many birthdays."

Yes, Grandfather, preceded by ninety-nine birthdays. Your Centennial Birthday!"

"My God," Braxton sighed. He shook his head and looked toward the prime minister for support.

"I must agree with the crown prince on this. England has never had a king reach the age of one hundred. This provides a genuine reason to bring the nation together to celebrate a milestone no monarch has achieved in over 1,000 years of history. It's a tonic, a rare opportunity to unite us all. It is —"

Braxton, holding a handkerchief, raised his hand as if to ward off further debate, coughing softly into his other hand. "Alright, alright, you win. But don't expect me to be at every single event," he sighed, resigned. "Perhaps a carriage ride for Trooping the Colors and a brief appearance on the balcony—no more." He grunted, settling back into his chair. "The rest of you, the family, can manage the festivities."

Prince Michael exchanged a smile with the prime minister. "Thank you, Grandfather. The nation will appreciate—"

The king snapped, "Do give it up. I said yes." He pressed the audience button on the side table. "Now, you two men run along, as I would like to speak to Lady Patricia. Tell her to come in as you leave.

The two men rose, bowed and exited the audience room.

The king's private secretary announced, "Your Majesty, Lady Patricia."

Patricia entered the audience chamber with a respectful bow. "Your Majesty," she greeted, her voice carrying warmth and formality, before adding with a familiar smile, "Uncle." She kissed him on both cheeks and sat next to him on the sofa, taking one of his hands in hers.

Braxton's gaze softened. "Patricia," he began, with a note of genuine pride, "you and Alexander have done incredible work. I've watched the progress closely—several billion raised and it's all going to exactly where it needs to be. Investments across the globe, in the Americas, Japan, China, Australia, Africa. Just look at what you've made possible."

Patricia's eyes glistened, a hint of gratitude in them. "Thank you, Sir," she said, her voice steady but carrying a touch of emotion. "Being able to help carry out your vision—it has been an honor."

Braxton leaned forward, his voice dropping to a gentler tone. "I knew you could do it. I always did. Keep moving forward with this, Patricia. You're building something that will last."

She nodded; a bit overwhelmed but maintained her composure. "I will. And thank you—for trusting me with your dream."

Braxton paused, then gave her a small smile. "There's one more thing. On my birthday, I'd like you to stand with me and the family on the palace balcony so we can greet the people together."

Patricia's eyes widened with surprise. "I'd be honored, Uncle," she murmured, a bit choked up.

Braxton chuckled softly. "Well, it's only fitting that a great-grandfather shares a moment like this with his family."

Tears filled Lady Patricia's eyes as she struggled to open her handbag in search of a handkerchief.

He pulled a tissue from a nearby box and handed it to her. They sat side-by-side as she dabbed her eyes.

Braxton turned and held her for a moment, warmth in his voice, he whispered, "Thank you, Patricia. You have made me very proud."

A few quiet moments passed as they held on, each internalizing the unspoken bond they'd shared for years, finally acknowledged.

On the second Saturday in June, Buckingham Palace gleamed under a brilliant summer sky as the Royal Family took their place on the grand balcony. The king looked out over the vast crowd gathered to celebrate his 100th birthday. Below, a sea of people stretched from the front face of the palace and down the length of the Mall, spilling onto surrounding streets; their voices rising in a chorus of cheers and well-wishes filling the air with palpable warmth.

The crowd's energy surged, their cheers echoing off the palace's stone facade, growing louder with each passing moment.

A vibrant crescendo, the sound of roaring engines filled the sky. Jets flew in tight formation, slicing through the air, their sleek silhouettes casting fleeting shadows over the palace and the crowd below.

The king raised his gaze as the planes swept overhead, their thunderous approach blending with the crowd's jubilant shouts, a powerful testament to the legacy of his reign.

Braxton's heart swelled as he looked down at the faces turned toward him, their admiration woven into every shout and wave—a birthday celebration unlike any other ringing through the city: a triumphant anthem.

A long way from the Cupula Inferno.

The king watched as the jets flew east to west over the Mall directly in front of Buckingham Palace. They then swooped south and vanished into the horizon, their red, blue, and white contrails blending into the cloudless sky.

"Do you see those jets disappearing? Notice the vapor they leave behind? Watch it disperse into the heavens," Braxton said to no one in particular.

The dissipating vapors captured the king, lost in contemplation until his attention shifted downward and out onto the crowd.

Much like those dispersing contrails, he thought, my meticulously crafted plans will disperse, take hold, and flourish across the globe; enduring well into and beyond the millennium.

Braxton caught Lady Patricia's eye, giving her a slight smile and a subtle, knowing wink.

NEXT UP:

MILLENNIAL MOGULS UNHINGED!

ACKNOWLEDGEMENTS

This third volume of *Braxton's Century* is the result of years of dedication, collaboration, and unwavering support from many incredible people. Over the past five years, your encouragement has been invaluable—thank you all for your tireless commitment.

A special and heartfelt thank you to Tamara Merrill, my steadfast anchor, and my own personal 'oracle' whose support has guided me on so many levels—Thank you! Thank you! Thank you!

To my San Diego Writer's Group, your insights and camaraderie have been instrumental throughout this journey. Craig McCleod, Tamara Merrill, Lynn Ravenswood, and the many others who have been part of our dynamic and ever-evolving group—thank you!

And to Trisha Gooch, my editor, who sat with me, reading word by word, page by page—your patience, expertise, and dedication means the world to me.

ABOUT THE AUTHOR

J.R. Strayve Jr., a U.S. Marine Corps veteran, is the acclaimed author of *Braxton's Century*, an alternate-history three-volume series renowned for its vivid storytelling and gripping narrative. His portfolio also includes the political thrillers *First Spouse of the United States* and *POTUS Down*, which delve into themes of ambition, identity, and resilience. Beyond his own novels, Strayve has ghostwritten both non-fiction and fiction works, along with numerous short stories and novellas. His writing, also featured in multiple anthologies, seamlessly blends his passion for history, politics, and the intricacies of the human experience.

WORKS BY JR STRAYVE JR

First Spouse of the United States

POTUS Down

Braxton's Century Vols 1 & 2 & 3

The Lieutenant & The Vintner

Vainglorious

Multiple Short Stories

Ghostwritten Works Include:

Broken Promises

No Hatred or Bitterness

Sin in the House of the Lord

<hr>

READER'S GUIDE

Introduction

Braxton's journey—spanning revolutions, world wars, and shifting empires—is one of power, ambition, and forbidden passions. Braxton's Century: Volume 3 brings his vision to its pinnacle, revealing the culmination of a dream born in his youth. This guide is designed to spark discussion about the novel's historical depth, its complex characters, and the provocative themes it explores.

Discussion Questions

Braxton as a Historical Force

1. How does Braxton's evolution reflect the transformations of the world from 1860 to 1960?

2. In what ways does he defy traditional power structures, and how does his vision challenge the status quo?

3. Do you view him as a hero, an anti-hero, or something in between?

The Dream Born in Youth

1. Braxton's dream, first conceived in his youth, drives much of his ambition. How does this vision shape his choices throughout the book?

2. Was his secrecy surrounding building the dream in to a reality justified? Could he have achieved it differently?

3. Do you think Lady Patricia can fulfill his dream.

Power, Betrayal, and Consequence

1. The novel explores the high price of ambition. What are some key moments where Braxton's power costs him dearly?

2. Which betrayals affected him the most—those from enemies or those from trusted allies?

3. Could he have avoided certain downfalls, or were they inevitable?

Forbidden Passion and Personal Sacrifice

1. Braxton's relationships often exist at the intersection of love, duty, and danger. How do these romantic and sexual entanglements shape his journey?

2. How does the novel portray the consequences of love in a world dictated by power and expectation?

3. Do you think that one person can love two people and if so, how do you feel Braxton and those he loved handled their relationships?

The Role of Women and Allies in His Life

1. How do the women in Braxton's life—whether as lovers, rivals, or allies—shape his path?

2. Does Braxton treat those close to him differently based on their gender, power, or personal loyalty?

The Dystopian Elements of the Novel

1. While rooted in historical events, Braxton's Century: Volume 3 also presents a dystopian undercurrent. What elements of the novel feel the most dystopian?

2. How does the alternative history in this book make you reflect on real-world historical events?

The Legacy of Braxton's Vision

1. In the end, do you think Braxton's vision succeeds? Does it live on in the way he intended?

2. How do you think a 'dystopian' history would remember him—visionary, tyrant, or something else entirely?

Personal Takeaways

1. Did any part of Braxton's journey resonate with you personally?

2. If you could ask the author one question about the book, what would it be?

Activities for Book Clubs

Historical Deep Dive – Research one of the real historical events referenced in the book and discuss how the novel's version compares to actual history.

Rewrite a Scene – Choose a pivotal moment in the book and rewrite it from a different character's perspective.

Character Debate – Assign different members to defend or critique Braxton's actions in key moments.

Soundtrack for a Century – Each member selects a song they feel represents a particular scene, character, or theme from the novel.

Final Thoughts

Braxton's Century: Volume 3 is a sweeping epic of power, legacy, and the cost of ambition. Whether you view Braxton as a revolutionary or a disruptor, his impact is undeniable. His story challenges us to consider who truly shapes history—the rulers, the rebels, or the dreamers who refuse to be caged.

Happy reading and discussing,

Contact thr author through his website: www.JRSTRAYVEJR.com